Archer of the Heathland

Book Five

Windemere

J.W. Elliot

Bent Bow
Publishing, LLC

Bent Bow Publishing
P.O. Box 1426
Middleboro, MA 02346

ISBN 13: 978-1-7336757-6-5

Cover Design by Brandi Doane McCann

If you enjoy this book, please consider leaving an honest review on Amazon and sharing on your social media sites.

Please sign up for my newsletter where you can get a free short story and more free content at: **www.jwelliot.com**

To Archers Young and Old

Book Five

Windemere

Note to the Reader

One of the persistent questions I have received about the Archer of the Heathland series is what about Redmond? What did he do all those years he lived off the island? And why did he come back? You now hold the answer to those questions in your hands. This is Redmond's journey home. This book also provides crucial backstory for the next volume (Book VI) in the series, in which Brion, Finola, York, and Gwyneth travel to the southland in search of Redmond. I hope you will enjoy this step back in time to before the death of Rosland and Weyland, before Brion's quest to save Brigid and Finola from the Salassani. Book VI will pick up where Book III *Vengeance* left off.

Enjoy,
J.W. Elliot

Frei-Ock Isles and the Southlands

PERTH

LISMOR

NAIRN

Parvni

Nanusan

Linnan

Creft

Ardell

Brecari

Taurini

Ballach

Salassani

Carpetani

Dunkeldi Kingdom

Dunkeldi

Dale

FAIR ISLE

FREI-OCK MOR

Mailag

Castle Bay

Alamani

Kingdom of Coll

Chullish

Barony of Whit-horn

Aldros

Rosyth

ROSYTHIA

Straits of Darden

Alborian Sea

Byrne Forest

Kazani

Alva

Kingdom of the Kassan

Pava

Alva River

SKIRDEN ISLE

Drun's Bay

Naymani

Kingdom of Deira

Roe River

Wych River

Duchy of Kirn

Royan

White Castle

Barony of Cassel

Hallstat

Earldom of Mayen

Langon

Duchy of Einbeck

Steamsisk Bay

Harrowden

Wolf River

Wind River

SOUTHLANDS

Blue River

Helder

Kingdom of Morcia

Medlock River

Gladd River

Beck Wood

Earldom of Hiede

Metz

Barony of Longmire

Barony of Windemere

Knoll River

Earldom of Tivoli

Azure Lake

Arras

Barony of Eliff

Denlani Mountains

Dart River

Barony of Gurloch

Denlani Mountains

Vermilion Dunes

Lands of the Dashneri

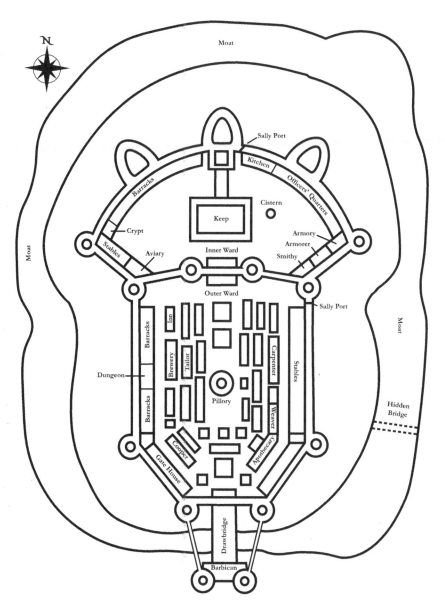

CASTLE WINDEMERE

Chapter 1
The Foresworn

he wail of a child lifted on the breeze. Redmond paused and crouched in the shadow of a rock outcrop. Waiting. Listening. The morning sun had not yet poked its head above the eastern horizon. Rocky, undulating hills bristled with pines and shrubs while the deep valleys still lay in gray shadow. A warm breeze rustled through clumps of grass and the delicate white flowers of the woodland asters, carrying with it the rich scent of pine. There was no smell of wood smoke or anything else that would suggest people were about.

Redmond's ears must have deceived him. There could be no children here. No one lived on the contested borders of the Barony of Longmire and the Barony of Windemere. This region of the Hallstat Kingdom of Morcia had been swept clean of inhabitants by the raids and counter-raids that left it a no man's land. No child could be making that sound.

The wail came again, and Redmond slipped an arrow onto the string of his longbow. He fell to his belly and crawled forward until he could peer down on the old road that snaked its way among the hills toward the north end of Long Lake.

"Shut up," a male voice growled. The slap of flesh on flesh split the air.

The voice came from directly below Redmond, concealed from view by a pile of boulders. Redmond stole over the lip of the hill to kneel behind a huge pine from where he could see them. A big man with a round belly the shape of a wine barrel, dressed in a pale green tunic and brown trousers, dragged a boy, who could be no more than ten or eleven years old, from inside a hollow log. They struggled not

1

fifteen feet below him.

"You run away again and it'll be the lash," the man said. He heaved the boy from the ground. The boy kicked and squirmed.

"Release the child," Redmond called as he gripped the string of his bow and stepped from behind the tree.

The two froze for an instant before the man spun to gaze up the hill at Redmond.

"Let him go," Redmond said.

The man whipped a knife from his sheath and pressed it to the boy's throat. The boy stared up at Redmond with wide eyes. This was no father disciplining a wayward child. Redmond had seen his kind more often than he would have liked in the Kingdom of Morcia. This man was a slave catcher or slaver himself. But why would they be here, so far from any inhabited town or village?

"You work for Lord Otto of Windemere?" Redmond asked.

"Just walk away and forget what you saw," the man said, "or you'll regret it."

Redmond glanced around dramatically. "And who's going to make me regret it?" he asked. "I only see the two of us. Besides, I have trouble forgetting things like this."

"Don't be a fool," the man said.

"You hurt the boy, and you're a dead man," Redmond replied. Ever since the Salassani raid on his village many years ago, he could not abide men who preyed upon women and children. Much to his dislike, slavery was a fundamental part of Hallstat society here in the southlands, and children were often the easiest targets.

The man edged his way up the road holding the child in front of him as a shield. He was moving south. Why south? What could there be along the southern shores of Long Lake that would attract slavers who traded in children? The southern villages were farther away than the northern ones.

"You're leaving me no choice," Redmond said.

The man stepped on a stone that rolled under his boot, causing him to stumble. The boy slammed his head back into the man's face in a desperate bid for freedom. The slaver dropped the boy with a curse. Then he lunged to grab him.

Redmond's arrow caught the slaver in the throat. He staggered backward, clutching at the shaft before he tripped and tumbled over the side of the road into the rocks and trees below.

The boy scrambled back to the hollow log and dove inside. Redmond let him go and bounded down the hill to check on the slaver. The shaft of the arrow had snapped in his fall, but the blood still leaked from the ghastly wound. His body lay at an awkward angle with one arm bent beneath him. A pine tree had arrested his fall. The man stared up at Redmond. There was no point questioning him. He wouldn't be able to speak with a wound like that. There was nothing Redmond could do to help him.

"You gave me no choice," Redmond said.

The man's fingers spasmed as they clutched at the broken arrow shaft. His eyes took on the cold, glassy look of death, and his body stopped quivering. Redmond checked the man's pockets but only found a bag filled with silver dust and a few small silver nuggets. He hefted the bag thoughtfully, climbed up to the road, and squatted beside the rotted tree.

"It's safe to come out," he said. "I won't hurt you."

A brown head poked out.

"He can't hurt you anymore either," Redmond said.

Redmond backed up so the boy could come out on his own without fear that he would harm him.

The boy crawled out. Dirt smeared his face where a red welt still burned. His clothes barely covered his thin body. He had a starved look about him.

"What's your name?"

The boy frowned. "Henry," he said in a tremulous voice.

"I'm Redmond. I work for the Baron of Longmire. You're on his lands, but I'm curious to know how you came to be here."

Redmond slipped his waterskin over his head, took a swallow, and handed it to the boy who drank greedily. When he finished, he handed it back to Redmond.

"I wanna go home," the boy said.

Redmond stepped over to sit on the log. "Tell me where that is, and I'll do what I can to get you there."

The distant blowing of horns echoed over the hills. Redmond snapped his head up. He had left his men not half an hour ago to scout the area. There had been no sign of soldiers from Windemere or anyone else until he came across the slaver and the boy. He lunged to his feet.

"Stay here, lad," he said. "I'll come back for you."

He tossed the boy the bag of silver and scrambled up the hill, racing toward the little bridge that controlled the pass which cut through the hill country around Long Lake. They had been ordered to prevent any of the Baron of Windemere's men from using the pass to prey on the villages clustered at the northern end of the lake.

The deep-throated bellow of the horns called him on over the rugged terrain. He ducked beneath gnarled trees and tore through the wild rose bushes. The horns ceased calling. An eerie quiet settled over the hill country. Redmond pounded over the broken ground and up the last rise.

He paused on the ridge in confusion. His men were gone. The valley was empty. The pass was unguarded. The distant crash of steel and the hoarse cries of battle reached his ears. Redmond leapt down the hill, sliding and lunging in a cascade of loose stone and soil. The sounds of battle could only be coming from farther up the road where it passed out into the broad valley beyond. But why had his men left their post? There was no sign of battle here. What or who could have driven them from the gorge?

Redmond pelted down the rutted road, now overgrown with grass and weeds, before he broke through the gap to the long, narrow valley that split the hills. The creek spread out on the grassy plain where Redmond's archers struggled over a tiny bridge. There were only one hundred and twenty of them, and a force more than twice their size encompassed them. It was an indefensible position, and Redmond could not understand why his men would defy his orders and advance to such a weak location.

A host of men-at-arms on horseback and on foot encircled them. Mail armor and steel helmets glinted in the early morning sun. Their ranks bristled with lances, maces, swords, and axes. The footmen closed with Redmond's men, while the knights on their big chargers waited behind a row of crossbowmen with their long, wooden shields planted at intervals wide enough to allow the knights to ride through.

Redmond recognized the big black horse with the white, speckled flank. It was Lord Dacrey's, one of the Baron of Longmire's commanders. Why would Dacrey be attacking Redmond's archers? Not

Windemere

pausing to catch his breath, Redmond raced down the sloping road. There had to be some mistake. He had to stop this.

"Lord Dacrey," he called when he came within earshot, but no one heard him over the tumult of battle.

"Stop," he called again.

His men were dying. Killed by their own comrades. His sword slapped against his side as his boots pounded the road.

"Hold!" he yelled again.

Lord Dacrey turned his head. He wore a distinctive helm with bronze flourishes that ran up the noseguard and over the top of the helmet. He whirled his horse around to face Redmond with a sharp, unintelligible command. Several knights reined their chargers around and lowered their lances at Redmond.

What was happening? Redmond slowed and jogged up the rise to stop before the threatening points of the lances.

"Stop this madness," Redmond panted.

Dacrey studied him before nodding. A mounted man-at-arms raised a horn to his lips and blew two sharp blasts. The attackers hesitated and then withdrew, leaving more than a dozen men dead or dying amid the bayberry bushes and marsh grasses lining the creek. Redmond's archers hesitated, uncertain what the respite might mean.

"What are you doing?" Redmond demanded.

"Following orders," Dacrey said.

"Baron Longmire ordered you to kill his own men?"

Redmond gripped his bow in a tight fist. He wanted to shoot the insolent smirk off Dacrey's face.

"Did I say anything about Longmire?" Dacrey sneered. "Tell your men to lay down their weapons and no one else will get hurt."

Redmond glanced at his men. They huddled together, some still with their longbows in hand. A dozen appeared to be seriously injured and others were spattered in blood. Jannik, the big redheaded Rosythian, stood at their forefront with his huge battlehammer clutched in his hands.

Redmond's men were sturdy bowmen drawn from all over the mainland and the Frei-Ock Islands to serve as mercenaries for the feuding barons and nobles of Morcia. But they had not been prepared for betrayal.

"You're surrounded," Lord Dacrey said. "Baron Dragos doesn't pay you enough to die to hold this little pass."

"And who is paying you now?" Redmond asked.

Dacrey's horse pranced sideways. "That's none of your concern."

"It's my concern," Redmond replied, "when my men are betrayed by Baron Longmire's own knights."

"Either surrender, or we'll leave your bodies to the crows," Dacrey said.

"What guarantee do you give us?" Redmond demanded.

He had grown weary of these squabbling barons and wished, yet again, that he had stayed in the Kingdom of Deira. At least there the nobles didn't prey on each other like they did in Morcia. He certainly didn't want to see his men die for no purpose. And he wondered how Dacrey had lured them out of the pass where they held an easily defensible position.

"You can choose to fight a battle you cannot win, or you can spend a few weeks in leisure while we convince your baron to withdraw his claim to lands that are not his own."

Redmond knew full well these lands had been granted to the Baron of Longmire after the King had confiscated them from the Baron of Windemere.

"Your baron?" Redmond repeated. "Then you admit you are forsworn? How can we trust a man who so recently sang a different tune?"

"I will personally guarantee your safety," Dacrey said, "and you may yet find more profitable employment."

Redmond scoffed. "You didn't answer my question."

"I'm giving you a way out of an impossible situation," Dacrey said. "Take it or leave it."

Redmond glanced at his men where they clustered on the other side of the bridge. Their position was untenable with the enemy both before and behind. They were exposed. There was no escape or redoubt to which they could retreat. If he didn't surrender, he would be nothing more than a butcher.

"Give us your word of honor spoken here before all these men," Redmond said, "that you will spare the life of every man here and guarantee their freedom."

"Done," Sir Dacrey said.

"I want an oath," Redmond insisted.

Windemere

Sir Dacrey removed his helmet. His dark hair spilled over his mail shirt. "I give you my word of honor, Captain Redmond, that you and your men will be spared and set free once this matter is settled." Some of Redmond's men dropped their weapons and raised their hands. What more could he do?

Redmond set his bow on the grass and unbuckled his sword. As he raised his hands over his head, he remembered the boy he had left back at the rotten log. What would happen to Henry now? Should he tell Dacrey where Henry was hidden? If he did, Dacrey might simply re-enslave him. If he didn't, the boy would likely starve out here on his own. Redmond glanced back up the road toward the pass. Henry crouched in the shadow of a boulder at the mouth of the canyon. The boy had followed him.

Chapter 2
A Shadow in the Dark

ight settled over the hill country, bringing with it a cold drizzle that spat upon the men huddled in a tight group under the watchful eye of the guard. Redmond wriggled where he sat with his back to a rotten fence post to see if he could find relief from the pinch of the leather straps around his wrists. His men were no longer secured in a line but left to lounge on the soggy ground with their hands tied behind their backs. The groans of the injured floated through the night, but otherwise, they sat in grim silence. No fires could be lit in the steady downpour.

Most of Dacrey's army moved off after disarming Redmond's men. They had tied their captives in a long line and forced them on the foot-bruising march to Windemere. By the grumbling of the guards and the way they drew their hoods up and hunched over against the rain, they weren't enjoying the march much more than Redmond and his men. The guards couldn't even seek shelter in the burned-out remains of the farmhouses that littered the valley. The destruction had been too complete.

Redmond made sure he was on the far edge of his company as they settled in for the night. He noted the location of the guards and the timing of their movements. It would be a dark night without any moon. When the moment presented itself, he would slip free and disappear into the hills. If he could reach Baron Longmire's men posted at the mouth of the Wolf River on the north end of Long Lake, he could lead them back to rescue his men before they reached the castle at Windemere. He would have preferred to seek the aid of the rest of his mercenary band posted farther south to protect the

Windemere

villages at the other end of the lake, but they were too far away. He might even find the boy, Henry, lurking in the darkness alone and scared. Redmond hadn't said anything to Dacrey about the boy and hoped he wouldn't find him. At least alone the boy had a chance of freedom. To leave the boy unprotected in the wild went against every inclination of Redmond's nature. But what could he do? The lives of a hundred good men outweighed the life of one boy. Still, Redmond hoped Henry had found shelter. Maybe he had gone back to his hollow log.

"You'll never make it," a voice said in Redmond's ear. He jerked around to see Jannik squinting at him. The rain soaked Jannik's beard, causing his mustache to droop. The big man knelt beside him covered in mud. He must have crawled on his knees halfway through the men. A man his size would have been noticed had he risen to his feet.

"One of us has to try," Redmond said.

"It'll only be a few weeks before Longmire sends word to free us," Jannik said.

"You trust them?" Redmond asked.

"Do I have a choice?" Jannik studied Redmond. He looked around at the men huddled together under the drizzling rain and sighed. "All right. I'll create a diversion on the other side when they change the guard. You better have a way of cutting those straps loose or you aren't going far."

"I'll figure something out," Redmond said. He didn't have his knives anymore. The Hallstat had searched him thoroughly.

"Don't get caught," Jannik said as he turned to shoulder his way into the crowd, sloshing through the mud on his knees.

Redmond's men rolled onto their sides in exhaustion, trying to gather what rest they could before the long march recommenced in the morning. A few snored. The guards paced their rounds as the rain continued to dribble and the darkness deepened. Dacrey sent almost one hundred men to guard them, which meant any attempt to overpower them would only result in more dead archers to no purpose. The Baron of Windemere used slaves in his salt mines, and Redmond couldn't suppress the nagging doubt that, given the chance, the Baron would send his men there, as well. It was better to run for aid than to trust men known for their duplicity.

Something squished in the wet ground at the edge of Redmond's hearing. He searched the darkness for the culprit. It was unlikely any game would be afoot in this weather, and he had accounted for all of his men—at least he thought he had. A dark shape materialized, crawling toward him. The blood pounded in Redmond's ears. It could only be an assassin sent by Dacrey to silence him, or it might be one of his own men coming to cut him free. Redmond struggled to his knees.

The shape approached. The dull-gray of a knife clutched in a white hand shone stark against the black mud. Redmond lunged to his feet. The hand raised and pulled back a hood.

Henry peered up at him. Redmond opened his mouth in surprise before he dropped to his knees.

"What are you doing?" Redmond whispered.

Henry held up the knife. "Turn around," he said. He sliced through the leather straps before starting off into the darkness.

Redmond grabbed him. "Wait," he said. Jannik hadn't created his diversion yet. Should he run now or wait? Henry peered back at him with a puzzled expression.

"We need a horse," Redmond said.

Henry nodded. "I have one."

Redmond glanced back at his men. A few of them were watching him.

"I'll be back," he whispered to them and followed Henry into the night.

"Get off me," Jannik's voice bellowed from the other side of the encampment. Guards shouted. The prisoners awoke. Some lunged to their feet and scampered off.

Redmond cursed. He hadn't expected to have a boy to worry about when he made his escape.

"Where's the horse?" he demanded.

Henry sprinted through the knee-high grass, splashing and slipping in the mud. Redmond raced after him. They hadn't gone more than a hundred paces when Henry slid to a stop before one of the burned-out buildings. The rich scent of charred wood and wet ashes filled the air. Redmond followed Henry as he stepped over a fallen beam to where a shaggy little pony stood with its head down. It must have been the horse the slaver had used to track Henry. That would explain where Henry had acquired the cloak and the knife. But Redmond wasn't sure the pony could carry both of them.

Henry jerked the reins free and led the horse out of the building. Redmond lifted Henry into the saddle and placed his foot in the stirrup when a voice boomed through the night.

"Hold!"

Redmond whirled to peer around the corner of the building. Three guards approached from the other side. Two held long spears. One held a crossbow. Though the string was likely wet, the crossbow would still be deadly at this close range. How had they seen them? The building obscured their view of the horse and Henry. Maybe they had only seen Redmond and knew he was an escaping archer. Redmond shoved the horse farther behind the building, hoping to buy a few moments' time.

"Follow the road through the pass," Redmond whispered to Henry. "Take the right fork and ride all the way to where the road crosses the big river. You'll find Baron Longmire's men there. Tell them what happened and that we're being taken to Windemere. Tell them Lord Dacrey has betrayed them."

Henry reached down to clutch at Redmond's tunic as if he wanted to pull him up onto the saddle behind him. Even in the darkness, Redmond sensed the boy's hesitation. He didn't want to be alone in the wild.

"I'm sorry," Redmond said. "Your horse won't be able to get away with both of us. Just stay to the road."

If the guards knew he had escaped, they would pursue them, but if he surrendered, maybe they wouldn't notice that the horse bore a tiny rider.

He slapped the horse's rump. It jumped into a trot. Henry bent low over its neck and kicked it into a gallop. Redmond watched them disappear into the night before he raised his hands above his head and stepped out from behind the building. The guards fanned out to encircle him.

"You scared my horse away," he said. "You can't blame a man for trying."

Chapter 3
A Life in the Balance

Redmond had saved his men from the sword—only to condemn them to the lash. Would it have been better to suffer a bloody death on a field of battle he could not win or to endure the lingering, paralyzing murder of servitude?

They were alive, but at what cost? And for how long? Two weeks of hard labor and still no news from Baron Longmire.

The door to the dungeon growled on its hinges, and the flickering light of a candle pierced the darkness. Redmond blinked against the stabbing light as the guard kicked at his boot.

"You're wanted," the guard said.

"By whom?"

"Just get up."

Redmond stood and stretched his stiff limbs. He glanced at the two dozen men who shared his cell. They trusted him. He was their leader. Another seventy-five men huddled in similar stinking cells each night only to be let out during the day to labor for the Baron of Windemere. Redmond followed the guard past the cell doors where the rest of his men languished, and he vowed he would find a way to set them free. Torches burned in brackets along the walls, casting a yellow-orange light. Black smoke from the torches filled the corridor with an acrid reek that competed with the foul smell of human filth.

The guard opened the last door and stepped aside. Redmond hesitated as the fresh, warm air washed over his face. The sun had already dropped below the horizon, and darkness settled into the streets of the little castle town. Redmond glanced at the guard and his conical, steel helmet. Was this a ploy to accuse him of attempting to escape? The guard jerked his head toward the door, so Redmond stepped up to it.

A woman leaned against the far wall of the street. She wore a plain, brown linen dress and a lightweight black cloak with the hood pulled up. It was too hot for the woolen cloaks used in the north. Though cloaks were in fashion among the Hallstat, the only reason Redmond could see to wear one this time of year was to hide your identity. He glanced at the guard, who motioned for him to follow the woman.

"Hurry up," the guard insisted.

"Are you going stab me in the back and say I was trying to escape?" Redmond asked. Given the treachery already heaped upon Redmond and his men, it seemed like a reasonable question.

The guard grunted. "If Sir Dacrey wanted you dead, he wouldn't waste time with such charades. The girl will tell you." He placed a hand on Redmond's back and shoved him into the street. "Be back by dawn."

Redmond's boots scraped on the cobblestones as he stumbled out to meet the woman. She spun and strode away, so he followed her. The narrow streets of the town pinched close together with barely room for three men to walk abreast. The main streets allowed wagons to pass, but the rest squeezed tight to use the limited space inside the walls as effectively as possible.

The curtain walls of solid stone loomed up forty feet into the blue-black sky where the moon dangled amid the shreds of clouds. Pale moonlight cast long shadows over the clusters of homes and shops that lined the inside of the walls and piled on top of each other. Smoke from cooking fires carried the aroma of roasting meat and baking bread. Redmond's stomach rumbled. The rations Dacrey gave them seldom did more than stimulate his appetite. Two weeks on the stuff had left Redmond with a permanent pit in the middle of his gut.

The young woman led him through the gates into the inner ward where the square keep stabbed eighty feet into the air. A few injured men propped against the walls, nursing their wounds, while silent, motionless figures of dead soldiers stretched out on the cobblestones with cloaks thrown over their faces. Other soldiers unsaddled horses and stowed gear.

A battle or skirmish had taken place. Did the Baron think Redmond knew something about it? Or did he plan to punish Redmond and his men in retaliation?

The Baron of Windemere lived in the keep with his family when he wasn't at court. He had ridden out earlier that morning with several of the other lords who had come for some kind of council. Redmond glanced up at the battlements atop the keep. Why had he been summoned? And why hadn't he managed to somehow keep his boot knife?

They circled around to the back of the keep where it was closest to the wall and mounted the steps that led to the battlements. Then they crossed the narrow drawbridge that spanned the distance from the walls to the keep some forty feet above the ground. The guard, who wore the dark blue surcoat of the Baron of Windemere over a mail shirt, nodded as the young woman passed through the open door into the deeper darkness of the interior. The air in the keep became close and stuffy, filled with the smells of straw, cooking food, mildew, and human occupation.

The young woman climbed the twisting stairs that wound to the right before pausing on the landing to glance back at Redmond. From the arrow slits in the walls of the keep that Redmond counted on the way up, he guessed they were on the fourth floor. The girl lifted the latch and entered. The odor of smoke, sweat, and old straw filled the room. A fire popped and flickered in the fireplace. Torches blazed along the walls. A small group of ladies and a few men stood to one side.

In the center of the room, a man knelt amid the straw on the floor beside a portly man who stretched facedown on a fur robe with his torso bared. Blood dribbled from a wound in his back. Redmond recognized the prostrate man as Baron Otto Selgrave, the Lord of Windemere Castle.

He knew better than to ask what happened, but the sight of the seriously injured Baron sent a nervous tremor through him. He and his men counted on the Baron to keep his word and exchange them for the prisoners the Baron of Longmire had taken. If someone thought Redmond or his men had anything to do with this, their situation would become perilous.

The young woman lowered her hood as the man who knelt beside the injured baron scrambled to his feet and stepped toward them. Redmond now recognized him as the apothecary and the young woman as the one he had seen around the apothecary's shop. Her long brown hair cascaded over her shoulders as she edged into the shadows. She studied Redmond with dark eyes.

"Thank you for coming," the apothecary said.

Redmond didn't bother to tell him he hadn't been given a choice. The apothecary didn't appear to be the type of man who spent his time crushing herbs and mixing potions. He stood taller than Redmond and was built more to heft stones or swing an axe than to bend over an apothecary's table. Specks of gray flecked his temples. He kept his hair cropped short. The deep depressions of the pox marred his face, but he had more the bearing of a warrior about him than a bent-backed herbalist.

"I need your help," the apothecary said. He gestured to the Baron lying on the fur robe. "Lord Selgrave took an arrow in the back," he explained. "He jerked the shaft out, but the point remains. I would leave it, but I think it's floating loose and near the heart. I fear it may be a mortal wound."

Redmond glanced at the unconscious noble. "Why me?" he asked.

"Word is that you have some skill with arrow wounds."

"Where's his surgeon?"

"He was killed in the ambush."

"The barber, then?" Redmond wanted to find someone—anyone—to treat the Baron other than himself.

"We don't have one," the apothecary said. "I've been doing all that work."

Redmond pursed his lips and inspected the cluster of well-dressed ladies and their servants that stood beside the Baron.

"And if he dies?" Redmond asked. He knew better than to work on a noble without some guarantee of safety.

Feet shuffled, and a slender woman dressed in a sky-blue gown that glistened with jewels approached. Her hair had been pulled up into a bun, and more jewels dangled from her ears. She was an attractive woman.

"I will protect you," she said. "No matter what happens."

Redmond bowed to her. "Thank you, My Lady," he said.

This must be Adelaide Selgrave, the Baroness of Windemere and

Countess of Hiede. Her beauty and guile were famous. Did he dare trust her? These Hallstat women could be as powerful, or more so, than their husbands. Some, like Lady Adelaide, even maintained their own small armies. She was as likely as not to kill him, regardless of what happened. But what choice did he have?

"I'll need a knife, some boiling water, and clean towels," he said.

The apothecary nodded to the Baroness, who gestured to a serving girl to get what Redmond wanted.

"And," Redmond continued, "whiskey, moldy bread, pincers, and wooden rods of various sizes."

The servant hesitated, and the apothecary smiled.

"Anything else?" Lady Selgrave asked.

"Yes," Redmond said. "Turpentine, honey, boiled barley, two goose quills, soap, and several white wax candles."

Lady Selgrave studied Redmond with interest before gesturing to her servant girl, who hurried away.

The apothecary grabbed Redmond's elbow and pulled him aside. "I've already given him two tablespoons of dwale to help him sleep."

"What do you use in your mixture?" Redmond asked. He knew of apothecaries who added bile and bull urine to their recipes, and he considered these more dangerous than the pure form of dwale.

"Poppy seed extract, hemlock, and henbane mixed with honey."

"Nothing else?" Redmond asked.

"No," the apothecary said. "I like my mixtures to be clean, and I like them to work."

Redmond nodded. This apothecary knew what he was about. "What may I call you?" he asked.

"My name is Tal, and this is my daughter, Emilia." He gestured to the young woman that had fetched Redmond to the tower. She bowed her head to him. "She will assist you," Tal said.

When Redmond gave him a questioning glance, he held up his big hands. "She has smaller hands," he said with a shrug.

A servant entered and set a pot of water to boil over the fire.

"Do you have steady hands?" Redmond asked Emilia.

She gave him a coy smile. "Steadier than most men's."

Her reply surprised Redmond. He had expected a quiet, demure young woman, but she possessed more spirit than he anticipated.

"Good," he said. "If you work with me, you'll need to wash your hands."

"Why?" Emilia questioned.

Redmond glanced at Tal. "Because that is the way Lara trained me, and I have found that clean hands and tools make for fewer infections."

"Who's Lara?"

Redmond ignored her question, slipped his padded linen jacket off over his head, and rolled up the sleeves of his tunic. He pulled his long, grizzled-brown hair back and tied it with a string. By then, the supplies arrived, and he knelt to examine the wound.

The oblong cut showed him it had been a broadhead, which meant it was probably barbed. He glanced at Lady Selgrave.

"Wasn't he wearing a mail shirt?" he asked. "No broadhead should have penetrated a mail shirt and a padded gambeson this deeply."

Lady Selgrave frowned and glanced at a soldier standing by the door.

"He removed it to bathe in the stream," he said. "That's when they attacked us."

Redmond considered the wound. To remove his armor had been foolish—especially at a time when King Rupert Thurin was so preoccupied with his border war that he let his barons and earls prey upon each other.

Redmond poured whiskey and turpentine over the wound. The Baron jerked and groaned. Redmond jabbed the pincers into the fire and washed his hands and arms with the soap and hot water. Emilia watched him before doing the same. He then picked up the knife, washed it with the whiskey and turpentine, and laid it beside the man on a clean cloth before washing the wooden dowels in the same manner. When everything was ready, he glanced up at the men standing nearby.

"Hold him," he said.

The dwale might have made the Baron drowsy, but even drugged men could respond to pain. The guards knelt to restrain the Baron, and Redmond used the tip of the knife to widen the wound. The Baron jerked, and the men sat on him to hold him still. Redmond inserted the smaller wooden dowel into the oozing wound. He slid his finger along the dowel, searching for the point, but he couldn't find it. It had gone deeper than he expected.

He slipped the dowel free and inserted the next largest dowel, working it back and forth to stretch open the wound. Then he inserted his finger again. Still nothing.

Emilia kept track of the dowels, handing him the next size up as he worked through them. He worried the point had passed to the other side of the Baron's body, in which case, there was nothing he could do. The last dowel scraped against something that was not bone. He slipped his finger in as far as he could reach. The barb on the broadhead cut his finger. He flinched at the stab of pain.

"Quills," he said to Emilia. She handed them to him. He trimmed them and then slipped the ends over the barbs of the broadhead. That way, they would not catch and tear at the flesh when he extracted the point.

"Pincers," he said.

Emilia withdrew the pincers from the fire, the tips now glowing red, and handed them to him. He poured whiskey over them. The whiskey sizzled and spat as it evaporated off the hot metal. He glanced at Emilia and Tal. Did they understand how dangerous this wound was? From the depth and location, it was obvious the point rested just behind the Baron's heart.

Redmond could end this man's life by simply giving the point a little push. The point would then penetrate the heart, and the Baron would bleed out. No one could blame him. He could tell them the wound had been mortal. Who would know? Redmond found Emilia watching him.

Their gazes met, and he realized that she guessed what was going through his mind. This was the Baron who had seized Redmond's men and forced them into hard labor. He had been in conflict with the Baron of Longmire for years and had murdered many innocent peasants whose only crime had been working their lord's lands. If he died now, maybe Redmond could help bring an end to the death and destruction and, thereby, free his men. He hesitated. Emilia's eyes narrowed. She probably thought he was going to do it.

Redmond slipped the large dowel free and inserted the smaller one so he would have room for the long, narrow tip of the pincers. Emilia held the dowel steady and pushed the ends of the quills out of the way. Then Redmond inserted the pincers into the wound. The blood boiled and hissed. Baron Selgrave jerked and cried out, and Redmond yanked the pincers free as the men struggled to restrain him. The Baron had almost killed himself. If the pincers had made contact with the broadhead while he was flailing about, they would have driven the point right into his heart.

After the Baron quieted, Redmond slipped the pincers in again until they grated against metal. He pinched the socket of the broadhead and hesitated.

One little push. One imperceptible jerk. That's all it would take. Emilia watched him with wide eyes. Redmond glanced at the apothecary, who gave a slight shake of his head. Redmond took a deep breath and slowly drew the point out. The quills guided the barbs free. The upwelling of blood that followed the point drew a gasp from the women who had remained to watch. Redmond dropped the point onto the Baron's back and poured whiskey over the wound again. The Baron flinched again and cried out, and Redmond had to catch the point as it slid off his back. Then Redmond held a clean cloth over the wound until the flow of the blood slowed.

"Hold it open," he said to Emilia. She used her fingers to keep the cut open as Redmond scraped the mold from the bread into the wound. Then he prepared a poultice of honey and boiled barley and pressed it onto the oozing gash.

When they finished, Redmond sat back and wiped the sweat from his brow with his sleeve. He struggled to his feet.

"If he doesn't take a fever and the wound doesn't fester, he should live."

Lady Adelaide bent to feel the Baron's forehead. Then she straightened with a rustle of her blue gown and examined Redmond from head to toe.

"You'll need to change the poultice twice daily," Redmond said before washing the blood from his hands and arms. "Only use boiled barley and honey and clean towels."

Tal patted Redmond on the back. "That was expertly done," he said. "Would you have time to talk? I have some questions for you."

"I'm supposed to be back at the dungeon by dawn," Redmond said.

"I'll speak to the guards," the Lady Adelaide said. "You can stay with the apothecary if you like."

Redmond bobbed his head in gratitude, and the woman spun with a swish of skirts that scattered the straw at her feet. He watched her back as she departed with a deep sense of foreboding. Something had changed in her demeanor—in the way she looked at him.

Chapter 4
The Apothecary and His Daughter

milia contemplated the tall stranger as he strode down the stairs beside her father. He carried himself with a confident grace, but he didn't give off the same arrogant dismissal of others she so often saw among the nobles. Nor had he been cowed by the presence of the beautiful Baroness—or the responsibility of treating a powerful baron. What piqued her interest the most was the fact that he considered killing the Baron. She had seen it in his eyes. One little push would have ended the Baron's life. Why didn't he do it? What stayed his hand? It wasn't simple fear. He didn't seem like the kind of man who would allow fear to control him.

Fear was something Emilia understood well. She had been living with it since she was a child. It had taken root in her heart on a cold winter's night in the city of Langon, when she was six or seven years old.

The door to her father's tiny apothecary shop had burst open to let in the bite of the winter wind that swirled around the shop, causing the flames to dance in the fireplace.

Baron Otto Selgrave of Windemere stumbled in, supported by a wide-eyed servant who wore a drooping hat. Emilia cowered against the stone fireplace, pulling her blanket tight around her tiny frame. Her father had pointed out the Baron to her a few days earlier and told her he had fought with him in the border wars.

The Baron mumbled something, but his mouth was horribly blistered. Bloody spittle dribbled off his chin. He hunched over with a hand on his belly, making hideous gurgling noises in his throat.

21

Tal sprang to his feet and helped the servant ease the Baron onto a bench at the table. Emilia's father was a tall powerful man who had once been a warrior. But when the plague swept through the southlands and claimed everyone in their family except her and her father, he had never gone to war again. He still bore the marks of the pox on his face. For some reason, she remained unharmed by the disease.

"Please," the servant said. "He's been poisoned."

"With what?" Tal asked.

The old servant shook his head, wagging his floppy hat. "I don't know."

"I have to know what it was," Tal insisted.

"I don't know," the old man wrung his hands. "It might have been lye."

Tal's face blanched. "Lye?" he said. "How would he swallow that?"

"It was in his mulled spiced wine. He only took a sip."

Tal raced to the pot of goat's milk warming by the fire. He poured a pint and brought it to the Baron. "Drink this," he said.

The Baron pulled away and groaned.

"You have to," Tal said. "If it was lye, it could eat a hole in your stomach."

The Baron stared at Tal for a moment, then nodded. Tal lifted the cup to his lips. Milk dribbled down the front of the Baron's fine tunic, but he managed to swallow.

"More," Tal coaxed. He kept insisting until the Baron drained the pint. Then he filled another and mixed it with the tonic he called dwale and made him drink that.

When he finished, the Baron grimaced and curled up on the bench in obvious pain. Tal retreated to his workbench and began mixing and grinding some new concoction. When he finished, he lifted a small bag from a hook on the wall.

"These honey candies will help soothe his throat," Tal said. Then he handed the servant the clay jar of powdered herbs. "This tea will help calm his stomach. There's nothing more I can do."

The old servant eyed the bag of candies and the pot of powder. "What is it?" he asked.

Tal shrugged. "Don't worry. It won't hurt him."

Most people thought of her father as a benevolent witch doctor, but few trusted him. If anything went wrong with one of his patients, they could become dangerous. When the servant still didn't look convinced, Tal continued.

"The candy drops have honey mixed with a blend of herbs."

"What herbs?"

"Horehound, hyssop, linden flower, sage, thyme, and few others. It won't hurt

him.

"And this?" The servant held up the clay pot.

"It's just a tea with chamomile, marshmallow, and my own dwale. It will ease the pain in his stomach and help him rest."

The servant scowled. "Will he survive?"

"I don't know," Tal said. "If he only swallowed a sip, he might be fine."

The Baron did survive, and Emilia thought she had seen the last of him, but a week later he reappeared, pounding on their door. This time, he wore his sword and his deep blue cloak. He brought half a dozen armed men with him. The blisters on his mouth had diminished, but he spoke in a quiet, raspy voice.

"You will pack your things and come with me."

Emilia darted to her father and hugged his waist. He placed a large hand on her head.

"My Lord?" Tal said.

"I have purchased your debt," the Baron said. "You are now my property."

Tal scowled and glanced down at Emilia. "But I was paying the debt," he said.

Emilia knew the merchant who owned the debt had been kind enough to let her father pay it off rather than send him to debtor's prison.

"Now you will pay it to me in the form of your services," the Baron whispered. "I may never recover from this attack. Your drops and tea are the only things that bring me any relief. I need you."

The Baron's gaze fell on Emilia. His flicker of interest there made a nervous tremor ripple through her belly. Tal pulled her close and straightened to his full height. He was several inches taller than the stocky Baron.

"I'll only go with you," he said, "if you swear in writing, that you will never lay a finger on my daughter and that you'll protect her from any other man."

The Baron scoffed and waved a hand at him. "Don't be a fool," he said. "I can take you both in chains if I desire."

Tal held his ground. "You will have to kill me first," he said.

The Baron scowled, clearly unused to being contradicted by a mere apothecary. He raised his fist as if to strike.

"If you refuse to protect her," Tal said, "You will never know when death will come."

The Baron hesitated. "Are you threatening me?" he demanded.

"I am merely pointing out that if you take my medicine, your life is in my hands."

The Baron stared for a moment and then gave a quiet laugh. He grimaced at the pain. "It is a small price to pay," he whispered.

Well, it was no small price to Emilia. The Baron's protection had been the only thing that kept her safe in the small castle town where soldiers, mercenaries, and nobles came and went and enjoyed free run of the place. Every other maiden had been meddled with at one time or another, some brutally. But Emilia had reached adulthood unsullied—for now.

And here, walking beside her father, was a man to whom the Baron would owe a great debt if he survived. Emilia studied Redmond's back as the seed of an idea sprouted in her mind.

The midnight air greeted them as Redmond, Tal, and Emilia stepped out of the keep. This southern clime never offered much in the way of relief from the heat. The warm breeze that blew in off the distant dunes beyond the mountains promised another hot day to come. Stars spread out in the great vault of the sky, broken by the dark silhouette of the battlements. Orange watch fires flickered in the darkness, casting dancing shadows up the stone walls and over the thatched roofs.

The muted clink of metal and jovial laughter drifted to them from the soldier's quarters that hugged the edge of the curtain walls on one side of the inner courtyard. The merrymaking for which the Baron's household was famous still persisted—despite the tragic ambush. The bodies of the dead had been removed, and no one mourned them.

Redmond followed Tal and his daughter as they made their way through the gates and into the outer ward where dozens of huts and buildings hugged the narrow, winding streets. A man dressed in fine silk stumbled from an alleyway and came up short as his gaze focused on Emilia. He grabbed her arm.

"You've found a pretty one," he mumbled to Redmond. "I'll take my turn." He smelled like sour grapes.

Before Redmond could respond, Emilia yanked her hand free, drew a knife, and pressed it against the man's throat.

"Don't touch me," she snarled.

The man blinked at the knife and grabbed her wrist with surprising speed for a drunk.

Windemere

"Emilia," Tal cried.

Redmond lunged, driving his fist into the man's ribs, which bent under the blow. The man grunted and fumbled with a sword that dangled at his waist. Tal grabbed the fumbling hand to prevent him from drawing it as Emilia backed away. Redmond slammed an elbow into the man's temple. The man slumped sideways against the wall and slid to the ground.

Tal checked to make sure the man was still alive. Then he straightened, casting a furtive glance around them, and grabbed Emilia's hand to drag her away from the scene. Redmond sped after them.

They raced through the shadows until Tal paused in front of a shuttered workshop, fumbled with the key, and ushered them through the door. He checked the street before shoving the door closed and locking it. Redmond watched them. He couldn't make out Tal's expression as he turned from the door, but a beam of moonlight slipped in through a crack to illuminate Emilia's face. She bore a ferocious expression. He kept underestimating this girl. She would have died fighting rather than submit to the indignity that drunk would have forced upon her.

Tal stepped away from the door. "Are you all right?" he asked Emilia.

She threw off her thin cloak and faced the fireplace. "Fine," she said.

Redmond blinked until his eyes adjusted to the dim light. A goshawk tied to a perch in a dark corner ruffled its feathers in response to Emilia's sudden movement. It blinked its orange eyes and puffed out the white and black barred feathers on its chest. White sand had been strewn on the floor underneath to catch its droppings and pellets. Emilia stroked its wing feathers to calm it, then bent to light the fire. The presence of the goshawk surprised Redmond. Falconry was a sport limited to the nobility or wealthy merchants. Common folk didn't have the time or resources to care for them.

"We have several more hawks in the mews outside," Tal said. "The Baron gave us a yard to weather them and to grow my herbs. It's small, but we get by."

The rich smells of spices and herbs filled the shop. Drying herbs tied in bunches dangled from the rafters. Shelves with glass and clay vials and pots lined the wall behind a workbench where a small mortar and pestle sat with various bags and tools of the apothecary's trade. A rectangular table with two benches stood before the fire, and two small doorways led off toward the back of the house.

"Who was that?" Redmond asked.

Tal watched Emilia's back as she prepared the fire. "He's one of Dacrey's men," he said. "Some minor noble from Harrowden." Tal paused. "It's a good thing you didn't kill him."

Redmond wasn't sure who Tal was talking about. He might be referring to the Baron or to the drunk they had just met. Emilia struck the flint, wrapped the charcloth with the glowing ember in the nest of grasses, and bent to blow on the spark. It smoked for a moment before bursting into flame. She placed it in the fireplace, feeding it with shavings until she coaxed it to a good, hot flame.

"*I'll* kill the next man that touches me," Emilia said while staring into the flickering fire.

Tal gestured to a bench at the table. "Please, sit," he said.

Redmond stepped over the bench and took a seat. Tal joined him with a glance at Emilia.

"Thank you for your help," Tal said.

"Anytime," Redmond said. "Now, would you mind explaining what's going on here?"

Tal shifted. "These are dangerous times."

Emilia stood and fed a few scraps of meat to the hawk.

"These Barons are up to something," Tal said. "Baron Otto and King Rupert have long been at odds, but this is something new. King Rupert is demanding new taxes and levies for his border war. Baron Otto called for a council of nobles, but the King refused. A few weeks later, the barons and other nobles started showing up here."

Redmond already knew most of this. He had served Justin Dragos, the Baron of Longmire, for two months now. The Hallstat King, Rupert Thurin, wanted to reclaim the lands his grandfather lost to the Kingdom of Deira in the east. Their border had become a permanent war zone with raids and counter-raids and the occasional all-out battle. Redmond spent some time on the Deira side of the border a few years before he traveled north to the Kingdom of the Kassan.

Kassan was a poor kingdom fighting the nomadic forest people. It was a bloody, vicious fight, and did not pay well. Eventually, Redmond and two hundred of his friends and fellow archers came south seeking better pay and better working conditions. Redmond and his friends had signed on with Baron Longmire because he was far away from the border and known to pay his men regularly.

"Baron Selgrave can't defy the King," Redmond said.

Tal laughed. "If you lived around Otto and his wife, Adelaide, long enough, you'd know they eventually get what they want. This is one of the best-situated baronies in the kingdom. Otto controls the salt mines in the Denlani Mountains. The gold that flows north from across the desert in exchange for the salt passes through his hands first. The King has to reckon with him."

"You think they're planning a rebellion?" Redmond asked.

"They're plotting something up there in that stuffy keep of theirs," Tal said.

"If things are so bad, why don't you leave and go to Royan or Arras?" Redmond asked. "There's more work for an apothecary in the cities."

Tal studied the table. "I can't," he said.

Redmond waited. Emilia clicked her tongue and disappeared into a back room.

"I have to serve the Baron of Windemere."

"Why?"

Tal fingered a stain on the table with his forefinger. "Because he holds my debt."

Redmond understood. The Hallstat employed many types of servitude that did not exist on Frei-Ock Mor.

"My father wasn't a wise man," Tal said. "He took on a debt he couldn't repay. When the pox took him and the rest of my family, I inherited his debt. The Baron bought it because he wanted my services."

"But he won't let you fulfill the debt?"

Tal shook his head.

"Why?"

Tal rubbed his jaw.

"Tell him," Emilia demanded. Redmond hadn't noticed that she had returned to stand in the doorway. "Tell him," she insisted.

"I make the drugs he needs to keep his slaves working in the mines."

Redmond stared. He had seen the slaves they dragged out of the mines. Their bodies were crusted white with salt. Their pallid faces and emotionless stares made them appear like the dead walking. Any man who participated in this business had to be the lowest and meanest of people. He had been growing to like the apothecary, but this revelation repulsed him.

Tal must have seen the revulsion slip across Redmond's face because he stood up and stepped over to the fire. Redmond glanced at Emilia, who watched her father with such an expression of tenderness and hopelessness it brought a burst of sympathy into Redmond's chest.

"What will this mean for Emilia?" Redmond asked.

Tal didn't face him. "For now, the Baron protects her, but if he dies…"

The popping of the fire rushed in to fill the silence left by Tal's unfinished sentence. No one spoke.

Tal spun and clapped his hands. "Enough about us," he said. "I want you to explain your methods. Why do you use mold? And why do you wash everything?"

The next morning dawned warm and bright. Redmond slept well on the floor of Tal's shop before the fire—far better than his men would have rested in the dark, fetid dungeons. His mind wandered over the events of the last two weeks as he crept from the apothecary's hut to return to his men.

What had happened to the boy named Henry? Had he made it to the Baron of Longmire's men? If he had, then why had no message arrived from the Baron to negotiate their release? Had the raid that injured Baron Selgrave been the only reply Baron Dragos would give to Dacrey's betrayal and their capture? Perhaps the Baron of Longmire decided to write them off as an unavoidable loss and had no intention of recovering them. After all, they were mere mercenaries—hired bows whose deaths would create no political difficulties in Morcia. They were expendable.

As Redmond approached the prison door, the guard waved him away. Redmond hesitated.

"Her Ladyship sends for you," the guard said.

Windemere

Redmond scowled. "Again?"

The guard shrugged off his protest. "It's not my problem," he said.

Redmond headed back up the street with a dissatisfied grunt. He was a fighting man, and he did not like getting involved in noble squabbles. As he approached the keep, he became supremely conscious of having no weapon. Nobles were a cantankerous bunch, and he knew better than to trust them.

The guards simply pointed Redmond up the stairs with a knowing smirk that sent a nervous shiver up his spine, making him wary. He missed the comforting weight of a sword at his hip and the bulge of a knife in his boot.

Everything about the keep set him on edge. Cool shadows closed about him as he stepped inside—just like they did at the entrance to the prison. The gray stone pressed in upon him as if to enfold him in a cold, mirthless embrace. The stairs wound up to the right, and the steps were uneven—all of which made it difficult for a right-handed intruder to fight his way up the stairs. But it also meant there was only one way out. The narrow arrow slits provided light, but no escape. Someone burned incense to cover the odor of human occupation. The sharp scent tickled his nostrils. This keep could well become his tomb.

A teenage servant girl with long brown hair and skittish eyes was waiting for him as he climbed to the floor where he had treated the Baron. She continued up the stairs to the next floor, where she ushered him into a room with walls draped in green silk. Candles burning in sconces cast a flickering light off a gilded mirror and dark wooden bedposts. The sight of the empty bed made him frown. The room smelled of incense and cinnamon.

The Baroness stood with her back to him. Her silver silk dress was open at the back exposing her creamy white skin and delicate shoulder blades. The door closed behind him with a quiet snap. Redmond glanced around, hoping to find some other servant still in the room. But he was alone—alone with one of the most powerful women in the kingdom. He clenched his jaw and flexed his fingers, trying not to fidget. This woman was dangerous. He needed to extricate himself from this situation as soon as possible.

The Baroness turned with a soft swish of silk and flashed him a beautiful smile. Redmond had rarely seen a more attractive woman. Her dark brown hair draped over her shoulder, and her silk dress revealed the contours of her body. She must have been in her late twenties or early thirties. Redmond shuffled his feet.

"I want to thank you for saving my husband's life," she said.

Redmond nodded.

"And I would like to make you an offer."

He waited.

"The captain of my guard was killed in the ambush." She paused. "And I want to offer you the position."

Redmond watched her, tight-lipped, uncertain how to respond. She knew nothing about him. He hadn't been in Morcia long enough to develop a reputation. She stepped toward him. Her sweet perfume preceded her.

"The position comes with certain…privileges," she said. Her voice grew soft.

Redmond stepped back. The Baroness scowled and hesitated.

"Do you understand what I'm offering you?" she asked.

"Yes, My Lady," Redmond said.

"And what is your answer?" Her eyes narrowed in guarded anticipation.

Redmond swallowed. He shifted his feet and glanced at the door. "I'm sorry, My Lady, but I must decline."

The Baroness pinched her lips tight. She scowled at him for a moment before spinning away from him.

"What is your reason?" she demanded with her back to him. She stood straight and rigid.

"I am promised to another," he said.

The Baroness faced him with a knowing smile.

"Ah," she said. "You're a romantic as well as a warrior and a healer. Do you also quote poetry?"

Redmond avoided her gaze.

The Baroness stepped toward him again. "I promise I won't ruin you for this lady love," she said in a low, seductive voice.

Redmond cleared his throat. "Thank you, My Lady, for the honor of your proposal, but I still have duties to my men."

The Baroness waved an annoyed hand. "You are a sword for hire," she sneered. "You owe loyalty to whomever pays you."

Windemere

"Until my men are free," Redmond replied, "I am bound to them."

A crafty smile spread over her face, and she clasped her hands together. "So if I release your men, you will accept my offer?"

Redmond hesitated. Was he willing to pay that price to set his men free? What about Lara? He had left her without so much as a goodbye. She might have assumed he was dead by now and married someone else. She might have been so hurt that she would never forgive him or accept him if he did go back, but he didn't know.

"When my men are free and back with Baron Dragos, I will be your captain—but only your captain."

The Baroness looked as if he had slapped her.

"Phah," she scoffed with a dismissive flick of her wrist. "Every man is free to betray those who trust him. They all do."

"Not me," Redmond said, though he had abandoned Lara, Neahl, and Weyland. But, in that instance, he had been given no choice. If he hadn't left the island and drawn the assassins after him, they might all be dead.

The Baroness narrowed her eyes with renewed interest.

"I will see what I can do," she said. "Leave me."

She spun away from him and disappeared into an adjoining room. The scent of her perfume washed over him. He was a fool. This woman was as powerful as any male noble, and she had a reputation of being crafty and vengeful.

Chapter 5
The Reed and the Flail

ady Adelaide Selgrave waved her servants out of her room and dropped into a chair at the table where several candles burned. A map of the Kingdom of Morcia covered the table. She bent to study it. The problem of their border with the Barony of Longmire needed to be resolved in her favor. She had lost a competent captain and needed to find a suitable replacement.

Unable to focus, she sat back, rubbing her eyes. This isn't the way she expected to spend her morning. She hadn't been rejected by a man since she was sixteen. Most men were too afraid to say no to her, but not this one. Why? Did he really have a secret love to whom he was faithful? If he did, he was the only man she had ever known who didn't sow his wild oats when the chance presented itself.

The sting of her first rejection still smarted after all these years. The poets and bards claimed that first love was the most exciting and the most painful. Maybe they were right.

"You said you would ask your father if we could marry," Adelaide had said. The bitter disappointment burned in her throat. Hans, the tall, blonde son of a lesser noble family fallen on hard times, held her hands in his. He gazed at her with earnest blue eyes. He was four years her senior. They had met at a tournament, and her father invited him to come train with his men.

Hans lifted a hand to trace the bruise on her cheek her father had given her that morning. Her father seethed with rage when he discovered that she and Hans were seen holding hands.

"Why did I have a pretty daughter if not to sell her to a powerful lord?" he said. "Hans is a good fighter, but he is a petty noble who will never amount to anything. I won't marry you off to any lord below an earl unless he comes with

a great fortune."

And now Hans stood in the secluded stairwell where they had spent many passionate moments to say he had betrayed her. That he would do nothing to rescue her from her father.

"I did ask him," Hans said. "He said 'no.'"

"You said you loved me." Adelaide choked on the words.

Hans dropped her hands. "I did. I mean, I do. But..."

"But what?" she demanded.

"Klara of Gurloch comes with a substantial dowry, and your father hates me. He says my family isn't good enough."

"We're both children of nobles," Adelaide said.

"She has a bigger dowry," Hans said. "My father would never agree to a union between us now."

A knot tightened in Adelaide's throat. "You're giving me up for a dowry? I'm worth no more to you than a piece of land and a bag of gold?"

"Be sensible," Hans said.

Adelaide grabbed his hands. "Take me away," she pleaded. "Let's go now."

Hans smirked at her. "You've listened to too many songs," he said. "In the real world, people marry for money—not love."

Adelaide slapped him as hard as she could and fled.

Those were the last words Hans had spoken to her before he left her to three more years of abuse at her father's hand. Now Hans and his wife Klara would be coming to Windemere to meet with Baron Otto. She hadn't seen Hans in all this time. She had purposefully avoided him.

Her older brother had died in battle, and she inherited her father's Earldom of Hiede and his vassals. She was a powerful woman now as a countess and a baroness. Even her husband had to tread lightly. He needed her, and he had good reason to fear her. Though she no longer needed Hans, he, too, would learn to respect her as he should have done.

Redmond's rejection wasn't the only reason she was disappointed. She had made inquiries about this Redmond of Frei-Ock Mor. He was a skilled warrior and a loyal servant. Loyalty was difficult to find in anyone, let alone a soldier. She had assumed she would be able to turn him the way she had Lord Dacrey. But this conquest was going to be more of a challenge. Still, she had all the advantages. Redmond would break, one way or another.

Redmond worked his way back toward the dungeon, trying to free himself of the haunting sense of impending doom. He and his men were entirely in Lady Selgrave's power. She could do with them as she wished, and still he had rejected her. What was he thinking? He had only made their situation worse.

His men filed toward the gate to resume work on the new barbican the Baron had ordered for the purpose of extending his fortifications to the other side of the moat. They still wore the same clothes they had when they were captured, though most had shed the heavy padded shirts they wore in battle. Salt from their sweat crusted on their now-stained yellow tunics. Their ragged, brown trousers and leather boots showed the wear of their heavy labor.

These were proud men, able to withstand the horrors of war and the deprivation of sieges, but Redmond could sense their growing frustration. Promises had been made and not kept. With each day of servitude, the chance of regaining their freedom diminished. Redmond fell in with his men, giving a nod to the guards.

Jannik sidled up to him.

"Where've you been?" he asked.

Redmond grinned. He liked Jannik and had served with him for years up in the forest of Byrne. Jannik drew a heavy 150-pound warbow and liked to wield a huge hammer in battle. Few men were more useful on a battlefield and few managed to maintain a more positive outlook regardless of the circumstances.

"Rubbing shoulders with nobles and apothecaries," Redmond said.

Jannik gave him a comical smirk. "You mean you need an apothecary to play with nobles?"

Redmond grinned. "They do tend to give a man a sour stomach."

Jannik elbowed Redmond. "You were gone all night. I've heard stories about that Baroness."

Redmond smirked. "You should know me better than that by now."

"I've never asked why you avoid women," Jannik said. "But that woman would tempt any man, no matter which way his appetites might tend."

A commotion erupted at the front of the line, and the men

stopped. Redmond and Jannik pushed their way to the front. The unfinished walls of the barbican cast a long shadow over the piles of sand and cut stone. The guards had drawn their weapons and forced the prisoners up against the far wall as two other guards dragged a Hallstat warrior from a pile of sand where he had been buried.

A shiver of recognition swept through Redmond, along with a deep foreboding. It was the drunken noble that assaulted Emilia the night before. Even from the shadow of the wall, Redmond could see that the side of his head had been crushed. White sand mingled in the clotted mass of broken bone, brains, and blood.

The captain of the guard straightened from inspecting the corpse and surveyed the prisoners until his gaze fell upon Redmond.

"You," he said. "Come here."

Redmond stepped forward as his men parted to let him through.

"Which one of your men did this?" the captain demanded.

Redmond restrained a smirk of annoyance.

"How could any of them do it?" Redmond replied. "They've been under close guard since we arrived."

The captain narrowed his eyes in suspicion. "That's true," he said. "You're the only one who was allowed to wander around last night."

A murmur erupted from the men behind Redmond.

"I didn't kill him," Redmond said. "I never even came near the gate."

The captain gestured to the guards behind him.

"Bind him," he said. "And make a count of the prisoners. I want to know if anyone is missing."

Redmond considered telling the captain to ask Tal and Emilia where he had been, but he didn't want to cast suspicion on them—especially since the dead man had attacked Emilia. He held his tongue as the guards slipped the rope around his wrists and cinched it tight. As the guards tied the knots, the Baroness appeared on the western tower to watch them.

Suspicion sprouted in Redmond's mind. Was she behind this? He didn't have time to ponder the thought because the guard dragged him away toward the keep. They hadn't gone far when a runner coming from the keep met them. He wore the light blue livery of the Baroness.

"Release him," he demanded.

The guards paused. "But the captain said—"

"Lady Selgrave has given her orders," he interrupted. "Release him."

The captain approached with the swish of a mail shirt flapping around his thighs. "What is this?" he demanded.

The guard gave a helpless gesture. "Lady Selgrave sends word to release him."

The captain scowled. "On what grounds?"

The messenger handed the captain a folded piece of paper. It crinkled as the captain unfolded it. He grimaced as he read and then crumpled the paper with a grunt of disgust.

"Untie him," he said.

Another guard jogged up to them.

"One is missing, sir," he said.

"Which one?"

"The short bald one."

"Find him," the captain said. "He can't have gone far on foot." Then he faced Redmond. "If I find you had anything to do with this, I'll hang you myself."

"In the meantime," the messenger said, "he comes with me."

Redmond sighed as the guards untied his hands. This Baroness was going to get him killed or drive him to kill someone.

Emilia met them at the door of the keep. She wore brown cotton trousers, knee-high leather boots, and a rust-colored tunic with a leather vest. A falconer's glove had been tucked under her belt next to a long dagger.

"I'll take him from here," she said to the messenger. The man gave a non-committal shrug and left them.

"You seem to have a nose for trouble," Emilia said.

"Yeah," Redmond agreed. "At least in Windemere."

"Looks like the Baron has taken an infection," Emilia said. "You have any more tricks up your sleeve?"

"Maybe," Redmond said.

Why hadn't the Baroness mentioned the infection when he met with her moments before? Had she wanted him to see the dead man dragged from the sand? Was she sending him a message? Maybe she would kill the Baron and blame it on Redmond.

Emilia paused at the door on the second level and knocked.

Windemere

"Come," Lady Selgrave said. The Baroness must have raced along the battlements to arrive before they did. Emilia followed Redmond through the doorway.

The room had one narrow window that let in a slanting ray of morning light. A fire crackled in the hearth. The Baroness rose from a chair to greet them. She was as alluring as ever in her pale green gown.

"If you keep getting into trouble," she said with a smirk, "I may not always be there to get you out."

"You know I didn't kill anyone," Redmond said.

Lady Selgrave raised her eyebrows. "Perhaps," she said. Then she pointed to the Baron who lay sweating and groaning on a fur-lined bed before the fire. "We did as you instructed, but he has still taken a fever."

Redmond knelt beside the Baron and peeled back the dressing to find the wound swollen and red. He pinched it and yellow pus oozed out.

"I've seen worse," he said. "But this has to be cleaned. I need a hollow cane and whiskey."

Lady Selgrave clapped her hands and a serving girl entered. "Get him whatever he requests," she ordered.

Redmond gave the servant a long list of items he needed and then rolled up his sleeves. He glanced at Emilia.

"Will you assist me again?" he asked.

Emilia nodded and followed his example.

Lady Selgrave folded her legs under her and sat beside the fire to watch.

Several servant girls filed in with the requested materials, and Redmond set to cleaning and washing his hands and the tools. When everything was laid out, Redmond picked up the long hollow cane.

"Hold it open," he said to Emilia, gesturing to the festering gash.

She used her fingers to push the wound open. Redmond inserted the cane into the wound. Pus welled up around the edges and spilled over Emilia's fingers, but she didn't flinch.

Redmond filled his mouth with whiskey, bent over the cane and blew the whiskey into the wound. Watery, yellow pus gushed out. The Baron jerked and moaned, and Redmond pressed a knee into his back to hold him. He repeated the procedure until the pus quit flowing. He extracted the cane and washed the area with turpentine before he scraped more green mold from the bread into the wound.

"You'll need to do this twice a day," he said, glancing over his shoulder at Lady Adelaide.

"I will see you are summoned," the Baroness said.

Redmond frowned but didn't say anything. He would rather train someone else to do it. The idea of becoming the Baron's personal physician was not a happy one. He wasn't qualified, and he wanted to keep a healthy distance from Lady Selgrave.

Emilia prepared the barley poultice and helped him wrap it in place.

"He'll need fluids," Redmond said. "He won't be able to sit up, but if you use a cane like this or a piece of straw, he should be able to get what he needs."

Lady Selgrave gestured to Emilia. "We'll need several quail and rabbits for the broth," she said. "See that your hawks don't maul them too badly."

"Yes, My Lady," Emilia said, curtsying.

"What was that all about?" Emilia asked as they stepped out into the streets.

"What?"

"The Baroness," Emilia said. "She couldn't keep her eyes off you."

Redmond grimaced. "You're imaging things."

Emilia wiggled her eyebrows at him. "I don't imagine things like that."

"It was nothing," Redmond said. He didn't want to discuss it with her.

Emilia walked beside him in silence for a few moments and then grabbed his arm. "This way," she said.

Redmond hesitated. He should get back to his men, but Emilia had raised his curiosity. She was a capable young woman with a mind of her own.

She led him up onto the battlements on the eastern side of the keep near the sally port. He followed her toward the front of the castle to a round tower where the walls made a sharp turn toward the gate. Emilia leaned against one of the merlons.

Windemere

"I have something to show you," she said.

"Okay." He nodded at her, urging her to hurry.

She pointed toward the moat. "It's there. See it?"

Redmond looked at Emilia. She was slender and attractive, and he sensed she had some ulterior motive for bringing him here. He leaned out over the battlements to peer down at the moat. His men still toiled on the barbican, and most of the soldiers had spread out to guard them. The reeds below rustled in the warm breeze that blew in off the dry lands to the south.

Redmond scowled. "See what?" he asked.

Emilia leaned closer, and he caught the scent of cinnamon and herbs. Her long hair draped over one shoulder. She clicked her tongue and pointed.

"Not over there," she said. "By that stump. It's a hidden bridge to cross the moat."

Redmond gave her a sideways glance to make sure she wasn't joking. She seemed serious.

"A bridge?" he questioned. "Are you sure?"

"I saw them build it last spring," Emilia said. "They tried to keep it a secret, but . . ." She batted her eyelids at him.

Redmond smiled. "But you have ways of finding things out," he finished for her.

She grinned. "It's a small village."

Redmond leaned back over the battlements and struggled to make out the outline of the structure beneath the water.

"Why are you showing me this?" he asked.

Emilia picked at the mortar with a slender finger. "If the Baroness gets her claws into you, you had better have a plan to get out of here. None of her lovers last more than a few years."

"I'm not her lover," Redmond said. "Nor am I going to be."

"If you say so," Emilia said. "But I saw the way she looked at you. It's only a matter of time."

"How old are you?" Redmond asked.

Emilia peered up at him. "I'm not yet twenty-two," she said.

Redmond watched her. Among the Hallstat, most women married before they turned eighteen. Why hadn't she? And why had she shown him the bridge?

"What are your plans?" he asked.

Emilia blew out her air in disgust. "What plans? I'm stuck here until Baron Selgrave gives me away to some scabby noble to be his plaything."

"You and your father could run away."

"And go where? The cities? The Baron would only track us down."

"Maybe the Baron would let you choose your husband," Redmond said.

Emilia watched him with a steady gaze. "Maybe," she said. "If the Baron owed him something." She reached out her hand to touch Redmond's. Her hand was soft and cool. Warmth filled Redmond's chest like he hadn't felt since the last time he had been with Lara. He found himself drawn to Emilia in a way that scared him, but he couldn't let himself form an attachment. He was still promised to Lara until she released him. Besides, he wasn't worthy of the earnest desire in Emilia's soft brown eyes. Not after leaving Lara the way he did. Not after betraying her trust. Redmond drew his hand away.

Emilia's expression fell into a frown. She blinked rapidly and whirled away from him. "You'd better get back before the captain accuses you of something else," she said and hurried away from him.

Redmond took a hesitant step to restrain her but stopped himself. He didn't have the right to encourage her. He would only disappoint her the way he had Lara. Every moment of that last evening when he had bid her farewell still burned bright in his memory.

He lifted Lara's cold hands in his as they stood in the quiet glade. Snowflakes fluttered down around them to perch on the green holly leaves. They collected in her blonde hair and on her dark cloak.

"I'll come back. I promise," he said.

She lifted her gaze to his.

"But you've already been gone for three years. How long will this take?"

"I don't know," Redmond said. "But I have to go. He's my brother. I can't abandon him."

Lara frowned. "He's going to get himself killed," she said. "When is he going to give up this obsession? How many Salassani does he have to kill before he's satisfied?"

Redmond brushed at a snowflake that landed on Lara's cheek.

"I don't know, Lara. I've been trying to convince him, but he won't let it be. Sometimes I think he's so full of rage that it's eating him up inside. But I promise I won't go again. The war should be over soon, maybe just a few more

months."

Lara shifted her feet and looked away.

"What?" Redmond asked. There was something she wasn't telling him.

Lara sighed. "I'll wait again," she said. "But only if you promise this will be the end of it. After what we've been through, we deserve a quiet life somewhere."

Redmond had broken his promise and abandoned Lara. He might have had good reasons, but it didn't change the fact that he had betrayed her trust. That betrayal had haunted his every step since then, but there was nothing he could do about it now. He strode off to join his men at the barbican. A few minutes later, Emilia swept past the sweating men with the goshawk perched on her arm. Several men paused in their work to watch her pass.

The sun rode high into the sky, burning down upon them with an intensity that sucked the energy and the moisture from their bodies. The warm breeze that purred through the reeds around the moat did little to freshen the men who toiled over the stones. Dirt and sand coated Redmond's throat. His lips cracked. Sweat soaked his hair and tunic. Even his feet seemed to be swimming in the sweat that trickled down into his boots. Not for the first time, Redmond longed for the cool wind that blew off the Aveen Mountains and the crystal blue waters of Comrie Lake where he had spent many hours as a boy swimming and splashing during the warm summer months.

Redmond paused to survey his perspiring men. How could he have avoided this? In all his long years of selling his skills in the wars on the continent, he had never been reduced to such indignity.

Yet, he hadn't spent much time in Hallstat country where the lords struggled to nibble away at each other's lands while the King focused on his war in the east. Lord Dacrey's betrayal had caught him off guard because he had been the first to welcome Redmond and his men to Longmire. When Dacrey approached Redmond's men in the pass, they naturally assumed he was acting under Baron Dragos's orders—only to find that, once he had them in the open and vulnerable, he ordered his men to attack. Perhaps Redmond should have pushed harder for a guarantee they wouldn't be used for hard labor, but how could he have known?

The Hallstat guards gave them a short break around noon and passed out the rock-hard bread, old cheese, and stale water that had become their daily fare. Some of the men played with the idea of dunking themselves in the moat. A few considered it seriously until a blob of human waste came floating by, and the wind kicked up the rancid odor of the moat. Redmond wasn't yet desperate enough to plunge into that water. Emilia's hawk soared above the fields that surrounded the keep with its leather jesses dangling out behind it. The faint tinkle of its bells reached his ears.

Before any of them had truly rested, his men were forced back to their labor, and the sounds of metal cracking stone and men grunting and swearing filled the air. Not long after, the clatter of horse hooves on the cobbled road broke over the noise. Men paused in their work to watch the rider approach. He wore the dark blue livery of Lord Selgrave as he galloped under the gate, calling for the captain. The two exchanged a few words, and the captain glared at Redmond before he strode away toward the keep.

Emilia carried the big red-tailed hawk out into the fields surrounding the castle. Because the Baron owned all the lands for several days' ride in any direction, she was free to roam in search of game. The quail liked to feed in the rye and barley fields and nested in the cover along the borders of the fields and pathways. It would have been easier to find them if she had a dog to flush them out, but the Baron kept his birding dogs for his own use.

Few large trees grew in the area around the castle, and there were no high vantage points from which to hunt, so Emilia brought the red-tailed hawk she had trained to circle in front of her as she beat the brush. This way, she scared the prey toward her hawk, not away from it.

When she had gone far enough from the castle to feel confident that game was about, she released the leather jesses she held in her gloved fingers and let the hawk fly. It jumped into the air with a flutter of wings, and she lifted her short walking stick to beat the brush. It was later in the day than she liked to start a hunt, but, as usual, the Baroness took no notice of such matters. Still, this is where Emilia preferred to be—outside the confines of the castle walls with all its stink and complicated relationships.

The sky above was clear blue with a thin wisp of cloud that did nothing to dampen the stifling heat. All around, the fields and pas-

Windemere

tures spread out, demarcated by hedges or stone-lined, split-rail fences. The Barony of Windemere marked the southern border of the kingdom of the Hallstat, and it was also one of the richest. Baron Otto controlled the gold trade that came over the jagged hills to the south in return for the salt he quarried from the southern flanks of the mountains.

Emilia had never been that far south, but she had seen the slaves who worked the mines. They were broken men—overworked and underfed—kept alive by the drug her father made for the Baron. The drug dulled their senses to make them easier to control, while still leaving them capable of long hours of manual labor. But it destroyed them. It was a cruel way to treat men. Still, her father had no choice. He either complied with the Baron's wishes or he ended up in the mines himself—and she would probably be sold as a sex slave in one of the cities.

Emilia gazed up at the hawk circling above her. If only she could enjoy such freedom—to fly wherever she wished. To be what she wanted to be. The thought was fleeting because the hawk wasn't really free. It had been trained to return to her hand for scraps of meat. Was she any different?

She always returned to the castle, to her father's house because she loved him and because, if something happened to him, even this pseudo-freedom would be stripped away from her. What if someday she broke those chains?

A hare bounded onto the pathway in front of her, and she gave a shrill whistle. The hawk had already seen it and swooped, but the hare was too fast and soon dove into a hole along the roadway. The hawk rose up to circle again. This wasn't the way hawks naturally hunted. They preferred to perch atop trees or cliffs or castle walls and wait for the prey to reveal itself. She couldn't keep him up there for too long or he would become tired.

A flutter of wings and a rapid chirping sounded as a flock of quail flushed from the barley field. Emilia whistled and, again, the hawk dove. It caught a quail in mid-flight and dropped to the ground. Emilia beat a path through the barley. The hawk had already killed the quail, so she fed it a scrap of meat and tugged the quail from its claws. She didn't want it to eat too much or it wouldn't keep hunting.

The flapping of wings above drew her attention, and she glanced up. A white pigeon fluttered away from the castle. She checked to see if anyone was about before lifting her hawk and tossing it into the air, giving it the shrill whistle. It circled, spotted the pigeon, and raced after it. These were the Baroness's own homing pigeons, and if she was sending a message now, it must be important. This was a dangerous game Emilia played, but she was far enough away from the castle that no one would know.

The dove struggled to evade the hawk, but the hawk brought it down, and Emilia trotted to collect it. The quails would have to go to the castle, but she and her father could eat the pigeon. She extracted the still-struggling pigeon from the hawk, wrung its neck, and untied the tiny scroll of paper attached to its leg. A rush of concern filled her chest, and her eyes opened wide as she read. Redmond needed to see this.

Redmond jerked his head up, wiping the sweat from his eyes, as a troop of Hallstat warriors came riding in. Behind them stumbled Peter, the man who had gone missing that morning. His hands had been tied with a rope, and he staggered after the last rider, jerked along by the trotting horse. When they reached the drawbridge, Peter tripped and fell headlong. But the rider didn't stop. He kept the horse at a steady pace, dragging Peter behind him, leaving a dark smear on the bridge and a red stain on the dusty white cobblestones.

The men stopped working to watch the display in grim silence. These were fighting men, unaccustomed to taking insults lightly and unwilling to die without a struggle. The Hallstat guards came out in force and herded the men back inside the walls toward the keep. They corralled them by the pillory where they tied Peter with his hands above his head. His shirt had been stripped off, and his raw flesh oozed blood where he had been dragged. The captain of the Baron's guard and Sir Dacrey stood beside him.

"I didn't do it," Peter gasped. "I didn't do anything. I escaped, that's all."

"Liar," the captain said. He held up a sword. "You were found with Lord Berard's sword."

"I found the sword," Peter cried. "I didn't know whose it was."

"Silence him," Dacrey said, and a guard stuffed a wad of cloth into

Windemere

Peter's mouth, which he secured with a rag.

"You." Dacrey pointed to a young man, named Sieger, standing near the front. "Come here."

Sieger hesitated until a guard grabbed him and yanked him forward.

Dacrey tossed him a whip. "Three hundred lashes should teach you all not to abuse our hospitality."

Redmond pushed his way to the front.

"Your word, Sir Dacrey," he said. "You gave us your word that no one would be harmed."

Dacrey spread his arms in a welcoming gesture. "And here you are, well-fed and well-housed," he said. "But a man who murders a nobleman cannot be allowed to go unpunished. Not even you would allow this." He raised an eyebrow at Redmond.

"He denies doing it," Redmond said.

"And what is that worth?" Dacrey scoffed. "The word of a low-born murderer." He gestured to Sieger. "Do it," he ordered.

Sieger stared at Redmond with unconcealed terror.

Redmond stepped forward. "I'll do it," he said. Better to spare this boy the indignity and shame than to avoid the horror himself.

"Shut up and get back in line," Dacrey ordered. "Or I'll have you all whipped one by one."

Sieger took a tentative step toward the stone stairs that led to the pillory.

"Now!" Dacrey shouted.

Sieger climbed the steps and raised the whip. He let it fall on Peter's back without much force. Dacrey sprang to Sieger, jerked the whip from his hand and lashed out with incredible fury. The whip struck Sieger's face, leaving a bloody trail that showed the whip had bits of metal or bone woven into it. Sieger cried out and tried to shy away, but Dacrey collared him and yanked him upright.

"You strike him like that every time, or I'll lash you until there's no flesh left on your bones." He jammed the whip back into Sieger's hand and shoved him toward Peter.

Sieger raised the whip and lashed it across Peter's bare back. Peter flinched but didn't cry out. Sieger swung again and again until he became too exhausted to deliver a powerful stroke, and Dacrey grabbed another one of Redmond's men and forced him to continue. Peter jerked and twitched at the bonds but never uttered a sound. Eventually, he sagged against his restraints, clearly unconscious. Dacrey didn't relent. Peter's back became a ragged pulp. His trousers were soaked in blood.

"He's had enough," Redmond growled. He ground his teeth. If he could get that whip and Dacrey alone, he would teach him how to treat men.

Dacrey raised his eyebrows and gestured toward the pillory. "Do you want to take his place?"

"You've made your point," Redmond said.

Dacrey glared at Redmond with a calculating expression before gesturing to the man with the whip. "Continue," he said.

And so it went on until the three hundred lashes had been given, and Dacrey cut Peter down. Peter fell to the ground and rolled down the steps. Redmond rushed to his side. Peter's ribs showed through, stark white against the bleeding mass of flesh. Redmond bent low to see if Peter was still breathing. He laid a hand on Peter's chest. No heartbeat. He gazed up at Dacrey as the rage burned in his face.

"You've killed him," he snarled.

Dacrey smiled. "That was the idea," he said. Then he faced Redmond's men. "Any more nonsense, and we'll give the same treatment to one man every day until the nonsense ends."

The men murmured, but no one challenged him.

Redmond stood. "The forsworn knight has shown his true character," he said.

Dacrey spun and backhanded Redmond across the face. Redmond stumbled and then lunged toward Dacrey before stopping himself. He straightened. He would save it for later. There was no point in giving Dacrey an excuse to kill him now.

"Wise choice," Dacrey sneered. "Now get back to work."

Redmond had seen worse brutality, but he hadn't been this helpless to stop it in a long time—not since the Salassani raid on his village at Comrie. The memory of that day had been seared into his soul. He was sixteen years old when the Salassani burst into his village and ripped his world apart, forcing him down the path of blood he now followed.

Windemere

Cries of alarm rang out around the village. Then the screaming began. "Salassani!" The shout was picked up and carried all over the village. At first, Redmond raced back toward his home, but flames engulfed it. His mother and sister were nowhere to be seen. People fled in all directions seeking shelter, while scattered groups of men stood to fight. Lara dragged her five-year-old brother by the hand. Frantic women and children knocked each other about. Lara's blonde hair flew out behind her, and her linen dress hugged her form. Redmond raced to her and scooped up the boy into his arms.

"Follow me," he shouted and rushed toward the lake. At first, he considered taking one of the boats out into the broad lake, but the Salassani were already on the long dock setting fire to everything.

Redmond wove in and out of the houses, dodging the fleeing people with Lara on his heels. There was only one place left to go—his secret hiding place under the great boulder by the lake.

A tall Salassani with bright blue war paint in the shape of a snarling bear barred their path. He grabbed Lara, who screamed and fought. Redmond set the boy down and snatched up a rock. He threw it at the Salassani with all his might. The rock flew true, smashing into the Salassani's face. The man screamed and dropped Lara before lunging toward Redmond, but Redmond dodged aside, scrambling to find another rock. Someone yelled. The Salassani paused before he grabbed up Lara's brother and sprinted back toward the edge of the village.

"No," Lara screamed and raced after the Salassani. Redmond threw another rock at the man's retreating back and sprinted after Lara, who disappeared into the clouds of smoke. Redmond found Lara with her skirt held up over her mouth and nose, stumbling amid the burning huts in search of her brother. The Salassani were still killing and burning all around them. Redmond grabbed Lara's hand.

"We have to go," Redmond said.

Lara blinked at him. Tears cut little trails through the soot on her cheeks. The smoke smelled of roasting flesh and burning thatch.

Lara shook her head and bit her lip, but Redmond pulled her away from the burning huts and led her to his secret hideaway. The great boulder stood alone on the edge of Comrie Lake, a hulking shadow in the drifting smoke.

Redmond fell to his hands and knees in the water, felt for the hole, and then ducked under the water to scramble up onto the cold, hard-packed earth on the other side. A crack in the rock above let in a ray of light. The smell of the burning village drifted in, but the sounds of the fighting and killing became muted.

Lara followed him through and collapsed into his arms, sobbing. Redmond held her, not knowing what else to do. He wished he was a bigger man—no, wished he was a great warrior so he could take revenge on the Salassani, find Lara's little brother, and bring him back. But he was only sixteen. He tried not to think of what happened to his mother, his little sister, and his older brother. How could anyone have survived? The raid had been so sudden and so violent.

After a long, cold night spent huddled next to Lara, they crawled out of their refuge to find the survivors picking through the smoking ruins of their village, searching for the living and the dead. Lara raced off to her home, and Redmond hurried toward his. The sight of the still-smoking ruin with the roof collapsed and the walls sagging in, forced a knot into his throat. The stone fireplace still stood, a blackened skeleton defying the destruction around it. Redmond kicked through the rubble, feeling the warmth through his boots until he stopped at the fireplace. Huddled in the back lay the charred remains of a woman clutching a child.

Redmond coughed on the sob that burned in his throat and collapsed to his knees. Ashes floated up to choke him. His mother had tried to save his sister by seeking protection in the fireplace. But the fire that destroyed their home had been too hot. Redmond reached in and lifted them into his arms. Bits of their charred clothing fell away and the stench of burned flesh filled his nostrils. He staggered through the blackened rubble and laid them on the trampled, burned grass.

The sobs tore from his throat. He had chosen to save Lara and her brother and let his own mother and sister die in the burning hut. He had failed them. How could he go on?

It was an agonizing memory—made all the more bitter by the years of hatred and revenge that followed. His brother, Neahl, had gone after the Salassani to rescue his wife. Weeks passed before he returned, scarred and disfigured with three fingers cut from his drawing hand.

The heath wars erupted after that, and Redmond and Neahl had joined the King's army. When it was over, Neahl convinced him and their friend, Weyland, to go back into the heathland to pursue the rest of the men who had raided their village. Redmond remembered, too, the sense of betrayal when he learned that Neahl and Weyland accused him of cowardice and had sworn to kill him for leaving them in battle.

He had never deserted them. His horse bolted after taking an arrow in the rump during their last battle together. As Redmond followed Neahl and Weyland, he learned they were being hunted by assassins sent by someone in Coll. Redmond intercepted and killed the assassins only to find he was also being followed. He didn't dare return to Lara after that. He lured the assassins off the island and killed them one by one.

In the foolishness of youth, he decided not to return to Coll, both out of a sense of betrayal and a fear that he might lead danger to Lara and her family. Now he couldn't go back. It had been too many years. There had been too much suffering. He probably wouldn't even survive long enough to go back.

For Redmond, the years of wandering the southland had been long and lonely. Now he was a prisoner of a crafty baron and his conniving wife. One of his men had already been slaughtered, and the rest depended on him to get them out safely. But the situation was getting worse. More unstable. Something else was going to go wrong—he could feel it in his bones.

Chapter 6
The Pigeon and the Assassin

I have news for you," Emilia whispered as Redmond stepped through the gates to the inner ward that evening on his way to clean the Baron's wound. She didn't have time to explain before a servant girl appeared to lead them up the spiraling stairs.

Redmond gave Emilia a questioning glance, but she shook her head and mouthed "later" to him.

The Baroness came to watch again but said nothing as they worked. The Baron still burned with fever, and Redmond wasn't sure he would pull through. Still, he cleaned the wound with whiskey and dusted it with the mold from the bread. When he finished, he washed his hands and straightened to face the Baroness.

She wore a light pink gown this evening, and she sat so her bare lower legs were visible. In any other context, the display of that much flesh would have been scandalous. Now it seemed threatening. Redmond chose to ignore it. He had more important things on his mind.

"You had one of my men killed," he said.

She feigned ignorance. "I did nothing but save you from a similar fate," she said.

"You know he didn't do it," Redmond said.

"I know he was found cowering in a haystack with Lord Berard's sword in his hands," she said. "What more proof do you desire?"

Redmond pursed his lips. "You're making it difficult for me to accept your offer," he said. The Baroness flashed him an annoyed glance.

Windemere

"Leave us," she said to Emilia.

Emilia raised knowing eyebrows at Redmond and left the room.

"You should have more discretion," Lady Selgrave said.

"And you should understand that my men come first," Redmond replied. "If you allow Dacrey to brutalize them, you leave me no choice."

Lady Selgrave lunged to her feet knocking her chair over. "Do not speak to me in that manner," she said. "You are nothing but a prisoner here. I have offered you the chance to save your men, and you insist on insulting me."

"I mean no disrespect, My Lady," Redmond said. "I ask you to spare my men. Release us, and we'll leave your lands for good."

The Baroness laughed. "You are not *my* prisoners," she said. She gestured to the Baron. "When my husband recovers, he'll decide what to do with you." She stepped toward Redmond with an alluring smile. Then stopped and plugged her nose. "You smell like a filthy dog," she said.

Redmond gave her a rueful smirk, feeling grateful for his body odor. "Working all day underneath your southern sun without the privilege of a bath is liable to make any man stink."

She backed away. "My offer still stands, providing you bathe regularly."

"When my men are free," Redmond said, "we can discuss your offer."

"Come back in the morning," she said with a gesture to Baron Selgrave. "I won't let anyone else treat him."

Redmond found Emilia waiting for him by the gate that led out of the inner courtyard. The evening light slanted through the village, washing it with a pure, yellow light.

"That didn't take long," Emilia said with a coy smile.

Redmond sighed and shook his head.

"Come with me," Emilia said and hurried away. Redmond followed her to the apothecary shop. They found Tal grinding herbs at his workbench. He jumped up as they entered, snatched a piece of paper from the table, and extended it to Redmond.

Redmond stepped to the fire to better read the note. The script was neat and distinctly feminine.

"I want your men here in no less than a week. They are getting difficult to control. We need their labor in the salt mines."

Redmond raised his head as the shock of what it meant coursed through him. "Where did you get this?" he demanded.

Emilia fell onto a bench by the table. She grabbed a chunk of bread and tore off a piece. "My goshawk caught one of the Baroness's homing pigeons," she said. She pointed at the paper in his hands with the chunk of bread. "That was tied to its ankle."

"She means to enslave us in the mines?" Redmond had long suspected the Baron might stoop to this, but with the Baron on what might be his death bed, he hadn't considered Lady Selgrave would act on her own.

"Probably not you," Emilia said with a wink. She tore a piece of bread with her teeth and chewed.

"It's worse than you know," Tal said. "She has ordered me to prepare the drug for them. I convinced her to let me introduce it slowly, so the men wouldn't notice, but I don't know how long I can hold her off."

"Can you substitute it?"

"It's dangerous," Tal said. "If they find out…"

Redmond paced. Then he stopped to study Emilia where she sat in apparent ease chewing on the bread. "Do you regularly intercept the Baroness's pigeons?"

Emilia shrugged. "Not always, but every now and then, it's good to see what they're up to. Besides, a good roasted pigeon provides variety to our bland diet."

"You *eat* the Baroness's pigeons?" Redmond asked in surprise. It was a brazen and dangerous act.

"You see," Tal said to Emilia. "I told you it was foolish."

"They'll find out," Redmond said.

"Nah," Emilia said. "Pigeons get lost all the time. When she doesn't get a reply in a day or two, she'll send another."

Redmond gave up arguing with her. He had bigger problems. Time had run out. He could no longer afford to wait and see if Henry had reached Baron Dragos and given him his message.

"I need to know the height of the walls," he said. "Do you have a ball of string or twine I can use?"

Windemere

Tal retrieved a ball of string from the back room.

"What are you thinking?" he asked, handing it to Redmond.

"I'm leaving tonight," Redmond said. "I need you to get word to Jannik. He's the big burly one with the full beard. Tell him I've gone to get help."

"What kind of help?" Tal said.

Redmond grinned. "The kind that knows how to storm a castle."

Tal scowled at him and glanced at Emilia.

"If you get caught," Tal said, "and they find out we helped you, Lady Selgrave will show no mercy."

"I understand the risk you're taking," Redmond said. "I won't betray you."

Tal scrutinized him uncertainly for a moment, then set his jaw and nodded.

"Is there a less obvious way outside the walls other than the gate?" Redmond asked.

"There's the sally port," Emilia said. "But it's guarded."

Redmond grinned at her. "But you know a way around the guard, don't you?"

Emilia flashed him a pretty smile. "I might," she said.

"Can you take care of that while I go measure the walls?"

Emilia stood. "It depends who's on watch."

"Thanks," Redmond said. "I'll be back."

He slipped out the door and raced through the streets, seeking the shadows whenever possible and relying on speed and quiet when it wasn't. Once the guard had passed on his nightly rounds atop the battlements, Redmond stole up the steps, tying a stone to the line and dropping it over the walls. He tied a knot at the height when the line became slack, wound it up, and hurried back toward Tal's shop.

He was passing the brewery, heading toward the pillory, when he encountered a slender figure draped in a dark cloak skulking along in the shadows. At first, he thought it might be Emilia, but this woman was taller and stepped as if unaccustomed to navigating the refuse of the streets. Redmond needed haste, but the obvious incongruity of this woman with the dark streets of Windemere sparked his curiosity.

The figure slipped into a dark alleyway and paused by a narrow door. A tall man with a longsword stepped out of the shadow of the doorway and embraced her. She pushed him away as her hood fell back, revealing Lady Selgrave.

"My Lady," Dacrey said.

Redmond crouched behind a barrel that smelled of apples.

"Not now, Dacrey," she said. "We have a more pressing problem. Your execution of that prisoner has created considerable animosity among the prisoners."

"I'll handle them," Dacrey said. "Men like these can only be governed by fear."

"But my reinforcements won't arrive for some time," Lady Selgrave insisted. "If you drive the men to rebellion before they arrive, we may not be able to hold them."

Dacrey raised a hand to brush at her hair. "Don't worry your pretty head about it. The apothecary's drug will take effect in a few days."

Lady Selgrave slapped at his hand. "You botched the job," she accused, jabbing her finger at him. "He wasn't supposed to be found for days, and your captain tried to blame it on the man who is treating my husband."

Dacrey stepped back. "Is that all he does?" Dacrey's voice filled with a sneer of mockery.

Lady Selgrave slapped him. "Do not forget your place," she said. She spun to leave, but Dacrey grabbed her and pulled her into a kiss.

"A few more weeks," Dacrey said after they separated, "and we will be in a position to seize Longmire. Then it's only a matter of time."

"I'm not worried about Longmire," Lady Selgrave said. "He's your problem."

Dacrey was silent for a moment as if in thought. "You have bigger plans?"

Lady Selgrave spun away. "Just keep these men under control until my reinforcements arrive."

Redmond shrank back into the shadows as Lady Selgrave swept past him. The scent of her perfume mixed with the sweet smell of apples.

Lady Selgrave kicked off her soiled shoes and draped the black cloak over the back of her chair. The candles flickered at her move-

Windemere

ment. Even the thin cloak had been hot and confining, but she needed to move about unobserved. She paused before a mirror to fix her hair. It wasn't that she was prim and fussy about her looks. She cared, of course, because her beauty was one of her most potent weapons, and she worked hard to keep it sharp. One never knew when the need might arise.

Pregnancy had been a real challenge—which is why she only let it happen twice. She had done her duty and given her husband two heirs. Once that was done, she saw no reason to allow it to happen again. She had sent her two sons to live in Hiede with their nursemaid, which left her free to pursue her political interests. Small meals and regular exercise riding horses over the green hills kept her mind and body honed and prepared for action, making her more attractive to the men and rousing jealousy in the women. Both could be turned to profit and power if one knew how to manipulate them.

"The fool," she said aloud and plopped down at her writing table. Dacrey had enough ambition to make him dangerous, but he had no vision. All he hoped for was a possible barony, while she had much, much bigger plans.

Feet shuffled against the floorboards. Lady Selgrave jumped to her feet and spun. Her hand found the handle of the knife she always wore in her belt. A hooded form stood in the shadows, silent and unmoving.

"Who are you?" Lady Selgrave demanded. A tickle of dread swept through her stomach. How had anyone been able to get into her rooms unseen?

"You look lovely, My Lady."

Adelaide didn't miss the note of mockery in the young female voice. She drew her dagger.

"Who are you?" she repeated.

The woman stepped into the light of the candles and lowered her hood. Adelaide straightened in confusion. It was a girl of about seventeen or eighteen. She had short-cropped black hair, dark eyes, and delicate features. She stood a full head shorter than Adelaide.

"You may call me Mara," the girl said.

"Get out of my rooms," Adelaide demanded as she stepped toward Mara.

"You don't want to do that," Mara said.

55

Adelaide stopped. This girl projected a commanding sense of confidence.

"I've come to make you an offer," Mara continued.

"How did you get in here?" Adelaide demanded, still unsettled by the girl's unexplained appearance.

Mara glanced at the open window.

Adelaide stared at her. "You didn't climb all the way up here," she said.

Mara gave her a blank stare. "You may believe what you wish, but I do have an offer for you. Will you hear it?"

Adelaide eyed the girl with interest. If the girl meant harm, she could have done it while Adelaide was primping in the mirror. She sheathed her knife and smoothed her dress as she settled into a chair.

"I belong to the Order of the Rook," Mara said. "Have you heard of us?"

Adelaide opened her eyes wide as a thrill of excitement and fear raced through her. Of course, she had heard of them. They were the shadowy organization that murdered for hire and manipulated every king on the isles and the mainland. Somehow, no one ever knew where to find them, and none of their assassins had ever been caught.

Adelaide bounded to her feet again with the realization that she might be their next victim. "Have you come to kill me?" she asked.

Mara grimaced. "If I had, My Lady, you would already be dead."

A shiver swept through Adelaide because it was true. "What do you want then?"

"To recruit you."

"What?" Adelaide dropped back into her chair.

"We need informants, and we have reliable evidence you will soon be in a position to be of value to us."

Adelaide scowled. "What evidence?"

Mara ignored her. "In return, we offer you information and assistance with your grand schemes."

"Have you been talking to Dacrey?" Adelaide demanded.

Mara let out a long, exaggerated sigh. "We have no need of Lord Dacrey, My Lady. This kingdom is unstable. We would help you bring stability and peace."

Pursing her lips, Adelaide chose her words carefully. "I don't know what plans you imagine I have, but I am just a countess. I'm not in any position to bring peace to the kingdom."

Mara clicked her tongue in annoyance. "Don't insult me." She stared at Adelaide with steady, dark eyes. Adelaide shifted in her seat. Her first inclination was to stomp over and slap some respect into the girl, but she hesitated. What if this girl *did* belong to the Order of the Rook? They would be valuable allies and dangerous opponents. Did she dare get on their wrong side when so much hung in the balance?

Adelaide gave her what she intended to be a disarming smile. "All right," she said. "What information do you seek?"

Mara slipped her hand into a pocket on her cloak. She withdrew a dark piece of cloth, stepped over to Adelaide and handed it to her. Adelaide flinched but accepted it. She held it close to the candle to find that it had a black rook stitched into the blood-red cloth.

"Keep this with you at all times," Mara said. "It is how we will identify you. We'll be in contact."

Mara stepped to the window and climbed onto the sill.

"Wait," Adelaide said.

Mara paused.

"What am I supposed to do?"

"Wait until you receive instructions," Mara said. "And do what you can to *not* destabilize Windemere before it is time to make your move." Then she slipped over the sill and vanished into the darkness.

Adelaide darted to the window and leaned out. A tiny figure rapidly descended the wall of the keep.

Chapter 7
Into the Night

milia rose from the shadows wearing her thin, black cloak as Redmond approached the apothecary shop. She handed him a satchel.

"A bit of food and water for your journey," she said.

"Thank you," Redmond said. He slipped the strap of the satchel over his shoulder and followed her into the night.

When they reached the sally port, the guard was nowhere to be seen, and the bars had been removed. As Redmond stepped to slip through the door, Emilia laid a hand on his arm. He paused.

"I'll send up the goshawk every morning to let you know how things stand," she said. "A blue ribbon means things are the same. Red means we are in real danger."

"Okay," Redmond said. "Thank you." He turned to leave again, but her hand restrained him.

"Come back," she whispered. The light of a watch fire flickered in her eyes. "Promise me you'll come back."

The words tore at Redmond. A knot tightened in his throat. They were almost the same words that Lara had spoken to him so long ago that night in the glade. He nodded and pulled his hand away to slip through the door.

Redmond slid down the rocky slope to the edge of the moat, eager to be on his way and anxious to avoid the feelings Emilia had stirred in him. He considered swimming to the other side, but the memory of the filth and waste he had seen floating in it during the day stopped him. He didn't want to risk using the underwater bridge in case someone saw him and discovered he knew about it. Nor did he want to make any noise that might attract the attention of the guards on the walls. Instead, he hugged close to the wall and worked his way around to the unfinished barbican where he could climb onto the scaffolding that spanned the moat. The drawbridge had been raised, but the scaffolding being used to construct the wall gave him a latticework to scramble across. No guard was posted on the unfinished barbican, but the measured tread of the guard on the tower behind him sounded clear and distinct in the calm night air.

Redmond crawled out onto the scaffold. The satchel dangled from his shoulder as he worked his way across. The water of the moat glistened darkly far below. A fall from this height would not only give him away, it could injure him severely. He focused on the narrow beams of the scaffolding, willing himself to stay calm and concentrate. Hand over hand, he inched his way into the night.

He was more than halfway across when his hand landed on a round metal object, like a chisel, that had been left on the scaffolding. The chisel rolled under his hand, and he lost his grip. His hand slipped free. He fell sideways, clinging to the scaffold with one hand and a leg wrapped around another beam. The chisel fell with a splash into the water below. Redmond froze with the satchel swinging from his shoulder.

The tread of feet on the battlements paused. The ensuing silence pressed in upon him, seeking to reveal him to the men now peering into the darkness in search of him. He held his breath. Whispered voices sounded, followed by more quiet as the normal sounds of the night returned.

Redmond took a shuddering breath and continued across until he reached the other side. While groping for a handhold on the unfinished stone, sand and bits of chiseled rock cascaded onto his head. He shifted his weight and tried again when a gloved hand grabbed his wrist.

Emilia waited until Redmond disappeared through the gate before slipping into the shadows to make her way home. She took the long route to the shop, following the wall past the gate to the inner ward and around toward the main gate and the unfinished barbican. Redmond said he would come back. She shouldn't let her fancies run away with her reason, but that expression on his face meant something. Was he beginning to care for her? A pleasant warmth filled her chest. No man—besides her father—had ever felt anything but lust for her. It might be useless to hope that Redmond would see her as more than a child. He was, after all, considerably older than she was, but she couldn't help but hope.

Now and then, she encountered the occasional night prowler like herself, but, by some unspoken agreement, they avoided one another. Less than two hundred people lived within the walls, and gossip spread quickly. It was best not to let others know you had been out at night—especially if you were a woman. Emilia paused. A dark shape was ascending the wall of the castle in the corner of the towers that overlooked the barbican.

It looked like a large spider moving silently in the dark. She paused and melted into the shadows to watch as the figure climbed over the battlements and disappeared over the other side heading toward the barbican. Emilia had never seen anything like it and couldn't decide what to make of it. It definitely wasn't Redmond. She had let him out the back gate. He should have crossed the bridge or swam the moat by now and been well on his way.

Who in the castle would be climbing at this time of night? The walls would not be easy to climb at any time—but in the dark? Most of the town's inhabitants occupied shops or served the Baron and his wife in some capacity or other. Try as she might, she couldn't imagine who might have the skill and the purpose to scale the walls of Castle Windemere.

Emilia considered approaching the guards at the gate to ask what they were doing letting someone climb over the walls, but, given the fact that Redmond had just escaped, it didn't seem like a good idea. She resisted the urge and continued on her way. What would the intrigues of the Baron and Baroness mean for her and her father? If they fell afoul of the King, they could bring their vassals, servants, and slaves down with them. And if they survived, Emilia knew what fate awaited her.

The Baron had started taking notice of her, despite her best efforts to remain unremarkable. Though the hawks gave her considerably more freedom than she might otherwise enjoy, they also brought her into frequent contact with the Baron and his wife. Such contact could be dangerous. Two years ago, the Baron told her how he planned to use her, which precipitated a crisis with her father.

She had been in the Baron's mews next to the keep dropping off one of the hawks who had weathered the molt when the Baron came in.

He paused in the doorway and passed an appraising eye over her.

"You've become quite the young woman," he said.

Emilia didn't miss the interest in his look. She finished tying the hawk to its perch and slipped the glove from her hand before attempting to walk past him. He raised an arm to stop her. She stepped away, eyeing him warily.

"I have a handsome young knight in want of a companion," he said. "Perhaps, I'll sell you to him."

Emilia blanched and swallowed. He dropped his arm with a laugh, and she fled to her father. Tal was far from amused. He stormed out of the apothecary shop to confront the Baron. Emilia followed, desperate to keep her father from making a rash mistake. But he wouldn't listen. Tal found the Baron still in the mews.

"What do you think you're doing?" Tal demanded. Being a strong, imposing man, he loomed over the Baron. The Baron narrowed his eyes.

"You should remember who you're talking to," he said.

"And you should remember your oath," Tal said. "I will hold you to it."

"Do not test my patience," the Baron growled, and he pushed past Tal. But the look he gave them when he glanced back told Emilia that, despite his anger, he knew that Tal could follow through with his threat.

Emilia understood her dilemma long ago. The only way out of this intolerable situation was to find a man who could protect her from the Baron or at least take her far away. A poor woman with no power, no family, and no lord to protect her would not last long where slavers roamed the land and barons preyed on each other. The Baron owed Redmond his life, and if she could get Redmond to agree to ask for her, maybe the Baron would let her go. After all, the Baron chafed at the fact that Tal had so much power over him. He would be anxious to be rid of Emilia.

The sound of shuffling feet brought Emilia out of her reverie. She cursed. It seemed like everyone was out prowling. She slipped behind a wagon that smelled of sheep and crouched low. A soft whimper sounded, and someone shushed the offender. Soon, a line of children clad in rags shuffled past her hiding place. An old woman led them, and a bent old man with a whip in his hands brought up the rear.

Emilia followed them, her curiosity now piqued. The Baron used slaves in his mines, but, as far as Emilia knew, he never used children. They wouldn't be strong enough. So why would he be smuggling children in under the cover of darkness? They couldn't be sex slaves. Not children this young. Emilia had seen the sex slaves brought in when the Baron was holding special feasts for his vassals, but they never brought them in the dead of night.

How did they even get in? The drawbridge was raised, and she had been at the sally port. There was no other way in—at least not that she knew.

The woman led the children to the dungeon where Redmond's men were housed. The entrance lay along the western wall of the castle, and the cells penetrated deep into the solid stone underneath. The woman whispered to the guard who opened the door for her. The children filed inside. Emilia crept closer, trying to hear what the man with the whip said to the guard. The only word she could catch was "silver."

Emilia swallowed the fury that gripped her throat. "Not children," she whispered. "I won't let them do this to children."

Redmond stifled the cry of surprise and almost tumbled from his precarious perch on the scaffolding as the hand gripped his wrist. A head poked out over the rock. It was a girl.

"Hush," she whispered. "You're making too much noise. You'll draw attention."

Redmond let her help him out onto a pile of sand. Fortunately, there were no guards on this side of the barbican.

"Who are you?" Redmond asked.

"Someone trying to get out of the castle unnoticed," she said. She glanced back to the gate and sidled into the shadows. She wore a mottled cloak that made her form seem to waver and join with the darkness.

"That doesn't answer my question," Redmond said.

She smirked at him. "I didn't ask your business. Don't ask mine." She disappeared through the unfinished gate.

Windemere

Redmond strode after her. She ignored him until they were approaching the first bridge that crossed the winding creek. Then she spun on him.

"Do you mind?" she asked.

Redmond raised his hands to show he was no threat. "I appear to be going the same way you are."

"I doubt it," she said.

Redmond pointed west. "I'm on my way to visit friends," he said.

Her eyes narrowed. "You're one of the prisoners. They'll catch you. You'll never make it."

Redmond shrugged. "That's my business. Now if you don't mind, I'm short on time." He stepped past her. It was a good two-day's walk to the borders of Longmire, and he needed to get as far as he could before daylight.

He broke into a jog on the road. In a few minutes, the girl was striding beside him.

"What did you say your name was?" she asked.

"I didn't," Redmond said.

"I'm Mara," she said.

"Redmond."

"Ah, I thought so," she said. "Your Baroness isn't going to be too happy to find you've escaped her net."

"She'll get over it," Redmond said.

Mara stayed with him—despite being a full foot shorter in stature. "I don't think so," she said. "But enjoy your freedom while it lasts. We may meet again." With that, she vaulted over a stone fence and sped to the south.

Lady Selgrave released a homing pigeon and watched it fly away over the fields. A lingering sadness tightened her chest as the pigeon disappeared into the blue-gray sky. If only she could lift up on the wind and fly away. If only she could be what she wanted. But it was no good getting sentimental. Her plans were in motion. Things were about to change.

She picked up another pigeon and stroked its soft gray feathers. The attic to the tower served as her pigeon coop. The Baron had his hawks. She had her pigeons. Hawks might be flashier and more awe-inspiring, but simple pigeons were far more useful. She maintained several coops for each of the places with whom she needed to communicate. Pigeons were less likely to be intercepted than horseback messengers, and few people thought seriously about them.

She raised pigeons here at the castle because the homing pigeons always returned to their original nesting site. She sent the pigeons she raised in cages to all of her correspondents, and they sent her some of theirs. By making sure pigeons were hatched and reared at all the locations with whom she wished to communicate, she kept up a steady, clandestine correspondence.

Her gaze drifted out over the rolling landscape around her. Where was the little assassin that had visited her the night before? She had inquired among the guards and her servants, but no one had seen the girl. The possibilities of this new alliance intrigued her. Having the most powerful force in all the lands working with her promised a more rapid and thorough resolution to her current challenges.

Someone clambered up the ladder and through the trap door behind her. Adelaide spun to give them a verbal thrashing. She wanted to be alone, but it was a soldier clad in her own light blue colors.

"Yes?" she asked, not trying to disguise the annoyance in her voice.

The man bowed. "My Lady," he said. "The captain of the prisoners is gone."

"Redmond? Gone?" Adelaide repeated.

"He didn't come to treat the Baron this morning or join his men for the work detail," the man said. "We can't find him in the castle."

"Have you searched the apothecary's hut?"

"Yes, My Lady."

"He couldn't have escaped without help," she said.

Adelaide ground her teeth in frustration. He was so brazen. She had given him his liberty in the castle, offered him a position of honor—and even herself. This is the way he thanked her? She narrowed her eyes in thought. Things now seemed clear to her. She noticed the way the apothecary's daughter watched him. The girl was young and foolish and would have her head turned by the first handsome man who didn't treat her like a piece of meat. Adelaide had seen it before.

Emilia must have intercepted the pigeon she sent yesterday as she planned, but it had not had the intended effect. Rather than driving him to her for protection, it had driven him to cowardice. She had thought better of him. Well, if Redmond chose cowardice over power and maybe even a dirty girl of no account over her, then she would use them both. The apothecary exercised some power over her husband that she had never been able to ascertain. Otherwise, how had the young woman gone this long without being called to the Baron's chambers or being given to one of his men? It was time Adelaide discovered what was going on. She shoved the pigeon into the confused soldier's hands.

"Take this," she said before clambering down the ladder.

"You're crazy," Rollo said. "What are you going to do with a castle?" A long scar ripped across Rollo's left cheek and into the hairline of his thick brown hair. He perched on a boulder before the fire with his big hands on his knees. It had been Rollo's idea to travel south in search of better pay and easier work, but Rollo had admitted that the Baron of Longmire hadn't met his expectations.

Redmond grinned. "I have plans."

"No doubt," Rollo said. "But what's in it for us? You just said we can't pillage the town or the keep."

Redmond had borrowed a horse from a pasture along the way and cut due west across the open countryside. It had still taken all night to reach the lands of the Baron of Longmire and the better part of the day to locate the mercenary encampment he expected to find in the southern passes. They had pushed out farther on the plains near the headwaters of the Wind River in response to Dacrey's betrayal.

Now he relaxed around a fire with several dozen of the best archers he knew. He had fought with them. They were stout and dependable. The Baron of Longmire paid them regularly, but he also gave them little action and little opportunity for real profit. Most of them had friends now languishing in the Baron of Windemere's prison.

"I'll give every man an equal share of all the legitimate plunder," Redmond said.

"Plunder?" Rollo exclaimed, slapping his knees. "You have to pillage to get plunder." He had always been the voice of reason for the group. He was shorter than Redmond but bulkier.

"There's a way to get far more plunder than mere pillaging," Redmond replied.

"Ransoms," someone said. "You're going to ransom all the nobles."

Redmond rested his elbows on his knees. "I'm going to hold my cards close, for now," he said. "But if we take the castle, every man here will be able to give up mercenary work altogether on what we'll get."

The men exchanged glances. "I'd need quite a bit to put away my bow," Rollo said. "I might even need a castle of my own with pretty servants to massage my weary feet."

The men chuckled.

"Dacrey is coming for Longmire," Redmond said.

Rollo scowled. "When?"

Redmond shrugged. "I don't know, but I heard him myself. He's coming for Longmire. You can fight him for a little pay, or you can fight for a fortune on ground you've chosen."

Rollo pursed his lips as the men whispered among themselves.

"And," Redmond continued, "we all have friends and comrades who are going to be sent to rot in the mines if we don't act."

"There are only a hundred of us," someone said. "We'll never be able to storm the gate, especially with a new barbican to guard it."

"Unity of action and clarity of purpose matter more than numbers," Kamil said. He had joined the mercenaries while they fought up north on the Alva River six months before and proved to be a skilled archer and tactician. Redmond glanced at the short recurved bow he held in his hands. He never went anywhere without it. It was a strange but powerful bow constructed of horn, wood, and sinew. Kamil pushed a strand of graying hair from before his face and smiled. He wore his hair long and untied and carried himself with a quiet demeanor that made him appear like a wise grandfather. But Redmond had learned not to be deceived.

"That may well be," Rollo said with a smirk of annoyance, "but there is still the matter of getting over those stone walls."

"I know a way," Redmond said.

"You say they're forty feet high?" Rollo asked.

"That's all," Redmond said. "Several good ladders and a couple of good bowmen will get us up and over the walls before they know we're there. The garrison is small since the Baroness sent a troop of men out a few days ago. When you release our men from the dungeons, we'll outnumber them."

"I still say you're crazy," Rollo said.

"Probably, but will you come?"

A murmur of interest swept through the men.

"Things have been a mite slow around here," Rollo said. "I could use a bit of excitement."

"We don't have much time," Redmond said.

Rollo's gaze ran over his men. "We're good to go," Rollo said. "Like I said, we haven't seen much action lately. All we do is sit around waiting for the Baron's next attack on Windemere or Gurloch." He grunted as he rose to his feet. "Give us five hours. We can leave at nightfall."

Emilia ducked behind a wagon and slipped into a side street. Lady Adelaide seldom came out among the people. Now she strode through the streets with purpose. Two guards wearing mail and carrying swords flanked her. This was no social call. Emilia checked Lady Adelaide's progress through the streets. She was making her way toward her father's shop. A horrible premonition that her life was about to change for the worse swooped down upon her. Lady Adelaide never visited her father's shop.

She must have found out about Redmond. She must know they helped him escape the castle, but how could she know?

Emilia slipped around behind the shop and through the gate in the wicker fence that enclosed the tiny herb garden. She stole into the small mews where they kept the hawks and falcons. The birds ruffled their feathers at her approach and then settled down again. Emilia clambered into an empty bin next to the hut where she used to hide from her father when they played hide-and-seek when she was a child. A large crack allowed her to see into the shop. Tal cast a questioning glance at the bin when the door burst open. He lunged to his feet, spilling the medicine he had been mixing all over the table.

Lady Selgrave stormed in, her face livid with rage.

"Where is he?" she demanded.

"Who?" Tal asked.

"You know who," she snapped.

"The Baron?"

Lady Selgrave stepped toward him with a raised hand. "Redmond," she snarled.

"With his men, I suppose," Tal said.

"Don't play dumb with me," Lady Selgrave sneered. "I know you and your daughter helped him escape the castle last night."

"I don't know what you're talking about," Tal said. "Redmond left here last night after he treated your husband. I haven't seen him since."

"Where is your daughter? Did she go with him?"

"What? No. I sent her out this morning to collect hyssop."

Lady Selgrave glared at Tal.

"Well," she said, "I think you're lying, and if you are, I am going to find out." She brushed at a stray lock of hair that fell before her eyes. "Have you administered the drug as I ordered?"

"Yes, My Lady."

"I just saw the men, and they don't seem much affected."

"I diluted the dose, so they wouldn't notice until it was too late."

"Well, increase it today," Lady Selgrave said, "and I want you to prepare a child's dose."

Emilia's stomach turned sour. She swallowed the lump that rose in her throat. Not children. She can't do that to children.

"My Lady?" Tal questioned.

"Don't challenge me," Lady Selgrave snarled. "Your life already hangs in the balance. If your drug doesn't work, you'll finish your days in the salt mines, and your uppity daughter will rot in the brothels of Royan."

"Help me up," Baron Otto demanded. His voice still had the air of command, though it was weak. Lady Selgrave scowled in resentment at his treating her like a servant, but she bent to help him into a chair before the fire. His face had taken on a pallid, gaunt look, and he trembled with the effort of raising himself. Otto had never been an attractive man, but he didn't need to be. The salt mines and the gold trade made him one of the richest men in the kingdom. Otto's fever had broken that morning, and he was already ordering everyone around.

"Dragos did this to me," he said.

"Probably," Adelaide said, "but you have no proof, and you have bigger problems now. The Barons and Earls are getting restless. You need to speak with them. Earl Cockren has already left."

Otto swore. "These men are cowards. They won't even stand up for their own rights."

Adelaide smiled at his ill-tempered ranting. Otto didn't care for anyone's rights but his own. She had never liked Otto. Theirs had been a marriage of political convenience. He had always been ambitious, but he needed her skills and connections to carry out his schemes. After Hans deserted her for a larger dowry, she had a dalliance or two before her father arranged her marriage to Otto.

"You said you would never marry me off to anyone lower than an Earl," Adelaide said.

"Yes, well," her father said, "we all have to make sacrifices. At least the Baron is titled, and he has the wealthiest barony in the kingdom. You could use his money to rebuild Hiede, make it great again."

"The King will never accept this match," Adelaide said. "It will make our families too powerful and Otto potentially more dangerous."

"I don't have to seek his permission," her father said.

Adelaide laughed. "Yes, you do. I'm his cousin," she said.

Her father waved her away. "When it is done, he can't change it."

Adelaide harrumphed. The King would retaliate. Rupert was no fool. He couldn't let a slight like this go unpunished. But the prospect intrigued her. The Earldom of Hiede was one of the larger estates in the kingdom, and, if combined with Windemere, which was one of the wealthiest, they could become a formidable power indeed. Now that her two older brothers had both died in the fighting along the border, she would inherit her father's estates. Any heir she might produce would inherit the largest estate in the kingdom, so she agreed. They married in secret in her father's manor house and rode north to Windemere. Baron Otto was young and foolish, but when he saw the small army she brought with her, he looked askance.

"My Lady," he said, "you have no need of such a force."

Adelaide smiled. "My Lord," she replied, "they will help you remember who I am."

Otto scowled but kept his peace.

Their first year of marriage had been a power struggle. The King seized Otto's lands that bordered the Barony of Longmire and even granted some of them to Dragos. He also seized the northern half of Beck Wood from the Earldom of Hiede and granted it to his brother, the Duke of Einbeck. Otto had raged and blamed her. Once, he even beat her, but a careful application of lye to his wine had put a stop to that.

She allowed him to take his pleasure once in a while, but he had never offered her love, and she had never given it. She permitted him his dalliances, and she enjoyed hers. Still, it was sometimes wise to remind the Baron with whom he dealt.

"Your apothecary and his daughter might have helped Redmond escape," she said.

"Who?" the Baron asked as he adjusted his seat in the chair.

"The captain of the men Dacrey captured. I warned them that when we found out how they did it I would send him to the mines and her to the brothels."

Otto scowled. "No you won't," he said.

Adelaide gave him a condescending smirk. "I know his potions ease your discomfort, but we can't allow disloyalty among our servants. Unpleasant things can get into our food."

Otto glared at her. He understood her reference. He had come stumbling into their rooms at Langon on his old steward's arm with his mouth blistered and bleeding after drinking the wine she had poisoned.

"What have you done to me?" he whispered in a raspy, labored voice.

Adelaide pinched her lips tight and pointed to the bruise on her cheek. Her father had abused her, but her husband would learn she was not a woman to be trifled with.

"You little witch," he coughed.

Adelaide left him to his suffering, but the lesson had been well-learned.

Otto eyed her now. "You can dispose of your own servants however you like," he said. "But you will leave mine to me."

Adelaide raised her eyebrows but chose to ignore him. "What will you do with the lords?" she asked.

"Invite them to a feast to celebrate my recovery," Otto said. "When they are softened up on wine and mead, we'll convince them to be reasonable."

Adelaide smiled. "Oh, I think we can do that," she said.

Windemere

"We have to leave—now," Emilia said. She grabbed her father's sleeve.

"You want to end up like that escaped prisoner?" he asked. "Or worse, in some brothel? We have to appease them. Baron Selgrave fears me. He won't let things go too far."

"It's not the Baron I'm worried about," Emilia said. "Lady Selgrave is up to something, and she will not hesitate to kill either of us if we get in her way. If she believes we helped her lover escape, it's only a matter of time."

"Redmond was never her lover," Tal said.

"You don't know that," Emilia said, "and it doesn't matter. She made him some offer, and he refused. We're tangled up in this now. We have to leave."

Emilia jumped as someone pounded on the door. Tal grabbed her hands. "Go," he said.

"Not without you."

"Go," Tal said again as the pounding repeated, and he pushed her toward the back door. The hawks cried out, and Emilia paused. Someone was at the back door. They were trapped. She glanced up at the hole in the wall and scrambled up into the rafters as the door burst open.

Emilia clung to the rafters of the stables. She had tucked herself up in a dark corner. The odor of the old thatch smelled like the floor of an ancient oak forest. The musky scent of horses drifted up from the stalls below. Spiders crawled over her cloak and the occasional scamper of tiny mice feet kept her awake. She pulled the cloak tight around her shoulders and struggled to keep in the tears. The day passed without incident as she listened to the sounds of the guards searching for her. She spent so much of her life worrying about herself that she never imagined the Baron would hurt her father—not until Lady Adelaide came storming into their shop.

A desperate, hollow ache filled her chest. If she lost her father, what would she do? Redmond might never come back—if he was even still alive. She watched the soldiers gather their horses and ride out after him. On foot and alone, he would never make it. She expected him to be dragged in, just like Peter, and whipped to death.

As darkness fell, the sounds of merrymaking drifted to her from the keep. During the long hours of crouching in the darkness, Emilia realized there was only one thing she could do, and it was about time to begin. Lady Selgrave left her no choice. An apothecary's daughter had knowledge that could be put to good use.

Her escape had been a close-run thing. Adelaide's guards had been at both doors, and she had climbed up into the rafters of the thatched roof through a narrow hole in the wall between the apothecary shop and the old weaver's shop. There she had crouched hidden for several hours before sneaking into the stables. Now she dangled from the rafters and dropped to the floor of the empty stall. She couldn't rely on Redmond. She couldn't rely on anyone. It was time to take matters into her own hands.

A cloak of darkness concealed Redmond's band of archers as their horses pounded down the road through the moonless night. It was fortunate that his men were posted in the eastern hill country that separated Longmire from Windemere. If they had been pulled back to Long Lake or to Longmire itself, it would have taken him more than a week to return.

The rumble of the supply wagons carrying the extra weapons, supplies, and the long ladders followed close behind. Redmond needed speed now more than secrecy. If he hoped to succeed, he had to get his men well-hidden near the castle before daylight so they could have time to scout the area and prepare for the assault. It would help if he could contact Tal and Emilia to warn them and to get information about what was happening in the castle.

By the time the sliver of moon had risen to spread a pale light over the rolling farm country of the Barony of Windemere, his men were spread out in a double-file line with scouts out front and behind and flankers on either side. They dropped down into the valley where the winding creek wiggled along the broad, flat plain. Castle Windemere squatted on the only substantial rocky knoll in the valley, still too far to be visible in the gray-black sky.

The scouts riding in front of the line wheeled and galloped back to the advancing column of mounted archers. Redmond kicked his horse into a gallop to meet them.

"Barricade," they said.

Redmond waved his hand in a circular motion, and the archers spread out to confront the threat. The black hulk of a wagon could be seen parked across the road where it crossed the wide, shallow creek. The shadows of men bustled about the barricade as if they had been surprised by the arrival of such a substantial armed force. Someone shouted orders to them.

Redmond cursed. "We don't have time for this," he muttered.

He signaled to the men behind him, who broke into three groups. The two side groups whirled to swing wide in a flanking movement, while the center group advanced toward the barricade. They dismounted and melted into the brush along the creek before commencing a steady and deadly shower of arrows into the thirty or forty men who manned the barricade.

Rollo and Redmond led the groups swinging around to either flank. Redmond's men splashed across the creek before dismounting to advance on the bridge. He needed to be sure no riders escaped to carry a warning to the castle, so he left a handful of men to shoot into the right flank while he crept toward the rear. His men worked in careful coordination, which is why Redmond selected them. They had served together for so long that each man understood his duty, and they required little direction.

Cries of dismay arose from the barricade as dark shadows rushed to find cover from the shower of arrows. For a moment, Redmond allowed himself to hope the guards at the barricade would surrender without much bloodshed. But the quiet thrum of bowstrings in front of him sent Redmond sprawling face-first into the tall, sharp-edged grass that lined the road. An arrow zipped passed him. One of his men grunted and fell to his knees.

Redmond peered through the grass, searching for the assailants. A branch shifted, and Redmond lunged to one knee, drew, and released before dropping and rolling to the side. The satisfying slap of an arrow striking a solid body sounded. He jumped up with a roar, jerked his sword from its sheath, and rushed the crouching shadows. His men followed him as they crashed headlong into the rearguard.

Rollo bellowed his battle cry on Redmond's left as he and his men swept the guard before them, pushing them back onto the bridge. The ring of steel on steel, the clank of steel striking mail, and the grunts and groans of the dying and injured filled the air. The guards on the bridge realized they were encircled and exposed and cast down their weapons to beg for mercy.

A rider broke from the underbrush near the creek and galloped away from them toward the castle. Redmond whirled, raced to where he dropped his bow. He snatched it up, nocked an arrow, drew, and loosed. The slap of another bowstring sounded behind him, and he spun to find Kamil grinning at him as he lowered his short recurved bow.

"Let us see whose arrow strikes first," Kamil said.

Redmond snorted. "You're crazy. You know that?"

He spun back in time to see the rider jerk and toppled from his horse. Kamil liked to remind him how superior his recurve bows were to the longbows Redmond used. But Redmond didn't have time for a debate at the moment. He whirled back to his men.

"Hold!" he bellowed. His men paused to be sure it wasn't a ruse before they gathered the guards, disarmed them, and tied their hands behind them.

"How many injured?" Redmond called to Rollo.

"Four injured, two dead," Rollo replied.

Redmond resisted the temptation to kick the captured guards into oblivion. He could ill afford to lose these men, and the battle had cost him precious minutes in delay. He grabbed one of the guards he recognized as a sergeant from Castle Windemere and pulled him away from the other men. The sergeant struggled to keep his balance with his hands tied behind his back.

"Explain," Redmond demanded when they were out of earshot.

The sergeant's eyes narrowed in recognition. "We were sent to find you," he said.

"You found me," Redmond said. "Now tell me what has happened at Windemere."

The sergeant's gaze drifted toward Redmond's men as they pushed the wagon out of the way and cleared the path over the bridge so their own wagons could pass. Redmond grabbed him by the collar and shook him.

"Speak or I'll leave none alive," Redmond snarled.

Windemere

The sergeant sneered. "You'll be too late," he said.

"Too late for what?" He jerked him again.

"The apothecary and his daughter will be executed at sundown, and your men will be sent to the mines."

A hollowness spread in Redmond's chest. "Why Tal and Emilia?" he demanded.

"For helping you, I guess," the sergeant said. "Rumor has it the apothecary's own poison is to be used in their execution." Redmond tried not to show his concern. That was the kind of thing the treacherous Baroness would do.

"How many men guard the castle?"

The sergeant shuffled his feet. "How should I know? Maybe a hundred. The rest are out searching for you. The Baroness is in a right state."

Redmond considered whether he should trust the man. Deciding he had little choice, he turned away. But the sergeant kept speaking.

"You'll never survive," he said. "They know you're coming."

Redmond stared at him. Was he leading his men into a trap? He dragged the sergeant back to where the other men had been tied to the wagon.

Kamil stepped up to him, holding two arrows in his hands. He handed one to Redmond.

"Your arrow struck, but mine delivered the killing blow," Kamil said.

"Sure it did." Redmond slipped the arrow into his quiver.

His desperate gamble to free his men might mean he was leading even more of them to death or captivity.

Chapter 8
Treachery

Redmond crouched in the shadow of a haystack as the light of dawn filtered through the low-lying clouds. The rich, fresh scent of the straw filled his nostrils as he blinked at the weariness in his eyes. He had managed to grab a few hours of rest before they set off, but the lack of sleep was taking its toll. Still, he had no time now. He left more than two dozen of the Baron's men tied to the wagon they used as a barricade. It would only be a matter of time before some traveler discovered them on the road and brought news of the battle at the bridge to the castle. Still, he hesitated. Something wasn't right.

The castle battlements loomed up dark and threatening on the hill that overlooked the long, narrow valley with its scattered fields and tiny hamlets. This was the last rich valley before the dry, hot lands to the south, and it was a major thoroughfare for the salt that flowed out of Hallstat lands and for the gold and spices from the east and south. It was a place worth defending, and yet, there was no sign the castle was prepared for an assault. Where were the guards that should have been pacing the battlements? Could they be hunkered down out of sight, waiting for him to show his hand?

Movement on the battlements caught Redmond's attention. A small figure peeked above a merlon and raised an arm. A hawk jumped into the air, trailing a long red ribbon. Redmond scowled. The sergeant told him that Emilia and Tal were to be executed, yet here was someone leaving him the signal Emilia said would show him they were in danger.

If Emilia and Tal were captured, how could she be sending up the hawk this morning? Redmond paused on that thought. The only possible conclusions were that the guard had lied to him or Emilia had betrayed him. Perhaps the entire thing had been a ruse to force him to act while the Baroness was prepared and he was not.

He didn't want to believe Tal and Emilia would betray him, but Tal was locked in debt servitude to the Baron. He would have little choice if the Baron demanded that he betray Redmond's trust. Since he fled from his home on Frei-Ock Mor, life had taught him that even good, well-meaning people could be twisted to evil purposes if the right pressure was applied. Baroness Adelaide would know how to intimidate Tal and Emilia.

The hawk soared up on the warm air flowing in from the south to circle the battlements for a few moments before a short whistle called it back to the outstretched arm. Redmond pondered the sergeant's words and the apparent contradiction of someone releasing the hawk and decided that he had to act. He crept back to his waiting men.

"We go now," Redmond said.

Rollo raised his eyebrows. "Um, you do realize," he said, "that it will be broad daylight in an hour?"

"Yes."

"And that we have had no sleep?"

"Yes, but it won't be long before someone discovers we passed the barricade. We can't wait."

Rollo nodded. "Then we breakfast in the keep," he said and slipped his helmet onto his head.

Redmond waited as the men dispersed into the fields surrounding the castle. They all wore dark colors, smeared their helmets with mud, and wrapped their weapons in dark cloth. Any reflection of light might give away their presence. The diffuse light of the coming dawn still shrouded their movements—but not for long.

The smell of rich earth mingled with the pungent aroma of sheep and cows. A rooster crowed somewhere in the distance. Castle Windemere would be a rich prize and one not lightly relinquished to a bunch of archers. Redmond led the men with the ladders around to the eastern wall toward the underwater bridge Emilia had shown him. He wrestled against the nagging doubt that he was being led into a trap—that Emilia and Tal had deceived him.

Despite their dark colors, Redmond's men would be plainly visible from the high walls long before they managed to cross the bridge. He scanned the walls expecting the cry of alarm at any moment. But the castle seemed to be asleep—too asleep.

If they knew he was coming, as the sergeant claimed, they would have sentries watching their approach, even if Redmond couldn't see them. It could only be a ruse to get him to make a mistake. Redmond needed to get the men on the walls to expose themselves. He needed to know where they were so he could clear a place for the ladders. Redmond crept as close to the moat as he dared and waited.

He glanced back to check his men. They were no more than dark shapes along the base of the hill. Redmond raised his bow. The bulbous tip of the arrow had been especially hollowed to emit a high whistle as it cut through the air. He glanced at the five archers kneeling next to him. They signaled they were ready. Redmond drew the arrow to his ear, aimed high to send the arrow over the battlements, and released. As soon as the string slipped from his fingers, he whipped another arrow from his quiver and drew.

Emilia reached the bottom of the stone steps when the high-pitched whistle shrieked overhead. She froze and flattened herself to the wall. Images of desert demons who were supposed to emit such a sound before they killed crept into her mind. She knew such things were fairytales to scare little children, but what could that screech mean?

The hawk perched on her arm flapped its wings, and she gripped the jesses to keep it from getting away. The slap of booted feet ran along the battlements above followed by cries of surprise and pain. Emilia stepped from her hiding place to flee when strong arms encircled her waist and lifted her from the ground. She choked on the cry of surprise as a hand clamped over her mouth. The hawk flapped desperately, and she released him. As he soared free, she wondered if she would ever see another dawn.

The screech of the whistling arrow cut the morning stillness. The guards on the walls rushed to see what caused the strange noise.

Windemere

Redmond had been right. They had been waiting for him, hidden and out sight. The quiet thrum of half a dozen bowstrings sounded. Arrows arced into the sky to vanish into the pale light. Cries sounded, and bodies tumbled from the walls as the arrows found their marks. The men with the ladders rushed forward without a sound. Redmond led them to the stump Emilia had indicated where he paused to check for the hidden bridge with the toe of his boot. His boot met a solid surface, and he eased his full weight on it.

The bridge held. Emilia hadn't been deceiving him—in that at least. The men splashed across the bridge knee-deep in the stinking water, heaved the ladders against the walls, and clambered up. Redmond led the way, while the archers on the ground gave them cover from any guards who might try to push the ladders away from the walls or otherwise oppose their assault.

The cry of a hawk made him look up to see the red-tail flapping its wings before circling over his men, the red ribbon streaming out behind it. Redmond wondered at its release a second time and the fact that no whistle called it back.

"Hurry." He waved his men on.

The ladders clattered against the stone, proving to be the right height. Redmond slipped over the walls and crouched, ready for a fight. No one opposed him. He raced toward the stairs, leaping over several men still writhing in their death struggle with arrows protruding from their bodies. A few raised themselves to lean back against the battlements. They made no effort to stop him, but the guard was alerted now and shouts echoed through the castle. Booted feet slapped the stones.

Redmond leapt down the steps two at a time and paused at the bottom to let his men catch up. When several dozen had gathered, he gestured for them to close around him.

"Any questions?" he asked. They shook their heads.

"Be careful," he said. "Something isn't right here. The castle should have been better guarded."

The men glanced at one another. They were in it now and had to see it through.

"Once the gate is secure," Redmond said, "and the prison is opened, converge on the keep. I may need your help."

Rollo grinned. "Don't take any liberties with the women," he said.

Redmond ignored him and raced toward the keep. He had to prevent Dacrey from finding refuge there, or it would be impossible to dislodge him. And he needed to find out where the other nobles were and why no one commanded the few guards they had encountered.

The streets were still shadowed in darkness, but lights flashed in the windows and heads poked out of doorways. Redmond slowed as he approached the gates that led to the inner court and the keep. No guards were posted, and the gates stood wide open. Redmond scowled and crouched in the shadows, working his way silently through the gate. The scrape of metal on stone and the grunts of men echoed in the darkness.

He raced across the open area and around behind the keep where the narrow drawbridge connected the keep to the battlements. The shapes of half a dozen men wrestled with bridge supports. Someone shouted from inside the keep where the winch would have been positioned to raise the bridge. It must have been a long time since the bridge had been raised because they were having trouble.

Redmond couldn't afford to let them raise the bridge and seal the door to the keep. He placed an arrow on his string and stepped around the corner. He drew and released. A man fell with a grunt. The other archers joined him and soon cleared the bridge and the winch. The last remaining guard leapt to the door and tried to shove it closed, but Redmond's arrow caught him in the eye. He slumped against the wall and slid to the ground.

Springing up the stairs and over the bridge, Redmond led the rest of his men. They leaned into the door to force it open despite the dead weight of the guard who had fallen behind it. Redmond propped his bow against the wall and drew his sword. His men rushed down the stairs to the rooms on the lower levels and quickly secured them. Then they crept up the stairs single file, twisting to the right. Redmond shifted his sword to his left hand, hugging close to the cold stone as he climbed. If the stairs were defended, it would be a hard fight.

The scrape of boots on stone above made Redmond pause. Whispered female voices echoed down the stairwell. A door banged closed, followed by the clank of a buckle. The black smoke of the sputtering torches burned his throat. The occupants of the keep were awake, but what were they planning?

"What's happening?" a male voice choked.

Redmond gave a rueful smile. They didn't seem to understand their keep had been compromised. He raced up the stairs and slid to a stop on the second landing to find the captain of the guard stumbling onto the landing, struggling to buckle on his sword belt. Two of Adelaide's maids cowered against the far wall. Another maid lay at their feet in a pool of blood.

Redmond paused. This isn't what he had expected. The flickering light of the torches revealed the captain's face, pale as ash. Vomit dribbled from his chin and soaked his tunic. A foul stench wafted to Redmond through the open door, and he stepped back, suddenly wary.

The captain pulled his sword from its sheath. He raised it and staggered toward Redmond. The sword trembled in his hand.

"They're dead," he murmured.

Six of Redmond's men pushed out onto the landing, and Redmond waved them on. They leapt up the stairs to the next floor. Another four men joined Redmond.

"Where's Dacrey," Redmond demanded.

The captain paused and blinked at him.

"She killed them," he said and staggered into the wall. The sword slipped from his grasp to thump onto the floorboards. A ragged cough gurgled in his throat. Bloody foam touched his lips and slipped down his chin. His eyes opened wide. He shuddered and convulsed before sliding to the ground, coughing and gasping.

Redmond stepped around him to the door that led to the Baron's quarters. He kicked it open with the toe of his boot. The sight that met his gaze sent a shiver of disgust through him. His men peered over his shoulder.

"By the desert wraiths," one of them cursed.

Food and dishes lay scattered about in complete disarray. A dozen Hallstat lords dressed in their finery lay crumpled on the floor or draped over the toppled benches and the long table that filled the center of the room. Some lay still. Others writhed in agony. But no injuries or blood could be seen that might indicate a struggle.

Near the center of the room, Dacrey raised himself on his hands and knees. He clutched a torn piece of green cloth with one hand

and reached for a sword that lay on the floorboards with the other. Redmond stepped up to him, kicked the sword away, and jerked the knife from Dacrey's sheath. He tossed it to the other side of the room before he kicked Dacrey onto his back.

"What happened here?" Redmond demanded.

Dacrey gave a ragged laugh. "You thought she was so delicate and weak," he said. "She will eat you alive."

Chapter 9
Sedition

Redmond," someone called from the stairway outside, but Redmond hesitated as he glanced around at the bodies. These were some of the most powerful men in the kingdom. If the rumor spread that he had done this, he wouldn't be safe anywhere in Morcia. He had underestimated the Baroness and the depths to which she was willing to sink. But why would she do this? These men supported her husband. Some were his vassals.

"Redmond," the voice called more urgently.

Redmond spun and raced back out to the landing.

"You'll want to see this."

He followed his men up to the fifth floor. The door to the Baroness's chambers lay open. Three guards in her livery lay in pools of blood. Redmond burst in to find his men standing in a wide semi-circle with their swords out. Lady Adelaide stood, dressed in her green gown with one hand on a high-backed chair where the Baron reclined. The Baron's chest was bare save for the white bandages that encircled him. He clutched a sword in his hand.

At their feet sprawled Emilia. Her white skin showed through her torn clothes. Large bruises spread on her neck and face, and her arms and legs had sustained several shallow cuts. That's when Redmond noted the bloody knife dangling in Lady Selgrave's hand and the torn sleeve of her green gown. Emilia was moving, which meant she was alive.

Redmond narrowed his eyes and flexed his jaw.

"My wife tells me," the Baron said, "that I owe you my life."

"It looks like I should have let you die," Redmond said, shifting

J.W. Elliot

his feet. The walls of the keep seemed to be closing in around him. Maybe this had all been a trap. There was only one way out of the keep, after all.

"What have you done to her?" Redmond demanded.

"My servants are no concern of yours," the Baron said.

"Perhaps," Redmond said, "but my friends are my concern."

"Phah," Lady Selgrave said. "You have no friends."

Baron Selgrave raised his hand to silence her.

"I owe you a debt," the Baron said, "and I would repay it."

"I don't think you realize—" Redmond began, but the Baron cut him off.

"You may hold the castle for a day," he said, "but you can't hold it forever."

Redmond enjoyed their ignorance. For once, the tables had turned decisively against them. "I don't intend to hold it," he said.

A momentary look of surprise swept across Baron Selgrave's face, and Lady Adelaide cocked her head in suspicion and scowled.

"I intend to sell it," Redmond said.

His men murmured behind him, and Redmond gestured to one of them to help Emilia to her feet. He lifted her up, and she staggered against him, but she remained standing.

"You can't do that," Baron Selgrave blurted.

"I can," Redmond said.

"No one would dare buy it," Lady Adelaide said.

Now Redmond laughed. "On the contrary, every baron or earl in the kingdom will be begging me to hand it over to them. Others appreciate the strategic location of your castle and the newly discovered silver mines you plan to exploit."

"How did you—" Adelaide began.

"Quiet!" the Baron barked.

Redmond smiled. He had guessed right. Henry hadn't been just any slave. The Selgraves had been using him to mine silver somewhere in the foothills between Longmire and Windemere. A boy his size would prove useful in getting down into the deepest, darkest pits.

"This is always the problem with you nobles," Redmond scoffed. "You never manage to understand that we, the pawns whose lives you so casually play with, have brains of our own. You can dismiss

84

us all you want, but in the end, without us, you're nothing."

Adelaide growled and stepped toward him. "How dare you," she snarled.

"And," Redmond talked over her, "some of us are honorable and loyal and cannot be turned by the wicked smile of a pretty woman." Adelaide stopped. She stared at him in open shock. Baron Selgrave shot her an annoyed glance.

"We are not your dogs," Redmond continued, "to be toyed with. Our lives matter."

Adelaide threw back her head and laughed. "You are miserable swine fit only to lick the dust from our feet. Get out of here before I—"

"Don't waste your breath," Redmond interrupted. "I've heard enough of your poisoned words to last me a lifetime. But I am curious why you murdered the lords under your protection. That seems like a deed too vile even for you."

"I'm starting a civil war," Adelaide said.

"Silence!" the Baron roared. Adelaide shot him a venomous look but held her tongue. "What do you intend to do with us?" he demanded.

"Well," Redmond said. "After you pay us a ransom worthy of your most magnificent station, of say ten thousand gold coins, I will put your castle up for auction and sell it to the highest bidder."

The Baron grimaced in pain as he struggled to his feet.

"Don't make us use violence," Redmond said. "Please drop your weapons, and you'll be treated with far more courtesy than you deserve."

A commotion sounded behind them and the door burst open. Redmond crouched and spun to find Jannik standing in the doorway with a sledgehammer in his hands. His gaze flicked from Redmond to the Baron and the Baroness and then back again.

"You want me to knock their heads for you?" Jannik asked.

Redmond grinned. "Not yet," he said. "They're worth more alive than dead."

"Hmm," Jannik said. "I can see that." His gaze passed over Adelaide, and she stepped back to stand beside her husband.

"What's happening outside?" Redmond asked.

Jannik waved a dismissive hand. "You missed all the fun," he said, "and if you don't hurry you'll miss the feast they're preparing in honor of our victory."

"Are all our men free?"

Jannik frowned. "Yes, though not all of them are sensible enough to know it."

"What do you mean?" Redmond asked.

Jannik poked his big chin toward Adelaide. "She's been trying to drug us," he said.

Redmond faced the Baron and Baroness. "Will you surrender quietly, or will you force us to get rough?"

The Baron dropped the sword to the floorboards with a thud. Adelaide scowled and then dropped her knife.

"You cannot hide from me," she spat.

"My Lady," Redmond said, "I would like nothing better than to never lay eyes on you again."

He stepped toward the door but turned back.

"Lord Selgrave," he said, "you owe me your life twice now, and I claim the lives and freedom of Tal and Emilia in payment of your debt."

The Baron scowled. "You are bold for a common archer."

"I am far more than a common archer," Redmond said. "Just ask your wife." He hadn't planned on humiliating them, but the sight of Emilia curled up in pain on the floor had made him reckless.

"Why you—" Adelaide began, but the Baron cut her off again.

"Done," the Baron said. "But when this is all over and we meet again, either you or I will die in the encounter."

Redmond pursed his lips. "Perhaps," he said. "The papers will be brought for you to sign and seal."

He gestured for his men to leave the room before he sheathed his sword and lifted Emilia into his arms. She was standing, but clearly disoriented. He didn't have time to let her stumble along beside him. It would be easier to carry her.

Jannik pulled the door closed behind him.

"Don't let them leave these rooms," Redmond ordered, "for any reason. Or have communication with anyone. No servant is to enter or leave."

"What about the feast?" the men asked.

"Don't eat food from within the keep," Redmond said. "It's been poisoned." Then he nodded to Jannik. "Jannik will see you're well supplied. Now I must go."

Jannik grinned. "This will be a night worthy of many a song."

He stepped past Jannik, but stopped. "A sledgehammer?" he asked. Jannik grinned and patted the oblong piece of steel. "I couldn't find my battlehammer, so I borrowed this little beauty. I have a feeling we're going to have a long, fulfilling relationship."

Redmond left him to fawn over his new weapon. He had more important matters to deal with.

Emilia groaned and clung to Redmond as he hurried down the spiral stairwell, careful not to let the uneven stairs trip him. She was coming around from whatever they had done to her. Her body was slender but strong. She smelled of spices and herbs. The warmth in Redmond's chest frightened him. He couldn't allow himself to become involved, not after what he'd done to Lara.

He paused to retrieve his bow and slip over his head before stepping into the broad daylight. The singing and drinking had already begun.

"Where's Rollo?" Redmond asked his men who guarded the entrance to the keep.

"At the gate," they replied.

"Please ask him to meet me at the apothecary's hut."

One of them crossed the bridge and jogged down the stairs. Redmond followed him through the gate and headed toward Tal's shop. As he passed, he encountered groups of his men working through the streets searching for any hiding castle guards. Some archers proved unable to resist the temptation to loot and were carrying their treasures. When the men recognized him, they cheered and chanted. "Redmond, Redmond."

Terrified women clutched their crying children close, and sour-faced men glared at him and his men. Redmond needed to get these people out of the castle. They would be a distraction he didn't need, and they might get hurt if it came to fighting—or rather, when it came to fighting.

As he neared Tal's hut, he encountered huddled groups of his men released from the dungeons. He scowled at the transformation in them. Men who had once been strong and courageous now cowered against the wall. They had become listless and timid, with the graying skin and hollow eyes characteristic of the drug used on the slaves in the salt mines. He had seen worse, but the sight of his men so reduced and debilitated caused a new fire to burn in his belly. These Selgraves had much to answer for.

Redmond lifted the latch on the door to Tal's hut and kneed the door open. He carried Emilia to the fireplace where he laid her on the soft furs.

"Where are you hurt?" he asked. She blinked up at him and licked her bleeding lips.

"You came back," she said.

"I told you I would. Are you seriously injured?"

She dropped her gaze. "I don't think so. Lady Selgrave was just getting started."

She raised a hand to Redmond's cheek. He gently pulled it away.

"Let me tend to your injuries," he said.

A tear slipped down Emilia's cheek, but she didn't resist as Redmond cleaned her cuts and administered a soothing balm to her bruises.

"She tried to poison me," Emilia said, and she licked at the cut lip again.

"Tried?" Redmond asked in alarm. He had seen the state of the poisoned nobles, and he couldn't have endured watching Emilia die like that.

"She broke the vial on my teeth," she said.

"Did you swallow any?"

"No."

Redmond sat back, running his hands through his hair and let out a long, slow breath. At least she was safe from that.

"Where is your father?" he asked.

"I think they took him to the keep." Emilia swallowed. "I escaped and hid until this morning when I sent the hawk up to warn you. They saw and came after me."

"We'll find him," Redmond said. He wrapped a blanket around her and set to lighting the fire and preparing a hot stew while Emilia rested. He was stirring the bubbling pot when the door banged open.

"There you are," Rollo boomed. Then his gaze fell on Emilia

wrapped in a blanket with parts of her bare shoulders still visible through her torn shirt. "I see you have no need of a feast," he said. Redmond smirked. "Don't dishonor the lady with your crude accusations," he said. "Emilia, this scoundrel is Rollo."

Emilia pulled the blanket tighter and nodded to him. Redmond pointed to the table.

"Now sit down and tell me how we fared."

Rollo seated himself, pulled off his helmet, and set it on the table. "May I?" he said, tearing off a chunk of bread from the loaf that lay on the wooden tray.

"The castle is ours," Rollo said. "We lost five men with a few more injured. Now, when do we get this great wealth you promised?"

"Baron and Lady Selgrave will be delivering a ransom of ten thousand gold coins from their treasury," Redmond said, "in return for their freedom. Then we offer the castle to the highest bidder."

Rollo beamed. "Yes," he said, "we shouldn't sell it for anything less than 500,000 in gold." Then he glowered. "You do realize Lady Selgrave has a small army approaching, and, if you set them free, the Baron will raise an army of his own. You can't sell the castle unless you hold it."

"That's the idea," Redmond said. "We hold it for a few weeks. When the ransom is paid and the castle is sold, we take all we can carry and head for the coast. We should be able to find a ship sailing for Kassan without too much trouble. I don't think we'll be welcome among the Hallstat after this."

"You think?" Rollo said, chuckling. "But we still have to pass through Hallstat lands carrying our loot."

"We'll worry about that when the time comes," Redmond said. "We have bigger problems."

Rollo cocked his head sideways and paused in his chewing.

"The lords are all dead," Redmond said.

Rollo's eyes opened wide. "You killed them?" he exclaimed.

Redmond glanced at Emilia, but she looked away.

"No, they had already been poisoned. Lady Selgrave said she did it to start a civil war."

Rollo cursed. "That's a problem we didn't need."

"There were a dozen powerful families represented in that group," Redmond said. "They're all going to come for us, but, for now, I need you to find the apothecary and bring him here. We also need to finish the barbican and prepare for a siege. After the men have feasted, set them to work preparing stones and oil. I'll need at least a hundred to dig long trenches beyond the moat."

Rollo snorted. "You plan to work them harder than the Baron did?"

"Maybe," Redmond said, "but they'll have a feast every night and a full share in the ransom. Besides, every noble within a hundred miles will be anxious to claim Windemere."

"Will the King allow it?" Rollo asked.

Redmond rubbed the back of his neck. "I don't know. That's not my problem. We take the money and run as soon as we can. Let them fight over it after we're gone."

A knock sounded, and Jannik entered, helping a stumbling Tal through the door.

Emilia let out a cry, tossed the blanket from her back, and dashed to her father's side. He smiled and reached for her. Jannik and Emilia helped him to a bench at the table.

"They roughed me up a bit," Tal said, holding his ribs.

Rollo stood. "Well Redmond, since you'll be playing doctor, I'll get to work. Someone has to make things happen around here."

"You don't fool anyone," Redmond said. "You're having more fun than a fox in the henhouse."

Rollo pursed his lips. "That may be, but I also want to survive to enjoy my time in the henhouse. Don't get so distracted that you forget who got us into this mess."

"Would you have done any differently?" Redmond asked.

Rollo studied him. "Probably not." Then he stepped toward the door.

"One last thing," Redmond called to him.

Rollo paused.

"We need to get the people out of the castle. Can you get that started? And send me the Baron's scribe, if he didn't get himself killed by Lady Selgrave."

Rollo grabbed the last of the loaf and left with a nod to Emilia.

Emilia was already stripping Tal's clothes off in search of his injuries. But Tal laid a hand on her arm. "Just get me some water and some of that stew I smell," he said. "I'm not bad hurt."

Windemere

"I'm glad to hear it," Redmond said. "Now, will the two of you tell me what has been going on around here?"

Emilia bowed her head and bent over the pot of stew. Tal's gaze followed her.

"I resisted as long as I could," Tal said. "I diluted the dose, but not everyone responds the same to the drug. I'm afraid some of your men had a negative reaction."

Emilia ladled Tal a bowl of stew and handed it to him.

"But why did they go after you?" Redmond asked.

Tal glanced at Emilia again and swallowed a mouthful of stew.

"When they found you missing," he said, "the guard that opened the gate for you was forced to admit what he had done and who paid him."

Redmond studied them. They weren't telling him something. "There's more, isn't there?" he asked.

Tal hung his head.

"Tell him," Emilia said.

Tal grunted and dropped his gaze to the floor.

Emilia clicked her tongue. "He refused to prepare the drug to be used on children," she said.

"What? Why would they need children to work in the salt mines?" Even as the words left his mouth, he realized he had been naive. Henry hadn't been drugged, but, if the children were giving them trouble, Lady Selgrave wouldn't hesitate to use the drug on them.

"They don't," Emilia said. "After I saw them sneaking children in here the night you left, I asked around. They plan to use them in some newly discovered silver mines on the border. They tried the full-strength drug on them. It killed them or drove them mad, so they needed a weaker dose."

Redmond nodded his understanding, but Emilia kept talking. He had already guessed that the silver mine existed and that they used children in them. How else could he explain Henry and the slaver he had killed?

"They didn't want to attract attention," Emilia said. "Children can go down in small holes and follow the seams. They can be kept in tiny camps well-hidden from unwanted eyes. I think they plan to extract enough silver to pay for a huge army and use it to seize Long-mire before Baron Dragos learns the mines are there."

Redmond passed a hand over his head. "He probably knows they're there by now," Redmond said. Then he let out a long sigh. "How do I keep getting myself into these situations?"

"More to the point," Emilia said, "how do you keep getting *us* into them?"

"Sure," Redmond said. "Blame me. But I had a little help and encouragement."

Tal laughed. "I haven't had this much fun since the border wars."

"Is this what fun feels like?" Emilia asked. "I'll pass next time."

"Where are the children now?" Redmond asked.

Emilia's smile faded. "I don't know."

"We didn't have time to find out much," Tal said. "They came for us late yesterday, and Emilia ran."

Redmond appraised her. "There aren't many places to hide in a castle this size," he said.

Emilia grunted. "I did more than hide," she said, frowning.

Tal gave her a questioning glance.

"I poisoned the Baron's food with the help of one of Lady Selgrave's maids," she whispered. When Redmond and Tal simply stared at her, she shrugged. "It seemed like the only way to stay alive. They were going to kill us all."

Redmond scowled. "But Lady and Baron Selgrave were unhurt. Only the nobles were poisoned."

"I didn't do that," Emilia said. "I only gave the maid enough to poison two people. She was supposed to slip it into Lady Selgrave's and Baron Otto's food."

"Well, someone introduced a lot more poison into the food served to the lords," Redmond said. "Lady Selgrave claimed she did it to start a civil war."

"It's going to start something." Tal said. "That's for certain."

Redmond dropped onto the bench and appraised Emilia.

"You never stop surprising me," he said.

Emilia gave him a smirk and spun away. "You're not the only one who can make plans of their own."

Redmond took a deep breath and let it out. "Once word gets out the lords are all dead, none of us will be safe in Morcia."

Emilia lowered her gaze to the floor. "I didn't do it," she said. "And even if I had, it would have been worth it to save my father."

Windemere

"Well, this could make our lives even more interesting for the next few weeks," Redmond said.

Emilia glanced at him sharply. "Why not just run now?" she asked. "Take your men and run for the coast before you get trapped in here."

"I could," Redmond said. "But I would have to leave almost sixty of my men behind who are either injured or still recovering from the drug and too weak to ride. I won't do that."

"But more of you will die defending this castle. Let's just go now."

"We're mercenaries," Redmond said. "We don't mind dying in battle. It's part of the job. But no man here would choose to suffer the indignity of dying a mindless slave over an honorable death in battle. I won't abandon a single man to that fate."

Emilia bowed her head and spoke almost in a whisper. "But you would lead them to a brutal death defending a castle you can't hold?"

Redmond clenched his jaw. How could he get her to understand? He had no good choices.

"If I left men to die in the mines when I could have done something to save them, I would never be able to live with myself. I would rather die."

"What have you done?" Baron Selgrave demanded of Adelaide once Redmond left his chambers. "You killed them all, and you let this adventurer seize my castle."

If the Baron hadn't been in such pain from his injury, Adelaide might have worried for her safety.

"I did you a favor," she said.

"By murdering the only supporters we had? Don't pretend you didn't kill Hans out of pure spite."

Adelaide scoffed. "You called them cowards, and, while you shivered on your fever bed, most of them were plotting against you."

"Fine," Baron Selgrave said. "Make an example of those, but why kill them all?"

"Because you might have cowed the others for a time, but they knew your plans. We couldn't trust any of them. This way, you get a crop of new young lords who will be more easily controlled."

He grunted. "Maybe, but you and your romantic flings are going to destroy everything we've worked for. Now one of your conquests has seized my castle."

Adelaide sneered at him. "It's a temporary setback," she said. "I'm more than a match for an ignorant archer."

Baron Selgrave raised his eyebrows at her, and she spun away in annoyance. She had better things to do than to quibble with Otto.

Redmond gazed at the women he had gathered in the lower room of the keep. Some wept openly, while others watched in stony-faced dislike. A few stood against the wall. Others sat rigid on the benches and chairs his men had gathered for them. Their fine clothes and elegant hair were disheveled. He cleared his throat considering how to begin.

"My Ladies," he said. "I regret to inform you that your menfolk were murdered by Lady Adelaide."

An outcry of disbelief erupted. "Liar," someone shouted in a high, piercing voice.

"Please, ladies." Redmond tried to calm them. When they quieted, he continued. "They were dead before we arrived. She poisoned them while they ate at her board."

Sniffles sounded. Someone coughed.

"Why would she do that?" a thin woman with a red silk handkerchief demanded.

Redmond shrugged. "I don't know. My men had orders not to harm them or you."

"Don't believe him," a round young woman said, who looked to be pregnant. She sneered at him. "These foreign rabble the lords are bringing in for their little wars are nothing more than animals."

Heads bobbed in agreement, but more than a few scowled and cast suspicious glances at the other ladies. They knew Lady Adelaide and her capabilities.

A woman with dark hair and a full figure stepped in front of the woman. "My name is Klara of Gurloch, wife of Hans," she said. "We all know Adelaide is a vile, conniving woman capable of any outrage. How many of your husbands has she tried to bed?"

The women glanced around at each other trying to hide their own shame.

Windemere

"Think about it," Klara continued. "Why would archers kill them when they could hold them and us for ransom? Adelaide doesn't deserve your loyalty."

Several women nodded in agreement.

"Thank you," Redmond said. "You may all believe what you wish, but we did not kill them as you will see for yourselves in a moment. If you will follow me." He opened the door and held it for them.

The women hesitated and eyed one another before filing out. Redmond's men escorted them to the room where their husband's bodies lay as Redmond had found them. Sobs and cries erupted as they passed through the door. One young woman turned aside and vomited against the wall. Others fell beside their loved ones and wailed in despair. Redmond resisted the urge to cover his nose and mouth at the horrible smell.

A middle-aged woman with red hair and a silver dress stopped just inside the door. Her back went rigid, and Redmond thought she might faint, but she whirled and launched herself on him.

"Murderer," she cried and slammed her fists into his face and chest. Redmond struggled to grab her arms. When he finally got a hold of them, he held her back.

"My Lady," he said. "I did not kill your husband. I do not murder helpless men. Lady Adelaide is plotting something against your king. All I want to do is save my men from the mines."

She jerked her hands free. The other women had turned to watch her.

"I am very sorry for your loss," Redmond said. "But we are not responsible for this." He gestured to the overturned tables and bodies with their grotesquely distorted faces and the dried foam and vomit on their mouths and clothes.

The women cast their gaze over the horrible scene. Handkerchiefs rose to cover mouths and noses.

"None of you will be harmed," Redmond said. "Prepare your things, and you will be escorted from the castle."

It may have been a futile effort, but at least he had sown the seeds of doubt among them.

Chapter 10
A Castle for Sale

R edmond leaned over the battlements, surveying the work on the barbican. With the death of all the nobles, it wasn't going to be a simple thing to sell the castle. Any powerful family who had a husband or father or son die here would be after Redmond's blood. That's why he had ordered his men not to kill the nobles. He planned to use them as bargaining chips, but now all he had were dead bodies. At least his men hadn't molested the ladies.

The castle was well-situated, but the two round towers on the front of the barbican were unfinished. If a large and determined army came, he wouldn't be able to hold the castle for more than a few days.

A long line of carts and wagons trailed into the distance as the peasants and villagers of the valley sought to escape the coming battle. Under different circumstances, they might have sought refuge in the castle itself, but no one knew what the new owners intended. Redmond sent all the occupants of the castle away, as well, and they joined the long file of refugees. He didn't need them underfoot or sabotaging his efforts to defend the castle, and he didn't want the distraction of women and girls for his men. Only the wives of the deceased nobles, Baron Otto, his wife, and a few of their servants remained.

Redmond's foraging parties spread over the countryside to gather in what food the peasants had left behind and to scout the approach of Lady Selgrave's army. The castle was strong, but they could not endure a sustained siege. They didn't have enough men or supplies.

Windemere

Redmond turned to Rollo, Jannik, and Kamil, the wizened older man from the east, who stood beside him. "Well," he said, "how would you defend this castle?"

"The first thing is to remove that underwater bridge we used," Rollo said.

"That can be done tonight," Redmond said.

"The barbican is our weakest point," Jannik said. "We'll never finish it before Lady Selgrave's men arrive."

"When able to attack," Kamil said, "you must appear unable. When preparing to use force, you must appear inactive."

Redmond turned to stare at the older man. Kamil's long, silver-streaked hair blew about his face in the wind that whipped up the walls of the castle. The sharp scent of foreign spices wafted from him. He wore a long, plain tunic with a wide leather belt buckled around the waist. Not many easterners condescended to live among the people of the southlands. Only those who fought in the border wars of the Kassan had seen them in action, and, once seen, they could not easily be forgotten. They rode short, shaggy horses and used powerful composite bows with great skill.

"What do you mean?" Redmond asked.

"They will expect the barbican to be incomplete and will focus their first assault there."

"I just said that," Jannik said. Though he came from the island of Rosythia and was a foreigner himself, Jannik never had much patience for what he called foreign rabble.

"So you must appear weak," Kamil said. "Leave the front of the barbican incomplete. Allow them to enter, and cut them down."

"What if they capture the barbican?" Rollo said.

"Let them," Kamil replied. "Then bring it down on their heads." He glanced at Jannik and the big sledgehammer he had leaned against the stone wall. "A few men with hammers such as those and the knowledge of where to strike a prepared weakness would do the job."

Jannik scowled, but he nodded, impressed despite his prejudice.

"Sounds good to me," Rollo said.

"Jannik?" Redmond asked.

"I'll get on it," Jannik grumbled. He shouldered his hammer and sauntered away.

"We might want a pit behind the unfinished wall," Kamil said to Rollo. "Sharpened stakes in the bottom will slow them down."

Rollo considered. "Sounds like the beginnings of a plan," he said. He stepped past Redmond and then paused. "Don't sit up here brooding all evening," he said. "The men missed you at the feasting."

Redmond nodded as Rollo strolled away.

"To subdue your enemy without fighting," Kamil said, "is the height of generalship. If you have to fight, then you have failed to know your enemy and yourself."

Redmond rubbed the back of his neck. "That may be true," he said, "but when you're stuck in a castle you don't have many options."

"Delay and disguise," Kamil said. "Give them reason to fear and to doubt."

Redmond regarded Kamil. He liked the older man and trusted him. "Will you take charge of organizing your delay and disguise ideas?" he asked.

"No," Kamil said.

Redmond started with surprise.

"The men will not follow me," Kamil said.

"All right," Redmond said. He had heard the men talk. Kamil was right. Everyone who knew him respected him, but he was too foreign for most of the men. "Then can you draw up plans for me to use?"

Kamil stared out over the valley. "It is strange how we struggle to keep from others what is rightfully theirs."

"Are you calling me a thief?" Redmond demanded.

"Yes," Kamil said. "Men of war are thieves. We steal life and breath from men who ought to have lived, and we seize their property to enrich ourselves." He gestured to the departing line of wagons. "Only the peasants who till the earth and eat from the sweat of their brows are not thieves of one sort or another."

Redmond grunted. Kamil was right, of course, but the world was seldom so simple. The sound of bells and a soaring hawk drew Redmond's attention. The hawk swooped down on a bounding hare. Emilia jogged up to stroke its feathers and feed it bits of meat until it let her take the hare and hang it from her belt.

Kamil stepped over to Redmond and leaned his elbows on the

battlements.

"It seems to me," Kamil said, "that you have chosen the path of aloneness."

Redmond frowned at him. "What's that supposed to mean?"

"It means that you should either find fulfillment in this path or chose another."

"Others forced this path upon me," Redmond said. Neahl's hard-headedness and the assassins that pursued him had driven him from Frei-Ock Mor years ago.

Kamil tapped his fingers against the stones. "No," he said, "others constrained your choices, but you chose your path."

"And you?" Redmond asked. "Is this the path you chose?"

"Yes," Kamil said. "I fled my people after I murdered the man who killed my mother. I could have remained and been executed. Or I could have followed the honorable path and ended my own life. I chose the coward's path. I was then enslaved but escaped and came west. It has taken me many years to find the path that I now walk alone."

"I'm fine," Redmond said.

"No," Kamil said. "You want others to believe you are a man of no emotion, that you are satisfied with the lonely life you lead, but you are not content. Those who watch have noticed."

"Who?"

"Your friends."

"I'm fine," Redmond repeated, wanting this uncomfortable conversation to end.

Kamil clicked his tongue. "Emilia's path has crossed yours, and you must choose whether to continue on your path of aloneness, join hers, or seek another." Then he walked away.

Redmond watched as Emilia's hawk caught a quail that jumped up from a field. Emilia was young and strong. He could do worse than take her and Tal to some distant land to build a new life. She would go with him, he had no doubt. But could he go with her?

Adelaide climbed through the private entrance in her chambers into the attic where she kept her pigeons It was time to turn the tables on Redmond and his band of ruffians. The sharp smell of the pigeons and straw greeted her. It surprised her that Redmond hadn't carted away her pigeons to keep her from communicating with her men outside the castle walls, but perhaps he was too preoccupied with his common wench. Regardless, she would take advantage of his mistake. He might have her trapped in the keep, but she could still make his life very difficult.

She read through the three new messages waiting for her before tying copies of her own to the legs of half a dozen pigeons. Word would spread that Redmond, an archer employed by the Baron of Longmire, had, on the orders of Baron Dragos, treacherously seized Castle Windemere and poisoned the lords he found there.

She checked to make sure Emilia wasn't out with her hawks before she released the pigeons. As she watched them fly away, she thought now might be a good time for the little assassin to reappear and help her out of this mess. But she would bide her time. Her men were coming, and Redmond was unprepared.

"Has anyone communicated with them?" Redmond asked the man guarding the upper rooms of the keep as he approached Lady Selgrave's rooms.

"Not yet," the guard said. "We leave the food at the door."

"Good," Redmond said. He pushed through the door.

Baron Selgrave looked up from a large leather-bound ledger. He now wore a loose silk undershirt. Glancing at the papers in Redmond's hand, he set the ledger aside.

"I see you've come for your pound of flesh," he said.

"I prefer to call it justice," Redmond said. He extended the bundle of papers. "If you would be so kind as to sign these manumission papers that release Tal, Emilia, and their descendants from their debt."

Baron Selgrave grimaced. "What else will you be wanting?"

"The ransom set for your release is 10,000 gold coins."

"I see," the Baron said. "You wish to rob me of my servants, deprive me of my castle, and reduce me to penury all in one stroke."

Redmond pursed his lips. "No," he said. "I wish to free myself and my men and two faithful and unjustly indebted servants. But, since you are unlikely to forgive and forget, I also need to provide the means for our escape from the wrath to follow."

The Baron sneered. "You're just a gold digger like the rest."

"You should consider," Redmond said, "that had you kept your word and restrained the abuse your vassals heaped upon my men, you would still be in possession of your castle."

"Phah," the Baron said with a dismissive wave of his hand.

Redmond bristled. "We surrendered under the promise of fair treatment, protection, and a quick release," he said. "But you decided to work my men as slaves and then intended to send us to your salt mines. No honorable man so radically reneges on his word."

"What are you talking about?" The Baron's eyes narrowed.

"Ah," Redmond said. "You claim to know nothing of the murder of one of my men or your orders to use Tal's drug to turn the rest into mindless beasts for your salt mines."

The Baron pinched his lips tight and reached for the papers, but Redmond had seen the Baron's surprise. Redmond handed him the papers and waited until he signed and sealed the wax with his signet ring.

"There," the Baron said, "take your piece of flesh and leave me in peace."

A door closed, and the soft tread of feet from an adjoining room brought Redmond's head up. His hand drifted to his sword hilt. Lady Selgrave stepped into the room, paused, then strode up to Redmond. She cocked back her hand and slapped him across the face.

"Do you betray everyone who trusts you?" she demanded.

Redmond let the slap burn on his cheek. "Trust was never asked for, nor given," he said. "And I know well what you and Dacrey had planned. If you desire to sneak about the castle grounds at night, you ought to at least try to disguise yourself."

"Why you," Adelaide shot her hand out to slap him again, but Redmond caught it.

"I believe once is sufficient," he said, squeezing her wrist.

"You will live to regret humiliating me," she said as she jerked her hand away.

"Perhaps," Redmond said. "But tomorrow morning, after the ransom has been collected from your treasury, I will escort you and any other noble ladies in the castle to safety. You may bring one trunk apiece for your maintenance."

J.W. Elliot

"You intend to keep me prisoner?" the Baron said.

"For now," Redmond said. "Lady Selgrave is prone to make rash decisions, and we need you here until your castle has been sold."

Redmond found Tal on the green to the west of the castle with Emilia exercising a couple of hawks. They each wore thick leather gloves on their left hands. Tal swung the lure over his head. As the hawk dove for it, he snatched it away. The hawk's jesses dangled out behind it, and the bells tied to its tail feathers jingled as it banked back up into the sky. Tal twirled the lure again, and this time he let the hawk catch it. The hawk dragged the lure to the ground to tear at the piece of meat tied there.

Emilia slipped the hood from the hawk perched on her arm as Redmond approached. The hawk ruffled its feathers and blinked.

"How long have you been training hawks?" Redmond asked.

Tal waited while the hawk at the lure finished the meat. "We started about ten years ago when the Baron needed someone to care for his birds during the molt. The birds did so well he had me take over the training of all of his birds." Tal whistled, and the hawk flew to his arm. He fed it another scrap of meat and then wound the jesses around his fingers to keep it from flying away again.

"Emilia does most of the training now." Tal stroked the hawk's feathers. "Baron Otto won't want to leave these behind."

"I think you can keep them as payment for your years of service," Redmond said.

He shifted his longbow to his right hand and drew the folded papers from his pocket. He handed them to Tal.

"He signed these this morning," Redmond said. "You and Emilia are free."

Tal stood blinking and working his mouth for a long moment before he took the papers.

"Thank you," he whispered.

"You shouldn't stay anywhere near here," Redmond said. "You might consider one of the port cities or move up north. I have a feeling Lady Selgrave will resent that fact that we've all escaped her clutches."

"Redmond," Emilia said with a sound of warning in her voice.

Windemere

Redmond flipped the bow back to his left hand and drew an arrow as he whirled around. Emilia pointed to the top of the keep.

A slender figure in a flowing gown stood atop the battlements. She raised her hands and a white pigeon leapt into the air with a flutter of wings. Emilia whistled and tossed her hawk into the air after it. The hawk soared up, circled, and shot out in pursuit of the pigeon. The pigeon swerved as the hawk's talons nearly seized it. Then it dove. The hawk followed in pursuit as the pigeon circled the keep. The two birds collided, but the pigeon rolled and fell away. The hawk dove after it.

"Watch out," Tal called, and Redmond jerked around. A lone archer rose from the bushes along the creek and drew his bow. He aimed directly at Redmond before jerking his bow up and loosing an arrow straight toward the hawk that was now diving toward them. Redmond drew and loosed his own arrow in a moment of desperate panic. It arced up and intercepted the arrow before it reached the hawk. Both arrows fell away with a clatter as the hawk caught the pigeon. Wings fluttered, and the hawk dropped toward the ground. Redmond jerked another arrow from his quiver and spun to shoot at the archer who was now sprinting over the open ground on the other side of the creek. The arrow caught him in the back. He stumbled and fell.

Redmond sprinted to the creek to make sure no one else was skulking in the bayberry bushes and reeds. He splashed through the creek and found the archer lying facedown a few paces from where Redmond's arrow struck him. The man had tried to crawl away.

The man wore a padded jerkin, but it had not stopped Redmond's arrow. The sharp broadhead had cut through the linen padding. His leather helmet had rolled from his head. He was clearly a lowly bowman and no noble.

The man blinked and tried to rise.

"Lie still," Redmond said as he knelt beside him, "and I won't kill you."

"You already have," the man said. "I can't feel my legs."

"What were you doing skulking about the castle?" Redmond demanded. "And why were you going to shoot me?"

"Just finish me," the man begged.

"I need information," Redmond insisted.

J.W. Elliot

"A few gold coins for a poor man with a family are reason enough," the man said.

"Who paid you?" Redmond demanded.

"How should I know? It was a dark tavern."

"All right, then how long ago?"

"Two nights."

"Do you know anything else that might convince me to save your life?"

The man coughed, and a dribble of blood touched his lips. "Unless you're a magician, there's nothing you can do."

Redmond glanced at the arrow. The man was right. The arrow entered the spine below the shoulder blades. If the man couldn't feel his legs, then the spinal cord had likely been severed.

"Where can I send word?" Redmond asked.

The man blinked at him. "Willow Hollow," he said. "My wife's name is Alma." The man coughed again and fumbled with a pouch at his waist. "Tell her I...that I'm sorry."

Redmond untied the pouch and pulled the strings open. It was filled with gold coins and a slip of paper.

"Don't hurt them," the man said.

"I won't," Redmond replied, "but tell me, why didn't you shoot me? Why did you change your aim to the hawk?"

"I'm not a murderer," he said. "Besides, any man that can shoot an arrow out of the air is a better archer than I could ever be."

"It was luck," Redmond said.

The man struggled to move. "Please, finish me," he whispered.

The rustle of grass brought Redmond's head up. Tal stood over him.

Redmond couldn't kill a helpless man—even if it would be an act of mercy.

Tal handed him a tiny glass vial without a word. Redmond hesitated and met Tal's gaze. Did Tal always walk around with a vile of poison in his pocket? He glanced at the arrow in the man's back and took the vial from Tal.

"What's your name?" he asked the dying man.

"Crispin," he said.

Redmond placed the vial in his hands. "This will help," he said.

Crispin swallowed. "Help me sit up," he said.

104

Windemere

Redmond snapped the arrow in Crispin's back and rolled him over. He lifted his head into his lap.

"I'm sorry," Redmond said.

Crispin swallowed. "Please give them the gold," he said.

"I will. I swear it."

Crispin lifted the vial to his lips and swallowed. Redmond laid Crispin's head in the green grass, straightened, and walked away. He couldn't watch the man die. If he had known the man only intended to kill the hawk, he wouldn't have shot him. The man had died for no good reason.

Emilia waited for them with both hawks. The dead pigeon now hung from her belt.

"Will he live?" she asked, gesturing toward the injured man.

Redmond lowered his gaze. "No," he said.

The wind whispered in the rushes along the stream as they watched Tal position the dead man's hands and retrieve his weapons.

"Was he an assassin?" Emilia asked. "Why did he try to shoot the hawk?"

"Someone paid him to shoot me," Redmond said, "but he says he couldn't murder me in the end, so he shot at the hawk, to scare us I suppose."

"I can't believe you hit that arrow," Emilia said.

"Me neither," Redmond said. "It was luck."

Emilia smirked as if she didn't believe him.

"Really," Redmond insisted. "I couldn't do that again if I tried. Besides, the arrow was only about fifteen yards away, and it was flying parallel to us. There's no way I could have hit it under any other circumstances."

Emilia lifted a tiny scroll she had pulled from the pigeon's leg. "Shall we see what her ladyship has to say this time?" she said. She unrolled the scroll.

Redmond bent to read it. The few words were written in an impeccable, flowing script that was beautiful to look at.

"Pathetic peasants!" it read. "You will not live long enough to enjoy your little romance."

"What the—" Redmond began and looked back to the top of the keep as another pigeon lifted into the air, banked to the right, and flew north.

"Well," Tal said as the pigeon diminished into a small dot against the blue sky. "It seems somebody should have taken those pigeons away from her."

Redmond cursed. "That woman is more trouble than a plague-filled blanket."

He glanced down at Emilia. She was blushing as she wrapped the hawk's jesses around her fingers.

"You realize how dangerous this is?" Baron Otto said as Lady Selgrave finished packing her trunk.

She smirked at him. Of course she knew. She hadn't been born yesterday.

"If the King gets here before we can secure the castle, he will use it to move against us."

"He won't," she said. "My army is coming, and, when combined with yours and those of the lords who now have a grievance against Redmond and his archers, we can storm the castle."

"My brother will come," Otto said.

"Yes, but we should also make other plans," Lady Selgrave said. "Can you arrange for one of your menservants to infiltrate the archers?"

"I already have," Baron Otto said. "I sent Lyle into the prison to spy on them when they first arrived, and he joined them when they stormed the castle. I can get a message to him."

"Good," Adelaide said. "Once I'm out of here, I will punish these ruffians one way or another."

Baron Otto studied her. "Why were you sending these archers to the mines? What were you and Dacrey plotting?"

Lady Selgrave whirled to face him with an undergarment in her hand. "I'm plotting to get your land back from Longmire and my land back from Einbeck. Those archers were just trouble—as they have now proven. I was trying to get rid of them before they did something like this."

Otto glowered at her.

"If you hadn't gone off and tried to get yourself killed," Lady Selgrave continued, "you would have been able to help. As it was, I had to do things on my own."

Windemere

"And the mines?" Otto asked.

"I had a group of children ready to send in, but they've disappeared. The men are already there opening the vein, but we can't spare more than a few. They're too difficult to manage, and their presence would be noticed. Children are easier to hide and easier to control. We can't get as much work out of them, of course, but, for now, it's the best solution."

"From now on," Baron Otto warned, "you talk to me first. If you hadn't antagonized these archers, none of this would have happened. You have to get control of your dalliances and choose your lovers more carefully."

"Me?" Adelaide replied. "Redmond was never my lover. And what about you and that little wench who keeps your hawks. What are you saving her for?"

Otto's face grew red, and he stepped toward his wife with a sneer. "I tolerate your excesses," he said, "but don't push me too far."

"And what is that supposed to mean?" Adelaide asked.

"It means you are still my wife, and the law is on my side."

Adelaide bristled. "I am a countess in my own right, and I outrank you in the peerage."

"Sure," Otto said. "But without me, you're nothing but an impoverished countess with a tiny army. It's silver from *my* lands you hope to use to build up your strength. Never forget that."

"Lands that now belong to Longmire," Adelaide reminded him.

The archers came out to gawk at the ladies and their servants as the four wagons trundled under the gate and out of the barbican. A few whistled and catcalled. Redmond didn't bother trying to silence them. It would be no use. It was a miracle someone hadn't forced his way into the keep to molest the women, and he was anxious to be rid of them.

A small guard of thirty men surrounded the wagons carrying the twenty ladies, all dressed in their finery. Most of them were the widows of the nobles Lady Selgrave had poisoned. Redmond had misgivings about letting them go, but he didn't need the headache of protecting and caring for them when he had a castle to defend. Besides, they would be a constant temptation to his archers.

J.W. Elliot

Behind the wagons carrying the ladies rolled the hay wagon piled high with the bodies of the dead nobles. Redmond's men hadn't killed any of the lords in their attack, but Adelaide's poison had been extraordinarily effective. Only Dacrey survived, and Redmond made sure he had a damp and dirty cell in the dungeon. Even if he hadn't wanted to give Dacrey a taste of his own medicine, he would have had to lock him up for his own safety. If he let Dacrey out, the archers would have found a way to exact their revenge upon him for murdering one of their own.

The women had looked on in wide-eyed horror as the bodies of the men were loaded onto the cart—all except Lady Selgrave. Most of the ladies had not believed Redmond's assertion that Lady Selgrave had poisoned them. Still, he needed to plant the seed of doubt in their minds regarding her. Her reputation might lend veracity to his claims that could come to his aid in the future.

Lady Selgrave perched alone on the seat with her back straight as a post without deigning to look at anyone. Her deep blue dress glittered in the morning light. It was one of the things Redmond had never understood. How could a person so blessed by nature with such physical beauty be so vile and ugly within? One would think such a woman would have pity for those not so blessed. But for some reason, Lady Selgrave turned her beauty into a weapon to ensnare and destroy. Only one of the women seemed willing to sit beside Lady Selgrave, but when she tried Lady Selgrave had discouraged her with an icy smile.

Emilia stepped out from the shadow of the barbican with a hawk on her arm and stared straight-faced at Lady Selgrave as she passed. Lady Selgrave ignored her. And yet Redmond couldn't help but see the contrast between them.

The heat of the day increased along with the dust from the wagons as they trundled over the rolling hills and across the creek. The barren mountains to the south stabbed upward in jagged peaks, barring the way to the scorched lands beyond. In between, the rolling hills and brush-lined creeks reminded Redmond of the lands around the village of Comrie before the Salassani raid—before Neahl returned crippled from the heathland demanding that he and Weyland join him in seeking vengeance.

"When are you going to be satisfied?" Weyland asked as they huddled around

the campfire caring for their equipment. "We almost didn't make it out of that one."

Neahl lifted his lip in a snarl and paused in scraping a file over the blade of his long spear. "Never," he said. "Not until the sound of Cassandra gasping her last breath stops haunting my dreams."

Redmond watched him. Neahl had always been a big, imposing man, but since the raid that killed his young wife, he had become even more surly and aggressive.

"You know, I'm sorry," Redmond said as he slipped an arrow he had finished straightening into his quiver, "but the rest of us have to go on living. Lara won't wait forever."

Neahl glared at him. "Are you with me or Lara?

"What's that supposed to mean?" Redmond bristled. He might be thinner than Neahl and only eighteen, but he was no coward.

"They murdered our mother and our baby sister," Neahl yelled.

Redmond jumped up and balled his fists. "And who found them?" he shouted. The rage burned his throat. He could still smell the horrible stench of roasted flesh as he stepped into the cabin. "And who buried them? I did, while you were off chasing the Salassani."

Neahl let his spear slip to the ground, and rose to his full imposing height. The muscles in his jaw flexed. He stepped close to Redmond so his hot breath washed over Redmond's cheek.

"They took everything we had, and I'm going to make them bleed."

Redmond held his ground. "You can kill them all, but it won't bring them back," he said.

Neahl ground his teeth. For a moment, Redmond thought he would slam one of those ham-sized fists into his face, but Neahl spun and stomped away.

"I don't know if he can give this up," Weyland said. "They've hurt him too badly."

Redmond bowed his head. "And now he's hurting us. We're all going to end up dead before the end."

Nearly twenty years had passed since then. Redmond had followed Neahl into the heathland again and again and then spent years in the wars between the Dunkeldi and Coll. If only Redmond hadn't listened to Neahl. If only he had let Neahl go alone, he could have been with Lara all these years. But he had no choice. How could he let his own brother, the only kin he had left, go off alone and get killed? It took him years to understand that to stop Neahl he had to leave him.

J.W. Elliot

The village where he planned to leave the ladies came into view, nestled in the wide arc of the shallow river. The road wound through fields and pastures with the shaggy longhorn cattle and black sheep common to the Hallstat. It was dangerous to venture into a village that would be swollen with those who fled Castle Windemere and its immediate surroundings, but his sense of honor dictated that he ensure the ladies were out of harm's way. He also needed to be certain word of his proposal to sell the castle spread to the right people.

He brought an escort of thirty men and hoped they would be enough to quell any potential problems. The wagons rumbled over the last bridge and into the narrow streets. The villagers fell back to watch the wagons roll through with guarded interest. Few of them had probably seen so many ladies dressed in their finery in one place—and never seated in the back of open hay wagons.

The wagons circled in the town square and came to a halt around the pillory. Its chains dangled empty. A town alderman with his customary pointed yellow cap broke from the crowd and approached Redmond. He eyed him curiously as if trying to decide how to address him. Redmond spared him the trouble.

"Alderman," Redmond said. "We deliver into your keeping the ladies from Castle Windemere."

The Alderman grimaced. "We have no means to care for them," he said. "We're a poor village with no proper residence for such nobles."

Redmond tossed a large bag of gold coins at his feet. "This should offset any cost you incur." Then he dismounted and climbed the stone steps to the pillory. He drew a small hammer from his belt and nailed the parchment to the post.

"The castle of Windemere is now up for sale to the highest bidder," he announced to all within earshot.

The alderman gaped. "Sir—" he began, but Redmond cut him off.

"I am not a sir," he said. "I am a simple archer, like these." He pointed to his men. "We were unlawfully forced to serve after surrendering honorably to Lord Dacrey and Lord Selgrave. Our men were abused, murdered, and drugged in preparation for service in the mines. We have resisted such injustice and seized the property of our abuser. We have no desire to keep it and will, therefore, sell it to whomever can deliver the highest sum in two weeks' time."

Windemere

"But—" the alderman tried again.

Redmond ignored him and gestured to his men. "Help them down," he said. Then he indicated the hay wagon with the bodies of the nobles piled one on top of the other. "You can deliver these to their families," he said.

The alderman gaped and blanched at the sight of the dead men and their grotesquely distorted faces. Redmond hadn't tried to clean them up.

"That's Lady Selgrave's handiwork," Redmond said. "She poisoned them. If you look, you'll see that none of them have wounds. We didn't kill them, and I expect you to make sure everyone knows who did."

The alderman wiped a hand across his mouth and swallowed.

"You can keep the wagon," Redmond said.

The ladies climbed down from the wagons with a rustle of silken robes. Some of the ladies cried quietly. Others stared in horror at the corpses in the wagon. Lady Selgrave slapped the hand of the archer who tried to help her down. She jumped off the bed of the wagon and stumbled, but caught herself and stood proudly. Something in her demeanor caught Redmond's attention. She didn't look as sullen as he would have expected. She looked self-satisfied.

Chapter 11
Too Many Corpses

R edmond's grip on the reins of his horse tightened as he surveyed the crowd more carefully. Some of the men did not have the bearing or dress of farmers and villagers. Instead, Redmond perceived the glint of mail shirts, the unnatural helmet-shaped hoods.

The ladies clustered to one side of the square as the four wagons rolled around the pillory to head out of town. Redmond vaulted into his saddle. His men paused in surprise at his sudden movement. He waved his hand over his head telling them to mount up and ride. As they scrambled for their horses, more than fifty men threw their village garb aside to reveal tunics bearing the coat of arms of Lady Selgrave. They raised their swords and spears and rushed Redmond's men with a harsh battle cry.

Villagers screamed and fled. Redmond caught Adelaide's gaze upon him. She had intended for Emilia's hawk to catch both her pigeons. Her men hadn't been a full week away. They had been a few days' ride. Adelaide had planned this.

Cursing himself for a fool, Redmond drew his sword and kicked his horse into the fray. The wagons congested the square, making it difficult for his men to find their horses. Several men jumped into the backs of the wagons and loosed arrows into the oncoming men-at-arms. He swept into the attackers.

His sword clanged off of steel helmets and slid across mail shirts. He wasn't doing much damage, little more than handing out head-aches and bruised or broken ribs. These men had been prepared for them, and most of his men wore the padded jerkins common to the poorly-paid archers rather than mail.

His blade found an opening and sliced across an unprotected throat. Blood sprayed everywhere.

His horse reared at the smell of the blood.

A man-at-arms thrust a spear into its belly.

The horse screamed and dropped backward on its haunches before tumbling sideways to thrash in agony. Redmond kicked free of the stirrups, landing hard on the cobblestone street. His bow cracked under his weight.

He wrestled free of the broken bow and the string in time to deflect a stroke aimed at his head. Then he swept his sword at the legs of his attackers.

It bit into bone.

Redmond jerked it free and spun, swinging it in a wide arc, trying to buy time to get his bearings. A soldier with a short sword lunged at him.

He kicked him in the groin while slashing at another that tried to get inside the reach of his blade. The man he kicked doubled over. Redmond slammed a foot against the side of his head.

A man-at-arms lunged at him but stumbled as a black-feathered ash shaft punched through his mail shirt. Redmond's men had the long, sharp-pointed bodkins meant for such work. At close range, they could be deadly.

Another man fell.

Redmond broke free and raced toward the departing wagons. His men, who had clambered into the wagons, rained arrows into the men-at-arms as they rolled away.

Half a dozen men-at-arms leapt into the cart carrying the corpses and slapped the reins to pursue Redmond's men. One of them held a bow.

Redmond sprinted to the wagon and caught hold of a trailing rope. The stench wafting back from the dead nobles made his stomach roll over, but he gripped the rope and leapt to drag himself atop the dead men.

An arrow thumped into one of them as Redmond scrambled toward the men at the front of the wagon. Horses' hooves clipped against the cobblestones, echoing off the walls of the buildings. The bouncing and rolling of the wagon nearly tossed him over the side.

He crawled over the bloated bodies that gave under his weight. The escaping gas made him retch. But he persisted until he could kick out at the men-at-arms.

Two of them lost their balance and fell screaming after he planted solid kicks to their ribs. He lunged onto the vacant space on the seat. His blade found another who crumpled forward and slid off the seat to tumble beneath the wagon.

A fist slammed into Redmond's head, making him reel.

He lashed out blindly and another soldier fell. A blow struck Redmond's wrist, knocking the sword from his hand. Redmond whirled and jumped forward onto the back of the horse pulling the wagon.

The bridge over the river was fast approaching. Redmond needed to stop the men-at-arms there. He couldn't afford to be pursued all the way to the castle, and he didn't know if Adelaide had other men secreted along the way.

Knife in hand, Redmond sliced through the chest strap and traces connecting the horse to the wagon.

The side poles fell away as one of the men in the wagon threw a javelin at Redmond. Redmond ducked, waving his knife at it in a desperate attempt to fend off the deadly point.

His knife collided with the wooden shaft, knocking it sideways— but not before the spear's edge sliced a long gash along his hairline and the wooden pole slammed against his head.

Redmond nearly toppled from the horse's back, but he clung desperately to its mane. The wagon lurched and flipped end over end to slam into the two upright support beams of the bridge.

Corpses spilled over the bridge and into the river as the wagon exploded into fragments. Redmond wiped at the blood streaming into his eyes. He looked back to the town where Lady Selgrave had scrambled onto the raised steps beside the pillory, her gaze fixed on Redmond.

Kamil bent over Redmond to watch as Emilia stitched closed the gash on his head. His unique smell washed over Redmond, and he tried to ignore it. Tal was off tending the other injured men while Redmond rested in the apothecary shop.

"It's a good thing we didn't try to run for it yesterday," Redmond said.

Emilia grunted.

"Adelaide was waiting for us," Redmond continued. "We totally underestimated how much she had planned in so short a time. I have a feeling there will be more surprises to come."

"I'm told women like a man with a scar," Kamil said, grinning at Emilia.

Emilia jabbed the curved needle into Redmond's flesh, and he flinched.

"Gently," Redmond said. "Kamil's the one annoying you, not me."

"I'm not so sure about that," Emilia said.

"Women are strange creatures," Kamil said as he straightened. "In my country, philosophers have spent centuries trying to unravel their secrets to little effect."

"That's because your philosophers are all men," Emilia said. She tied off a knot, snipped the string, and stabbed the needle into Redmond's flesh again.

"Perhaps," Kamil said, "but women seldom know what they want from a man or why their hearts wander."

Emilia clicked her tongue and smirked at him. "That's easy," she said. "Women's hearts wander because men's hearts wander." She jabbed the needle into Redmond's scalp.

"Easy," Redmond said, raising his hands in surrender.

"And," Emilia continued, "a little respect and kindness are pretty much all any woman wants."

Kamil grinned as she jammed the needle in again. "I like this one," he said, pointing at her.

"We should change the subject," Redmond said, "before Emilia stabs the needle right through my skull and into my brain."

"But I'm having so much fun," Kamil said with a laugh.

Jannik and Rollo strolled in, each grasping a mug of ale.

"Just in time," Redmond said. "Kamil is going to show us his ideas for defending the castle."

Emilia snipped the line again and sat back. "There," she said, "now you'll be attractive to all of Kamil's women."

Rollo and Jannik exchanged confused glances. Redmond rubbed both hands across his face. "Forget it," he said before they could ask what she meant. "Let's hear them, Kamil."

J.W. Elliot

Kamil settled on a bench at the table and spread out a rough sketch of the castle and the area surrounding it.

"Disguise and delay," Kamil said. "Appear weak where you are strong and strong where you are weak."

"Are we going to play a riddle game again?" Jannik asked with obvious irritation.

Kamil smirked at him. "It is only a riddle for the weak-minded."

Jannik scowled and balled his fists.

"None of that," Redmond said. "We need each other here."

"Then tell him to quit insulting me," Jannik said.

"Ride out to meet them," Kamil said, ignoring Jannik's comment.

Rollo furrowed his brow. "You did notice that there are few defensible places out there on the open plain, right? And we are most likely going to be outnumbered."

"Exactly," Kamil said. "Which is why you should ride out to meet them."

"I don't follow," Redmond said.

Kamil gave him a condescending smile. "They will not expect you to leave the protection of the castle. If you do, you will delay them, and you will appear far stronger than they anticipated."

"Or too stupid to know when to hold a strong position," Jannik said.

Pointing to the map, Kamil said, "Here is the village where they attacked you." He pointed to where the road followed the creek. "And here is a hill sloping down to the creek with a cutaway opposite the road."

"I remember it," Redmond said.

"You take a hundred archers and conceal yourself on the other side of the ridge. When they approach, you rain arrows down upon them and then retreat before they can respond. The creek and the cutaway will slow them down."

"And what if they have flankers?" Rollo asked.

"I will take twenty of our best riders," Kamil said, "we will give cover for any unexpected movements of the enemy."

"You mean you intend to fight from horseback?" Jannik said.

"Yes."

Longbow archers, like the men who fought with them, generally dismounted before battle, and men like Jannik who preferred heavy bows, could not shoot effectively from horseback. But Redmond had seen Kamil ride and shoot his short bows from horseback. He was extraordinarily effective in combat.

"I like it," Redmond said.

"Me too," Rollo said. "But we have to disengage after the initial shock, or we'll be caught in the open."

"This is true," Kamil said. "Which is why we need to make the approach to the castle more difficult than it would appear. We can draw them in along the path we choose."

Redmond motioned for him to continue. "Go on," he said.

"You already have several trenches dug." Kamil pointed to the map. "We should cover them with wickerwork and sod to conceal their presence and leave a narrow path between for our horses to ride through here." He traced the map with his finger. "The last to pass will spread caltrops across the opening. If we maintain sporadic contact, we can draw them into the field within range of the archers on the walls." He glanced at Jannik's sledgehammer. "While they are struggling in the trenches, a sortie of heavily-armored men led by Jannik can cut them to pieces."

Rollo was nodding by the time Kamil finished.

"Now that sounds like a battle plan, doesn't it, Bessie?" Jannik said, stroking the handle of his weapon. "Hammer on bone and steel. Just the way I like it."

"Agreed," Redmond said. "But if anything goes wrong, I want every man back into the castle as quickly as possible. We cannot afford to lose men."

"I want to fight," Emilia spoke up. The men turned to stare at her. She had been sitting quietly, following their conversation. Meeting their gazes with an embarrassed blush, she held her ground.

"I'm serious," she said.

"Have you ever fought?" Jannik asked. "Or even held a sword?"

"Well, no, but—"

"It's too dangerous," Redmond said. "There will be plenty of work caring for the injured."

"You're already shorthanded," Emilia said.

"She's right," Kamil said. "In my country, we expect ladies to become expert in polearms before they wed. We had an empress who kept 2,500 women with glaives and halberds as shock troops. They were never defeated in battle."

"Why is everything always better in your country?" Jannik growled.

Rollo thumped the table with his fist and stood. "We have things to prepare." He gestured to Jannik, who followed him out the door with one final glare at Kamil.

Emilia scowled at their retreating backs. "I want to do something to help," she said. "I'm not a doll."

Redmond opened his mouth to speak when Kamil said, "Wait here."

He left Redmond and Emilia to an uncomfortable silence. If she had some training or experience, Redmond might have been willing to entertain the idea, but a siege of a castle was no time to learn how to fight.

Kamil returned carrying one of his short recurved bows and a quiver of arrows. "I have a bow you will be able to draw," he said. "But it is not a warbow and will do nothing against mail or plate armor." He handed her the bow which he had already braced. "Try it," he said.

Emilia jumped to her feet. Her cheeks flushed with excitement. She grabbed the bow and pulled the string to her ear.

"That's heavy," she said.

Kamil chuckled. "Not really," he said. "It's heavy for you because you're a woman, and you haven't trained. With time, you'll be able to draw a heavier bow."

Emilia gave him a pinched grimace, and he laughed.

"Do not be so easily insulted when men speak the truth," he said.

"They so seldom do," she said with a smirk.

Kamil ignored her. "I'll teach you to shoot it, and I'll find you a spear, but you must leave the sword work to the men."

"I'll only agree," Redmond said, "if you promise to stay on the walls. I don't want you down at the gate. If they break through, you have to swear you will try to escape out the sally port and get away."

"He's right," Kamil said. "You can learn to loose an arrow in a day, but it will take you years to become skilled at archery. A bow is a long-distance weapon, and, if the battle closes, you can flee. If you try to match an experienced man with a sword, he will cut you down."

Emilia frowned as if she didn't like hearing she was poorly

equipped to defend herself.

"Remember," Redmond said. "The idea of this whole exercise is to survive, not to die needlessly."

Emilia considered. "Okay."

"Good," Kamil said. "To the butts. We will shoot until your arm is weak."

Redmond rubbed his head, wishing the splitting headache would subside. He didn't like the idea of Emilia being in the battle, but he couldn't stop her. If she confined herself to shooting arrows into the mass of men and kept her head down, she might do some damage without getting hurt. But something told him Emilia would formulate plans of her own, and there wasn't anything he could do to prevent that. He may as well let Kamil give her some training. It was better than refusing and having her show up in the middle of the battle with no idea how to survive.

He got to his feet to head to the armory. With so few men, he needed to get as many of them in mail shirts and steel helmets as he could. Armor may be hot in the southern climate, but it could reduce fatal strikes to mere bruises or broken bones, leaving more of his men alive and able fight.

Redmond paused as he remembered the bag of gold Crispin had given him. He withdrew it from the cabinet and pulled the strings open. The note crinkled as he unfolded it.

"My darling," it read, "the children and I miss you so much. Please take care of yourself and come home safely. Love, Alma."

Redmond folded the paper. Once again, he had killed a man who should have lived. His arrow had cut short a life and left a family waiting with empty arms for the news that the man they loved was dead.

"Why?" he said out loud. "Why do we do this?"

He remembered the warm summer day on the open heathland where he and a soldier named Aengus had been pinned down by a single archer on a field of battle. Aengus had not survived, but Redmond had waited until nightfall, approached the archer's hiding place by stealth, and shot an arrow through his throat—only to find that the archer was a boy watching over his injured father. The words Mortegai, the boy's father, had spoken then came back to Redmond.

"Why do we do this?" Mortegai asked. "Why do we fight and kill and die for

some other man's dream? What will any of us gain when the kings have ended their squabbles?" He pointed at Redmond with a spoon from the stew he was eating. *"You and me?"* he said. *"What do we get out of it but broken hearts and ruined lives?"*

"What indeed?" Redmond whispered and set out in search of the armory.

Lady Adelaide smirked in satisfaction as she crumpled the note in her hand. She waved the messenger away. The tent flap closed behind him, and she bent over the table where she spread a map of the Barony of Windemere. She ran a finger thoughtfully over the polished back of a mahogany chair. Oil lamps cast a golden glow over the thick woolen rug, chests, and the bed with its silk coverlets that sat in the far corner. She saw no reason to live in discomfort while on campaign.

Redmond wasn't the only one who could lay cunning plans. She had been scheming for years, and she wasn't about to let him or anyone else spoil her plans now. She was so close—only a few months from success.

Dacrey had been her latest conquest in preparation for the final undoing of King Rupert. He had been easily compromised by the sight of a pretty face and a wanton smile. His hatred of Baron Dragos of Longmire made him easy pickings—and a useful tool. She had already weakened Dragos and diverted his attention away from the hill country on his side of the border where her spies discovered the new veins of silver. A few months of digging should yield enough to buy off the poorer nobles who pretend to possess sufficient honor to refuse to betray their sovereign and an army large enough to break those who did take their oaths seriously.

Redmond surprised her with his noble bearing and humility. At first, she found his rugged handsomeness enticing and thought she might play with him for a bit of diversion. When he refused her with claims of already being promised to another, she found herself even more drawn to him. Had she finally met a man who knew how to love the way a woman needed to be loved? Had she finally met a man who would remain faithful regardless of the cost? Or had he simply lied? He couldn't possibly be promised to Emilia already could he?

Windemere

Then he seized her castle and humiliated her in front of her husband. Perhaps that is why she hated him so much now. Perhaps she hated herself for her weakness—for allowing the stirrings of real romance one more time. That is what made his betrayal sting so deeply. He could not be manipulated by her beauty, even after she had been willing to give him her heart, as well. He had to know, didn't he?

Something rustled behind her. She spun to see Mara's slight figure standing inside the tent. The girl lowered her hood. The look she gave Adelaide confused her.

"What do you think you're doing?" Mara said, her fists planted on her narrow hips.

"Pardon me?" Adelaide replied. She had forgotten how forward and disrespectful the girl could be.

"I asked you *not* to destabilize Windemere," Mara said. "Was that so hard? Now you have the entire kingdom in an uproar, and you are nowhere near ready for the chaos you've unleashed."

"Me?" Adelaide said. "That fool archer took my castle. Before then, everything was working according to plan."

Mara glared. "And you know full well that you sought to punish him by enslaving his men. For a woman of so many conquests, you seem to have little understanding of men."

Adelaide spun away from her to master the urge to wring the girl's neck. If Mara were her servant, she'd have her whipped to within an inch of her life.

"What do you want?" Adelaide asked.

"A little more discretion from you for starters," Mara said. "And I came to warn you that King Rupert has taken an interest in Redmond's offer to sell the castle."

Adelaide cursed and spun back to face Mara.

"Then we will have to take it back before he arrives," she said.

Mara raised her eyebrows and lifted the tent flap.

"Wait," Adelaide said. She reached to grab the girl but thought better of it.

Mara narrowed her eyes.

"Why are you helping me?" she asked.

"Because those are my orders," Mara said.

"That's not what I mean," Adelaide said. "Why is the Order of the Rook helping me?"

Mara brushed a lock of hair from her face. "It's usually about money, My Lady," she said. "Rumor has it that King Rupert doesn't pay his bills."

"Oh, I thought—"

"What?" Mara sniffed. "You thought the masters of the Order had some affection for you? Don't be foolish. They don't do anything unless it benefits the Order somehow. You're just a pawn like the rest of us."

"You insolent girl," Adelaide spat, and she stepped toward her.

Mara cocked her head to the side. "Really, My Lady?" She glared as though daring Adelaide to touch her.

Lady Selgrave paused and regained control of herself.

"The truth is seldom what we might like," Mara said and pushed the flap aside to melt into the night.

Adelaide spun and threw the wad of paper at the table.

"Those upstart archers are going to discover that I am no one to be trifled with," she snarled.

Chapter 12
Disguise and Delay

edmond lay on his belly with his face pressed close to the earth. The rich smell of fertile soil, mixed with the fresh scent of crushed grass, filled his nostrils. Eighty archers spread out on either side of him. The clop of horses' hooves and the creak of leather floated to him on the morning breeze.

They had ridden out under the cover of darkness to assume their positions on the high bank above the creek. The sun rose behind them to burn off the morning haze, though shreds of mist still clung to the low places as if desperate to hide from the heat of the coming day. Kamil had chosen the location well.

From their position on the hill, the sun would be shining directly into the eyes of Adelaide's army. Redmond glanced at the men around him and felt proud to be fighting with them, but he also would have liked to have Weyland and Neahl by his side. Those two were the most cunning and determined fighters he had ever known. He spent his life trying to live up to their expectations and to match their skill.

A whisper rippled down the line. "They've come around the bend."

"Wait," Redmond whispered.

He raised his head to peer through the tall grass. The first of the men-at-arms reached the end of the long cutaway where his men were hidden. He gripped his bow more tightly as the first row passed. They were well-mounted and well-armored with gleaming helmets and shining mail. The officers' horses were also armored. Every man carried a shield and a lance. Behind the men-at-arms marched the crossbowmen and the pikemen. It was a formidable army. Redmond would never allow his men to meet them on an open field. It would be suicide.

The blood pounded in his brain as he readied himself for action. A horn rang out wild and clear on the still morning air. Redmond lunged to one knee, nocked an arrow, and loosed. His men joined him as the soldiers on the road paused in confusion. The first volley cut into them, punching through mail and cutting into the unprotected flanks of the horses. The horses reared. Men cursed. A few tumbled from their mounts. Officers shouted orders.

"The crossbowmen," Redmond called in warning as the crossbowmen spun to face Redmond's men.

His archers managed another volley that sliced into the poorly-armored crossbowmen before they swung long rectangular shields called pavises from their backs and planted them in front of them. The shields protected the crossbowmen while they reloaded their weapons.

Chaos erupted as the line stalled, and men struggled to find cover from the bite of the arrows and to organize a response. Cries came up from the back of the line as Kamil's horseback archers swept across the flank, raking them with arrows. They wheeled away and circled back for another attack.

The crossbowmen consolidated a line with their pavises in front of them and shot their bolts at Redmond's men. Most of the bolts flew high because the sun blinded the crossbowmen, but it wouldn't take them long to recognize their error.

"Down," Redmond shouted.

Most of his men ducked the bolts, but a few fell, mortally wounded.

This is what he had feared. They had little cover and couldn't shoot the longbows from their bellies.

Once the crossbowmen loosed, his men leapt up and shot two arrows to their one.

And so the rhythm of the shooting continued until a few of the crossbowmen figured out the archers were waiting for them all to loose before rising and sending two or three rapid volleys into the exposed flanks of their armies. A bolt narrowly missed Redmond's head as he rose to shoot.

It was time to leave.

Windemere

Redmond scrambled back and signaled for the horn to sound. Once he was below the rise, he paused, and the horror of what he saw left him rooted to the spot. Over the rolling hills behind them streamed an army of several thousand, and they were riding up behind his unsuspecting men.

"Retreat!" Redmond yelled and sprinted for the horses picketed nearby. "Retreat," he called as the horn sounded again.

All the along the hill, his men scrambled for their horses.

As they disengaged, the officers on the road organized, and a group of horsemen charged across the creek and around the cutaway.

Under normal battle conditions, Redmond would have had his men stand and shoot the horses out from under their riders, but he could not afford to let his men get trapped between two armies. He whirled his horse and raised his bow.

"To me," he shouted. "To me."

Most of his men were mounted now, though a few of the injured still struggled to mount their nervous horses. The army to the rear disappeared behind a small rise. Redmond helped an injured archer into his saddle, then kicked his horse in between the two forces in a desperate attempt to get his men clear of the converging armies.

The new army pounded over the rise.

Redmond and his men were finished.

Out of nowhere, Kamil rode in front of them with his twenty mounted archers and swept them with two volleys of arrows.

The first two ranks of galloping horses collapsed, while those that followed trampled the fallen or tripped and sprawled to the ground themselves.

The charge stalled as Kamil whirled and rode along the flank, loosing another volley.

A cheer exploded from Redmond's men as they raced between the two armies into the open field.

Redmond swung around in the saddle, canting his longbow so it didn't strike his horse, and loosed an arrow into the charging men-at-arms.

His men followed his example before Kamil swept in between Redmond's men and their pursuers to shoot more arrows into them.

Riding hard for the castle and safety, Redmond splashed through the creek and over the road.

He chanced a glance back. Kamil and his horsemen shot over their horses' rumps at the men-at-arms who pursued them. The pursuit fell back to avoid Kamil's arrows, and he raced ahead to catch up with Redmond's men.

"Keep going," Kamil shouted. "We'll draw them in."

The castle loomed over the plain a mile away. Redmond veered off the main road down a dirt path that would lead to the east side of the castle rather than the front gate. The route was shorter, and it would let his men ride straight through the ditches they had constructed.

They were within two hundred yards of the castle when a line of pikemen burst from the side of the trail and rushed to bar their way.

For a moment, Redmond thought they were his own men who had somehow confused who he was, but then he recognized the light blue tunics of Adelaide's soldiers.

Redmond jerked on the reins of his horse, but he was too late. His horse impaled itself on the long pikes as Redmond somersaulted over its head to slam into a pikeman.

He let go of his bow and struggled to get his knife free as the pike-man attacked. He clutched the knife and drove it into his enemy's neck before rolling free.

Warm blood gushed over his hand. Redmond swept his sword from its sheath and sliced into the backs of the men still holding pikes.

His horsemen milled about. Only the men in the front could challenge the pikemen. A dozen horses were down, flailing about. The pikemen struggled to hold Redmond's men, but their weapons were too long for close fighting and most of the pikes remained embedded in the horses. The butt end of one pike had been driven so deeply into the soft ground that the body of the archer impaled upon it dangled above the battlefield—a grotesque scarecrow of death.

The pikemen fled as more dismounted archers closed with them. Redmond grabbed a riderless horse and swung into the saddle. He waved his men on until they reached the path through the ditches. They rode in single file while Redmond waited.

Kamil came galloping over the rise, his hair streaming out behind him. He rotated in the saddle and loosed an arrow. He let his men get in front of him and waited while they filed through the gap.

Windemere

"I lost my caltrops," Redmond shouted.

Kamil grinned at Redmond and jerked a strap loose on his saddle. He handed the bag of caltrops to Redmond before he rode between the ditches.

Instead of making for the castle like the rest of the men, Kamil spun in the saddle and shot arrow after arrow into the advancing, disorganized ranks of men-at-arms now sweeping through the marsh and into the open field where they spread out in a long line.

Redmond scattered the triangular-shaped caltrops as best he could. They had been forged so that one sharp point always stuck up no matter how they fell. This way, when men or horses tread on them, they would receive a serious injury to their feet. It wasn't much, but it was the best they could do. Then he kicked his horse toward the barbican.

"Let's go," he yelled to Kamil.

Kamil gave a whoop of pure enjoyment and raced after Redmond. They clambered between the unfinished barbican and over the drawbridge before reining their horses to a halt.

"Now that is how a battle should be fought," Kamil said.

Redmond leapt from his horse's back and rushed to Jannik who stood dressed in a mail shirt with a steel helmet on his head. Jannik clasped the sledgehammer in his gloved hands.

"Are you ready?" Redmond asked.

"I wouldn't miss it for the sight of a Rosythian beauty." Jannik grinned.

The thrum of strings sounded from the battlements.

Redmond snatched a spare bow and quiver from the stack by the gate and raced up the steps. Emilia had positioned herself behind a merlon on the round tower. She smiled at him as he slid to a stop beside her, but her lips trembled.

His archers loosed again before the foremost horses plummeted into the pits. Those behind either tried to leap the falling horses, tripped over them, or fell in on top of them. The screams of injured horses and dying men echoed over the walls of the castle. The riders at the back pulled up, but they were still in range of the archers from the battlements.

Jannik's hoarse battle cry rang from the barbican below. He and fifty men rushed out to hammer and hack at the unhorsed men. As the slaughter commenced beneath them, the archers on the walls kept Adelaide's men who would have come to their aid at bay.

When the rest of the army emerged from over the green hills, Redmond sounded the horn to recall Jannik and his men to the castle. He needed to get them to safety and the drawbridge raised before they were overrun.

Jannik glanced up when the horn rang over the battlefield but kept at the grisly work, swinging his huge sledgehammer with deadly force. When one of the last of his men grabbed his arm to pull him away, he finally withdrew.

"Raise the bridge," Redmond called as Jannik pounded over it.

The gears ground and creaked as the bridge came up.

Redmond gazed out over the battlefield. Men and horses writhed in agony in the trenches and scattered over the field as far back as the archers' arrows could reach. The two armies joined and drew up beyond the range of the archers to survey the bloody field. Redmond glanced down into the space inside the gate. A couple dozen men, some with horrible injuries, huddled against the walls.

It had been a costly victory. Redmond bowed his head. He had gambled everything on the ability of his men to hold off more numerous armies for weeks and that the King or some other noble would be willing to purchase and secure the castle.

He hadn't counted on having to face the armies of a dozen noble families. Lady Selgrave's murderous schemes had complicated everything. What if all of his men died despite his best efforts to save them? He raised his head as the wail of an injured man carried over the battlements. Their situation was probably hopeless, but he had to keep fighting. The other option was surrender and the certainty of a lingering death in the mines.

A rider broke from the ranks of horses, bearing a white flag tied to the tip of his spear. Redmond doubted he would like what the man said, but he agreed to let him ride forward and deliver his message. He signaled to have the white flag raised, and the rider came up to the edge of the field where his comrades lay dead or dying.

"Lord Dwayne of Windemere," the rider shouted, "acting on behalf of his brother Baron Otto Selgrave, whom you have ignobly captured, requests permission to remove their dead and wounded from the field of battle."

Windemere

His horse pranced sideways, apparently alarmed by the smell of so much blood.

"If he will return our injured comrades, as well," Redmond called out.

The rider hesitated. "We found no injured enemies," he called.

A cry arose from Redmond's men all along the battlements. "They slaughtered them," they called.

Redmond waited until they fell silent. "You would ask us to give you the honor you denied our helpless comrades?" he asked.

"Forgive me," the rider replied, "but your men are traitors and common archers. They have no claim to the codes of chivalry, especially after so dastardly an ambush."

"Let me shoot him from his horse," Jannik said in Redmond's ear.

"Then your men will receive the same treatment," Redmond called. "Any man who attempts to remove a dead or injured man from the field will be shot on sight."

"Lord Dwayne bids me offer the following conditions for your surrender," the rider said.

Archers all along the wall shouted insults that drowned out what the rider said. He waited to continue until the hooting quieted.

"Captain Redmond and his co-conspirators will be allowed to go free with whatever loot they can carry. But we will have the right hand of every archer who has drawn a bow or raised a sword against Lord Otto Selgrave or any of his vassals."

A cry of disbelief rang over the castle. Swords beat on shields. Jannik rose up with his great warbow and drew the arrow to his ear.

"Wait," Redmond said, laying a hand on Jannik's arm.

Jannik let the bow down and glared at Redmond. "If you won't kill him, then I will," he said.

"Not yet," Redmond said. "Not under the flag of parley."

He leaned over the merlon so the messenger could see him clearly. "You may return to your master," he said, "and tell him that Lord and Lady Selgrave are tyrants justly deprived of their property by men whom they betrayed. We will not bandy words with liars and cowards who murder wounded men. If they believe they can take this castle, we beg them to try so we may show them that any archer is better than soft nobles and their dogs who live off the labor of others."

129

"You're not trying to make friends, are you?" Rollo said.

"Not really," Redmond replied.

"So be it," the rider called. He reined his horse around and rode back to the waiting army. The archers on the castle walls cheered.

"When do you think they'll attack?" Jannik asked.

"They have a lot of daylight left," Redmond said. "They won't want to waste it. Get the braziers burning and the marksmen in place. We don't want those crossbowmen taking shelter in the trenches."

He turned to Rollo. "How many men do you reckon they have?"

Rollo pursed his lips. "Two and a half, three thousand maybe."

"Can we hold them?" Redmond asked.

"That army is not prepared for an assault on these walls," Rollo said. "They'll try for the barbican first. They think we're a bunch of rabble."

"We are," Redmond said.

Rollo laughed. "Yes, but we're rabble to be reckoned with. We know how to defend a castle. This will be like those sieges up north."

"I hope not," Redmond said. "We usually starved before much happened."

"They'll come today," Rollo said.

Chapter 13
Battle's Fury

Emilia couldn't do it. She stood on the battlements with the still-unfamiliar bow gripped in her hand. She wore a thick padded jerkin that increased her discomfort in the rising heat of the day. The steel helmet was too big for her and she had to buckle it so tight that the chin strap pinched. As far as she could see to the jagged, blue-gray mountains in the distance, the rolling hills of Windemere spread out in alternating patterns of green and brown with the occasional blue line to mark a stream or pond.

Over it all flapped the dark blue standard with the silver tree of the Baron of Windemere and the light blue standard with its band of silver stars for Lady Selgrave. The late morning breeze stretched the banners out over the heads of the thousands of men come to retake the castle.

Sweat beaded on her upper lip. She raised a trembling hand to wipe it away. What was she thinking? All around her, strong men, archers with long experience in battle, silently watched the lines of soldiers spread out over the field below them like a disease.

She spun and leapt down the steps, conscious of eyes that turned to watch her retreat. Bursting through the door of the gatehouse, she dropped her bow and threw the helmet from her head. It clanged against the hard-packed earth as she leaned against the wall and slid to the ground, grasping her head in her hands. She had to get control of herself.

The door pushed open, and she glanced up. Her father stood there with a concerned scowl on his face. He slipped to the ground beside her and rested a hand on her knee.

"I'm a coward," she said with dry sobs.

Tal grabbed her hand and squeezed it tight. "You don't think every single man up there doesn't feel the same way?" he asked. "They've just learned to channel it."

Emilia tried to control the pounding in her head and the trembling that spread through her entire body.

"You don't have to fight," Tal said. "No one expects it of you."

Emilia let the tears slip from her eyes. "Yes I do," she said. "You won't always be here to protect me."

Tal bowed his head.

"I need to learn how to protect myself," she said. "How to face this fear."

"Battle is an awful thing," Tal said. "You saw the carnage this morning. It is one thing to watch it and quite another to cause it."

"I know," Emilia said.

"No, you don't know," Tal said. "When you see the light fade from the eyes of a man you've killed, that blank face filled with the horror of coming death will never leave you alone. It will haunt you, gnaw at you."

Emilia studied her father. Why had he refused to be a soldier, and why did he become an apothecary? She always assumed it was because his family died, and he had to stay and care for her, which must have been part of it. But Tal had also sold his armor and weapons.

"Is this why you don't join the battle?" she asked.

Tal stared at the wall, his face blank.

"He was twelve years old," Tal said. "The Naymani ambushed our patrol in the hills above the Medlock River. I saw one of them pop up to shoot at us, and I shot him through the throat. Then we stormed their position and I…" Tal paused and swallowed. "I came around a rock to find a boy not much older than you were at the time. He lunged at me with his sword, and I cut him down." Tal raised his hands to study them. "His blood sprayed everywhere."

Tal blinked and wiped his hands on his trousers. "As I saw the terror and pain in that boy's face, I realized I was nothing but a paid murderer, killing so other people could profit. I vowed I'd never kill again—not if I could help it."

He gazed at Emilia with a pleading expression as if he needed her to understand. "I may not be a great man, but at least I can help people who are suffering. I can save some of them."

Emilia watched her father with a furrowed brow. It was like she had never known him. This is why he hated working for the Baron so much—why he refused to make the drug for the children. She reached over and hugged him.

"You're a great man to me, Father," she said.

Tal hugged her back and then held her at arm's length. "I don't want you to fight," he said. "I don't want you to get hurt, and I don't want you to have to live with the guilt and horror that haunt me every day."

Emilia bowed her head. "And what will happen if they take back the castle?" she asked.

Tal stared at her, but he knew the answer as well as she did.

"They aren't going to let any of us live," she said. "If I don't fight now, I'll just have to fight later on, and I won't have conquered this fear."

"In battle, fear is your constant companion," Tal said. "But I understand why you believe you have to do this." He shifted and clasped her hand in his.

"Now, listen to me. You have not been trained. You have no skill in fighting."

"Everyone keeps reminding me of that," she said, the panic rising in her once again.

"That means," Tal continued, speaking over her, "that you have to be smart. Use the bow from the battlements, but if they get inside the walls, you have to come down to the ground and avoid one-on-one fighting. If you have to hide, then do it. If you can escape out the sally port, do it."

Emilia furrowed her brow. She didn't want to be the one who ran. Tal saw the expression and squeezed her hand.

"No. Listen. There is no shame in surviving to fight another day. If you can't hide or get away, get yourself a spear. Don't let them get close. If they do, run until you can surprise them. Strike at the face, throat, arms, and legs, anywhere that is not protected with armor."

Emilia nodded.

"And remember, they are stronger and more experienced than you are. Don't let them get close."

A horn sounded, and Emilia stood. She picked up her bow and

retrieved her helmet. A rush of affection filled her chest despite the trembling fear. She might not live to see his face again.

"I love you," she said.

Tal came to his feet and pulled her into a hug. "My precious child," he said. "You have become a strong woman, like your mother."

"We're going to have to do something about that," Redmond said, pointing to where the enemy wheeled a siege engine onto the field. It was a torsion-driven catapult with huge ropes wrapped around the beams. Redmond had seen one before, though it was still relatively new in the west countries.

"You see?" Kamil said. "You have borrowed this weapon from my people."

Redmond glanced at Kamil who wore a smug look of pride on his face.

"We do everything more thoroughly than you westerners," Kamil said.

"That's nice to know," Redmond said. "Do you have a *thorough* solution to keeping that thing from knocking our archers off the walls?"

Kamil grinned. "Care for a little wager, famous western archer?" he asked.

Redmond smiled. "Of course, famous eastern archer."

Kamil drew six arrows from his quiver. Three had two white fletchings and one black, while the others had all white fletchings. Kamil handed the three with the black cock feathers to Redmond. The arrows were yard-long, barrel-shaped, ash arrows with broad, crescent-shaped points on them. Redmond had seen such points used in naval combat to cut rigging but had never used one.

"Our bows are evenly matched in draw weight?" Kamil asked.

"I suppose so," Redmond said.

"Then the first archer to hit the torsion bundle on the catapult owes the other a barrel of fine wine."

Kamil wore a black ring on the thumb of his right hand. Redmond watched as he nocked an arrow on the right side of the bow and hooked his thumb around the string.

"You easterners do everything backward," Redmond said.

Windemere

"But we easterners are superior archers," Kamil replied with a broad grin.

Redmond smirked. "We'll see."

He surveyed the catapult. It had a wooden throwing arm that had been forced between the twisted ropes so that, when the arm was drawn back with a winch, it created incredible tension in the ropes. When the arm was released, it would cast a stone at the walls of the castle. Since the ropes were the key to the entire system, if they were cut while under tension, it would destroy the machine's ability to cast. But the catapult was at the extreme range for an archer. Neahl had been the expert at long-distance shots, not Redmond.

"How big is that rope bundle?" Redmond asked.

"Oh, I'd say about six feet across and a foot deep."

Redmond smirked. "This is your idea for disabling that thing?"

"I will concede to your superior wisdom, should you have another," Kamil said.

Redmond laughed. "All right. Let's do this, but I've never hit anything at this range with a wind like this."

"Nor have I," Kamil said. "That's what makes it fun."

The armies organized behind the catapult in preparation to advance on the field. The men at the catapult cranked the winch to draw the arm back.

"May the best archer win," Redmond said.

"I intend to," Kamil replied.

Redmond checked the wind, gauged the distance, and drew the arrow to his ear. He leaned back, bending at the waist, so his arrow would fly high. The barrel shape of the arrows would give them greater hang time, and the wind that blew from their rear might give them more range. He loosed his string about the same time Kamil did.

Both arrows soared up to vanish into the sky. Redmond waited. A flash of white passed by the catapult, but he couldn't tell where the arrows landed.

"I believe you missed," Kamil said.

Redmond glanced at him and smirked. "I believe you did, too"

"Again," Kamil said.

Redmond nocked another arrow, made a few adjustments to his aim, and released. A few other archers tried their luck at the men working the machine, but their arrows fell short. Redmond caught sight of his arrow drifting sideways with the wind. It flashed down into the center of the machine, but he couldn't tell where it struck.

The men working the machine paused.

"You cannot afford to miss again," Kamil said as he nocked his last arrow. "I have no more crescent points. So make this one count."

Redmond ignored him. He had the range now. He drew and released. Two arrows plunged toward the catapult. They struck. The men working the machine released the lever and the ropes burst. The machine bucked and rolled forward as the ropes lashed at the men standing nearby.

A cheer burst from the archers on the walls.

"One small victory," Redmond said before turning to Kamil. "I believe you owe me a barrel of wine."

Kamil feigned surprise. "You would take credit for my shot?"

"Two of my arrows hit that rope," Redmond said.

Kamil slapped him on the back. "We'll see when we drive these fools from the field," he said.

Emilia climbed the steps as the archers cheered all along the battlements. She found Redmond and Kamil laughing and joking as though they weren't about to die. She snorted in disgust. How could men be so casual about facing death? She strode out on the tower overlooking the drawbridge and the unfinished barbican on the other side of the moat. Redmond had let the drawbridge down to make it seem as if they were unprepared.

Two stone archways had been built to connect the barbican with the castle walls. They were so narrow only one man could cross at a time. If the barbican fell, the defenders could retreat to the safety of the castle.

Piles of stone had been stacked against the battlements. Braziers smoked with tiny fires. Several large cauldrons of boiling oil sat on the wall that overlooked the gate. Archers clustered on the towers, and, along the walls. Bundles of arrows lay in neat rows. Beside the braziers rested stacks of arrows with tips tied in oil-soaked cloths. Bags filled with combustibles had been attached to the long, narrow foreshafts. Emilia had spent several hours helping Kamil prepare them after he had worn her out practicing the bow.

Redmond's men erected a wooden framework like a tiny house with wooden shutters that stretched out over the walls. The structure allowed them to shoot down on the attackers and then close the shutters for protection. Holes bored into the floor let the defenders drop stones and oil down on any who came right up to the gate. They constructed the frameworks only along the wall overlooking the gates, one of the towers, and above the two sally ports because these were the weak points that had to be defended.

The sidelong glances of a few archers clearly showed their disapproval of her being there, but she ignored them. She rammed the helmet onto her head and cinched the buckle tight. Her mouth felt like cotton, and she licked at her lips with a dry tongue. She wiped at the sweat that beaded on her upper lip.

"Here they come," someone called.

Redmond caught her gaze and held it. She nodded to him, trying to appear more confident than she felt. He returned the nod and resumed his examination of the army advancing on foot with their shields held in front of them. The crossbowmen led the line with their pavises in one hand and their crossbows in the other. As the army crossed into the range of the strongest longbows, arrows arced through the air. The clatter of arrows against steel and wood echoed dully over the battlefield. Here and there, an arrow found a mark and a man fell, but the line came on like a relentless tide.

Emilia nocked an arrow on the string even though her bow could never reach that far. She wished her hands would stop shaking. The crossbowmen stopped behind the first trench where their friends and comrades lay dead and dying. They planted their shields in a great arc before the barbican and raised their crossbows.

A knot crawled into Emilia's throat. The thrum of a thousand crossbows stuttered over the battlefield. She ducked behind a merlon as the bolts clattered and ricocheted off the stone. The archers rose and replied with a volley of their own as the rest of the army pushed on toward the gate, scrambling over the bodies in the trench.

"Wait," Redmond said. He picked up a fire arrow and lit it in the brazier. Another hidden trench collapsed, and the soldiers let out a cry of surprise as hundreds of them dropped through the latticework. As the line faltered momentarily, Redmond raised the burning arrow, drew, and released. Archers all along the wall followed his example, and dozens of flaming arrows arced through the sky to land amid the men struggling in the trenches. The arrows ignited the oil they had dumped in the trenches the day before.

Flames burst out all along the trenches. Soldiers screamed in pain and terror. Some tried to roll free of the scorching flames. Others jumped back with their clothes on fire, spreading the flames amid their comrades. Several broke free and raced, screaming back over the field, setting the waving fields of grain surrounding the castle ablaze, while others rushed toward the waters of the moat. Few of them made it, but those that did found themselves the target of the archers on the walls.

Great black clouds rolled over the battlefield back into the faces of the oncoming army. The crossbowmen fell back. Emilia swallowed the sour taste in her mouth as her stomach rolled into a knot. What a horrible way to die.

The fires in the trench revealed the gap in the line the archers used to escape pursuit. The first soldiers to rush into the gap stalled as the caltrops bit into their feet. But it was the work of a few moments before they cleared the path, and the army pushed past the flickering flames.

"Looks like it's not hot enough for them," Kamil called.

Soldiers poured through the gap and neared the barbican.

The lines closed. Men behind and on the sides locked their shields to form a shield wall.

Arrows slammed into the shields, making the advancing groups of men look like misshapen hedgehogs. They disappeared behind the barbican when Emilia realized she was the only one not shooting arrows at the enemy. She stepped up to the wall and loosed an arrow at the crossbowmen who were shooting sporadically through the flames and smoke.

Her arrow vanished into the bunched men. It probably hadn't done any damage because they were too far away.

The men in the shield wall reached the entrance to the barbican but had to break their formation to scramble over the piles of stone.

Rollo and several other men, who had been stationed on the partially completed tower, heaved a pot of hot oil over the wall. It splashed onto the shields, causing the men to cry out and break formation.

The archers on the ground launched a volley into their ranks. Redmond spun and sent a burning arrow into the oil, igniting it. The men scattered.

For a moment, Emilia thought the battle had been won, but a knight on foot, dressed in mail armor with a steel breastplate and steel plates on the front of his arms and legs burst through the flames. He leapt over the crumbled wall, followed by dozens of men using their shields to deflect the arrows and stones from above. The knight somehow jumped over the trench, but his men found it. Soon the trench filled with the bodies of the injured and dying. Their comrades simply stomped across their bodies to join the fight.

The knight gave a tremendous battle cry and crashed into the archers who formed to oppose them. Emilia shot an arrow into the mass of men behind the knight. It bounced off a mail shirt.

"I'll let you play up here," Redmond said to Kamil and raced down the stairs to join the men on the other side of the bridge.

Jannik climbed on top of a pile of rocks, bent his great warbow, and sent a shaft into the armed men around the knight. One fell as the shaft buried itself in his chest. At that range, no mail shirt could stop the heavy arrows Jannik shot. He aimed at the knight, who stumbled with the impact of the arrow, but the arrow stuck in his steel breastplate. He broke its shaft and kept swinging his long, two-handed sword.

"I'm no use back here," Emilia said. She had to get closer for her bow to have any effect. She sprinted across the stone archway to join Rollo and his men who were shooting arrows and lobbing stones onto the heads of the attackers from the finished barbican tower.

More men rushed through the gap by the barbican. The archers fell back. Emilia leaned over the wall to shoot straight down. Her arrow found a mark and buried itself in the neck of an attacker. He clutched at the feathered shaft and stumbled away.

She shot again and again, but her bow was not powerful enough to do damage unless she hit an unprotected area, and she was too inexperienced to do that consistently. So she discarded the bow and picked up the rocks.

Her first rock knocked the helmet off a man-at-arms and sent him sprawling. She gave a grunt of satisfaction.

"That's more like it," she said as she heaved another stone over the wall.

Jannik discarded his bow and picked up his sledgehammer as Redmond joined him. Together, they waded into the fray.

Jannik's great voice boomed over the sounds of battle. "Come to Papa," he bellowed.

Emilia lost track of the battle as she concentrated on throwing rocks down on the attackers until a hoarse cry from Redmond made her pause. Jannik slammed his hammer into the head of an attacker and sprinted for the wall. He was going to knock it down.

"Come on," Rollo said and followed his men as they raced across the archway back to the wall one at a time. Emilia spun to race after them when something crashed into her helmet. She stumbled and fell.

Her head slammed into the stone wall, and her helmet flew off. Pain exploded behind her eyes. Her vision blurred. She crawled to her knees as the stone beneath her gave way, and she was falling.

Chapter 14
The Wall

Redmond jumped aside as the wall came crashing down. Stones bounced and tumbled. One slammed painfully against his leg. Attackers collapsed under the pile of rubble. Dust choked the air. A human form with long brown hair and a slender body cascaded with the stones. Men-at-arms scattered to avoid the falling stones, but Lord Dwayne came charging through the dust and debris with his sword raised for a killing stroke. His plate armor was dented and covered in dust.

Redmond slipped sideways and deflected the blade. Lord Dwayne advanced but lost his footing on the loose stones. He stumbled and recovered. Redmond leapt out of the way of a wide-swinging stroke that would have disemboweled him. Jumping inside Lord Dwayne's guard, he delivered a terrific blow to his breastplate which left a thin dent, but otherwise did no damage. The jolt from the blow jarred his hands, and Redmond nearly dropped his sword.

Lord Dwayne stepped back and swung again. They circled as Redmond struggled to get inside his guard and find an unprotected place to strike. But he was tiring, and Lord Dwayne drove him back. Redmond's sword rang off the metal helm and breastplate and slid off Dwayne's steel greaves. Redmond might be the better swordsman, but the plate armor kept Lord Dwayne so well protected that Redmond couldn't stop him. Jannik's hammer would have been helpful, but he was nowhere to be seen.

Redmond tripped over a fallen body, sprawling onto his back. His sword bounced out of his hand as the breath rushed from his lungs. Lord Dwayne raised his sword and rushed in for the kill.

Emilia lay facedown amid the rubble, dazed and choking on the dust. Warm blood dribbled into her eyes. She struggled to stand but found her legs trapped amongst the stones. The battle raged about her. Steel crashed. Men roared and screamed. Something twitched beneath her, and she looked down.

Her gaze focused on the startling blue eyes of a man staring up at her. She recoiled as the man spasmed again. Bile rose in her throat. Panic gripped her chest. She jerked at her feet, desperate to get free. The rocks gave. She rolled a few stones off her legs and yanked again. Her legs came free. She rolled down the mountain of rubble. When she tried to stand, a sharp pain shot up her leg, and her ankle gave out.

Through the dust and confusion, she saw Redmond locked in combat with a man wearing a breastplate and steel on his arms and legs. She crawled forward, dragging her injured leg. Her hand fell on the shaft of a spear. Her fingers spasmed around it as if they needed something to clutch. Pounding sounded in her ears. Redmond was in trouble. He tripped and fell. The knight raised his sword.

Emilia grasped the spear in both hands and threw herself forward. The spear bit into the back of the knight's thigh. He jerked away from the pain and stumbled sideways. Redmond lunged to his feet and slammed into the knight. A hoarse shout of warning rose above the din of battle. The knight stumbled into the wall of the last remaining arch as it came crashing down on top of him.

Redmond staggered away from the shower of stone and debris, still trying to understand what had happened. The pile of rubble sealed the entrance to the barbican. The few men-at-arms who remained on the inside were cut down. The attack stalled as the cry went up that Lord Dwayne was slain. The attackers fell back.

Someone pushed past Redmond. Kamil dug through the rubble.

"Emilia," Redmond whispered and staggered over to join Kamil, ignoring the pain on his shin where the rock had struck him. Emilia lay on her belly with a bloody spear still clutched in her hands. Redmond tossed the last remaining stones from her body and helped

Windemere

Kamil pull her free. Kamil lifted her in his arms.

"This girl saved your life," Kamil said and carried Emilia's limp body across the bridge.

Adelaide watched in horror as her army broke itself on the walls of her home. The wind carried the horrible odor of burning flesh as it rolled black clouds over the green lands before the castle. She had climbed into the loft of a barn, trembling with the excitement at the coming battle and the prospect of shaming the arrogant archers.

Now the ache of despair burned in her throat and coiled around her chest. How would she recover from this catastrophe? Her army lay scattered over the field in front of the barbican, and Lord Dwayne had not returned. Some stragglers still fell as arrows from the archers found them struggling to reach the safety of the marsh and the rest of the army. Hundreds had fallen. All of her plans now lay in ruins. If the King came with his army, she would have to withdraw.

Adelaide balled her fists and clenched her jaw. If she couldn't seize the castle by force, she would take it by guile.

Redmond hesitated, torn between his concern for Emilia and the need to make sure his men were prepared for the next assault. Jannik ambled up to him with a satisfied smirk on his face.

"That went well," Jannik said. He had lost his helmet, and he was covered in gore. Redmond couldn't tell if any of the blood was Jannik's.

Redmond snorted. "It was risky," he said. "We can't afford to do that again."

Jannik patted his sledgehammer. "Nothing like a good hammer," he said. "Not even plate armor is a defense."

"Yeah. I could have used you about ten minutes ago," Redmond said.

"I can't be everywhere at once," Jannik said with a shrug.

Redmond rolled his eyes but chose to ignore him. His men were resting or trying to extract their injured comrades from the rubble.

"I've got to see to Emilia," Redmond said. "Can you and Rollo make sure the dead are stripped of their armor? Distribute it among our men. We also need to collect all the usable arrows we can find. And get that drawbridge cleared so we can raise it." He glanced back. "We should probably pull Lord Dwayne from the rubble. I'll take his helmet to his brother."

Jannik slapped Redmond on the back. "You need to relax," he said. "They won't be back in a hurry."

"We need to hold this castle," Redmond said. "Right now, that's all that matters. I'll be back."

He followed Kamil to the apothecary shop where Tal knelt to treat the injured who had managed to get that far. Tal sprang to his feet with concern at the sight of them and helped Kamil lay Emilia before the fireplace. She grunted and opened her eyes.

"You've been a busy girl," Kamil said.

Emilia reached a hand to her head. Redmond knelt beside her and raised her head to give her a drink from a waterskin.

"When we told you to come *off* the walls if they broke through," Kamil said, "we didn't mean come down *with* the walls."

Emilia gave them a feeble smile. "It was quicker," she said.

"No doubt," Kamil said.

Tal washed the blood and grime from her face.

"You should have seen her," Kamil said. "She slid down that collapsing wall like some kind of warrior goddess, grabbed a spear, and saved Redmond's life."

"Thank you, by the way," Redmond said. He brushed a hair from her face. A rush of affection for this brave young woman filled his chest. "You never stop surprising me."

"Let me care for her now," Tal said. "Thank you for bringing her to me."

Redmond stood with Kamil.

"Stay strong, little sister," Kamil said.

Redmond glanced at him as they left them.

"What?" Kamil asked.

"Little sister?"

"You westerners worry me," Kamil said. "You're too serious and too literal."

"She's young enough to be your daughter," Redmond said.

Kamil smirked and waved a dismissive hand. "I don't need or want a daughter, but I do miss my little sisters."

Chapter 15
Infiltration

my Lady?" Adelaide's guard called from the flap of her tent.

Lady Selgrave roused from her study of the correspondence that had been pouring in that morning. She had been trying to figure out how to transform this mess to her advantage. If she failed to retake the castle before the King's army arrived, her plans could be set back for years. She needed to silence Redmond, the apothecary, and his daughter. They knew too much.

"Come," she said.

The flap opened, and the big mason, named Walter, who had overseen the building of the barbican, stepped in, followed by a round woman and two children. Walter kept his hair cropped short. He wore a long gray tunic and brown trousers. His wife was more stout, but she had an infuriatingly kind face. Though Adelaide normally liked to handle these matters alone, she signaled for the guard to stay. She didn't know how the mason might react.

"Your archway has collapsed," she said.

"Yes, My Lady." Walter's voice was deep and resonant.

"I thought you said you would build it to withstand siege engines."

"My Lady," Walter said. "The archways weren't finished, but they wouldn't have fallen unless someone weakened them and then knocked them down."

"They did that on purpose?"

"Yes, My Lady."

"Hmm," she said. "Well, this has created a nice problem for us." She glanced at the children. The oldest was a girl about the same age as her youngest, maybe five or six. She was an adorable child with

145

round cheeks and deep-brown, observant eyes. Adelaide would have preferred a different method, but, as always, she was prepared to do what needed to be done.

"Come here, child," she said to the oldest.

The girl glanced up at her father, and he nodded. She stepped forward.

"You're a pretty little thing," Adelaide said. Then she drew her knife and pressed it to the child's throat. A cry of dismay came from the parents, and Walter lunged forward. The guard grabbed him and held him back.

"This is what you're going to do," Adelaide said. "You are going to infiltrate the castle and open the sally port for my men. When we attack the sally port, you are going to cut the cables that hold the drawbridge."

"My Lady, please," Walter begged. His wife was openly weeping.

These people were so weak and simple. They didn't understand there were things more important than their own little lives.

"I'll be keeping your family here to ensure you do not lose your head. Understand me?" she said, glaring up at Walter.

He swallowed. "Yes, My Lady."

"You know a way to get into the castle undetected?"

"Yes, My Lady."

"Good. Now make sure the drawbridge comes down after dark and before the moon rises."

"I'll do whatever you ask," Walter said. "Just please don't hurt them."

"Oh, I won't be hurting them," Adelaide said. "You will—if you fail."

Redmond passed under the gates to the inner ward as the afternoon sun burned down on the castle. No breeze blew to provide relief. Lord Dwayne's helmet hung heavy in his hands. The Baron had a right to know his brother was dead. He rounded the corner of the keep and stopped. The girl in the mottled cloak slouched on the bottom stair. Redmond glanced up at the guard to the door of the keep. He didn't seem to know or care that she was there.

"I didn't expect to see you here," Redmond said.

Windemere

Mara stood and stretched. "I wondered how long it would take you to inform the Baron that you'd killed his brother," she said. "I've been sweating here for an hour."

"Sorry to burden you," Redmond said, "but I do have a castle to defend."

"Yes, about that," Mara said. "You've been making my life rather difficult." She brushed a hair from her face.

"Once again, I am sorry," Redmond said, his voice thick with sarcasm.

Mara spread her hands in a gesture of disbelief. "When I helped you escape, I had no idea you'd sneak back and seize the castle. What do you think you're doing?"

Redmond smirked. "Surviving," he said.

Mara considered him before letting out a long sigh. "I'm probably going to get into trouble for this, but I figure things are so messed up now I might as well let you continue."

"Thanks," Redmond said. "That's awfully kind of you." He didn't bother to tell her that one young woman wasn't going to be able to overpower a couple of hundred men. Mara apparently didn't notice his sarcastic tone.

"I know," she said. "Besides, I like you."

Redmond glanced at the helmet in his hands and walked over to sit in the shadow of the wall. He studied the short, slender woman. She couldn't be any older than Emilia, but here she was up to her neck in all the intrigues of the Morcian court. He hadn't known the Order of the Rook used young women like this.

"Are you going to go tell Lady Selgrave about the strength and disposition of my men now?" he asked.

Mara wrinkled her nose. "Maybe," she said. "If I decide to."

"Will I have to fight the Order of the Rook to survive?" Redmond asked.

Mara pursed her lips in thought. "Nah," she said. "You'll be kept plenty busy with every noble family in Morcia howling for your blood."

"She told them I did it, didn't she?" Redmond asked. "She's making them believe I poisoned all the nobles."

"Of course," Mara said. "You're not surprised, are you?"

"No, not really," Redmond turned the helmet over. "But it does complicate my one and only objective."

"Survival?" Mara asked.

Redmond nodded.

"Perhaps I can help you there," Mara said.

Redmond shifted in his seat. He winced as he leaned back against the wall. The new injuries were starting to stiffen. "I'm listening," he said.

Mara settled herself on a stone step."I don't suppose you've noticed that they're draining the moat?"

Redmond scowled. "It did escape my attention," he said.

Adelaide must have told the army about the hidden bridge. If they were draining the moat, they were also planning an attack on one of the sally ports. Maybe he should consider a sortie to disrupt the draining. But could he afford to lose more men on escapades like that? Not really. Adelaide would expect an attack, and his men would be caught in the open.

"The King is also on his way," she said. "It seems he might be interested in your offer to sell him a castle you don't own."

"Ownership is a slippery legal term," Redmond said with a smile. "Why don't we use the word 'possess?'"

Mara smirked. "Sure, whatever you say."

"How long have you been doing this?" Redmond asked.

Mara licked her lips. "My whole life," she said and stood. "Well, I've given you a chance to survive the night," she said. "After that, you're on your own."

Redmond stood with her. "Thanks," he said.

She glanced at the helmet. "I wonder how the Baron will take the news that he's lost his only brother," she said before climbing the steps. "Oh, and I would appreciate it," she called over her shoulder, "if you would ask your archers not to shoot me. They make climbing the wall more difficult than I would like."

Redmond smiled at her brazenness. "I'll get the word out," he said. "Just make sure you don't compromise our position. I'm afraid they wouldn't take too kindly to that."

She waved at him and slipped over the wall.

Baron Otto glanced up as Redmond stepped into his room. He

was lounging before the fire in an unbelted tunic. His gaze focused on the helmet, and he frowned.

"Your brother has fallen," Redmond said.

The Baron stared at him straight-faced. "Did you kill him?" he asked.

"No," Redmond said. "He almost killed me though. The wall of the barbican fell on him." Redmond wasn't about to tell him that Emilia stabbed Lord Dwayne from behind or that he pushed him into the crumbling wall. Baron Otto already had plenty of reasons to dislike them. There was no point in fanning the flames.

Baron Otto reached for the helmet. Redmond handed it to him. It was dented and still had flecks of blood on it, though Redmond didn't know to whom the blood belonged.

"He was a good man," Baron Otto said.

"I'm sorry," Redmond said.

Baron Otto jerked his head up to glare at Redmond. "Are you?" He sneered.

Redmond scowled. This man had no right to censure him for trying to survive and keep his men from a languishing death in the mines.

"Yes, I am," Redmond said. "And you should be sorry for all of my men who perished. All they wanted was to remain free of your mines."

But Otto didn't seem to be listening. "My sons and I are all that is left of the Selgraves," he said. "He was my only brother."

"I've lost my entire family, as well," Redmond said, "save one brother."

"Leave me in peace," Otto said.

Redmond turned to leave.

"Thank you," Baron Otto mumbled.

Redmond glanced back.

Baron Otto held up the dented helmet. "For bringing this to me. It was nobly done."

Redmond nodded and closed the door behind him.

Walter knew the castle better than anyone. He had repaired or built most of it at one time or another over the last twenty years.

J.W. Elliot

Few people knew the sewer of the keep drained out into the creek a quarter-mile downstream from the castle. He excavated the channel himself over a period of four years. The Baron didn't like having to bother with chamber pots. The Lady couldn't stand the smell of them. Each level in the keep had its own garderobe, and they all drained down through this tunnel.

Walter waded across the creek until he stood over the grated entrance. He removed the hammer and chisel from his belt and set to work. After an hour of chiseling under the burning hot sun, he had a hole large enough for him to slide through. He tied a scarf over his nose and mouth to hold out the worst of the stench and pulled on his gloves. When he built the tunnel, he set iron handles in the walls to make it easier to work. Now he would use them to save his family.

He poked his head into the hole and pulled it out. "By the desert wraiths," he said, "that is vile." He steeled himself. "I'm doing this for my family," he mumbled as he sucked in a deep breath of the last fresh air he would have for some time. He grabbed the bundle of torches and climbed in.

The stink smote him like a punch in the face, but he grabbed the first handle and pulled himself up. He had to do this. He knew Lady Adelaide from long experience. She may look sweet on the outside, but inside, she craved control more than anyone he had ever known. There would be no hesitation in killing his family. She had done it before to other servants.

The ascent took the better part of the afternoon. When he raised the trap door in the storage room of the keep, the ventilation holes near the ceiling that let in the light showed that dusk was already falling. That was the easy part. From here on, every move he made might mean the life or death of his entire family.

Walter let the trap door down quietly and rolled out onto the cool stone floor. The stuffy air of the storage space had never tasted so sweet. He rummaged through the boxes in search of clean clothes. It wouldn't be possible to avoid notice if he walked around smelling like an outhouse in clothes stained with filth. When he found a wardrobe chest, he stripped off his clothes, tossed them in a corner and pulled on a new pair of trousers and a new tunic. He even found a pair of boots that fit him, more or less.

In this outfit, he wouldn't be so obvious. He stole up the stairs and waited until the change of guard. The sound of voices and the thump of wooden bowls on a table-board reached him through the closed door. Walter picked up a tray piled high with dirty bowls and waited as the guards engaged in small talk. His mouth went dry, and he tried to lick his lips. His legs trembled. When the old guard left, he strode out the door as if he belonged. The new guard glanced at him.

"Kitchen," Walter said, raising the tray for the guard to see. The guard grunted and let him go.

Walter swung around to the kitchen in case the guard was still watching, deposited the tray beside a growing mountain of unwashed dishes, and lifted a barrel onto his shoulders. He passed under the gates to the outer ward where he found a stack of weapons and armor that was apparently being stored until their owners wanted them. He discarded the barrel and lifted a large padded jacket over his head. Then he slipped on a helmet.

This time of day, the castle was usually a busy place as people hawked their wares and peasants from the nearby villages came to buy and sell. This afternoon, the castle was deserted with the exception of the guards on the walls. This had been his home since before he had married. He had apprenticed here. So why did he feel like such a scoundrel in his own village?

No one paid him much attention as he stole into the stables by the sally port and began checking the feed and water for the horses. It would be dark soon. He needed to stay close and seize the opportunity to get to the door when it presented. He brushed a horse and then stepped out to see where the guards stood that were watching the sally port. They all seemed to be on the tower and focused their attention outward. Walter noted a large pile of cut stone lying next to the gate. What did the archers have planned?

He leaned against the walls of the stable, chewing on a piece of straw until the guard passed to the other side of the tower. Then he strode over to the alcove where the gate was set in the wall and hunched down in the shadows. He had once brought his wife here, before they were wed, for a quiet moment. How things could change.

Walter dabbed at the sweat that stung his eyes and struggled to control his nervous breathing. This wasn't his element. He was no spy. He knew how to shape stone, not how to engage in intrigue. He slipped up to the gate and crouched in the shadows to study the lock. The wall was four feet thick here, and the iron-bound door had been set so the stone face on the outside protected the edges of the door from being pried open.

Slots had been cut in the stone to allow two iron bars to slip in and nestle into openings that held the bars against the door. Wedges had also been pounded into the crack where the door met the stone floor. It was a simple matter to knock the wedges away and lift the bars free. He tested the door to make sure it would open and then slipped back to the entrance carrying the bars.

The slap of booted feet on the stones above told him the guard was moving back to this side of the tower. Walter raced to the rock pile, dropped the iron rods behind it, and hefted two of the stones. He waited until the tread of boots stopped before tossing the stones on the pile. Then he waved a hand at the guard and ambled off toward the front gate. He stepped into the stables and took a long, ragged breath. The ploy worked, but he couldn't leave the bars there for someone to find.

Daylight was fading. He had to get down to the front gate or his family would die. He crept back to find the guard had passed on, so he raced in, snatched up the two iron rods and darted for the cover of the shadows. The sound of voices laughing and joking moved toward him, and he swerved into a side street.

He waited for the punch of the arrow in his back, but nothing happened. If they caught him now, he was a dead man. He slipped back to the storage building between the stables and the gatehouse. After working his way to a back corner, he rested against the stone and slid to the ground with the iron bars still in his hands. His heart beat against his ribs, and his hands trembled. When the alarm sounded that the sally port was under attack, he would rush to finish the job.

Lady Selgrave secured the clasp of her dark cloak. It draped over the black trousers and black tunic she wore. She didn't like the rough feel of trousers against her legs, but she couldn't afford to be tripping over her dress tonight. She had become so used to silk that she had forgotten what linen felt like against the skin.

Windemere

When she stepped out of her tent, she paused to gaze up at the dark hulk of the castle. A light burned in the window of the Baron's rooms, and she could imagine the fit of rage he was in at seeing his castle so manhandled by a mob of low-bred archers. Had he been told that his brother was dead? It was good for him that she was at liberty to protect their interests.

Still, the sight of the castle made her pause. Something wasn't right. She expected watch fires set on the battlements, but, from where she stood, the castle walls appeared to be deserted. Well, foolish men die more quickly.

She strode off to meet the party of forty men she had handpicked to sneak in through the sally port and begin the slaughter. Ten expert crossbowmen accompanied them whose task it was to keep the walls clear while her men infiltrated the castle. Everything depended on Walter's ability to open the gate, but she was confident he would find a way. His motivation was certainly strong enough, and he knew the castle better than anyone alive. She had to lead the men to show them the location of the bridge, and she wanted to be close enough to witness her triumph when the castle fell.

The men, all dressed in black, clustered on the edge of the army behind a peasant's farmhouse. They had wrapped their weapons in dark cloth to keep any reflection being seen from the battlements and to muffle any sounds they might make. Several hundred more men similarly clad were arrayed along the rise in front of the barbican in readiness for an assault on the drawbridge when it fell.

Lady Adelaide led the men away from the castle as the last rays of the fading day slipped behind the horizon. She swung wide and then brought them back toward the moat. When they reached the last rise, she fell on her belly to wait for the cover of darkness. She could barely make out the stump that marked the corner of the bridge. She pointed to it.

"It's just there," she said.

"What if the door isn't open, My Lady?" the captain asked.

"It will be," she said. Because if it wasn't, Walter and his family would pay.

Darkness settled over the fields and transformed the castle into a black heap of stone with a single eye where the Baron's candle burned in his window. The castle was strangely silent, watchful. This might be her last chance. Her scouts told her an army was approaching from the north and would arrive on the morrow.

The men crept down the hill, dark shadows against the grass. When they reached the moat, they stalled. Why weren't they crossing? Adelaide scurried down the gentle slope to join them.

The captain pointed to the jagged edges of what had been the bridge. Adelaide cursed under her breath. She waved them on, and the men slipped into the now-drained moat and waded across in the muddy water that came up to their waists. Adelaide crouched as they stole silently up the hill toward the sally port. She wrung her hands and clenched her teeth. How had her spies not seen Redmond's men destroying the bridge?

The men paused at the sally port. Nothing happened. Adelaide's heart sank. Walter had failed. She had been so certain that a big stonemason like him would find a way. One of the men broke away and scurried down the hill. He slipped into the water and waded across.

"Wasn't it open?" Adelaide whispered when he was within hearing.

"Yes," he said, "but they built a stone wall behind it. We can't push it over."

A shout rang out and her men at the sally port scampered back down the hill followed by a shower of arrows. The crossbowmen released their quarrels and cries of pain echoed in the stillness.

Adelaide fled up the hill toward the front gate. That was her last hope now. Walter wouldn't dare fail her twice.

Chapter 16
A Rescue in the Dark

he shouts and cries of battle drew Walter from his hiding place. Lady Selgrave's men must have already entered the sally port. One last task remained to save his family. He crept out the door and joined the throng of men rushing toward the gate. A set of stairs climbed halfway up the wall into a corridor that passed through the walls onto a catwalk where the winch that raised and lowered the gate stood.

Walter didn't need the winch to drop the gate, but that was the easiest place to cut the cables. He found a guard there and walked up to him as if he had nothing to hide. The man scowled at him and opened his mouth to question him when Walter slammed an iron bar against the man's helmet. The blow rang in the confined space. Walter jumped on the man to silence any cry he might make when someone called out behind him.

"Hold," the voice commanded. Cold steel touched the back of Walter's neck.

Walter raised his hands and stood. Dread spilled into his stomach. He had failed. His family would die.

"Please," Walter said as he recognized the tall, thin leader of the archers.

"How did you get in here?" Redmond wrinkled his nose. "You stink," he said.

"The sewer," Walter said.

"What sewer?"

"There's a long tunnel in the keep that flows out into the river."

"Right," Redmond said. "You unbarred the sally port, didn't you?"

Walter nodded.

"Well, I can guess what you are doing here, but I'd like to know why."

"Please," Walter said again. "She has my family."

Redmond scowled. "Lady Selgrave?"

"Yes."

"Of course she does," Redmond said.

"I have to cut the cables, or she'll kill them."

"I can't let you cut the cables," Redmond said.

Walter stepped toward him but stopped as the point of the sword jabbed into his throat. "Please," he said again. Tears spilled from his eyes. His chest burned.

"Let me finish," Redmond said. "I can't let you cut the cables, but I will let you lower the gate as soon as those men out there are close enough."

Walter stared, uncertain if Redmond was playing with him or not.

"Then we'll see about rescuing your family."

A wild hope leapt into Walter's throat. Maybe all was not lost.

"You won't kill me?"

Redmond gave a short laugh. "Not today," he said.

"But why? Why would you do that for me after what I tried to do?"

"Because Lady Adelaide has destroyed too many lives already," Redmond said.

The man Walter had struck groaned.

He glanced at him and said, "Sorry."

"Redmond." The voice came from above, and Walter glanced up. A face appeared in a hole in the rock. "They're here."

"Let's do it," Redmond said to Walter. He sheathed his sword and sprang to the winch. "Release the pin, and we'll let it fall just like they expect."

Redmond pulled on the lever to relieve the pressure on the pin that held the bridge closed so Walter could slip it free.

"Ready," Redmond yelled. A scuffle of movement on the walls above and a clatter of weapons from the ground below told Walter that Redmond's men had been prepared for this, but how?

"Stand back," Redmond said and released the winch. The draw-bridge creaked, and the cable hissed as it zipped through the hole in the wall. The bridge slammed to the ground with an earth-trembling crash. Walter raced after Redmond as he bounded down the steps and under the wall to where a new stone wall had been erected to block the gate. The wall had arrow slits for the row of archers that crouched behind it. Spearmen stood ready behind them.

Walter wondered at the newly built wall. He gaped at Redmond, who smiled.

"What?" Redmond said. "You didn't expect me to invite them in without a welcoming party, did you?"

Through one of the slits, Walter watched as the shapes of men bounded over the rubble on the other side of the moat. The thump of boots thudded on the bridge. Then the bowstrings sang. Arrows whipped through the air into the surprised men. Rocks and arrows rained down from above. Several men raced through the deadly shower and scrambled on top of the newly-erected stone wall. The men with spears waiting behind the archers stabbed at their unprotected faces. The charge faltered, and the men fell back behind the broken barbican.

"Don't waste your arrows," Redmond yelled before turning to Walter. "Where is she holding your family?"

Adelaide fidgeted on the rise above the moat watching in horror as the men who surged onto the bridge faltered and fell back. She couldn't understand what had happened. The sally port had been opened and the gate had fallen like she planned, but Redmond had been one step ahead of her. If he had walled off the sally port, maybe he had walled off the gate, as well. That was the only explanation. He must have captured Walter and tortured her plans out of him. Or maybe Walter had betrayed her.

"Fool," Adelaide cursed. Everyone kept failing her. She would have to try something else. But first, she had a promise to keep.

"Why are you helping me?" Walter said as he and Redmond hurried over the bridge now dressed in the armor and tunics of Lady Selgrave's men. In the dark, no one would notice the holes and bloodstains.

"I don't like it when innocent children suffer," Redmond said.

They slowed as they clambered over the rubble from the collapsed walls. Redmond paused, surprised to find men still crouching behind the pile. Some had arrows punched through their mail shirts.

Redmond bent to help a wounded man stand. "It's too dark for them to shoot now," he said. "Lean on me." He gestured with his head for Walter to follow his example, but Walter didn't understand the gesture. "Help him," Redmond said.

Walter's eyes opened wide, and he bent to lift an injured soldier. Redmond didn't have time to explain that carrying the enemy's wounded would make it much easier for them to infiltrate the camp. Together, they hobbled across the field into the sheltering darkness. They navigated the bodies of horses and men and the network of trenches that crisscrossed the field, but they eventually deposited the men among the other injured and crept into the camp.

"Her tent is near the center," Walter whispered. Redmond followed him until they found the large white tent with two banners fluttering overhead. Torches blazed all around it. Redmond pulled Walter behind a nearby tent.

"Are you sure they're in there?"

Walter wrung his hands. "I don't know. That's where I left them."

"Okay," Redmond said. "You wait here."

Redmond stepped out into the space between the tents, when a hand grabbed his arm and jerked him back. Redmond whirled, ready to give Walter a thrashing, but it wasn't Walter. Mara stood there in the mottled cloak, staring at him with her hands on her hips.

"Now what are you doing?" she whispered.

Redmond's face grew hot, and he growled. "You're starting to make a nuisance out of yourself."

"Me?" Mara said. "I'm *supposed* to be wandering around Lady Selgrave's camp." She poked a finger at Redmond. "You are supposed to be surviving over in that castle you now *possess*." She spat the last word at him.

"Lady Selgrave is going to kill three innocent people," Redmond said.

Mara smirked. "What's new about that?"

"Two of them are children," Redmond said.

Mara scowled. "You risked your life to sneak into her camp to rescue some children you don't even know?" She glanced at Walter.

"Where are they?" Redmond said.

Mara chewed on the edge of her bottom lip in indecision. She threw up her hands. "Oh, hang it," she said. "You're set on getting me into hot water with my superiors. Follow me."

She strode off into the shadows between the tents. In ten minutes, they had crossed to the far side nearest the marsh. She squatted behind a pile of boxes.

"Is that them?" she asked. A woman and two children sat strapped to the wheel of a wagon. Walter stepped forward, but Redmond grabbed him and pulled him down.

"You stay here," he whispered to him. The last thing he needed was Walter rushing in and creating a problem. He approached the guard as Mara melted into the shadows.

"Lady Selgrave wants the prisoners," he said as he approached.

The guard straightened. "Who are you?" he asked.

Redmond spread his hands in front himself to show he wasn't a threat before launching himself onto the guard.

He kicked the man in the stomach. Grabbed his head and drove his knee into the man's face before sweeping his feet from under him. Then he gripped him in a stranglehold.

The man struggled, but he couldn't cry out. He thrashed for a few seconds until he went limp. Redmond let him down, slipped his weapons from their sheaths and threw them away. Then he rushed to cut the woman and children free.

Walter raced to help him when a cry rang out over the camp. It was a woman's voice.

Redmond glanced back as he lifted the two children into his arms. Lady Selgrave rushed toward them with several armed guards racing behind her.

"Let's go," Redmond said. "Run."

He sprinted into the darkness, desperate to reach the cover of the marsh. The twang of a crossbow loosing a bolt sounded behind him.

Emilia awoke with a splitting headache. She stared up into the shadows of the roof. The snores and deep, rhythmic breathing of sleeping men surrounded her. The air smelled like the soldiers' barracks. She grimaced at the unpleasant aroma and tried to think what had awakened her. The sound came again. Something had disturbed the hawks in the mews.

She pushed herself to a sitting position, fighting the nausea that made her reel, and clutched the floor for stability. Every muscle complained at her movement. She felt like she had been run over by an ox cart.

Grabbing the edge of a bench, she pulled herself to her feet. It had been a while since she checked on the hawks. Maybe some critter had gotten into the mews. She grimaced as she put weight on her right ankle. It had been banged up and twisted badly by the falling stones. After the wave of nausea subsided, she limped over to the back door that led to the small garden and the mews where she kept the hawks and stopped to listen.

The noises confused her. They sounded like rats gnawing a piece of fruit with an occasional groan and rumble. No creature she had ever heard made noises like that. It certainly wasn't her hawks.

She pushed the door open to peek out. In the center of her herb garden crouched a group of creatures with long matted hair. Now and again, one would reach out a small hand to tear up an herb or plant.

"Hey!" Emilia shouted as she shoved the door open and hopped out to shoo the odd creatures away.

They jumped up to scamper into the shadows. Emilia paused as a shock swept through her. They were children!

"Wait!" she called.

One tiny child became tangled in the gate. Emilia grabbed him.

The child struggled and bit and then screamed a horrible, terrified scream that brought a knot into Emilia's throat.

"It's okay," she said. "I'm not going to hurt you."

Something bowled into Emilia, knocking her sideways. She released the child as she slammed into the soft, rich earth of the garden.

Dozens of little hands clawed at her eyes and face. Emilia was struggling for her life.

One pair of hands got a hold of her throat and squeezed.

Windemere

A shrill cry burst over the encampment as Redmond sprinted for cover. Walter and his wife raced behind him. A bolt zipped past his head, and he ducked behind a stray boulder. The children clung to him. One of them whimpered. He glanced back. Walter lifted his wife into his arms and rushed after them. A bolt protruded from his wife's leg.

"We have to go," Redmond said and sprinted toward the castle. He didn't have time to wonder where Mara had gone. Navigating the battlefield in the dark with two terrified children in his arms as soldiers chased after them required all his attention.

He leapt over a fallen horse and then slowed to clamber over the stinking bodies in the trenches. Then he paused and gave a shrill whistle that would signal the archers on the walls not to shoot them. He set the children down and rushed to help Walter with his injured wife.

When they had gathered on the edge of the moat, Redmond paused to rest.

"Is anyone else hurt?" he asked. The children stared at him. Walter shook his head. "We can't risk lowering the bridge again," Redmond said. "So we'll have to wade the moat."

He glanced at Walter's wife.

"I know it hurts, but it's best to leave the bolt in for now until we can look at it. And you must keep the injury out of the water."

She pinched her lips tight and nodded.

"I'll carry the children over and then I'll come back to help you."

Redmond splashed into the putrid water, trying not to think about what he was wading through. He scrambled up the muddy slope to deposit the children on the other side and then returned for Walter and his wife. The woman was short but round and heavy. It took both of them to get her up onto the bank without dipping her injured leg in the water.

While they rested, Redmond gave another short whistle and an arrow zipped past them to bury itself in the mud. Redmond untied the line attached to it and walked over to the wall. He motioned for the children to join him. One by one, his men above pulled each of them up until they stood on the battlements, dripping with fetid muck, but alive.

Walter offered Redmond his hand.

"Thank you," he said.

Redmond shrugged. It had been easier than he had imagined, and it left him with a nagging feeling that something else was coming for him—he just couldn't see it.

The hoarse bellows of male voices cut through the clutching, scratching chaos as Emilia clawed the fingers from her throat. Tal loomed over her, snatching children from her body. They climbed up on his back and grabbed his legs. One of them sank her teeth into his thigh. Tal howled as he tried to disengage the clutching, biting children.

Kamil appeared, grinning for all he was worth as he dragged Emilia from the children.

"Oi!" he yelled. "Stop trying to claw us to death."

Other men arrived, and soon the ten children were being restrained.

"What is this?" Kamil demanded.

The dirty, frightened children stared at them with wide eyes. They ranged in age from about ten or eleven to the youngest who couldn't be more than three or four years old.

"Where did you come from?" Tal asked.

"They were being sent to the mines," Emilia said as she clung to Kamil for support.

"The salt mines?" someone asked.

Emilia shook her head and then grabbed her forehead with her free hand. Her head felt like it was splitting in two. "The silver mines," she mumbled.

"What silver mines?" someone asked.

Emilia didn't have the energy to explain.

"But they weren't in the prison," one of the men said. "We searched the entire dungeon."

Tal stepped to the oldest child, a girl about ten or eleven years old, who was restrained by one of the archers. He knelt in front of her.

"We aren't going to hurt you," he said. "We aren't the people who brought you here. Can you tell us what happened?"

The girl hesitated. "We killed them," she said. She lowered her head and matted hair fell over her eyes.

Windemere

"What?"

"The man and woman who brought us here. We killed them."

Emilia's throat tightened. She should have done something that night they brought the children in.

"Where were they keeping you?" Tal asked.

The girl bit her lip and pointed toward the gatehouse.

"Okay," Tal said. "Why don't you come inside, and we'll fix you some stew."

Tal signaled to two of the men to check the gatehouse, and they bounded off into the darkness.

The smallest child wriggled free from the man who was holding him and scurried to clutch at Emilia's leg. She bent down. He wrapped his arms around her neck and began to wail.

Dawn burst over the eastern hills, igniting the peaks with coral fire. At any other time, Redmond would have reveled in the beauty of the scene—but not today. He had dragged himself from a bed in the barracks after washing the filth of the moat from his body and clothes and grabbing a few hours of sleep. Redmond passed his hands over his face and rubbed vigorously at his eyes. Rarely had he been this tired. He glanced down from where he leaned against a merlon at the sound of the waking castle. They had lost too many men. The battle had begun with two hundred, but he was down to one hundred fifty able to fight. Fifteen had been killed, ten more would be crippled, and the others had injuries too serious to allow them to shoot a bow.

Now the dawn revealed to him that Adelaide's camp had swollen by some thousands. Their tents spread over the rolling hills like a plague. Their horses roamed the nearby pastures. He didn't have enough men to hold the walls. All he could hope to do was to hold the gates. If he retreated now into the inner ward, he would have a better chance with his small force. But that would mean giving Adelaide's men the cover of the village. He didn't like the thought of them being that close.

"Let me know if you see any movement," Redmond said to the archer standing beside him. "I'll be in the apothecary's hut."

Laughter greeted him as he approached the open door of the hut.

He stuck his head in to find Jannik apparently wrestling on the floor with a scrawny boy dressed in rags.

"Ouch," Jannik said. "Let go of my thumb."

Redmond grinned. The boy had Jannik's thumb in his mouth and was biting down hard.

"You tangled with the wrong little warrior," Kamil cackled.

"The kid's a cannibal," someone else added. Another wave of hilarity rippled around the room.

Rollo reached over and collared the child. "Let him go," he said. When the child refused to comply, Rollo gave him a sharp slap on the rump. The child released Jannik and attacked Rollo, who held him out at arm's length.

The group of injured men lounging around inside the hut roared with laughter.

"Stop it," Emilia said. "Bring him to me."

"Gladly," Rollo said as he deposited the child in Emilia's lap where she sat at the table. "The little villain is going chew right through every man here if we aren't careful."

Emilia hugged the child, but he squirmed around to glare at Jannik and Rollo. Jannik remained on the ground holding his thumb, looking for all the world like an overgrown baby.

"The little scamp," he said. "It was *my* piece of bread."

Redmond stepped through the door as the men guffawed and slapped their legs in pure merriment. "By the size of you," Redmond said, "you've had plenty of bread already."

Jannik clambered to his feet. "I think I'll go up on the walls where it's safe," he said.

Redmond paused to stare at him. "What is that?"

"What?" Jannik glanced down at the dented armor breastplate.

Redmond had put a few of those dents on there himself and would have recognized it anywhere.

"Why are you wearing Lord Dwayne's armor?"

Jannik grinned. "I'm the only one big enough to wear it, and it seemed like such a waste to leave this nice piece lying around."

"Sure," Redmond said. "But don't get any ideas of grandeur. You're still just an archer."

"An archer with a pretty breastplate that tells everyone I'm no one to be messed with."

Windemere

"Everyone but a little kid with a set of sharp teeth," someone hollered.

Jannik scowled and pushed past Redmond as another round of laughter followed him out the door. Redmond settled onto the bench beside Emilia. The bow Kamil had given Emilia lay on the table. Kamil must have collected it from the battle site. It was battered but otherwise sound. She clearly hadn't given up her desire to learn to fight.

"How are you feeling?" he asked.

"I'll be all right," she said.

Redmond tickled the child who so recently had Jannik in a death grip. "What are we going to do with all these little ones?" he asked.

Emilia ran a tender hand over the child's head. "The older ones might know where they're from and who their parents are, but the little ones, like this fellow, are going to be more difficult."

"We can't leave them here," Redmond said. "When Adelaide gets her castle back, she'll re-enslave them."

"I know," Emilia said. Redmond considered her. She had washed since the battle and had pulled her hair back. Even with all the cuts and bruises, she looked so young and vulnerable. If life had thrown her a different roll of the dice, she might now be a mother herself, married to some well-to-do merchant or farmer and nurturing a family of her own.

"You look good with a child on your lap," Redmond said.

Emilia glanced at him and blushed.

"I heard you brought in the mason last night," one of the men called from across the room. Most of the men knew Walter by sight since he had been directing their work and had labored alongside them—which is why Redmond had been so surprised that Walter managed to simply stroll into the castle without anyone challenging him.

"We did," Redmond said.

"He could be a handy man to have around with you making us build all these walls."

"I'm afraid we've run out of time to build any more walls," Redmond said. "Adelaide's army has been joined by the armies of some of the nobles she killed. Things are likely to get warm around here."

That silenced the men. Redmond stood. "If any of you can draw a bow or throw rocks over the wall, I'm afraid we're going to have to ask you to join us."

A few of the men struggled to their feet. Others exchanged shameful glances. Redmond left them to decide on their own. They knew the score. Kamil and Rollo followed him out.

"You sure know how to throw a bucket of cold water on a party," Rollo said.

"I'm afraid I've led us into a trap," Redmond said. "Adelaide wants her castle back, and she's convinced all the families of the nobles she murdered that we did it."

"She's playing a much bigger game," Rollo said. "We just got in her way."

"I realize that, but, if that army attacks this castle, they'll swarm over the walls. We don't have enough men to repel them."

Kamil laid a hand on Redmond's shoulder.

"You know," he said, "unlike your longbows, which eventually follow the string and so lose their cast and become good for nothing but the fire, my bows are alive."

Redmond glanced at him, trying to anticipate where this conversation was going.

"I create my bows from bone, sinew, hide, and hoof," Kamil continued. "They have to be aged until they are strong enough to bend. But eventually they grow old and tired, and we set them aside to let them rest and regain their strength."

"Is there a point to this?" Redmond asked.

"You, my friend," Kamil said, "are like a long-strung bow. You have grown temperamental and overstressed, bending under the burden of the guilt you carry. You need to rest your soul for a time or you will surely break."

Redmond stopped to stare at Kamil. Had his inner turmoil about Lara and Emilia and his concern for his men become so obvious? He thought of how beautiful Comrie had been with its fields and high pastures surrounding the deep, crystal-blue lake. It would be good to go home—to leave this all behind. But he couldn't.

Rollo grunted. "Very nice sentiment, Kamil," he said. "But he can rest after he's extracted us from this little mess he's got us into."

A shout rose from the wall and all three of them sprinted up the steps to discover what new danger threatened them.

Chapter 17
The Ruse

delaide had thrown off her black clothing of the night before and spent a good hour making sure she radiated health and beauty before letting the newly arrived lords into her tent. She wore the green silk gown that fit her figure well. She had learned that it distracted the men—made them easier to manipulate.

One disaster had followed another. Her time was running out. She had been foolish and over-confident. She had placed her trust in bumbling idiots with no vision. There remained one last pawn to play, and she had already set it in motion. This move she saved for the last because the secret was too important to reveal without good cause. Things had now become desperate. In a few days or even hours, the castle could fall into the King's hands and then few of her secrets would be safe. She needed a distraction while the pawn was on the move.

The servant shuffled his feet by the entrance to the tent while she finished her note. She shot him an annoyed glance and dusted the paper before folding it and sealing it with hot green wax.

"This is only for Captain Redmond. Do you understand?"

The servant nodded.

"If he will not accept it, you bring it back. No one else is to read it. Is that clear?

"Yes, My Lady."

"Good. Now get out, and don't let anyone see you."

The servant took the note and slipped out of the tent. Adelaide stepped up to the tent flap and signaled to the guard. One of them jogged off into the camp. It was better to make the lords wait on her rather than her go crawling to them. It would train them for how things should be.

The lords arrived, dressed in their military regalia with gleaming helms, flowing cloaks, and bejeweled swords. Most of them were the younger brothers and heirs of the lords she had murdered a few days before. But there were several grizzled uncles and captains with long military experience. Adelaide suspected that, in more than one case, the uncles and captains were the ones in charge.

She smiled sweetly as they entered and extended her hand for each of them to kiss. She didn't miss the lingering gaze of the men as they filed in to stand in a semi-circle around her table.

"My lords," she said. "I am sorry for your loss. We were taken by surprise while our men were off dealing with a border matter."

She smoothed a wrinkle in her dress, drawing the men's gaze to her body.

"These ruffians from Longmire stole into the castle at first light, murdered our guards and many of your lords."

She glanced at the young men who stood with solemn faces and tried to judge which of them would be the easiest to turn to her wishes. More than a few of them refused to meet her gaze, and she read doubt and distrust in the faces of some of the older men. She would have to work hard to keep them reined in.

"Unfortunately," she continued, "my husband, Lord Baron Otto Selgrave, was unable to resist them, having recently suffered a grievous wound at the hands of assassins sent from Longmire. No doubt this was part of Longmire's plan for robbing us of our home."

She tried to look the part of the injured wife of a beloved husband, frail and weak—in need of protection.

"Now I beg you." She ran a hand over the polished surface of the table. "Do not let this outrage go unpunished. We have each been deprived of loved ones."

"What do you propose, My Lady?" asked Lord Merek, the brother of the Baron of Eliff. He had the same strong jaw as his brother and the same stocky build, but he had a kinder face with short-cropped hair and dark stubble on his chin.

"They only have enough men to hold the gates," she said. "If we attack along the entire length of the wall, we will simply overwhelm them with numbers."

A few of the men shuffled their feet.

"Would it not be better to wait them out?" Lord Merek asked. He glanced at the other men. "We have seen the battlefield, My Lady. Your army lost more than half its men, dead or wounded, to these ruffians."

Adelaide gave them a simpering smile to avoid clenching her jaw and throwing the table at the simpleminded upstart. Just because she killed his brother and he would be elevated to a barony didn't mean he could speak to her like that.

Before she could answer, a young whelp who couldn't be more than seventeen years old spoke up. She recognized him as Warin, the brother of the Earl of Tivoli.

"Has anyone offered to purchase the castle back from them?" Warin asked. "If they get paid, they'll have to leave the castle."

Adelaide kept smiling. "Why would I pay for my own castle when we have the power to take it back with force?" she said. "I've already paid them a ransom."

"With all due respect," Lord Merek said, "these are *our* men's lives. We would spend them wisely. Those archers have shown they are capable of defending that castle against superior numbers. Why not wait them out or offer to purchase the castle before someone else does?"

"Because," Adelaide said with controlled patience, "the seizure is illegal, and if you reward any rabble that gets ideas of grandeur, you might all find yourselves in my position."

A few of the them seemed to see the wisdom of her argument, but others still refused to look at her.

"My sources tell me," said a short round man that clearly spent too much time at the barrel, "the King intends to purchase the castle from them." He was a minor noble from the city of Arras.

"He can't," Adelaide said.

"He can," Lord Merek said. "If the King is coming, then I say we wait to find out what he intends."

"Do you mean to challenge him?" Warin asked.

Lord Merek glanced at him. "Not I," he said. "I have more important problems to deal with. I have no desire to tangle with the King."

Adelaide watched as her plans crumbled yet again. She was about to press her position when a horn sounded long and loud over the encampment.

The lords exchanged glances and rushed out of the tent.

Redmond, Rollo, and Kamil slid to a stop on the battlements as a lone man approached the crumbled barbican waving a white flag. He wore the light blue colors of the Lady Selgrave, but he was no warrior.

"I have a message for Captain Redmond from Lady Selgrave," the messenger shouted.

"Speak," Redmond called.

"It is written," the man said.

"Then read it you blasted fool," Jannik bellowed.

"It is for his eyes only."

"I see," Kamil said to Redmond, "you have become so elevated that we mere archers are no longer good enough to hear the same words Lady Selgrave would speak to you."

Redmond glared at him. "Does she actually think we'll parley with her?" he asked.

"She thinks *you* will," Rollo said and gave Redmond a knowing wink.

"Well, I'm not going down there to get it," Redmond said.

Kamil grabbed an arrow and tied a line to it. He drew and released. The arrow narrowly missed the messenger's head, as he dove aside.

"You did that on purpose," Rollo said.

Kamil shrugged and grinned. "Tie your message to the line," he called.

The messenger fumbled with the arrow and the line for a moment and then stood. He waved his white cloth, and Kamil dragged the line in.

Rollo caught the note that dangled on the end of the line. "Don't these people know how to tie knots?" he muttered as he inspected the strange, tangled blob of line that served to secure the paper to the rope.

"Apparently not," Redmond said. "Shall we?"

Rollo handed him the letter. "It's for *your* eyes only," he said.

Windemere

"Just open it," Redmond said with an impatient wave of his hand. Rollo broke the seal and handed it to Redmond. "I don't read so well," he said. "That script is too pretty for me."

Redmond grabbed the note and read it aloud.

"Captain Redmond, I will pay whatever price you demand if you and your men will surrender the castle to me this morning. My armies will withdraw, and I will bring the sum within a week's time. You have no hope of holding it now that my armies have been reinforced by thousands of men. Save your men by accepting my offer. If you refuse, they will be slaughtered."

"She's a cheery lady," Jannik said after Redmond finished reading.

"Why is she offering to buy it now?" Rollo asked.

Redmond gripped the note tightly and gazed out at the enemy camp.

"Because," he said, "she knows the lords don't want to send their armies to break on this castle like hers did. They're going to wait until we come out. That's when we're most vulnerable."

"We can't stand a siege of more than a week or two," Rollo said. "We don't have the supplies."

"We don't need to," Redmond said. "If they don't come soon, it will be too late."

"Spit it out," Jannik said. "What are you hinting at?"

Redmond swatted at the note with the back of his free hand. "Isn't it obvious?" he said. "She knows the King is coming. We have to hold on until he gets here."

A horn blast rang over the hills as a new banner fluttered on the western horizon.

Emilia hobbled along behind the little boy, using a spear as a makeshift crutch to keep her weight off the injured ankle. It was feeling better, but she didn't want to reinjure it. She had no delusions about what was coming. Even if they sold the castle, they would still have to escape. The boy had been so insistent that she let him take her hand and pull her toward the gatehouse by the front gate.

Redmond, Jannik, Rollo, and Kamil all debated something on the battlements where a group of archers clustered to listen to them. Emilia paused and was about to ask them what was going on, but the boy tugged on her hand, and she followed him into the gatehouse. She left the door open to let the light into the murky interior. What did the boy want so badly? He had been tugging at her and pointing for more than a quarter of an hour before she gave up and let him drag her to the gatehouse.

The place had been used as a sleeping quarters for the archers as was obvious by the piles of rucksacks, weapons, and scraps of food. Emilia wrinkled her nose at the smell of dirty men and moldy bread. A rat scurried away. Emilia secretly hoped it annoyed the men in payment for their having left such a mess.

The boy slipped into a back room and pushed on the stone wall.

"What are you doing?" Emilia asked.

He glanced up at her with a wrinkled brow. Then he pushed again.

Emilia studied the wall. She hadn't had time to question the children about where they had been hidden. The oldest girl had pointed toward these rooms, but Emilia hadn't thought much of it. The men Tal sent to search the gatehouse had found nothing, and they had assumed the children were just frightened and confused. She placed a hand on the rough cool stone and leaned into it. It gave with a harsh scraping sound.

A crack appeared. She shoved harder, and the door rotated open, grinding against the floor. The door stood about four feet high, so she had to bend over to peer into the darkness of a room beyond. A horrible reek of rotting flesh smote her in the face. She retched and covered her nose.

The boy scampered in, apparently oblivious to the smell, and bent over a pile of rags in the back corner. He rummaged around until he came up clutching something in his hands. By then, Emilia's eyes adjusted to the darkness and the breath caught in her throat.

The room was about twenty feet square and had no furniture. The ceiling was barely high enough for a man to stand. In the corner, the face of the old woman who had been herding the children stared at her with her mouth opened in a grotesque scream. At her feet lay the old man, bloated in death.

"Come here," Emilia said, gesturing urgently to the boy. "We have to go."

The boy glanced at the old woman and kicked her.

"Stop that," Emilia said. "Come here." She pointed to the ground in front of her. This was a place of death. She couldn't imagine what horrors had driven the children to murder these people or how they had done it. She didn't want to know.

The boy cocked his head and listened.

Emilia heard it, too.

It was a quiet rhythmic sound. The boy squatted on the floor and scraped at the dirt. A golden outline burned around a square slab set in the floor.

Emilia fell to her hands and knees. She crawled into the chamber to grab the boy. There could be only one reason light would be shining through a crack in the floor, and she was alone and injured.

Terror gripped her throat.

"Come on," she said in a harsh whisper. "Now."

The boy resisted.

He held up the wooden horse he retrieved from the old woman's body. It must have been a present from someone he loved, and the old woman had taken it away.

Emilia grabbed him and dragged him through the door. The stone in the floor shifted and slid aside, grinding over the dust-covered floor.

Light burst into the room.

A helmeted head poked through, and a man stared up at her.

Redmond watched in silence as another army spilled over the hills to the northeast. The army didn't attempt to join the one encamped before the gates of the castle. Instead, it spread out on a hill above the river. Spears and helmets glinted in the morning light. A long line of horsemen, maybe a thousand strong, detached itself from the army and swept down the hill. They forded the river and came on galloping straight for the gates of the castle. The hope that had leapt into Redmond's throat died. This wasn't the King's army.

"Man the walls," he called.

"Here we go again," Jannik said as he reached for his great warbow.

Adelaide pushed past the surprised men and raced to the edge of the encampment where a crowd of men had gathered. An army swarmed onto the northeastern hills, but she ignored it. She stared at the gate, willing it to open. It had to happen now. This was her last gamble. It couldn't fail.

She clutched at the long sleeves of her dress just to have something to hold. Her fists clenched and unclenched. The men on the walls scrambled about, but she couldn't tell whether it was in response to the arrival of the new army or the pawns she had unleashed on the castle. Even now she could snatch victory from defeat and from right under the nose of the meddling King.

Emilia scrambled backward as the man clambered out of the hole in the floor. His armor and weapons clanged against the stone. She pulled the door closed and wrestled a bed in front it before scrambling to her feet, ignoring the pain in her ankle.

The spear she held in front of her was foreign and heavy in her hands. She struggled to recall everything Kamil and her father had taught her about fighting.

But her mind went blank. She couldn't think. She struggled to breathe.

The man shouldered the door open and kicked at the bed. He had his sword out.

Emilia was going to die.

"Run!" she cried to the boy.

The boy bent and picked up a discarded knife.

"Just go," Emilia said as the desperation constricted her throat.

Why wouldn't the boy listen? It had been funny when the boy picked fights with Jannik, but this was for real. These men had been sent to slaughter them, and Redmond didn't even know they were in the castle.

Emilia cried out and retreated, shoving the boy behind her until she stood in the doorway to the gatehouse. She considered running for it, but she wouldn't get far with her injured leg.

"Redmond!" she called as loud as she could without taking her gaze off the man.

Others now loomed behind the man.

"Redmond!" she screamed as they rushed.

Windemere

She faked a jab of her spear toward his throat and then drove it into his thigh. The blow jerked the spear from her hands. She fell back, stumbling through the doorway.

The men burst out into the streets.

"Redmond!" she shrieked again.

A bowstring thrummed, and an arrow slammed into the man's back.

Emilia glanced up. Jannik nocked another arrow as Kamil took aim.

She grabbed the boy and fled as dozens of armed men poured into the streets from the gatehouse.

The castle was lost.

Chapter 18
Comrades Lost

edmond realized the threat too late. He had thought to question the children where they had been hidden, but it didn't occur to him there might be a secret passage into the castle. The men who checked the gatehouse reported nothing unusual. He should have searched it himself.

Now a new army emerged on the horizon arrayed for battle, and an enemy had infiltrated his castle. He had seen situations like this before. Castles frequently fell when their defenders lost heart simply because a few attackers managed to get inside.

It had been a fool's dream to believe he could cheat fate and keep his men from the mines. It had been even more foolish to try to outsmart Lady Adelaide in her own country and in her own castle.

"Hold the gate," he called. "Do not drop the drawbridge for any reason." He leapt down the steps two at a time.

"To me," he called as he bounded into battle. He needn't have been surprised. Death had always been the most likely outcome of any attempt to escape Windemere with nothing but a handful of archers.

His men came from all around the castle to converge on the new threat. They understood that their lives depended on keeping this castle.

Men wearing Lady Selgrave's light blue tunics poured into the streets. His archers on the walls thinned their ranks one by one, but they kept coming. He had to plug that entrance.

Redmond cut into the first man he found. His sword slid across a mail shirt, but the blow had been hard enough to double the man

Windemere

over. Redmond kicked him in the face and sent him sprawling.

He slipped his blade underneath the man's mail shirt, plunging it into his belly, ripping it free, and jumping to the next man.

A great roar rose up outside the walls. Redmond's heart fell. If the army assaulted his walls now they would surely fall.

It had been a well-executed plan—lure them into a false sense of security through several failed attempts and then attack them from within and without simultaneously.

All they could do now was sell their lives as dearly as possible.

Emilia stumbled down the cobblestone street, ignoring the pain in her ankle. The cries and clash of battle drove her on. She struggled to breathe as the horror of the disaster unfolding behind her, in the place she had called home for most of her life, constricted her throat. How could such a strong castle, protected by stalwart and experienced fighting men fall to a simple ruse?

She burst into the weaver's shop where Sibyl, the mason's wife, kept the children. Walter lunged to his feet with a spear in his hands. He shoved a big hammer through his belt. The children crowded into a corner, huddled together like a pack of frightened kittens.

"They're in the castle," Emilia panted. She set the boy down to give her arms a rest.

"Has it fallen?" Walter asked.

"Not yet, but something is happening outside. We have to save the children. We have to get them out of here."

Walter glanced at his wife. "There's the sewer," he said.

Emilia stared at him. She had no idea what he was talking about. "The garderobe?" she asked.

"No," Walter said. "The entrance is in the storage room in the keep. It leads out to the river."

"Does Lady Selgrave know about it?"

"Yes."

Terror gripped Emilia's throat. "She'll send more in that way," she said. "We have to warn Redmond."

She spun to find her father hastening toward her with a pack on his back. He carried another one in his hands.

"The castle is going to fall," he said. "We need to leave now."

"What about Redmond and the others?"

"He knows," Tal said. "He told me to take you and flee if it looked like we would be overrun."

Emilia glanced toward the gates. The crash of battle echoed down the streets. How could she leave Redmond like this? After all he had done for her and her father? But he wouldn't want her to sit here and wait to die. He wouldn't want her to sacrifice the children just so she could stay with him.

Tal poked his head into the weaver's shop. "Grab the children," he said, "and any supplies you can carry. We'll try the sally ports."

"No," Walter said. "It's blocked, and we would be seen anyway."

"Walter knows a way," Emilia said. "Let's go."

She snatched the pack from her father and slipped it on before lifting the boy into her arms. Her ankle throbbed as she whirled to leave. She bit her lip against the pain.

"Come on." She waved to the children as Walter wrapped an arm about Sibyl's waist to support her. A red stain showed through the bandage around her leg. She used the butt-end of a spear with her free hand for added support. The children followed them, clutching one another.

All the men set to guard the entrance to the keep had abandoned their posts. Apparently, they had concluded the keep was lost as well, or they had run to join the fighting at the front gate. Walter led them in, stumbling down the steps. Loud voices sounded above, and a door slammed. Walter fumbled around in the dark of the basement until he found a resin-soaked torch and a tinder box. He struck the flint and steel until the torch caught. Then he bent and lifted a trapdoor in the floor. The air that blew in from the open door made Emilia gag and retch. One of the children bent over and vomited.

"That's your way out?" Tal asked.

Walter scratched his head. "It's the only way."

The clatter and din of battle approached the keep. Emilia peeked through an arrow slit to see archers locked in a running battle with Adelaide's soldiers as they spilled into the inner court. Redmond's men were being driven back.

"They're coming," Emilia breathed. "Hurry."

"After you," Tal said, and they climbed down the ladder into air so heavy and thick with stench that Emilia could have cut it with her knife.

Battle surged around Redmond. The cobblestones became slick with blood and littered with bodies. Men roared their battle cries and screamed in their death agony. The horrible, sickening fetor of combat filled his nostrils as he slashed and parried, kicked and punched in the wild, chaotic choreography of battle. The rush of soldiers in blue poured from the gatehouse, like a gaping wound gushing blood. Redmond's men struggled in grim determination to stop the flood before it overwhelmed them.

Jannik bounded down the stairs wielding his big sledgehammer. He roared as he bowled into Adelaide's men. "Come to Papa," he bellowed. "Bessie will give you a kiss." The sledgehammer fell with brutal force, crushing helmets, shattering bones. Adelaide's men scattered before him like leaves in a hurricane. A group broke away, sprinting toward the inner ward as if they hoped to find sanctuary there.

"After them," Redmond called as he swung and hacked at armor and swords.

Kamil's voice rang over the battle. At first, Redmond thought he was singing, but in a pause in the battle, he glanced up to see that he was chanting in his own language to the rhythm of his shooting as he emptied his quiver with lethal precision into Adelaide's men. Kamil enjoyed battle far more than was natural.

A cordon of Redmond's archers contained the flow of intruders and forced them back until only a handful still fought with ferocious desperation by the gatehouse. Their comrades retreated through the door.

Jannik hammered away at one flank while Redmond led the push on the other. At last, the men broke and scrambled into the gatehouse. Redmond followed to see them disappear down a tunnel in a hidden chamber. He stood with Jannik at his side, panting and trembling with the exertion.

"Block that entrance," Redmond said to Jannik. "I have to see to the walls."

He whirled and rushed back to the steps, taking them two at time. He hadn't forgotten the army that appeared on the hills just as the invaders burst into the castle. The strange silence that greeted his ears sent a chill to his heart. What had happened? Why weren't his men fighting to hold the gate? Had the army chosen to attack the walls? He hoped not. He didn't have enough men to defend them.

Redmond slid to a stop beside Rollo, who stood with his hands behind his back facing the field in front of the castle. The horsemen that Redmond had seen riding out to attack the castle had formed a line in front of the barbican and were now facing Adelaide's army.

"What the—" Redmond began and then stopped. Now he recognized the colors. It was the pale yellow of the Baron of Longmire with the black rearing horse in its center.

The journey through the festering darkness of the sewer had nearly undone Emilia's sanity. She washed in the river above where the sewer emptied for half an hour, but she still couldn't get the smell off her clothes and body. Her ankle throbbed, and her arms ached from carrying the boy down the iron rungs and through the sloping channel of the sewer. The sun burned down with a special vengeance as if it hoped to burn off the stink they had introduced into the world. Even the wind tried to blow it away as it swept through the cattails and willows, swirling around the depression where the high bank hid the entrance to the sewer.

A blue jay fluttered to a branch, where it bobbed for just an instant before it gave an annoyed screech and flew away.

"Even the birds can't stand the smell," Emilia mumbled as she wrung out her hair.

"We need to go," Tal said.

"I don't hear any sound of battle," Emilia said. She glanced up the walls of the castle barely visible over the rise.

"It's probably over," Tal hefted his pack. "When the enemy gets inside and you're trapped, most men surrender."

"I'm not sure we should have left them," Emilia said. Her mercenary interest in Redmond had changed, and she would have willingly remained with him and fought to the death. "What if they could have come with us? I mean we all might have escaped."

"We haven't escaped yet," Tal said. He gestured to Walter and Sibyl. "Let's go."

They worked their way up the river away from the castle, following

Windemere

a narrow game trail as they tried to keep below the bank of the river. The smell of wet earth and the occasional sweet scent of a flower forced through the stink that clung to Emilia's nose. But always that lingering smell of the sewer laced everything.

She paused to cut a piece of willow bark with her knife and slipped it into her mouth to chew. The bark had a bitter, earthy flavor. But she hoped it would dull the ache in her ankle.

When they came around the bend north of the castle, Emilia chanced a glance back. The stone walls soared up into the bright afternoon sky, silent and solemn. She wasn't just leaving Redmond. She was leaving behind everything she had known for over ten years.

Adelaide watched as the horsemen filed out in front of the castle and turned to oppose her army. She wrung her hands, waiting for her men to raise her standard over the walls. The distant sound of steel clashing against steel and shouts and cries drifted to her. The attack had begun. Her men were inside. The castle would surely fall. It had to fall.

She had saved this move to the last. No one knew about the tunnel but her and the old man and woman she employed to bring the children in before shipping them off to the silver mines. Not even Otto knew of it. She paid the men well to build it in secret and had then quietly executed them. Some secrets had to be protected at all costs.

Two hundred soldiers had entered the tunnel, more than enough to overwhelm the archers. They would have come up right behind the gate when the archer's attention was fixed on her offer to buy the castle and on the newly arrived army. It was a perfect plan. It had to work. Her fingers tingled, and she realized she had squeezed them hard enough to cut off the flow of blood. She released them and smoothed her dress. The sounds of fighting faded and disappeared. Any moment now her flag would rise above the castle.

A rider, bearing the yellow banner of the Baron of Longmire, broke from the army that gathered on the hill. He wore a shining helmet and a breastplate and clutched the staff of the Baron's colors as he galloped over the field. The banner streamed out behind him snapping in the wind. He pulled up in front of the ruined barbican. Redmond strode out to the east tower to hear what the messenger had to say.

"Greetings," the messenger called. "My Lord Dragos, Baron of Longmire, sends congratulations to his archers for their daring and skill in capturing and holding so imposing a fortress. He begs admittance to your castle so he may parley for the purpose of purchasing your prize from you."

A cheer rang out from the men on the wall, and Redmond couldn't help but smile. A rush of relief swelled in his chest. Maybe they would survive.

Redmond leaned out through a crenellation so the messenger could see him.

"I am Captain Redmond of Baron Longmire's mercenaries," he called. "You are most welcome. We would beg Baron Longmire to understand that our position is a delicate one in which much treachery has been at play. Therefore, we hesitate to let any into our fortifications until some security has been given."

The messenger's horse pranced sideways. "The Baron offers his son as security if it is deemed necessary," the messenger said, "and begs me to inform you that his royal majesty Rupert Thurin, King of Morcia, will arrive later today with an interest in your prize. Will you meet with them?"

"Gladly," Redmond called back. "But a hostile army even now encamps in front of this castle, one that has made several attempts against us. We would parley on our doorstep rather than within our walls."

"I will so inform the Baron."

The messenger dipped his flag in a salute, whirled, and galloped away.

Rollo pounded Redmond on the back. "We did it," he said. "We held on."

Redmond glanced at the bloody sword he still held in his hand and wondered why he hadn't sheathed it. Then he smiled up at Rollo.

"I didn't know if we could hold out."

He took a deep breath, allowing himself to enjoy the moment even though he knew their troubles were far from over.

"We should keep the men vigilant," he said, "in case this turns out be a ploy, too. And I think we should prepare to leave." He laid a hand on Rollo's shoulder. "Thank you, my friend."

"We archers have to look out for each other," Rollo said. "No one else will. Besides, I'm looking forward to owning my own castle and getting a nice foot massage."

Lady Selgrave held her breath as the rider carrying Baron Longmire's yellow banner with the rearing black horse faced the castle. Adelaide grabbed the long bit of sleeve that hung down past her hands and twisted it around her fingers. Any minute now. But nothing happened. A cheer burst from the castle. Adelaide dropped her sleeve and let out her breath as the uncomfortable heat of disappointment spread through her chest. The messenger rode away and with him her hopes of taking the castle. She gazed up at the keep that towered over the castle. Baron Otto would never forgive her.

"My Lady?"

Adelaide spun to find the captain of her husband's guard standing with the other lords.

"Yes?" she snapped.

"We should withdraw," he said.

Adelaide stared at them and ground her teeth as the heat rose in her face. "What about my husband?" she demanded.

"The King will release him," he said, "even if he chooses to keep the castle."

"I want those archers," Adelaide said.

Lord Tyron of Cassel stepped forward from the gathering of nobles. He was a short man with a scraggly beard and shifting eyes. "They have to leave the castle sometime, My Lady, and if they are slowed down by their loot, they will be all the easier to bring to heel."

"They will seek the fastest route out of Morcia," she said.

"In that case," Lord Tyron said, "they have only two choices. They must run east or west. We can send out scouts to watch for them and leave men here to keep an eye on the castle. They can't escape us."

Adelaide gazed up at the castle. "They had better not escape again," she murmured.

"I will lead my men away today to get in front of them," Lord Tyron said. "We'll catch them."

Lord Merek clicked his tongue. "This is a fool's errand," he said. "My men will not die so you and the King can renege on your word." He whirled to leave.

"Lord Merek," Adelaide snapped.

He paused and looked over his shoulder at her.

"If you abandon me now," she said, "I will not forget."

"Nor will I," Lord Merek said with a sneer.

Redmond descended the steps, struggling against the weariness. It would be good to be free of the castle at last, even if it meant rejoining Longmire's army for a time. At least he would no longer have to shoulder the burden of keeping his men alive without support in the face of overwhelming odds. He needed to check on Tal, Emilia and the children and let them know it was time to prepare to leave. If all went well, they could be on the road tomorrow.

His men dragged the bodies of the dead into the guardroom, leaving dark, bloody stains on the cobblestone streets. He worried there might be other tunnels like this one somewhere in the castle, and he was anxious to get out before Lady Selgrave could work more mischief.

He paused. The door to the apothecary hut stood open. He entered to find his wounded men peering up at him.

"Where's the apothecary?" he asked.

"He grabbed two rucksacks and ran that way," one of the men said, pointing away from the front gates.

Redmond strode to the weaver's shop where the children had been staying and found the door slightly ajar. He pushed it open. It too was empty. He stepped back out into the street, trying to understand what had happened. Could they have gone to hide somewhere else? He stopped one of his men who was searching the buildings for any more of Adelaide's men who might be hiding.

"Have you seen the apothecary or the mason?" Redmond asked.

"No," he said. "But we did find a few of the enemy hiding in the stables."

"Good," Redmond said. "Keep them secure. We may need to bargain with them."

The archer avoided his gaze.

Windemere

"What?"

"We didn't leave any alive," he said.

Redmond considered the man. He could scold him for being bloodthirsty and reckless, but he knew better. These men had been threatened with the salt mines and bodily mutilation simply for being archers. They had endured assaults and sleepless nights. Their injured friends and comrades had been mercilessly butchered. When the enemy fell so easily into their hands, they were unlikely to show much restraint.

"Okay," he said, "but make a thorough search. Those children and the apothecary have to be somewhere within the walls."

An hour later, Redmond and Rollo strode over the bridge to await the royal procession. The last of Lady Selgrave's battered army straggled over the hills. She had good reason to withdraw from the field. The combined armies of the King and the Baron of Longmire numbered around seven thousand men.

To prepare for the royal visit, Redmond had cleared the area in front of the barbican of rubble and bodies. The sickly sweet odor of rotting corpses filled the air, but, if the breeze blew just right, it was hardly noticeable.

His men gathered the armor and weapons so that every archer now had a mail shirt and a good steel helmet. They replenished their supply of arrows and many upgraded their weapons. Redmond wanted them properly outfitted because he had no delusions about an easy escape. He had offended half the nobles in the kingdom by depriving them of the castle. They would be out for blood, even if he and his men did ride with the Baron of Longmire.

A party of horsemen bearing the King's purple standard and the yellow one of the Baron of Longmire descended the hill where the army was busy setting up tents.

Redmond glanced up at his men arrayed along the towers and the wall. Baron Otto had flung back the shutters and stood at his window, impassive, to watch the sale of his castle. Redmond left his weapons behind as a sign of good faith, but he wanted his archers to have his back in case anything went wrong. Jannik waved his great bow at him, and Redmond smiled and shook his head at his boyish exuberance. He could hardly blame them. Few of them believed they would survive this long.

The horses galloped up in a cloud of dust that stirred the vile smell of the corpses. Redmond and Rollo knelt before the King.

"Rise," the King said. "We stand upon the field of your victory, not mine."

The King was older than Redmond expected with a fine white head of hair and a wispy beard. But he was still muscular and commanding with a sharp jaw and a steady gaze.

"Thank you for coming, Your Majesty," Redmond said.

The King dismounted as did Baron Longmire and the six knights who accompanied them. None of them wore their helmets, but they all wore mail shirts. The King and the Baron had solid breastplates to which the mail had been woven to form the rest of their hauberk.

The King and the Baron took their seats on the benches Redmond had provided. The Baron sported a bushy red mustache. His face always burned a dull red.

"Well, Captain Redmond," the Baron said. "I should be angry with you for running off with my archers, but I can see you've put them to good use." He glanced around at the stripped corpses. "I declare, man, you have some nerve."

The King smiled. "I like a man who knows how to take chances. If I had a few thousand stalwart men such as you have here, I could drive those pesky Naymani from my lands." Then he clapped his hands. "But we haven't come to talk politics. I believe you have a castle for sale."

The King's jovial mood was infectious, and Redmond found himself smiling.

"Yes, Your Majesty," Redmond said.

"I hope you realize that I could simply take it if I chose," the King said.

That wiped the smile from Redmond's face. He glanced at the army on the hill.

"Yes, Your Majesty."

"But, I owe you something for ridding me of some traitorous nobles and weakening my most vocal opponents." The King's gaze strayed to Baron Otto's keep. Redmond followed his gaze. Baron Otto still watched them.

Windemere

"We didn't kill the nobles," Redmond said. "Lady Selgrave poisoned them."

"Ah." The King grinned. "Now, that is interesting. Can you prove it?

Redmond shrugged. "They were dead or dying when I arrived. Lord Dacrey survived. He can tell you."

"And where is he?" Baron Longmire interjected.

"In the dungeon."

Baron Longmire's already red face brightened. "I will be happy to get my hands on that turncoat, that forsworn fool."

"You do understand," the King said, "that given the constant disturbance on my eastern border, my resources are somewhat constrained. But I'm prepared to pay 200,000 gold coins."

Rollo shifted beside Redmond, and he glanced at him. Rollo wanted more than twice that sum.

"Do you have a better offer?" the King asked.

"No, My Lord," Redmond said.

"Good. If this is acceptable, I will send the wagon with the payment after we finish here. Now, we have the matter of your other prisoner," the King said. "Will you release Baron Selgrave into my hands?"

"We don't want him," Rollo said.

"Neither do I," the King smirked. "But we must deal with the nobles we have." He stood and smoothed his tunic. "I assume you will rejoin Baron Longmire's army."

Redmond glanced at Rollo. "Given the fact that we are now probably the most wanted men in the kingdom," he said, "I think it best we find a rapid exit."

The King gestured to Baron Longmire. "They're your archers," he said.

The way the King said this, it sounded as if he was suggesting the Baron owned them—that they were his peasants or slaves. The insult had not gone unnoticed. Rollo scowled and Baron Longmire gave the King an irritated glance before speaking.

"We can escort you back to Longmire," he said, "and then *you* can decide what to do."

Baron Dragos glanced at the King, and Redmond sensed that some unspoken agreement between them had already been struck.

He watched them, trying to see what he was missing. Baron Dragos shifted in his seat.

The knights mounted, but the King waved Redmond over for a private conversation. Redmond glanced around at his men on the wall. He had no reason to trust the King.

"Well," the King said, "you have done me a favor. I'll do you one in return."

"Okay," Redmond said.

"I understand you come from Frei-Ock Mor."

"Yes."

"War is about to erupt on Frei-Ock Mor again, and if you have any friends in Coll, you should warn them and get them out if you can."

"What do you mean, Sire?" Redmond asked, but the King smoothed his tunic and avoided Redmond's gaze.

"I've said too much already, but you would do well to heed my advice."

With that, the King mounted and road away.

Redmond stepped over to stand beside Rollo. The Baron of Long-mire hung back until the others had trotted out of earshot.

"Your messenger reached me," he said.

Redmond stared at him in confusion for a moment before he realized the Baron was speaking of Henry, the brave little boy that had come to rescue Redmond the first night they had been captured.

The Baron glanced at the King and back at Redmond. "I wanted you to know," he said. Then he kicked his horse into a gallop and shouted over his shoulder, "Very interesting contents in that pouch he carried."

Adelaide Selgrave threw off her cloak and picked up a handheld mirror. She poked a stray hair back into place and bent over the map on the table. She led her army away from the castle to show the King she would not contest his purchase of it, but only far enough to demonstrate she entertained no hostile intent toward the King. The game was still afoot. She may have been checked for now, but her pawns were still moving. Redmond and his men would never escape.

"Do you really care that much about how you look?"

Lady Selgrave jumped and whirled to face Mara. The little assassin stood in the corner of her tent.

"What do you want?" Lady Selgrave asked.

"Information," Mara said. "The Order has discovered that you have found some new silver mines."

"I don't know what you're talking about."

"Oh please," Mara sneered. "Don't play innocent with me. The Order wants to know how you plan to exploit the mines and how you'll do it without the King's knowledge."

"It's none of their business what I do."

Mara raised her eyebrows. "I see," she said and stepped toward the entrance to the tent. "I will send that report to the masters of the Order. I'm sure they will be interested to note that one of their informants has become a turncoat." She stopped at the tent flap. "The last turncoat died a painful death."

"Oh, all right," Lady Selgrave said. "But you haven't been much use to me yet. I want something in exchange for the information."

Mara faced her and waited.

"I want you to help me get revenge on these people."

Lady Selgrave gestured toward the castle. When Mara still didn't say anything, she continued.

"I sent a mason into the castle to open the gates, and he betrayed me. I also have two servants in there who tried to poison me and Lord Otto. I want them found."

Mara blinked at her and pursed her lips as if she were thinking. Lady Selgrave spun to pace before her table.

"Redmond wouldn't be able to take them with him if he's going with the Baron of Longmire as my spies believe. That mason knows there's a sewer under the keep that drains into the river north of the castle. He'll try to use it to escape me. I want them found and brought to me."

Mara simply stared at her without expression.

"That's all I want from you," Lady Selgrave said. "Just find them and bring them to me. Then I'll tell you everything your masters want to know about the silver mines."

"You believe they've already left the castle?" Mara asked.

"Yes."

"Why would they leave before Redmond?"

Lady Selgrave considered how much she should tell this girl. She

J.W. Elliot

knew so little about her and had been forced to accept that she was from the Order on the girl's word alone. For all she knew, the girl could be working for someone else—maybe even the King. But it would be risky to assume too much.

"One of my men," she said, "who survived the attempt to infiltrate the castle saw them running toward the inner ward. My servants carried packs on their backs, and they were leading a bunch of children. I'm guessing they left because they thought the castle was overrun. But you can get into the castle and see if they're there, can't you?"

Lady Selgrave had seen this girl scale the keep. She would be the perfect person to find the mason, the apothecary, and his daughter.

Mara nodded. "I'll bring them to you if I can find them, but if you fail the Order, I am not responsible for what happens to you."

Chapter 19
The Broken Bargain

here are they then?" Redmond demanded as Rollo informed him that Emilia, Tal, Walter and his family, and all the children could not be found within the castle. He gathered Rollo, Jannik, and Kamil in Tal's shop, which had become a headquarters as well as a hospital, to plan their next move.

"They must have fled the castle," Kamil said.

"But how?" Redmond demanded. He plopped down at the table. "They didn't leave by any of the gates, and we would have seen them if they had gone over the wall."

Then he paused as he remembered that Walter came in by the sewer that burrowed under the keep. Redmond had it guarded, but, during the confusion of the attack, they might have slipped out without anyone noticing. He told Tal to take Emilia and run if they were overwhelmed, and the fact that dozens of men had broken into the castle would have made it look like a defeat.

Redmond passed a hand over his head. "They went through the sewer," he said. "The mason led them through the sewer."

"What sewer?" Rollo asked.

"In the keep," Redmond said. "It channels the waste from the garderobes in the keep out of the castle to the river."

Jannik frowned. "Are you planning on using the sewer to get us out?" he asked. "Because if you are, I'm going to protest."

Kamil grimaced. "I'd rather die up here in battle," he said. "There are some things worse than death."

"You two are a little dramatic," Redmond said. "I have no intention of going through the sewer. We're going to need our horses if

191

we hope to get out of here."

The thought of Emilia out there with Tal and a bunch of kids, with Lady Selgrave on the loose and vengeful, expanded a sickening pit in Redmond's stomach. Tal might have been a warrior once, but none of the rest of them were. If Lady Selgrave's scouts found them escaping the castle, she would make sure they suffered, and then she would make sure Redmond knew they suffered. He couldn't leave them, especially since it was his coming and his plans that put them in danger. He had abandoned people he cared about once before. Never again.

"We can't help them now," Redmond said. "But we'll need to find them before Lady Selgrave does."

Rollo shifted as if he had something to say. Redmond thought his pragmatic friend might tell him to worry about saving his own hide, but he didn't.

"We shouldn't wait on Baron Longmire," Rollo said. "There was something odd about the way he offered to escort us."

"Agreed," Redmond said.

"You don't trust them?" Jannik asked.

Redmond glanced at Rollo, and they both shook their heads.

"To them," Rollo said. "We're expendable. They have no legal reason to care if we live or die. We're tools they employ while we're useful. Once we leave this castle, we're no longer useful, and we'll have money the King desperately needs to fight his wars with Deira."

"And the money we extracted from the Selgraves," Kamil added.

"So, in other words," Jannik said as he passed a pensive hand over his beard. "They're going to pay us to get us out of the castle, and then they're going to rob us and kill us one way or another."

"I think so," Redmond said. "Which is why we should leave tonight. We rotate the guard on the gates, the tunnel, and the sewer so the men can get some rest. I don't want any more uninvited guests."

"What about the wagon?" Kamil asked.

Redmond studied him. "You think they might smuggle someone in with the wagon?"

"I would," Kamil said.

Jannik gave Kamil a sideways glance. Redmond had thought that Jannik might be overcoming his distrust of Kamil, but that glance was full of suspicion. He considered asking what was bothering him but decided against it.

"Right," Redmond said, "then the wagon stays off the bridge on the outside of the barbican. We'll unload it from there."

"If it comes," Rollo said.

The wagon did arrive an hour later with a guard of fifty men clad in mail bearing the royal coat of arms. Redmond met it on the same spot where he entertained the King.

"We were ordered to deliver it into the castle," the leader of the guard said.

"This will do," Redmond said. "We'll unload it from here."

"But my orders were—" the man said.

"No one is entering the castle until tomorrow," Redmond talked over him.

The men exchanged glances but apparently were unwilling to risk a battle so close to the walls where over one hundred archers stood ready.

"You'll answer to the King," the guard said.

"I understand," Redmond said.

The guard's desire to enter the castle made Redmond even more suspicious. Maybe Kamil was right. He kept an eye on the guards as he reached to remove the canvas covering. Their horses pranced as if their riders were transmitting nervousness to them. Redmond paused, then flipped the canvas away.

He tensed, expecting men to leap from the wagon, but nothing happened. Iron-bound boxes filled the bed of the wagon. Maybe he had been too paranoid. He signaled to the archers to come unload it. Twenty-five of them stepped out onto the bridge. Within half an hour, they had unloaded all the boxes, and Redmond started to relax when something caught his eye.

The last archer in the line had fresh soil marks on his knees. Redmond tried to remember if any of his men had knelt down while retrieving the boxes, but he was certain none of them had. They were stacking the boxes in the barracks which had wooden floors, so why would any of them have wet stains on the knees of their trousers?

"Stop," Redmond called and drew his sword. The men paused and glanced back. The one with the wet stains faced him.

Redmond strode up to him.

"Who are you?" he demanded.

J.W. Elliot

The man tried to appear shocked and confused by the question. "Captain?" he questioned.

Now that Redmond could see his face, he knew this man was not one of his archers or one of the men that had joined them from the dungeons.

"Set the box down," Redmond said. Jannik jogged out to see what the matter was. He clutched his big hammer, ready for action.

The man set the box down and raised his hands. "What's going on?" he said. "I didn't steal any of the money."

"You recognize him?" Redmond asked Jannik.

Jannik peered at him. "No," he said.

"Me neither," Redmond said and gestured toward the waiting guard with his sword. "You had better rejoin your men," he said.

"Captain Redmond—" the man began, but Redmond interrupted him.

"My men don't call me captain," Redmond said.

Uncertainty swept over the man's face, and Jannik shot out a hand and collared him.

"Wait," the man said.

The clatter of hooves sounded as the guard rode onto the bridge. Redmond whirled to face them.

"He's under the King's protection," the guard said.

Jannik gave the intruder a shove, and he stumbled toward the men on horseback. "Then take him back to the King," he said.

"And tell the King," Redmond said, "that this treachery is beneath him. We negotiated in good faith."

The guard snorted. "You're simple thieves," he spat.

Jannik stepped toward him, his hammer raised, but Redmond restrained him.

"Take your wagon and leave," Redmond said.

The guard whirled as the intruder climbed up in the wagon beside the driver.

"It's like you often say," Jannik remarked loudly. "You can never trust a noble."

Redmond turned to follow his men back into the castle when Jannik placed a hand on his arm. He bent close.

"How did he know?" he whispered.

"Who?"

Windemere

"Kamil," Jannik said. "How did he know they would be smuggling someone inside the wagon?"

"What are you getting at?" Redmond asked.

Jannik glanced up at the walls as if to see if Kamil was spying on them.

"I saw him leaving the keep two days ago."

"So?"

"So what was he doing in the keep—if not conspiring with Baron Otto?"

Redmond scowled. "I think you're letting your dislike of foreigners confuse your thinking."

Jannik's gaze darted to the gate and back to Redmond's face. "And you're too trusting. I saw him coming out the keep when he had no business there. Where was he when you were meeting with the King?"

Redmond shrugged, but he couldn't remember seeing Kamil immediately before or after he met with the King. Kamil had come up to them from the direction of the inner ward.

"No," Redmond said, shaking his head. He couldn't believe it of any of his men—certainly not Kamil.

"Well you had best keep an eye on him," Jannik said. He patted his sledgehammer. "Me and Bessie won't be far away."

Adelaide refused to stand as the King's emissary entered her tent. She knew the man well. He had been a frequent visitor at her father's manor in Metz and his castle in Beck Wood. The King probably chose him for that reason—assuming a childhood acquaintance might make her more malleable.

Marquess Leo Brom of Langon smiled at her. His beard had grown longer in the intervening years. Gray now streaked his long dark hair. He peered down at her over his hawkish nose. A blue robe with pointed sleeves nearly concealed his hands. Lady Selgrave had never liked him.

"Adelaide," he said as if he had real affection for her. "You look lovely."

Lady Selgrave glowered. "Have you come to mock me?" she asked.

Leo pulled back as if surprised. "Of course not," he said. "The

195

King sends you his best wishes and an offer."

"The King has interfered in a personal matter," she insisted, "and has humiliated me and the Baron by coming to oppose us with an army in our own lands and purchasing our castle from a band of ruffians and outlaws."

Leo bestowed a fatherly smile upon her. "Now, don't be like that," he said. "The King came to help you out of a difficult situation."

"I'm no longer a child," Lady Selgrave said.

"Any man can see that," he said. His gaze swept over her body. Normally, this gave her a sense of power over men, but not this time. She shivered in disgust.

"What do you want?"

Rubbing his hands together as if he were enjoying himself, Leo said, "The King sends his greetings as I said and his best wishes for your good health."

Lady Selgrave raised her eyebrows at the meaningless formalities and waved a hand at him to hurry up.

"King Rupert has purchased Castle Windemere for 200,000 gold coins."

"So little?" Lady Selgrave said. "Those archers are fools."

"Perhaps," Leo continued, "but the King would like to return the castle to its proper owners."

"Why hasn't he sent emissaries to Baron Otto?" Lady Selgrave knew better than to trust King Rupert.

"Because, the archers have refused anyone admittance to the castle while they hold it, and you are in command of the Baron's army, for the time being."

Lady Selgrave narrowed her eyes. That could only mean the King wanted her army for something. She was not sending them to the frontier to be wasted on the useless border wars under any circumstances.

"However," Leo continued, "the King could use your help in a tiny matter."

Lady Selgrave waited tight-lipped.

"The King can ill afford the 200,000 gold coins at present and would like to recover them."

Now it was coming clear. Lady Selgrave sat up straighter. The King was going to be duplicitous as always.

Windemere

"He also knows the archers extorted 10,000 gold coins from you and assumes you might like to have that money returned."

"Of course," Lady Selgrave said.

"The King will return the Castle of Windemere to its rightful owners under the following conditions. First, you agree to assist him in recovering the gold from the archers. And second, you and Baron Otto withdraw your opposition to the head tax."

Lady Selgrave scowled. "The King wastes our resources and men on a war he cannot win," she said. "And he still holds lands that he stole from us without cause."

The Marquess gave her his paternal smile again. "And you are wasting resources and men here when a simple payment could have solved the problem. Please remember that your father knew he was playing with fire when he arranged your wedding, and he was willing to take the risk. The King could hardly turn a blind eye to such an insult, as you well know. Consider it the price of being allowed to become a baroness as well as a countess rather than some lower lord's plaything."

"How dare you!" Lady Selgrave lunged to her feet.

Leo continued that irritating smile.

"Your father would advise you to accept the King's offer," he said, "especially given the fact that you have no other options. If you refuse, the King will imprison Baron Otto for sedition and rebellion and for the murder of the lords who died while under his protection."

"The archers murdered them when they attacked the castle," Lady Selgrave insisted.

The Marquess gave her a simpering smile and clasped his hands together. "You and I both know those archers had no cause to kill men for whom they could have received large ransoms. The King has also seen the bodies. The lords were not killed by archers, they were poisoned while feasting at Baron Otto's board."

"I was there," Lady Selgrave said. But her continued defiance was getting her nowhere.

"You may maintain the charade," he said. "But the King knows the truth. You accept his offer, or he will have you both arrested for murder and sedition."

"He can't do that."

"He can, and you'll find that the lords who have gathered to you will quickly disappear once they learn the truth of how you have manipulated them. I believe you will find that once a woman develops a reputation of being vengeful, only the naïve or despicable will follow her."

"Oh, all right!" Adelaide said and sat down again. "What to do you want me to do?"

"The King cannot attack the archers as he has finalized a truce with them, but you and the other nobles remain free to act. The archers are expected to surrender the castle tomorrow. They will most likely travel with Baron Longmire to the coast. Baron Longmire has instructions not to intervene should you intercept them. You may then take whatever vengeance you desire and what monies may be yours. The rest is to be returned to the King."

Lady Selgrave smiled now for the first time since the Marquess entered her tent. "For once, the King's priorities and mine seem to have aligned," she said. "Will I be given complete freedom to deal with all the archers as I see fit?"

"You mean their leader? What's his name? Redmond, I think?"

"Yes," Lady Selgrave said.

"He is your plaything," Leo said. "The King will turn a blind eye, so long as his terms are met."

Lady Selgrave nodded. "I accept."

As the shadow of evening spread over the castle, Redmond stepped into the mews behind the apothecary shop with the thick leather glove on his hand. He had no experience working with hawks, but he couldn't leave these birds here to starve or leave them to the Baron—not after seeing how much Emilia and Tal cared about them. He held a piece of meat in the gloved hand the way Emilia had done.

He untied the hawk from its perch, held up his hand, and whistled. The hawk jumped to his hand with a flutter of wings and tore at the meat. Redmond carried it outside and threw his hand up. The hawk took off with a jingle of the bells tied to its tail. Redmond watched it soar up over the curtain wall with its jesses trailing behind. Then he did the same with the other hawk. Would Emilia and Tal see them fly and know he had been thinking of them?

Windemere

The men emptied the Baron's stables of horses and collected enough from the battlefield so every man, injured or whole, had a mount. Redmond would not leave his injured men behind for Adelaide to torture. Each archer filled his saddlebags with his share of the treasure. That way, those who survived would still be able to profit, and it would make it that much more difficult for the King or Lady Selgrave to reclaim the money if they tried. It also meant his men could be mobile without the need to worry about cumbersome wagons. They had packed what food was left—and there was precious little of that. They would have to scavenge off the land as they rode.

Each man carried one hundred twenty arrows, a bow, a sword, and a shield. Redmond had also seen that at least half of them had a lance, spear, or pike. All of them now wore a mail hauberk and a steel helmet scavenged from the dead.

They hadn't had time to repair the mail shirts that had holes where the bodkin points had torn the rings apart, but that would hardly matter. At least his men were as well armored as the men-at-arms they would face in open country. And he knew pursuit was inevitable.

Redmond strode through the outer ward. He had two more visits to make before he left the castle. One of his men still guarded the dungeon, and he opened the door for Redmond. The dungeon retained the moldy smell mixed with the powerful stink of sweat and human waste. Redmond's boots scraped against the damp stone floor as he descended holding a torch aloft. He let himself into the room where Dacrey was kept.

Dacrey stirred and blinked up at him but didn't try to rise. He was chained to the wall and slouched on a pile of straw. Redmond wrinkled his nose at the unpleasant smell.

"Finally come to gloat, have you?" Dacrey said.

"No," Redmond replied. "I wouldn't waste my time on you. But I thought I should tell you as a matter of honor that we have sold the castle to King Rupert. He has been informed of your treachery, and you will be delivered to Baron Longmire tomorrow."

"That's noble of you," Dacrey said. "Why didn't you kill me with the rest of them?"

"Because I don't kill men who are defeated," Redmond said.

Dacrey scoffed at him. "You're a fool," he said. "Lady Selgrave will have your head before the end."

"Speaking of Lady Selgrave," Redmond said. "What can you tell me about her plans?"

"Ah, I see," Dacrey said. "You're hunting for information you can sell to the King."

"I now have more money than I can spend," Redmond said. "My only interest is in getting my men out safely."

"I don't know anything," Dacrey sneered. He shifted, making his chains rattle.

"Was she planning on dethroning the King?" Redmond asked.

Dacrey peered up at him with a surprised and thoughtful expression.

"She never told me," he said. "She said if I helped her, she would support my claim to Longmire."

"Why Longmire?" Redmond asked.

"Leave me alone," Dacrey said.

"If you help us, I will speak for you to the King and the Baron."

"I don't need your help."

"Okay," Redmond said. "Then, with any luck, we will never meet again."

Redmond closed the door behind him and climbed the stairs, pondering on the ability of the promise of power or wealth to make men and women do terrible things—to betray people who trusted them. He stepped out into the warm evening air and strode toward the keep. He needed to pay one more visit to Baron Otto before leaving the castle.

The man the King tried to smuggle inside disturbed him. One spy like that could have caused a lot of trouble, such as warning the King of their plans to sneak away or leaving signs to lead the King's men to them, poisoning the cistern, or simply opening one of the gates.

All of those potential tragedies had been avoided for now, by the mere luck of wet knee stains. The spy must have dropped from the wagon as it passed behind the rubble of the barbican and waited there, kneeling in the mud, to join the archers who came to unload the wagon. It had not escaped his mind that King Rupert and Baron Dragos could be conspiring together.

As Redmond approached the keep, he remembered the first time he entered there as an unarmed prisoner anxious to save his men. Now he came as a conqueror, ready to flee for his life because he couldn't hold the castle forever.

He found Baron Otto dressed in a long black tunic, reclining before the fire with some ponderous tome he had acquired from somewhere.

"How are you feeling?" Redmond asked.

The Baron glanced at him and grunted. "I'll soon be well enough to go into battle," he said.

"That's encouraging," Redmond said. "Fortunately for us, we will be gone from here tomorrow, and you can haggle with the King for the return of your castle."

Now the Baron looked up. "Tomorrow?" he said.

"Baron Longmire has offered to escort us back to his lands," Redmond said.

Baron Otto sniffed. "Good riddance," he said. "I hope you'll have the honor to leave the homes and shops undamaged. My servants and peasants have done nothing to you."

Redmond smirked. "We don't make war on innocent people," he said. "Nor do we enslave them and send them to die in the mines."

The Baron waved him away. "Leave me in peace. Take your men and get out of my home."

Redmond whirled to leave but glanced over his shoulder at the Baron. "You should know," he said, "that your wife has a secret entrance into the outer ward she has been using to smuggle children to work in your new silver mines."

The Baron scowled.

"And," Redmond continued, "she forced your mason to sneak in and try to open the gates by threatening to kill his wife and children."

The Baron showed no sign of concern, but Redmond thought he had surprised him. "You should consider that she is not working for the same goals you are," Redmond said. "She's using you like she uses everyone else."

"Get out," the Baron said.

"Gladly," Redmond replied and strode from the room.

Dusk had fallen by the time Redmond stepped out of the keep. The air was still warm, but the sky was cloudy. That made for a darker night, which worked to his advantage. His men were already lighting the watch fires and had dismantled the stone wall blocking the traitor's gate.

Redmond found a new horse and checked his gear one last time. Neahl had beaten into him the necessity of being vigilant about his equipment. "The time you don't take care of it," he liked to say, "is the time you'll need it most."

Kamil stalked past carrying an armload of eggs he had pilfered from somewhere.

"What are you doing?" Redmond asked.

Kamil gave him a roguish grin. "I'm cooking up a little surprise just in case something goes wrong with our plans."

"Eggs?" Redmond asked.

"You'll see," Kamil called over his shoulder as he strolled away.

Redmond watched him go, pondering what Jannik had told him.

By the time he finished checking his gear, it was time to set the plans in motion. He ordered runners to set up the decoy sentries and led the rest of the men into the inner ward. The rear sally port had two doors—one with steps for foot soldiers and the other with a slatted ramp for horses. All the horses had cloth tied over their hooves. The men's weapons had been painted or tied with cloth to quiet them and to avoid any reflection that might give away their presence. They needed stealth if they were to escape undetected.

Kamil rode up with his short recurve strung and in a leather case tied to his saddle so he could pull it out quickly. The shapes of several more were wrapped in cloth and tied behind his saddle. Redmond harbored a secret jealousy of Kamil's short bows and the ease with which he used them on horseback.

Most longbow archers carried their bows in their hands and dismounted to shoot. Redmond had learned to shoot his longbow from horseback because he didn't insist on heavy draw weights, but a longbow could be difficult to use from horseback. If he had more time, he might have asked Kamil for a chance to give it a try. But he wasn't sure he could discard the longbow that had served him well for so many years. Maybe he was nostalgic, but now wasn't the time to worry about it.

Kamil glanced up at the keep as if contemplating something. Redmond didn't want to distrust Kamil, but despite his efforts, he couldn't help remembering Jannik's warning.

Windemere

Rollo rode up and signaled that the men were ready. Redmond checked the watch fires on the walls and the silhouettes of the decoy guards. Helmets had been rammed onto the top of sacks filled with straw. Spears and bows had been tied to make them stand upright. If someone were watching closely, they would realize the guards never moved. But if the King remained true to his word, Redmond hoped they would take no notice of it until he was far away.

"Let's go," he said and led his horse toward the sally port. The gate was tall enough to allow a rider to gallop out, but Redmond wanted to be as unobtrusive as possible. He led his horse out onto the hillside and down toward the moat. This was going to be a long night.

Baron Otto Selgrave stood atop his keep hugging close to the shadows as the warm breeze played in his hair. The easterner who shot the odd-shaped bows looked up as if he knew he was there. The man had come in and out of the keep over the last few days, and the Baron had spoken with him on one occasion. If the easterner was looking up at him, maybe he was contemplating their conversation.

Redmond and his men led their horses down the hill and across the moat. They were only dark shapes in the night, but they were moving north. Baron Otto smiled. They were going to ride for Langon then.

Baron Otto placed his hands on the battlements to lean over and peer down at the last of the riders. A man lifted his face up to the Baron and raised a hand. The Baron recognized him. A thrill shivered up his spine. It had worked. His man was now on the inside and traveling with the archers. Together, with his man and that foreign fellow, the scoundrel wouldn't last long. Redmond wouldn't even know until it was too late.

Chapter 20
The Smashed Hedgerow

omeone is out there," Emilia whispered. She clutched a knife in one hand and rolled to a kneeling position from where she had been lying beside the children. Darkness overtook them several miles north of the castle, footsore and hungry. They had eaten a cold meal of dried meat and stale bread before settling down to sleep. Tal assumed the watch, and Emilia was drifting off to sleep when the rustle of some branches jerked her awake.

The day had been warm, and Emilia's clothes, now damp with sweat, still stank of the sewer. The little boy who attached himself to her lay beside her in the tall grass, breathing quietly and rhythmically. He still clutched the carved horse he had taken from the body of the old woman. The other children spread out around them huddled together in little groups, while Walter and his family snuggled up against a boulder.

They selected a hollow for their encampment that had been created by an old cutaway the river carved out of a long, sloping hill in ages past. Upriver, a huge boulder guarded the northern entrance to the hollow and to the south a thick stand of beech and pine concealed them from view. The hill was bare except for the grass. The road ran along the top, but they were well-hidden from unwanted eyes.

Tal rose to his knees and crawled to a boulder that jutted out of the darkness, peering south into the copse of trees. The rustling sound came again, and a dark shape detached itself from one tree to slip to the next. Emilia noted two more shapes slinking through the shadows, heading straight for them. Whoever they were knew they were there.

Emilia's mind raced as the blood pounded in her ears. How could anyone know they were there? They had taken every precaution to move quietly and unseen, and they met no one. Then she remembered. Lady Selgrave knew about the sewer. She probably knew Walter had used it to get into the castle and would have expected someone to use it to escape.

A child tossed in his sleep and gave a cry. The advancing shapes froze or melted into the shadows. Emilia wished she had grabbed some other weapon besides a knife before leaving the castle. Her mouth went dry. The crouching shapes slipped from the trees not fifteen feet away.

Emilia swallowed and tightened her grip on the knife. She wouldn't let them take her or any of the children. Their freedom had been dearly purchased. She wasn't about to let it go without a fight. The shapes of three men loomed over them. Emilia prepared to spring when a smaller shadow leapt from the tangle of bushes along the river. For a moment, Emilia thought it was one of the children. But the slight figure slammed into the men, wielding what looked like sticks.

The slap and smack of something hard striking flesh rang in the darkness, followed by bellows of pain and cursing from their attackers. Tal crouched to scan the area for more attackers. Several loud thwacks sounded, and then the fall of heavy bodies hitting the ground. The slender figure stepped toward them and lowered her hood. Emilia stared. It was a young woman no older than she was, dressed in black with short-cropped hair.

"You need to go," the woman said.

Tal stepped in front of Emilia. "Who are you?" he asked.

"I am called Mara," she said. "Scouts are searching the entire river bank. If you're found, they won't play nice."

Tal glanced at the children. A few of them were still asleep, but most watched them with big, frightened eyes. Walter and Sybil hugged them close.

"Is there a clear path to Langon?" Tal asked. "We need to get out of the country."

"Follow me," Mara said. "I'll take you somewhere you can hide for now."

"How do we know we can trust you?" Emilia asked.

"Redmond trusts me," Mara said.

Hope leapt into Emilia's heart. "Redmond sent you?" she asked.

"Not exactly," Mara said.

"Are they alive?" Emilia asked.

"Yes, " Mara said. "You didn't need to run. They sold the castle to the King and should be riding out with the Baron of Longmire tomorrow."

Emilia was surprised by the surge of relief that warmed her chest. Redmond was still alive. He might still come for her.

"Now, we had better get away from the river," Mara said.

"How did those men know we were here?" Emilia asked.

"The same way I did," Mara said. "I followed your trail and your smell."

Emilia was glad the darkness kept Mara from seeing her cheeks burn. Tal bent to rouse the children, and soon they were traipsing through the night in search of a better hiding place.

The golden blush of morning found Redmond and his men riding hard to the north, following the river. They encountered a few scouts, but his flankers dealt with them. The men and horses were tiring. They needed rest, having led their horses for several hours on foot. The ploy slowed them down, but Redmond hoped it would make it more difficult for their pursuers to find them and discern their direction.

Redmond led his men onto the road that followed the Wind River. They would be able to travel more quickly now. A few more miles, and they would swing west. He wanted the King and Lady Selgrave to believe they intended to head for Langon. He hoped they might find some sign of Emilia and the others, but they hadn't. If he hadn't needed to get his men safely out of Morcia, he would have gone in search of them.

A shout rang out over the pounding of the hooves. Redmond swung around in the saddle. One of his scouts raced toward him. He slowed to let the man catch up.

"An army is approaching from the east on the other side of the river."

"How many?"

Windemere

"No more than a thousand."

Redmond cursed. "How did they find us so quickly?"

"They're riding hard," the scout said. "They'll catch us in less than half an hour."

Redmond signaled for the men to follow, and he veered off the road to the west, riding up and over a green hill. It was sooner than he wanted to leave the road, but he had little choice. Somehow, Lady Selgrave's men had anticipated what they would do, or someone had revealed their plans. That nagging doubt about Kamil returned with a vengeance. The only way an army could have caught them was if they already knew the direction of their escape and kept to the road all night.

The rolling hills passed as the horses pounded through the countryside. Redmond kept his eyes open for any defensible position where his small army would stand a chance against a superior force. At the crest of one of the taller hills, he spied a stone manor. He adjusted his path to come up straight on the manor.

A cry came from the men behind him, and he swung around. The light blue banner of Lady Selgrave fluttered above the hills. Then the riders came into view briefly before Redmond raced down the last hill to the manor. A thick stand of oak and maple pushed up against one side of the manor, which had an austere, hulking appearance. It was built of black stone, with arrow slits along the walls and battlements around the roof. For a moment, he considered bursting into the manor and seizing it for his men's defense, but that would be suicide. Once they went in, they would never get out. He had to find a position that would allow them to defend themselves and escape if the chance presented itself.

A garden with low stone walls and hedges set in geometric patterns branched out on the other side of the manor. Redmond veered toward the spot in the garden where a fountain splashed into a sizeable pool of water. The pool was enclosed in a large square with thick hedges on three sides and a low stone wall on the other. His horse galloped through the tall, dry grass that covered the hillside and leapt over the stone wall. Redmond pulled the horse to a halt and slipped from the saddle.

"Form a square," Redmond called. "Around the fountain. Form a square. Horses on the inside. Injured men, keep them from bolting."

Jannik dropped to the ground beside him, strung his great warbow, and stepped up to the low stone wall. The pursuing riders crested the hill as the last of Redmond's men pelted for the garden.

"Archers ready," Redmond called, as he drew his own bow to his ear. The riders were in range now. "Loose," he called. A volley of arrows jumped into the sky, arcing toward the oncoming riders. By the time the arrows struck home, the riders had covered a good sixty yards. Redmond's men knew what they were about. They aimed low so their arrows bit into the ranks of the enemy. Men screamed. Horses neighed. Riders and horses tumbled down the slope, tripping the horses behind them. The pursuit slowed and descended into chaos as riders tried to avoid the deadly tangle.

"Loose," Redmond called again, and the arrows flew again in a shower of death to slice and punch into the flesh of man and beast. "At will," Redmond called as the rest of his men reached the safety of the wall and hedges. Arrows flew in a scattered, stuttering volley. The riders still on horseback and the new ones who came over the field held up their shields and came on despite the punishment.

"Pikes," Redmond called as the first of the riders raced toward them. A bristling wall of spears thrust over the stone wall. Each pikeman rammed the butt end of his shaft into the ground and stomped his foot on top of it. The horses shied, but a few slammed into the pikes. The pikemen held, and the archers loosed arrows at point-blank range into the milling horses and men.

Jannik drew his bow. He loosed an arrow that punched through a raised shield and into the face of the man that carried it. The man tumbled off the back of his horse.

The warriors seethed about the square, swinging around to each flank, seeking an entrance. But Redmond's men formed a square with the stone wall on one side and thick hedges on the others. Pikemen held the perimeter, while his archers bunched in the middle, sending volley after volley to slam into the enemy. The musky stink of sweating horses and churned earth mingled with the foul, coppery reek of blood and entrails. Horses screamed and reared, surging about the prickly square. Men cursed and roared their battle cries. Steel crashed. Men grunted and cried out, creating the overwhelming cacophony of battle.

One flank bent inward as several riders forced their horses through the hedge. For one horrible moment, Redmond thought the square might collapse, but his men held. The attack stalled as horses and men floundered. A horn sounded over the battle and the riders withdrew, leaving their dead and wounded comrades behind.

Redmond stood panting, trying to assess the extent of the damage to his men. A few staggered back from the line with injuries to their faces and arms, but none had fallen. The mail shirts over the padded gambesons and the steel helms had done their work well. But they couldn't stay here. They would be exposed to crossbow fire when the crossbowmen came up.

"Hey," someone yelled. "What are you doing?"

Redmond spun. A short, round man with a bald head strode toward them. The door to the manor stood open behind him where a woman cowered with several children.

"Get out of here!" The man waved a hand at them. He wore an orange tunic with brown pants and boots with the pointed toes that were becoming the fashion of the rich in some parts of Morcia.

Redmond checked that the riders were not preparing for another attack at that moment before he stepped to meet the man.

"We beg your pardon—" Redmond began.

"I should think so," the man interrupted. "You can't just trample my garden." He glanced at the dead and dying men. "And who is going to care for them?"

"As you can see," Redmond said. "We are under attack and unable to leave at our leisure. As soon as those men leave us be, we will happily be on our way."

"Those are Lady Selgrave's men," the man said. "Are you traitors?"

Redmond took a deep breath. He didn't have time or energy to bandy words with this man. "No," he said. "We're being wrongly pursued because we refused to submit to the injustice of the mines."

The man stepped back.

"You came from Castle Windemere?" he asked, in a low voice that wouldn't carry.

"Yes."

"Is there one called Redmond among you?"

Redmond inspected the man more carefully. Then he glanced around. How could this man know his name? "I am he."

The man cast a glance at the ground so he didn't step in a pool of blood and came to the edge of the hedgerow.

"I have some people here who might belong to you," he said in a barely audible voice.

The man could only mean Emilia and the others. Redmond tried not to show the joy that leapt into his heart. "Are they well?" he asked.

"Yes," the man said. "But they can't stay here. I don't have an army to protect them, and if Baron Otto ever found out..." He let the thought linger in the air between them.

"I know," Redmond said. "Keep to the house with your doors locked. My men won't disturb you, but I can't say the same for Lady Selgrave's. If she finds out you have her servants hiding with you, she will attack. Keep them hidden. We'll take them with us when we're able to leave," Redmond said.

The man's face paled. "Agreed," he said.

"You better get back into the house," Redmond said, "with a show of wanting us to leave."

The man nodded understanding and waved his hands.

"You can't stay here," he shouted. "Get off my land." Then he whirled and hurried to the house.

Redmond watched him disappear into the manor and then faced the hill where the number of soldiers kept increasing. These horsemen didn't seem anxious to make another attempt on Redmond's position.

Rollo stepped up to him. His face was splattered with gore, but he was smiling. "They won't want to try that again," he said.

"When the crossbowmen arrive, they'll come again," Redmond said. "And we have no shelter. We can't stay here."

Rollo glanced at the manor. "The frightened part of me would say to seek refuge in the manor, but the thinking part says if we allow ourselves to be bottled up in there, we won't come out alive."

"I know," Redmond said. "If we can hold on until nightfall, we might be able to slip away." Then he glanced at the horses. Some of them were drinking from the fountain, while others nibbled at the grass and the hedges. "But if we have to endure a shower of crossbow bolts, we could lose our horses."

"We're going to have to detail men with shields to protect them," Rollo said.

"Agreed," Redmond said. "Can you see to that? Some of the injured may be able to help. I'm going to treat those I can."

They spent the next several hours gathering spent arrows and shields from the fallen soldiers and letting the men rest. Like all men accustomed to battle, they were able to sleep wherever they could find a spare patch of ground. Redmond found that most of the wounds had been superficial because the riders couldn't close with his men and because his men were well-protected with the mail armor he had insisted they all wear. He treated them as best he could and then dropped to the ground to rest.

He leaned his back against a tall stone, so he could face the manor. Emilia was in there. He had thought he would never see her again, and the prospect had left him more disheartened than he cared to admit. She was so like Lara—yet so different. But he was being foolish. He was too old for her, and he still needed to know how Lara fared before he could commit to a different path. The King's warning that Coll would be attacked by someone gave more urgency to this idea. Maybe he should go back to Coll. Maybe he could find Neahl and Weyland and warn them. Maybe Lara would let him help her one last time.

Or maybe, he should go with Emilia and Tal into a neighboring kingdom and begin a new life. He had already closed the door on his life in Coll. Why reopen it? With his share of the money, he wouldn't need to work as a mercenary ever again. Perhaps he could retire his bow and join Tal as an apothecary and healer.

Redmond awoke with a start to blink up at the burning sun. Sweat soaked his gambeson, and he wished he could take it and the mail shirt off. The sun now stood well overhead and was dipping toward the west. He scrambled to his feet, concerned that he had slept so long and that it was so late in the afternoon. Kamil stepped over to speak with him.

"Rest well?" he asked.

Redmond grunted. No one rested well on a field of battle.

"What's happening?" he asked.

"Nothing," Kamil said. "They appear to be waiting for something or someone. They've set sentries around us, so we can't break free

211

without giving the alarm."

"The crossbowmen," Redmond said. "They're waiting for the crossbowmen, so they can give cover."

"Perhaps," Kamil said, "but two new banners arrived a few minutes ago. One was red and the other gray. I think they were waiting for the rest of the angry lords to arrive with their men."

"They sent their fastest riders to run us to ground," Redmond said, "so they could bring up the larger force."

Kamil pointed. "Look. They've dismounted. They're forming up."

"To your feet men!" Redmond shouted. "They're coming again. Let's remind them why they withdrew the last time."

He turned to the men with the shields who were prepared to protect the horses. They all held two shields, one in each hand.

"Remember, those horses are our only way out of here," Redmond said.

By their stern faces, it was plain they understood all too well what was at stake.

"Archers," he called. "Aim high at the crossbowmen. We need to remind them that a longbow has the greater range. We must keep them back."

His men assembled at their positions and looked on in grim silence. They knew they would receive no quarter. They had to conquer or die.

"When the footmen approach," Redmond shouted, "send your shafts straight into their faces. We have to hold a few more hours before we'll have the cover of darkness."

The soldiers now on foot advanced down the hill. The line of crossbowmen spread out and came behind them.

"Steady men," Redmond called. "They'll show you no mercy. We stand or fall today. You are fighting for your lives and for your freedom."

The men cheered and beat their weapons against their shields. Redmond's throat went dry as the ranks of soldiers came on. It was an unnerving sight. They were heavily outnumbered. If they survived the next half hour, it would be a miracle.

He glanced around. Should he have tried to make a run for it? No. It would have been suicide. He glanced up at the manor. A face peered out a window. It was Emilia. Warmth spread in his chest, and he raised a hand to her. She placed a palm on the window, and Redmond looked away.

That was another reason he needed to survive this day. If Emilia and Tal were captured, Lady Selgrave would make sure they suffered. They were depending on him, too.

"Archers," Redmond called as the crossbowmen stopped at the extreme range for their weapons and planted their pavises in the ground.

"Aim high," he called. "Rain the arrows down over the top of the shields."

He bent his bow and raised it to an extreme angle.

"Loose," he shouted.

Bowstrings slapped. A hundred arrows jumped into the pale blue sky.

"Again," Redmond yelled.

Another storm of arrows launched upward as the first volley fell among the crossbowmen.

A few men fell, but most of the arrows either missed entirely or stuck fast in the wooden pavises.

"Again," Redmond called.

He didn't want the crossbowmen to get off a concentrated volley before the soldiers coming down the hill were in their way. A few crossbowmen shot their bolts, but most were cowering behind their pavises as the footmen came on.

"Again," Redmond said.

He would get one more volley before he needed to concentrate on the oncoming footmen.

The arrows lanced into the air. There were fewer crossbowmen now, but the pavises protected most of them.

The footmen advanced within twenty paces of their formation. Spears bristled before them, and their mail and steel helmets reflected the afternoon sun.

"Now the footmen," Redmond bellowed.

The archers lowered their aim and loosed. The arrows zipped past the heads of their own pikemen to slam into the oncoming enemy. Most lodged in the enemy's shields, but a few found an unprotected area.

At this range, the needle-sharp bodkins would punch through the mail rings and gambeson and into the flesh beneath. The heavy ash shafts the longbowmen used gave them incredible penetrating power.

Kamil held a dozen arrows in his bow hand and loosed them with such rapidity that Redmond paused to watch him. Kamil continually surprised him with his short recurved bows and the skill with which he used them.

A rain of crossbow bolts cut into his men. Redmond ducked behind a hedge. A few bolts found unprotected places such as faces and thighs, but most slammed into mail or steel helmets. The crossbowmen were so far back their light bolts did little damage.

One plunged into a horse's neck, despite the men shielding them. The horse reared and burst through the hedge to gallop straight into the ranks of the oncoming men. She bowled a few over, but the rest scrambled aside to let her pass.

Jannik's powerful warbow shot his arrows with such force they drove through the shields. The advancing line faltered before the men formed a sufficient shield wall to protect their vitals from the arrows.

"Aim at their legs," Redmond called.

Soon arrows were slamming into unprotected thighs, knees, and shins. The line slowed again, but the injured were quickly replaced by those behind. Another shower of crossbow bolts arced into their square. One struck Redmond so hard in the chest that it knocked the wind out him. For one desperate moment, he thought he had received a mortal wound. But the bolt fell away to reveal several broken rings in his mail and a dent in his gambeson.

When the soldiers had advanced to within ten paces, they charged with a roar that shook the earth.

"Hold your ground!" Redmond called.

Kamil's arrows found exposed eyes and throats. Jannik's punched through mail and armor. Redmond loosed arrow after arrow, but still the men came on.

The extreme ends of the line swung to close in on them from all sides. They hacked and slashed their way through the hedges to be met by a wall of pikes and slashing, stabbing swords. The line stalled at the stone wall and the hedges. The fighting proved fierce and deadly.

Windemere

Redmond dropped his bow and drew his sword as a familiar figure broke through the hedge. He wore the distinctive helm with the bronze flourishes on the noseguard that rose up over the top of the helm.

"Dacrey," Redmond breathed.

The sight of Lord Dacrey among the fighting men gave him pause. Redmond had left him locked in the dungeon, and Baron Dragos of Longmire said he wanted to get his hands on Dacrey. But here he was fully armored. It could only mean one thing—the Baron of Longmire had betrayed them, as well.

Rollo had been right. Longmire never intended on helping them reach safety. Redmond rushed to meet Dacrey as he hacked his way through the hedge.

Dacrey sneered when he recognized Redmond. "You're the man I wanted to meet," Dacrey said.

He lunged at Redmond, but Redmond parried the blow. The sounds of the battle raging around him became a dull, indistinct roar.

"You should know when you are beaten," Dacrey said.

"And you should know when you have met your match," Redmond replied.

He lunged forward with a series of rapid strikes aimed at Dacrey's face. Dacrey stumbled backward, struggling to deflect the blows. They separated as Redmond paused to catch his breath.

"The King says if I bring him your head and his money," Dacrey said, "he'll forgive my indiscretions regarding Lady Adelaide and Baron Otto."

"Does Longmire know you're plotting to steal his land?"

"It's not his land," Dacrey growled.

He sidestepped and slashed at Redmond's legs. Redmond leapt out of the way. Their swords clashed. The blow jarred Redmond's hands. But he slipped to Dacrey's off-side and delivered a ringing blow to his helmet. Dacrey staggered backward.

Redmond tried to exploit the opening, but Dacrey recovered and drove him back.

"Whose land is it?" Redmond asked.

"Mine," Dacrey growled again. "He stole it from my father, and I will get it back."

Dacrey swung at Redmond's head. Redmond raised his sword, but the stroke had been a fake. Dacrey twisted his wrist and slammed the sword into Redmond's side. The blow knocked the wind out of him. He staggered back, bruised and dazed, sure that Dacrey had cracked some ribs.

Without the mail shirt, that strike would have severed him in two. Dacrey elbowed Redmond in the face and raised his sword for the killing blow. Redmond sank to a knee and drove his sword upward under Dacrey's guard into his exposed throat. Dacrey's sword fell to slam against Redmond's helm but without much energy. He staggered backward, clutching his throat as the blood gurgled out. His sword slipped from his hand, and he sank to his knees.

The roar of battle rushed back into Redmond's ears as Dacrey slumped to the ground, his bronze-lined helmet covered in droplets of his own blood.

Emilia peered through the window of the manor with her heart in her throat as Redmond engaged Dacrey. The battle surged around the square formation Redmond had established. The soldiers came on and on. How would any of Redmond's men survive?

"We have to help them," she said. She spun to face Tal and Mara, who watched over her shoulder. Walter, his wife, and the children huddled together in a back corner.

"We can't do anything from here," Tal said, "or Lady Selgrave will send her men into the manor."

"We can't just watch them get slaughtered," Emilia insisted.

"I'm a healer now," Tal said.

Emilia spun on him. "I admire your wish to do no more harm," she said. "But sometimes you have to. Some things are worth fighting and dying for. I'm worth defending," she said. She jabbed a finger toward the children. "They're worth defending. You're going to have to choose sometime if your conscience and principles are more important than the lives of your family and friends."

Tal bowed his head. Emilia cringed. She had chastised her father. He had given up everything to be there for her when she was most vulnerable. She lifted his hand into hers.

"I'm sorry," she said.

Windemere

Tal raised his head. A tear glistened on his cheek. "You're right," he said.

Mara stirred. "I might as well tell you," she said. "Lady Selgrave sent me to find you and bring you to her."

Tal stepped back from her, and Emilia straightened. Emilia had started to like Mara, even though she didn't know anything about her.

Mara raised her hands. "Relax," she said. "I've obviously decided not to do that." She gestured to the window. "It didn't occur to me that Redmond would appear in the only safe place we could find within fifty miles." She scratched at her neck. "But I have an idea, and I'm going need you two to help me."

Tal narrowed his eyes at her. "And what help might you require?" he asked.

"Follow me," Mara said.

Chapter 21
Flight

The battle surged around Redmond as he and his men struggled to hold back the tide of soldiers surging about their tiny square. A warm wind kicked up, stirring and mixing the odors of death, sweat, and churned earth.

Jannik hammered at any head or body part that pushed through the hedge. Rollo held his ground with a short sword in one hand and dagger in the other. Kamil discarded his bow and used a curved blade to hack and slice at weak places in armor.

Redmond's men were tiring. They couldn't last. Not outnumbered and surrounded like they were. They edged back from the wall and hedge, giving ground, closing in upon their own lines.

A new cry erupted from the soldiers still on the hill. Redmond hacked at an arm that bore a sword and spun to see what the new threat was. Clouds of smoke billowed up on the sides and in back of the army. Orange flames jumped about as the smell of burning grass drifted down to them. A rider in a black cloak bearing a torch swept over the grassland, bending low to ignite the dry grass. A long line of orange flame trailed out behind him as if he were some kind of legend sprung to life. Redmond could hardly believe what he was seeing.

Another rider galloped between the crossbowmen on the hill and the footmen attacking Redmond's formation. A line of flickering flames erupted behind the rider. Several crossbowmen shot bolts at him, but he swept on.

The cries grew louder. The men attacking his formation paused. When they realized that a fire now separated them and their reinforcements, they hesitated and slowed their attack, uncertain what to do. Redmond raced to the men protecting the horses.

"Your bows," he yelled. "Your bows."

The crossbowmen would be too preoccupied now to loose any volleys. Redmond's men snatched up their weapons and shot arrows into the faces and backs of the soldiers who now concentrated on finding a means of escaping the approaching flames. The attackers broke and fled toward the back of the manor, away from the rolling flames and the biting arrows.

Redmond's men gave a half-hearted cheer. Many sank to their knees, trembling with exhaustion, still unaware of what had saved them. The horses jostled each other as they smelled the smoke.

Redmond shouted orders. "Gather the horses in the fountain," he called, "and splash water over everything."

The grass had been thoroughly trampled around the wall and the hedges, but he couldn't take the chance that it wouldn't catch. A few of the men continued to rain arrows into the retreating army while those who were able slipped off their helmets, dipped them in the pool, and threw water over the grass all around their formation.

The roar of the fire reached Redmond's ears as the wind whipped it toward the manor. Whoever started the fire might have saved them from death on the point of a spear or a sword only to broil them in the hungry flames now rolling down the hill toward them. The horrible greasy smell of roasting flesh swept before the wind as the fire reached the bodies of the dead and dying. Screams of agony filled the air. Redmond's stomach tightened at the smell. He swallowed and blinked, trying to keep in the rising sickness. Fire was a horrible weapon, though it had saved them several times over the last few days.

The fire scorched the green lawn in front of the manor. It blazed up to the stone wall spitting hungrily, but the water and the trampled grass provided little fuel. The heat became unbearable as the flames swept around them into the garden. His men tossed helmets of water at the places where the fire caught the hedges or over their own heads until the air was thick with steam, smoke, and ash. Eventually, the flame lost its biting fury.

The green foliage of the garden didn't burn well or hot, and the fire sputtered and went out after leaving long, black scars through the once-green and lovely garden. Horror at the scene mingled with an overwhelming sense of relief. Against all the odds, they had survived.

Soldiers staggered past Emilia as she swung around behind the manor. They took no notice of her in their haste to escape the flames. She had discarded her torch after making the mad dash behind the army. Clouds of gray smoke billowed into the sky. The screams of dying men and horses split the air. She didn't want to see them die, but she had to know if Redmond and his men had survived.

She slipped from the saddle, crept around the side of the manor, and pressed against the cool, rough stone. The air was thick with greasy smoke and mist, but Redmond stood beside the fountain with his helmet in his hands, staring up the hill to where the remains of Lady Adelaide's army had retreated in disarray. Somehow, many of them had escaped through the flames.

Emilia stepped around the wall and sprinted through the choking smoke. Redmond faced her. Soot and sweat streaked his face. He smiled as she pushed through the hedge and threw her arms around his neck. The joy at seeing him alive and happy to see her forced a sob from her throat. Redmond embraced her briefly and then pushed her gently away with a groan of pain.

"My ribs," he said, putting a protective hand over them.

"I never thought I would see you again," Emilia said.

"Was that you?" he pointed toward the scorched hillside.

Emilia wiped at the tear that trickled down her cheek and nodded. "It was Mara's idea."

Shock swept across Redmond's face and then he laughed. "That girl seems to be everywhere," he said. "Where's Tal?"

Emilia gestured to the manor. "He might not be back yet," she said. "He took the longest route behind the armies."

Redmond glanced up at the sky. "A few more hours," he said, "and we can find a way out of here." He faced Emilia. "You'll come with us, won't you?"

Emilia's heart swelled. "Of course," she said.

"What about the children?"

Emilia frowned. "Walter and his wife said they would care for them. The lord of the manor already agreed to hide them until the army leaves."

"Good," Redmond said. "We'd better see to our injured men."

An hour later, a white flag of parley fluttered on the crest of the hill, and a lone rider walked his horse over the blackened hillside.

Redmond had placed scouts around his formation to give them advanced warning of another attack, especially from the woods on the other side of the manor. The afternoon had been quiet as the sun sank toward the western horizon. Redmond could hardly believe he and his men were still alive. He waited for the rider to approach within hailing distance and then signaled for him to stop.

"Do you wish to surrender?" Redmond called.

A ripple of laughter passed through his men.

"Your arrogance will get you no further," the voice called back. Redmond recognized it as belonging to Baron Otto.

"Our arrogance has defeated your armies thrice now," Redmond said. "You should learn the lesson and leave us be."

"I offer you one last chance," Baron Otto said. "Surrender now, and I will let you live."

"You will forgive me if I don't trust you or your word," Redmond said.

"You have little choice," Baron Otto said. "You have fought well, but it is only a matter of time. Luck will desert you in the end."

"But strength and skill will not," Redmond said. "We know your intentions and the cunning and treachery of your foul wife. Let us be, and we'll leave your lands for good."

"So be it," Baron Otto said. "Before the sun sets tomorrow, I will have your heads on the end of my pikes."

"Each head will cost you thirty," Redmond said.

Baron Otto whirled and galloped back up the hill.

"You have a way of making lords and ladies dislike you," Kamil observed.

Redmond chuckled. "It's the southern heat," he said. "It seems to affect their brains."

Jannik strolled up to him with his sledgehammer over his shoulder. His face was lined with streaks of black, and he had sustained a sizeable cut on the side of his head.

"And I was just starting to have fun," he said.

"Well, I'm sure you'll have plenty of chances to play before we reach the coast," Redmond said.

Jannik patted his sledgehammer. "Me and Bessie will always be ready."

Watch fires flickered all around them as the gray twilight descended into hazy darkness. Redmond kept his men low and quiet for the last few hours of the day to give them rest and to deceive the Baron that he intended to stay on ground that had proven strong for them. Now that the cover of night descended, he set his plans into motion. His men packed their gear and prepared to ride.

Redmond strode to the manor door and knocked. Tal yanked it open and ushered him in.

"It's nearly time to go," Redmond said.

He handed the owner of the manor a bag filled with gold coins. "This should help pay for the damage we've done," he said.

The man refused to take it. "I'm sorry I couldn't do more," he said.

"Please," Redmond insisted. "It comes from the sale of the castle. At least some of that money ought to do some good here in the King's own lands."

The man considered. "All right." He took the bag, testing its weight.

Redmond handed another bag of coins to Walter.

"I don't know if we'll ever meet again," Redmond said. "But you're a brave man, and you deserve better. This might help you set up trade somewhere else. I would go far from here if I were you."

Walter took the bag. "Thank you," he said.

Most of the children clustered around Walter and Sybil. But the little boy that had attached himself to Emilia clung to her neck as if he understood she was going to leave him. Redmond stepped back to the lord of the manor. He stood a full head taller than the balding man.

"Thank you for taking them in," he said.

"I lost my father to Baron Otto," the man said. "It was the least I could do."

Windemere

Redmond faced Walter. "I wish you all the best," he said. "I would ask you to come with us, but it would be more dangerous than leaving you behind."

"We'll take the children to Arras," Walter said. "We should be safe there."

"I hope so," Redmond said. Then he turned to Emilia. "It's time." Emilia held the child close to her bosom. "I'll miss you," she whispered. A tear glistened on her cheek.

"Momma," the boy said.

Emilia's eyes opened wide and a sob escaped her throat. She squeezed the child. "I have to go," she said. "Walter and Sybil will take care of you now." She set the child down, but he clung to her leg.

"Momma," he said again.

Emilia patted him on the head and looked pleadingly at Redmond. He swept the boy up into his arms. "It's all right, little man," he said. "Momma has to go away for a while." He handed the child to Sibyl. The child stretched his chubby arms for Emilia and began to cry.

Emilia sniffled and hurried out the door without another word. Redmond and Tal followed her out. They found the men ready to depart. Their horses' hooves had been covered in cloth and the bridles had been wrapped so they wouldn't jingle. The soot from the fire gave them ample material to blacken their faces and hands.

Redmond signaled to Kamil. "Let's go," he said.

The two of them slipped into the darkness. Now was Kamil's chance to show his true loyalties. If Jannik was right about him, Kamil could easily betray them to the Baron's men. Redmond wouldn't believe it of him until he saw it. Still, he knew he was taking a risk letting Kamil go with him. Just to be sure, he sent Rollo behind Kamil to keep an eye on him.

Redmond took the left flank as he crept to the edge of the garden. The dark shapes of guards paced on the edge of the light cast by their watch fires. He would have to eliminate two of them in rapid succession, or they might sound the alarm.

The firelight would blind the men to the darker shadows of the night, and Redmond used that advantage to creep on his belly across the open space to the nearest fire. He waited until the man turned his back to peer away from the encampment and then straightened.

He leapt on the man and dragged his knife across his throat. His blade slipped across an aventail of mail that protected his throat from just such an attack. The man gave a muffled cry through the hand Redmond clamped over his mouth. Redmond jerked the aventail up and plunged his blade into the man's throat. He let him down quietly only to find that the nearest guard was striding around his fire to get a better view of the commotion. Redmond crouched, trying to decide how best to approach the man before he gave the alarm when a slight figure loomed up behind the guard. A few solid whacks sounded, and the man dropped to the ground like a sack of grain. Mara strode toward Redmond.

"It's a good thing us women are around to save you," Mara whispered.

Redmond smirked at her and headed back toward the camp. They had only a few minutes before the guards would be discovered. Kamil strolled in smiling.

"It's like the good old days," he said.

Redmond snorted. Kamil found pleasure in the oddest things. Rollo appeared behind him and shook his head to Redmond to indicate that he had seen nothing to suggest Kamil had betrayed them. Redmond scowled, but he didn't have time to puzzle out his suspicions.

"Lead the horses until we're through the gap," Redmond said. His band had been thinned by the engagement, so there were spare horses for Tal and Emilia.

It took the better part of half an hour for the men to pass through the lines. Redmond led them on for another half mile on foot before they mounted and galloped over the rolling hill country toward the lake and the coast beyond.

Lady Selgrave stood on the blackened hillside gazing down on the garden next to the manor. The fountain had ceased to flow, choked with soot and the bodies of the dead. The hedges and flowers had been trampled. Bodies and armor lay scattered about over the scorched earth and in piles in front of the stone wall. The square where she had trapped Redmond and his men stood empty, save for the bodies of the dead stretched out in awkward postures. Some still moved as the crows and ravens hopped among them. Baron Otto had sent men to search the field for the injured who had survived the fire and to begin the grizzly work of clearing them from the battlefield.

The rich aroma of burned grass filled her nostrils as the warm wind played with her green dress. Once again, Redmond had escaped her. He and his men had slipped away into the night. Mara had not been seen, and Emilia and Tal had disappeared. Lady Selgrave couldn't remember a time when everything had gone so wrong.

A few days ago, she and Baron Otto had been poised to force the King to the bargaining table and to assert the power of the nobility to control the exchequer. She had been weakening him and his allies at every opportunity so that when she was ready to make her move all the cards would fall into place. But now her army lay shattered on two battlefields. The King was asserting his authority, and, after the deal she had made to support his new head tax, it would be months or years before she would be in a position to make her play.

She ground her teeth in rage. Redmond would pay. Someday, she would make him pay for what he had done to her. Baron Otto rode up beside her to watch his men pick through the corpses.

"Don't worry," he said. "My man is still with him."

Lady Selgrave shielded her eyes from the morning sun as she glanced up at him. "How do you know he wasn't killed in the battle?" she asked.

Baron Otto snorted. "Not Lyle. He has never failed me. He probably feigned an injury to avoid the worst of the fighting. He'll get Redmond before the end."

The Baron paused and smiled down at her. "Besides, I have planted a seed that I'm convinced will bear fruit before the end."

"Well that didn't work," Rollo said as they paused to watch the rider in orange vanish over the hill behind them. It was a scout from Cassel, which was the home of one of the lords Lady Selgrave had poisoned. Redmond hadn't seen those colors in any of their previous battles, which meant this army had never been at Windemere. It must have been swinging wide to cut them off before they had even left the castle. That was the only way they could have ridden ahead of them. But how had they known? Or was it just a gamble?

Redmond and his men had ridden hard for three days as he led them through the rolling hills on the borders of the Barony of Longmire. Long Lake now stretched out to their left as they worked their way toward the northern end before swinging west to the sea and the port at Harrowden.

"If they catch us on the open plain," Kamil said, "it will go hard for us."

Redmond glanced at the lake below them. He and his men had fought skirmishes with Baron Selgrave's scouts in these hills weeks before.

"The bridge," he said.

Redmond led his men this way partly because he wanted the cover of the hills to conceal their movements, but also because he had known that if anyone followed him, he would have options in how to deal with them. The track they now followed skirted the edge of the lake and crossed a wide chasm cut by a stream that poured from the wooded slopes above.

"Yes," Kamil said. "Make your weakness your strength."

Jannik scowled at him. "You spend too much time thinking in riddles," he said. Then he patted the handle of his big sledgehammer. "Bessie and I prefer to wade into the fray."

"There'll be plenty of time for that," Redmond said. "If we drop the bridge, they'll have to go around. It'll delay them by at least two days."

"That's not as much fun," Jannik said.

Rollo harrumphed. "Yes," he said, "but it keeps your ugly head attached to your neck for a few more days."

Jannik smirked. "Suit yourself."

In another hour, they reached the narrow bridge. The jagged walls of the chasm fell away to a ribbon of white water far below. Gnarled oaks and pines clung to the rocky soil. The rich scent of moist earth lifted on the spray boiling from the long waterfall to their right. Green moss clung to everything within reach of the mist. This was the only crossing for miles.

Redmond hastened his men across before releasing Jannik and his big sledgehammer on the wooden supports of the bridge. His men scattered out along the narrow trail to rest as the thud of the ham-

Windemere

mer echoed in the canyon. The bridge sagged to one side when an arrow slammed into the railing beside Jannik's head. He paused to stare at it.

"Let's go," Redmond shouted to his men as he scrambled to remount. Jannik continued hammering at the supports.

Kamil had already mounted and loosed an arrow as a party of orange-clad riders galloped onto the trail behind them. The arrow buried itself in a horse's neck. It reared, spilling its rider onto the trail.

"Give Jannik cover," Redmond said as he nocked an arrow and loosed. They had to get that bridge down or they would be fighting a running battle all the way to Harrowden.

The riders paused as the injured horse bucked and flailed about. Redmond's arrow found its mark, and the remaining riders whirled to escape behind the cover of the hillside.

"Come on," Redmond shouted to Jannik. "That's good enough."

Redmond rode his horse behind a great pine tree as he studied their back trail. There would be more of them.

A flash of orange on the bluffs above the bridge caught his attention. An archer rose to one knee and drew.

"Down," Redmond shouted as he kicked his horse toward Jannik.

He loosed an arrow, but his shot flew wide in his haste. The archer flinched to avoid it, and Jannik glanced up as the archer released his string. The arrow leapt from the bow in a flash of white goose feathers.

A surge of panic burned in Redmond's throat. Jannik was about to die. As if by command, Jannik paused in his hammering to watch the arrow streaking toward him. Redmond snapped a hurried shot at the arrow in the wild hope he might be able to hit an arrow in flight a second time. The two arrows passed each other in the air.

Jannik didn't stir as if he had frozen in terror. What was the matter with him?

The arrow zipped past his face. Redmond stared as a thin red line dribbled blood down Jannik's cheek.

Kamil loosed an arrow, and the archer on the bluff tumbled to the rocks below.

"Now!" Redmond shouted.

Jannik gave the bridge one final blow, which sent it crashing into the canyon, before he scrambled over the rocks to his horse. Arrows began to click and bounce against the stones around them. A few slammed into the trunks of trees. Jannik raced after the rest of his men while Redmond and Kamil loosed several more arrows to give them cover before dashing down the trail.

"What's the matter with you?" Redmond shouted when he caught up with Jannik. "Do you have a death wish?"

Jannik scowled at him. "I didn't know which way to move so I took my chances and stayed put."

Fighting men knew they risked being killed or maimed every time they went into battle. This constant tension gave them a certain amount of fatalism when confronting danger. It could also give them nerves of steel. How many men could have stood there and faced an onrushing arrow without flinching?

"Sometimes," Redmond said, "I get the feeling you like to see how close you can come to dying."

"I almost moved," Jannik said with a shrug, "into the arrow."

"They're herding us," Rollo said as the last of the injured men came in from a skirmish with a new band of soldiers.

Redmond nodded to him. "Pigeons," he mumbled. Redmond and his men had forded the Wolf River and skirted the village on the northern end of the lake before setting out across the plains that rolled on toward the coast. Fields interspersed with pastures in a confusing network of hedges and stone walls that had to be navigated. Dark clouds formed on the western horizon, promising some relief from the constant heat of the sun, but they would also bring rain that could slow them down and soak their bowstrings. Their scouts had already fought several skirmishes with new bands that had been swinging around in an attempt to flank them.

Rollo glanced at Redmond as if he had lost his reason.

"Lady Selgrave's pigeons," Redmond said.

Rollo smirked. "No. I think it was warriors that attacked our men, not her pigeons."

Redmond didn't bother to respond to the taunt.

"Those scouting parties could only be here," he said, "if they had prior warning and set out long before we left Windemere. The mountains didn't slow us down that much. She's using her pigeons to communicate with them or someone is leading them."

"Like I said," Rollo replied. "They're herding us like sheep."

Redmond kicked his horse into a trot. Three armies approached from the north and the south, as well as from behind.

"They want to trap us with our backs to the sea," Redmond said. He knew how dangerous their situation was, yet they had no choice but to run. To the west was the sea and their only hope of escape.

Evening of the seventh day found them riding down a sand dune onto the long beach that led northward to Harrowden. Gulls soared overhead. Their cries rang over the soft murmur of the waves that lapped at the pebble-strewn beach. Bunches of seagrass clung to the sandy soil, desperately seeking to keep it from sliding into the sea. The smell of fish filled the air. Far across the bay, tiny lights from the city of Helder twinkled in the distance. With Stennack Bay on their left, they could ride north without fear of attack from that quarter at least.

Redmond pulled them into a wide alcove above the high tide with a steep cliff rising far above them. A pool of water caught a rivulet that seeped from the rock. There was plenty of grass for the horses to crop. They had run out of grain days ago. The horses would not be able to subsist on grass alone for long. Redmond permitted his men small cooking fires to prepare their first warm meal since they had left Castle Windemere because their light would be shielded from enemy eyes by the sandy rise.

He slid from his saddle and stepped around to caress his horse's cheek. His ribs still ached from the blow Dacrey had given him, but he was on the mend. Exhausted men and horses set about preparing for the night.

Rollo dropped from his saddle beside him. "One more day and we should be at Harrowden," he said.

"Maybe," Redmond said. "If they don't trap us before then."

"What's bothering you?" Rollo asked.

"How did they catch us so quickly on the Wind River?"

Rollo considered. "Well, once they knew we were headed north, all they had to do was take the road to cut us off."

Redmond was shaking his head before Rollo finished. He stepped around to undo the girth strap. "We should have had six or seven hours' head start," Redmond said. "And since the chasm, they have been hot on our trail, like they were being led."

Rollo pondered. "You think one of our men is betraying us?"

"I think so," Redmond said. He glanced around to make sure he was not overheard. "Jannik suspects Kamil."

Rollo smiled in disbelief and then let the smile fade from his face as he saw that Redmond was serious.

Emilia and Tal approached, followed by Kamil and Jannik.

"Feels like a picnic," Jannik said.

Emilia grimaced at him. "Feels like my backside's burning, and my legs are stiff as fire irons."

Kamil dismounted. "Don't you ever take this girl riding?" he asked Tal.

Tal flipped the reins over his horse's neck. "Not much opportunity for that when you're an apothecary."

Kamil wiggled his eyebrows at Emilia and grinned at her. "I know some stretches that will make all the pain go away." He rubbed his hands together.

Emilia eyed him warily. "I don't trust you," she said.

"Nor should you," Kamil replied.

"I've got some salve that will help," Tal offered.

"Him I trust," Emilia said, pointing at her father.

Kamil laughed and ambled over to care for his horse. Redmond exchanged a glance with Rollo and slipped the saddle and blanket from his horse's back. He had instructed his men to remove the saddles each night, brush the horses, and give them an hour to browse without the saddles. Before they slept, they always saddled the animals and packed their gear in case they needed to make a hasty getaway.

Redmond watched his men. That nagging doubt kept playing at him. One or two had joined them from the prisons in the castle, but they all fought well and had no reason to love the Baron of Windemere. The rest he had handpicked to come south with him. None of them would betray their friends—or would they? If Jannik was right about Kamil, Redmond would have to do something about it. If Jannik was wrong, then it could be any of his men. Collectively, they carried 200,000 pieces of gold. A man might be tempted to betray his friends for far less. Redmond left his horse to graze beside the pond while he strolled among his men—partly to stretch his legs, partly to see if he could find any reason for the suspicion that troubled him.

A group of the men had gathered to pry limpets and mussels from the rocks. Apparently, they had grown weary of the stale bread, dried meat, and hard cheese that had become their daily fare. Some men played at cards while others rolled dice in a wooden bowl.

Goosebumps raised on Redmond's arms, and he experienced that weird sensation that someone was watching him. Of course, that was ridiculous. With over one hundred men settling in for the night around him, someone was probably looking at him. Then why did he sense evil intent and danger? He had learned long ago not to discount his instincts, even when he didn't understand them.

Redmond tried not to react. Instead, he bent and picked up a stone from the beach. As he did so, he glanced behind him. A man spun away and melted into the crowd. Redmond hurried back the way he had come, thinking he might recognize the man, but it was now too dark for him to see anything distinctly. He returned to the fire where Emilia and Kamil were debating the correct method of boiling the huge pot of periwinkles they had gathered.

"I tell you," Kamil insisted, "it leaves them fresher and more savory if you wait until the water is boiling to throw them in. Let them simmer for about five minutes, and they come out tender and tasty."

"But," Emilia countered, "if you don't cook them thoroughly, they'll make you sick."

"Right now," Jannik said, "all I care about is getting them into my stomach to lay alongside that nasty, moldy cheese I just ate."

Kamil threw up his hands. "Ah, you westerners have no refinement," he said and retreated to the fire he had started a few feet away.

Redmond crisscrossed his legs as he settled to the ground and tried to eat when the smell of sulfur reached him. He grimaced at Kamil. "You call that refined cooking?" he said.

Kamil gestured for him to join him. Redmond scooted over as Kamil stirred a bubbling brew that smelled awful.

"I told you I was cooking up something," Kamil said.

Redmond noted the pile of eggs Kamil had collected at the castle. How he had managed to transport them all this way without breaking them Redmond would never know. Each egg had a hole in the top and the bottom.

"If you want fire that will cling to anything and be difficult to put out," he explained, "you just mix a bit of pine resin, quicklime, sulfur, charcoal, and saltpeter."

Redmond nodded.

"You want it to be runny, so it will expand when it's lit. This isn't like your regular fire arrow. It's meant to burn even if they pour water on it. It will cling to anything it touches."

"And the eggs?" Redmond asked.

Kamil handed him one. It was hollow. He placed a small plug in the bottom.

"Hold this," he said. He inserted a tiny funnel made from birch bark into the top opening, lifted the pot of the stinking liquid, and poured its contents into the funnel. When he finished, he stuffed a wooden plug into the opening and sealed it with wax. Then he pulled out several copper cones filled with dried grass. He packed each egg carefully into the cones and placed them in his saddlebags.

"I'm still trying to figure out how that works," Redmond said.

Kamil held up a copper cone and an arrow with no point on it. "Just tie this arrow to the bowstring and place the egg and dry grass in the cone. When it's time to shoot, you light the grass on fire, attach it to the shaft and shoot."

"It works?" Redmond asked.

"Of course," Kamil said. "I'll show you."

Redmond studied Kamil as he packed the cones. The man did not have the feel of someone who would betray his friends.

"Can I ask you a difficult question?" Redmond said.

"Hmm?" Kamil grunted but didn't look at him.

"How would a man know if his friends had betrayed him?"

Kamil stopped what he was doing and turned his head slowly to peer at Redmond. His lips pinched tight. He set down the half-packed cone as if to free his hands. Redmond tensed. Had he judged incorrectly? Had Jannik been right?

"You are referring to the fact that we have been found twice and that our enemies seem to be driving us?"

Redmond nodded.

Kamil pulled at his wispy beard as he studied Redmond.

"A wise man makes contingency plans," Kamil said, "so if one path is broken, he may have others to choose from."

He glanced down at Redmond's hand, which had crept toward the hilt of his dagger. Then he cocked his head to the side with a curious expression on his face.

Chapter 22
The Archers of Windemere

hey rode out long before dawn, keeping their horses at a steady canter. Emilia ached from head to toe. She tried to remember what it was like to exist without pain. The heavy mail shirt Redmond insisted that she wear chafed her neck despite the hot gambeson she wore underneath. A short sword slapped at her thigh even though she didn't know how to use one, and she held a long spear in her hand. The helmet banged against the back of her neck. Why couldn't they ever find one that fit her?

Did all men have such big heads? Maybe some just had inflated egos. A shield bounced against her back from the strap that crossed her chest. She had never considered how much gear a warrior had to carry. Being a falconer was far simpler and far more comfortable.

Her father rode beside her, arrayed in the same outfit. She hadn't seen him dressed for war since she was a small child, and she had forgotten how imposing he could be.

She had spent the last several days trying to forget the child who had called her "Momma," but his words left a peculiar ache in her chest that gnawed at her. Her thoughts constantly strayed to him and the other children. Had she done the right thing in leaving them behind? Would they be safe?

Kamil tried to take her mind off her fears by teaching her how to use the spear and the bow when they camped. She happily accepted his offer until the stiffness set in. Last night, she could hardly walk, let alone practice. Her father's salve helped, but it had been difficult to find a place where she could have enough privacy to apply it. A steady rain drizzled from the sky, and Redmond called the army to

233

a halt.

"Unstring your bows and put the strings under your helmets," he said. "If we have to fight, we want dry strings."

None of the men grumbled at this because they respected Redmond and knew he was right. Kamil had given Emilia her short bow again, which she carried in a sheath tied to her saddle on the left side. The quiver of arrows hung on the right. Emilia unstrung the bow and placed the string under her helmet before she rode on.

The rain was a nuisance, but at least it held off some of the heat. She glanced at her mail shirt and clicked her tongue in disgust. It would rust before long. She was going to have to clean it and oil it once they reached safety.

Gray clouds hung low in the sky, transforming the ocean into a steel-gray color that was strangely beautiful. Gulls cried overhead. Brown cormorants with orange beaks nested on the rocky bluffs. The whole world compressed itself into this peaceful scene. Emilia could almost believe everything would be all right—that they would escape and Redmond would go with them to some foreign city where they could begin new lives as free people.

Emilia grew up knowing she would remain an indebted servant to the Selgraves until Baron Selgrave sold her or until she died. To be free of him, at last, left her with a bittersweet sensation. She relished her freedom to go where she wanted, to marry whom she pleased. But she also missed the familiar surroundings of the castle and the joy of training the hawks. Her life might have been far worse. Her father had protected her from the hard, menial labor and the advances of unscrupulous men. Other girls her age had not been so lucky. But now she was free—really free. And yet, beyond her hopes that Redmond might choose to stay with her, she had no idea what she was going to do with the rest of her life.

The sound of pounding of hooves broke through her thoughts. A rider paused at the crest of the long sloping hill to their right and then urged his horse down it toward Redmond, who signaled the company to a halt. The messenger was one of the scouts he had sent out that morning.

The man reined his horse up before Redmond. "A detachment of Lord Tyron's troops are just over the rise," he said. "They're riding like they know where to intercept us."

Windemere

"How long?" Redmond asked.

"Maybe fifteen minutes."

Redmond cursed and stood in the saddle to survey the terrain around them.

"They'll have the high ground," Rollo said as he gazed up the hill. "The horses won't be much use fighting up that."

The hill had a bank about three feet high where the ocean waves had nibbled away at the land. Then it climbed in a steady slope to a rocky crest. On either side, bluffs of gray stone streaked dark with rain loomed through the morning haze. The hill was narrow enough that their little army could spread across the bottom. The attacking army would be forced to descend through that gap.

"They'll have to come down here," Kamil said. "You won't find a better place."

"Pikemen to the cutaway," Redmond yelled. "Archers, I want two lines behind the pikemen. Space yourselves out."

The men dismounted, and the horses were led to the edge of the lapping sea to keep them out of the way. Emilia grabbed her bow, but Tal shook his head and motioned for her to put it back.

"Take the spear," he said. "You'll stand right behind me in the line. You take care of anyone who gets past me."

Emilia nodded and tried to swallow, but her mouth was dry. She hadn't done so well in her last attempt at playing soldier. She had hoped she might escape without having to do it again before she had some real training.

The drizzle of rain stopped. The clouds overhead thinned, as if the heavens paused to watch the battle. Kamil slipped away to the cover of the rocks and bent to build a fire. Emilia watched for a minute. Did he think he would have time for a cup of his fine tea or something?

The sound of thousands of pounding hooves filled the air. She faced the hill. Her hands gripped the shaft of the spear until her fingers went numb.

Redmond's men were settling into their positions when the first of the horsemen crested the hill. They reined in their mounts and whirled away. Then a line of them appeared, horses blowing, hooves stomping. They lowered their lances.

"Here they come," Redmond called. "Aim low. Bring down the

horses."

The riders advanced, kicking up a spray of rock and debris that cascaded down the slope in front of them. The occasional rock broke loose and tumbled down the hill to slam into the shields the pikemen had strapped to their arms.

Emilia held her spear ready with both gloved hands. The straps of her teardrop shield pinched her arm. It was cumbersome and heavy, but Tal insisted she use it.

"It'll save your life," he said.

"Ready," Redmond called.

The double line of archers bent their bows.

"Loose."

White goose feathers streaked upward, distinct against the gray sky and the green hillside. Horses reared. Some fell. Others broke ranks and galloped down the hill straight at them. Jannik's great warbow brought them down.

They and their riders tumbled down in an avalanche of loose stone and soil. Volleys bit into the oncoming men. Decimating their ranks. Tearing flesh. Punching through mail shirts. Quivering in shields. Some of the surviving horsemen kicked their horses down the hill, lowering their lances. The horses leapt over the line as their riders tried to spear the men below them.

Pikes slammed into the horses' chests and bellies. The momentum of the charge carried them over the heads of Redmond's men, dragging the pikes with them. The archers behind the pikemen broke ranks to let them pass through, then wheeled to deal with the survivors.

Unhorsed soldiers staggered down the hill to hack away at the pikes thrust at them from the front of the line. One hammered Tal's spear out of the way and raised his sword, but Emilia's spear stabbed him in the face.

He screamed and swung the sword wildly before Tal recovered and drove his spear into the man's belly. Bile choked Emilia. Her stomach threatened to heave. Then the mass of the enemy arrived, and the melee surged around her.

That peculiar sound and smell of battle settled over Emilia. Screams of agony mingled with battle cries, the crashing of steel, the grunts and groans of struggling men, and the hollow thump of blows on mail-covered bodies. Gore stained the hillside and dribbled over the cutaway to pool at their feet.

Emilia jabbed and thrust, desperate to keep her father safe. To her left, a group of soldiers broke through the line. She turned as a man in a brown tunic rushed the archers behind her.

She fell to her knee, planted the shaft in the sand the way Kamil had taught her, and presented it at the man's chest. The man rammed himself onto the spear, but his mail shirt protected him from the worst of the blow. He swatted the shaft away with his sword and leapt across the distance separating them.

His sword slammed into Emilia's shield, sending a painful jolt through her arm and into her shoulder. By then, the archers had recognized their danger and spun to face him. He delivered a terrible blow to the helmet of the man on her right, and he fell to the sand. Emilia stabbed at the soldier's unprotected knee. The spear scraped against bone. The man bellowed, and the archer on her left dispatched him with a vicious thrust.

Trembling and panting, Emilia whirled back to the battle. The attack washed up on the wall of Redmond's defenses and broke. Those still on horseback retreated back up the hill.

Archers and pikemen rushed out to dispatch any of the wounded close enough to be a danger to them and to recover spent arrows.

Emilia licked her lips. She tasted sweat and blood.

Tal spun to her. "Are you all right?" he asked.

Blood splattered across his face. It dripped from the shaft of his spear.

She nodded.

"We held them," Tal said.

Another banner crested the hill, and men dismounted. This banner was black with golden sheaves of wheat. Emilia recognized it as the banner of the Baron of Tivoli.

"I want fifty archers behind," Redmond called. "The rest of you get a spear or pike and form a line. We'll attack them before they can form ranks. Archers, harry them as long as you can and then join us."

Redmond waved his sword over his head.

"This day," he called, "they will remember the archers of Windemere."

The archers roared with a single voice and rushed up the hill.

A coppery flash passed overhead. Something slammed into the foremost of the men lining up on the hill and erupted into flame. Men screamed and tried to extinguish the clutching flames, but to no avail.

Emilia glanced back. Kamil stood beside his little fire. He drew back his bow with a copper cone on the end of a shaft that had no fletchings. He released, and the cone jumped from the bow, leaving the shaft behind. It flew overhead to crash into the enemy. Their lines wavered. Kamil's surprise had a dramatic effect.

"Stay with me," Tal called, and Emilia clambered over the embankment beside her father.

The weight of the unfamiliar mail shirt made her legs burn. Arrows zipped overhead, but she paid no attention to anything but keeping up with the men jostling her as they scrambled over the dead and dying that littered the hillside.

Once, Emilia tripped over the leg of a dead man and caught herself with her hand. Her glove splashed into a pool of gore. She tried to ignore the bile that rose in her throat and stumbled on.

The disorganized ranks of the enemy struggled to reform on the crest of the hill as arrows punched under the shields and fire burned everything it touched. The smell of burned clothing and charred flesh lingered in the air.

By the time Emilia and Tal reached the summit, the flames from Kamil's fire had swept through the tall grass, leaving a blackened trail of smoking earth and burning corpses. Here and there, patches of flame still consumed a writhing body. The enemy formed into a ragged line with their shields up. More men galloped to join them from over the hills behind.

Jannik was the first to slam into the shield wall they presented with his heavy sledgehammer. Men scattered as he swung the hammer from side to side.

"Meet Bessie!" he roared.

The hole he created allowed the rest of the archers to drive through the line. Soon, the entire hillside became a chaotic fray of struggling men.

Emilia fell to her knees below the crest of the hill and jabbed her spear up under the triangular shields and slashed and hacked at the unprotected legs.

Windemere

A man slipped past the archers and threw himself on her. The weight of his body knocked the wind out of her, and she dropped the spear as she tumbled backward with a shriek of surprise.

All around Redmond the battle surged back and forth. The roar and clash of it echoed in his ears. The bitter smell of it filled his nostrils. He could hardly believe his men had even reached the summit of the hill. By all rights, they should have been crushed in that first rush. He had never seen men face such overwhelming odds with so much courage.

Redmond kicked at the bottom of a shield, forcing the top down to create an opening. He jabbed his sword at the man's face before slamming into the shield. This was their last chance. If they couldn't hold the field now, they would be swept into the sea.

A high-pitched scream rang above the sound of battle. It was a woman's voice. Redmond disengaged and spun. Emilia disappeared over the hill under the body of a huge warrior.

"No," he cried as he cut and hacked his way through the throng. He had to reach her. He couldn't let her die like this. Not because of him.

He leapt over the bodies as the desperate horror clutched at his throat. On the southern rise above the battlefield, a new banner burst from the grassland, followed by a sweeping arc of armored horsemen. Hope withered in his chest. They could never survive. But he wouldn't let Emilia die.

Emilia's lungs spasmed as she struggled to breathe. Terror gripped her throat.

The man clung to her as they tumbled and bounced down the hill. Her father's desperate cry punched through the melee as if from another world. They stopped rolling and slid for a dozen feet until they slammed into the corpse of a horse. Air rushed back into Emilia's lungs. The man had lost his helmet, and he fumbled with the knife at his hip. With a wild gleam in his eyes, he raised his hand. The long, slender blade descended.

Redmond slipped and fell on the hillside made slick with blood. A cry of dismay burst from his men as the news of another banner on the hill spread. He scrambled to his feet, grabbing up a discarded spear. The man on top of Emilia raised his hand for the killing stroke. Redmond cocked back his arm to throw when an arrow zipped past his head.

Emilia's hand spasmed against something long and hard. She grabbed it up and thrust it at the man's throat in desperate terror. The broken end of a sword plunged into his throat at the same time that an arrow slammed into his head.

The man grunted and fell sideways. Emilia blinked at the spray of blood and looked up the hill to find Kamil standing behind the line of battle with his bow in his hands. He raised the bow to her and rejoined the fray.

Redmond stared at her with a look of desperation, holding a spear loosely in his hand. The expression on his face pulled a knot into her throat. He had been afraid for her.

A shout rose up from the men above. "Longmire!" they called. Redmond spun away from her and raced back to the battle.

Emilia crawled to her feet and scrambled back up the hill. She drew her sword as she reached the summit to find the attackers falling back. She paused. Her heart fell as the yellow banner of the Baron of Longmire descending a hill in the distance followed by his army.

They were doomed.

She fell to her knees in exhaustion, gasping for breath. It had been all for naught. A few hours from safety and real freedom, they had been brought to heel by the one man who should have been their friend. The archers paused in their pursuit of the enemy as if uncertain what to expect. Emilia raised her head when Tal appeared beside her and dragged her to her feet.

"Are you all right?" he demanded. "I saw you fall but couldn't break free." She gave him a feeble nod.

"We have to go," Tal said. He dragged her back toward the hill

Windemere

when the archers gave a cheer. Tal and Emilia whirled. The armies of Longmire crashed into the exposed flank of the enemy, who scrambled to face the new threat. But they were swept from the field. Emilia watched in disbelief as the enemy broke and fled before the combined forces of the archers of Windemere and the Baron of Longmire.

Redmond surveyed the battlefield with his sword held loosely in his hand. His archers scattered around the crest of the hill, watching as Baron Longmire's army chased the enemy across the prairie. It was hard to believe that he and his men were still alive. He had been forced to fight on ground he hadn't chosen against a force with numbers far larger than his own. Yet his men were far superior to the soldiers they faced.

Pride swelled in his chest at the dogged determination, courage, and discipline his men displayed. Few companies of archers or soldiers could have withstood the assaults these men had weathered time and again over the last few weeks. Their ranks had thinned, but more than a hundred of them still stood on the field of victory.

Redmond walked among them seeing to their wounds and congratulating them on a battle well-fought. The men were so exhausted that few offered any reply. Now and then, Redmond passed the body of a fallen comrade. He knew each face and remembered the first time he had met them. A few of those who had joined them from Baron Otto's prisons lay crumpled in death with the others. Maybe Redmond's suspicions had been wrong. Perhaps there had been no traitor among them.

His men collected the dead and wounded, separating them from their fallen enemies. Redmond paused. The great sledgehammer Jannik called Bessie lay half-buried in the mud. A grisly, severed hand still clutched the handle. Redmond froze as a lump formed in his throat. Jannik's body lay a few feet away, still wearing Lord Dwayne's armor. It hadn't done any more to protect him than it had its previous owner.

A knot of men gathered around him. Redmond hadn't thought a man as large and powerful as Jannik could fall. He had never met the man who could stand against Jannik when he was in full battle rage.

Emilia fell beside Jannik and laid a hand on his brow. The stump of Jannik's arm still dribbled blood. His helmet had been smashed in on one side, and a bloody dent in his skull gave him a grotesque appearance.

Redmond swallowed at the lump in his throat. He wanted to say something, but no words would come. Jannik had been his companion in many an adventure from the far northern forests to the Vermilion Desert. He thought himself inured to the horrors of war, but when a man such as Jannik fell, he found himself repulsed by what he did for a living. Kamil was right. He had become nothing but a paid robber and a murderer. He wanted to leave it all behind.

That odd, disconcerting feeling that someone was watching him rippled through his body. He snapped his head up and spun. An arrow leapt from a bow not more than twenty paces away. Redmond gave a strangled cry and twisted in a desperate attempt to avoid the arrow that streaked toward him. The arrow dove low and punched through the mail shirt at his thigh, stabbing into his leg. Redmond hit the ground and rolled, snapping the shaft. He came up on one knee ready to face the next arrow, but he found the man rushing toward him.

A roar sounded, and Tal lunged in front of Redmond, a spear in his hands. Redmond's assailant slid to a stop, spun, and sprinted for the safety of the hill. A string slapped, and a white-fletched shaft slammed into his back, punching through his mail shirt. The man stumbled but kept running. Another arrow drove into him, and the man tumbled over the crest of the hill. Kamil raced to the edge of the hill, drew, and released.

Redmond yanked the bodkin point from his leg. The mail and padded gambeson had kept it from inflicting a debilitating wound. But it left a round hole in his thigh nearly half an inch wide. This assassin had little experience with a bow or he would have aimed at a more vulnerable spot and would have had another arrow in the air before Redmond could recover himself. Tal offered him a hand up, and Redmond rose.

"He was one of Baron Otto's men," Tal said.

Redmond nodded. "He was in the prison with us and joined our cause after we took the castle," he said. "That's why they always knew where to find us."

Windemere

"Probably," Tal said.

Kamil stepped up to them.

"Thanks," Redmond said to him. At least now he didn't need to doubt his friend anymore.

"He's dead," Kamil said. Then he gave Redmond a big grin. "You owe me two barrels of fine wine now."

Redmond smiled despite the sorrow that filled his chest. "We never had the chance to check that catapult," he said. "And if you spent less time with your fine wines, you might shoot like a longbow archer."

Kamil harrumphed. "Your longbow is just a stick. My bows are works of art—highly tuned instruments of war."

"Sure," Redmond said.

Rollo strode up to them, followed by the Baron of Longmire riding a huge gray and white charger. The smile died on Rollo's face as his gaze rested on Jannik's body. He removed his helmet and came to stand over his old friend. Redmond stepped to him, wincing at the pain in his leg, and placed a hand on his shoulder. Rollo blinked rapidly and kept swallowing. He opened his mouth to speak and then closed it.

The Baron kicked his horse over to look down on them.

"I'm sorry we didn't arrive sooner," he said. "You were hard to find."

"Only to some," Redmond said, casting his gaze over the bodies that littered the battlefield. "We didn't expect you," he said.

Longmire leaned forward in the saddle.

"I'm sorry," he said again. "King Rupert asked me to help him recover the money he paid to you for the castle. I argued against it, but he can be a stiff-necked man."

"What ever happened to Henry?" Redmond asked.

Longmire smiled. "I've made that little scamp a page," he said. "He has more courage than half the men who serve me now."

"And his family?"

Longmire frowned. "Dead," he said. "He was taken in a raid on Kirn that Selgrave's men tried to blame on me."

Longmire's gaze strayed over the battlefield, and he shook his head in disgust.

"These are dark times," he said. "I fear worse times will come. But a man of honor never goes back on his word." He looked back to Redmond and his men. His gaze lingered on Jannik's body. "I have sworn to protect you as long as you are my mercenaries, and I will do so. We should leave the field. There's another force farther south. They are no more than a few hours behind me."

Redmond glanced at Jannik's body. "After we collect our men," he said.

Then he bowed his head and trudged to the hillside, stepping over the dead. He descended the hill, found a sizeable stone outcrop and dropped onto it to stare out over the steel-gray sea. The heavens opened, and the drizzle returned to wash away the horror of battle.

Chapter 23
Farewell

The townsfolk of Harrowden kept a wary eye on them as Redmond led his men into the town just as the sun splashed a golden glow over the sea to the west. Harrowden nestled at the end of a wide bay between the stony shore and the rocky bluffs behind. An open delta where a shallow river flowed into the bay was checkered with fields, pastures, and tiny farmhouses. The town collected around several long wharves that jutted over the water. Ships bobbed at anchor, their tall masts towering above the buildings and shops that spread out in a maze of roads and alleyways. The heavy scent of fish filled the air.

"Well," Rollo said as they reined their horses to a stop in front of a tavern, "it may not be a castle, but I'm going to find someone to feed me a hot meal and massage my feet."

"I'm going to see if anyone in this town knows how to cook," Kamil said. "I haven't had real food in months."

Redmond turned to Tal and Emilia. "You better get in there," he said, "before these two take all the good food and decent rooms." He glanced at Jannik's saddlebags, heavy with gold, that sat behind Tal's saddle. He thought Jannik would prefer they have it.

"Oh, I wouldn't let my little sister starve," Kamil said. He jumped from the saddle and raised a hand to help Emilia down. She winced as she slid to the ground.

"Ouch," she said. "Does it ever stop hurting?"

"I can show you those stretches," Kamil said.

"I'll pass. I'd rather have a hot bath and a soft bed."

Tal glanced over at Redmond as the others dismounted.

"Coming in?" he asked.

Redmond squinted up at the windows of the tavern before looking back at his friends.

"I can't," he said. "I have something I need to do."

They all watched him curiously.

"I have a promise to keep."

"Crispin?" Tal asked.

Redmond nodded.

"We'll be gone before you get back," Rollo said.

"I'm sorry," Redmond said. How could he tell them that after everything that had happened over the last several weeks, he needed time alone to decide what to do?

"I'll come with you," Tal said and placed his foot back in the stirrup.

"No," Redmond said. "I need to do this alone."

Tal paused with a hand on the pommel of his saddle.

Rollo stepped over to Redmond. "Surely you can rest for one night," he said.

Redmond was tired, but it wasn't the type of weariness mere sleep would wash away. Emilia blinked at him with a confused expression. Redmond passed a hand over his face feeling the scruff of days without shaving.

"I'll be back," he said. "It won't take long."

"You have come to the parting of the roads," Kamil said. "Choose your path well."

Redmond nodded to him. "I will," he said. "Goodbye, friends. We'll meet again."

He reined his horse around, then paused, and turned back to Kamil.

"Why were you in the keep with Baron Otto?" he asked.

Kamil shrugged. "Replenishing my supply of fine tea," he said as if it were a matter of little importance.

"You stole his tea?" Rollo said.

Kamil raised his hands in a gesture of innocence. "I just borrowed a bit. He won't miss it."

Redmond grunted in disbelief. The things Kamil found important amazed him.

Kamil hesitated. "He did ask me if I ever tired of being mistrusted and hinted that he would pay me well if I helped him."

Emilia gasped, but Redmond never took his gaze from Kamil's face. He had convinced himself that Kamil had never considered betraying them. Had he been wrong?

Kamil smiled. "I told him that even if he appreciated the taste of excellent tea, which is a rarity in this land of barbarians, I could not be purchased for any price. I'm far too valuable."

Redmond gave him a wry smile and shook his head. He raised a hand in farewell and rode eastward, away from the setting sun.

Redmond set the heavy bag of gold on the narrow board Alma, Crispin's wife, used for a table. She was a robust woman with sad, blue eyes and long, brown hair she wore in a braid. Three children huddled around her. Redmond had traveled for three days to find Willow Hollow on the borders of the Barony of Longmire and the Duchy of Kirn. He gazed across the table at Alma where she sat in a hut on the edge of town. Her fingers played with a stray piece of straw.

"I'm sorry," Redmond said. "His last thoughts were of you and your children. He asked me to bring to you this."

He pointed to the bag. Redmond had filled it with five hundred gold coins and would have added more, but he didn't want to cause the woman any more trouble. People might believe her husband had amassed a small fortune in his travels and fighting, but their credulity would only go so far. He couldn't have them accusing her of stealing it—or worse, practicing witchcraft. Countryfolk could be very intolerant of those who enjoyed unaccountable success.

Alma blinked back her tears. "How did he die?" she asked.

Redmond glanced at the table and folded his hands. This woman didn't care about the money. She had loved Crispin. Redmond considered how rare a thing that kind of affection was in the world. He had seen so much infidelity and lust he had almost forgotten such tender loyalty could exist between a man and a woman.

He hesitated. He couldn't tell her he had shot her husband in the back. She would never accept money from such a man, and it would only add to her grief. Redmond needed to help her. A few gold coins couldn't bring back her husband, but at least Redmond would know she wouldn't want for food and lodging because of him.

Redmond contemplated the kindly woman and her three frightened children. How many more families across Morcia would be receiving the news that their husbands and fathers were dead?

"He died in battle," Redmond said. "Crispin was a brave man who cared a great deal for his family."

"Yes," Alma said. "Thank you for coming all this way to bring me word. Will you eat with us?"

Redmond stood. "No. Thank you," he said. "I need to get back." He stepped to the door and lifted the latch before glancing back at her.

"I am sorry," he said. "Truly, I am."

Alma nodded and wiped at the tears. Redmond stepped out into the warm afternoon sunlight. He had hoped fulfilling his pledge to Crispin would relieve some of the burden of sorrow that weighed him down. An important duty was now done, but it brought him no relief.

Redmond mounted his horse and headed back toward Harrowden and the waiting ships.

Adelaide stood at the window of her room contemplating the rolling farmlands of Windemere, the distant hills that were no more than a gray smudge and beyond to Harrowden where Redmond would be preparing to depart. She rolled an arrow between her fingers. She considered the irony that his band was being called The Archers of Windemere. Word of their exploits was being noised abroad, along with word of her shame. Not only had she failed to recover her own castle from a small band of foreign archers, but she also lost her army and years of work and intrigue.

She hated Redmond even more than she had hated her father. And yet, she couldn't help but admire what he had achieved. Few men she knew would have even tried, and none would have succeeded. If she had met him when she was young and unattached, maybe she could have been the one that seized hold of his heart—the one to whom he remained loyal despite another's attempts to capture him. She would give anything to find such a man—almost anything. But he had mocked her. Rejected her. Humiliated her. People who humiliated Adelaide Selgrave had to be dealt with, one way or another. He might escape her for now, but he could not escape forever. Emilia and Tal would be easy to track. When she found them, she would find Redmond.

Emilia stood in the shadows of the tavern next to the pier where their ship rode at anchor. It would sail in the morning with the outgoing tide. She peered up into Redmond's face. He had a thick scruff of a beard, and he had pulled his hair back to tie it with a string in a way that made him look younger. Lines of weariness spread from the corners of his eyes. She had made her father wait until Redmond returned before purchasing their passage to Pava.

"Won't you come with us?" she asked.

Redmond hesitated as if undecided. A war of emotions played across his face. He wanted to come with her, but something still held him back.

"I can't," Redmond said. "I have unfinished business on Frei-Ock Mor."

"Will you come to us afterward then?"

"Perhaps," Redmond said.

A peculiar ache filled her chest. How could he leave her after all they had been through together? Emilia placed her arms around his neck and leaned in to kiss him. Her lips brushed his, but he gently pushed her away. Shame and confusion burned her cheeks. She dropped her arms and searched his face, trying to understand.

"I thought…" she began but didn't continue. She bowed her head.

Redmond placed a finger under her chin to raise her head. She let him do it.

"I can't," he said. "Not now. I'm promised to someone else."

Emilia tried to swallow the horrible knot that formed in her throat.

"What do you mean *not now?*" she whispered. If he was promised to someone else, didn't he mean *not ever?* When she first met Redmond, she had seen him as a means of escaping an intolerable situation. He had freed her, but not in the way she had expected. Now she had become a prisoner again. Her heart belonged to him. She allowed herself to believe he had formed similar feelings for her. She was sure he had.

"I don't know. I thought I could, but…" he trailed off. "I don't deserve your affection. If you knew what I had done, you wouldn't want me."

Emilia scowled at him in confusion. What could he mean he didn't deserve affection?

The muscles flexed in Redmond's jaw.

"I'm not free to give you what you want," he said. "Not now. I'm sorry."

Emilia spun away so he wouldn't see the bitter tears, but he grabbed her shoulders and pulled her to him. He wrapped his strong arms around her.

"I will always care for you," he said.

Emilia allowed her tears to stain his linen tunic.

"I will be waiting," she whispered.

When they parted, she pulled a little bell from her pocket. It was the kind she tied to the tails of her hawks.

"Keep this," she said. "And remember me." Then she whirled and fled.

Mara stepped out in front of Redmond two days later as he prepared to mount the plank to the ship that would carry him home.

"You're leaving then?" Mara asked.

"Why is it that you always show up when you're least expected?" Redmond asked.

Mara wiggled her eyebrows at him. "Because I'm always one step ahead of you."

Redmond sniffed. "I take it Lady Selgrave hasn't tried to punish you for helping us?"

"She doesn't know," Mara said. "But I have been chastised by the Order."

"Sorry." Redmond rubbed his eyes. The weariness still hadn't subsided.

"They accused me of willfully disobeying orders because I became too attached to my contacts."

"Well," Redmond said. "Whatever your reasons, I thank you. I don't know if we could have made it without your help."

"You couldn't have," Mara said with a grin.

Windemere

Redmond laughed.

Mara placed a piece of red cloth into his hand. It had a black rook stitched in it.

"I told them I've been cultivating an important contact who may even become a recruit," she said.

"I have no desire to be a spy or an assassin," Redmond said, trying to give her back the cloth.

Mara stuffed her hands in the pockets of her black trousers. "You'll need me again someday," she said. "Keep the cloth. If you're ever in Morcia and need help, send it to the slave dealer named Nicolas. He lives on Water Street in Royan. He'll know how to contact me."

Redmond fingered the cloth. "Thanks," he said.

Mara kept watching him as if she were struggling to decide something. She stepped closer. "I know you've heard about the war that might be coming to Coll." She glanced at her boots and kicked at a piece of wood. "There may be even bigger things in motion," she said. "I can't tell you what they are, because I don't know for sure. But I may need men like you before too long. Can I call on you if I need to?"

"All right," he said. He owed her that much.

Mara smiled and stepped past him.

"Wait," Redmond said.

She turned.

"Will you keep an eye on Tal and Emilia for me?" he asked.

Mara smiled. "I knew you had a soft spot for that girl."

Redmond shrugged.

"I will," Mara said, "and I'll make sure Walter and Sibyl and those kids are safe, too."

"You're very generous," Redmond said.

"I always collect," Mara said. She winked at him and melted into the crowd.

Redmond grasped the taut rope that raised the foremast of the ship and let the wind blow through his hair. The rope was stiff with tar and rough to the touch. Emilia and Tal had sailed the previous morning with Jannik's share of the earnings from the sale of Windemere. They would put it to good use in the city of Pava—far from the lands of Baron Otto and Lady Selgrave. He tried to forget the brush of Emilia's lips on his. If it had not been for Lara and the threat of war to Coll, he would have stayed with Emilia. He almost had. Someday he would sail to Pava and find them, no matter what happened.

He breathed in the sea air and smiled as a weight lifted from his heart. Home. He was heading home, at last. His men were safe from the mines, and it was time he cared for his own affairs. Eighteen years of avoiding them had done little good. He would see if Neahl and Weyland had survived Neahl's mania to kill Salassani, and he would find Lara. He would explain. She may not be able to forgive him, but at least she would know the truth. And he would warn them of the coming war. Together, they could find a safe place where they could wait it out.

The south coast of Rosythia materialized from the sea on his right, and the white cliffs of Whit-horn rose up on his left. In the center, the green blur of Laro Forest accentuated the purple outlines of the Aveen Mountains far to the northwest. The wind carried the smell of pine and oak and rich earth—the smell of home. Joy leapt into Redmond's heart. Tears stung his eyes. He would be able to rest from war for the first time in more than twenty years.

Author's Note

his story brings together two unrelated events from the Hundred Years' War (1337-1453), in which the English crown of the House of Plantagenet and the French crown of the House of Valois contested each other's right to rule the kingdom of France. I have, of course, taken considerable literary license to suit the needs of the *Archer of the Heathland* series and the story about Redmond and what finally drove him back home to Frei-Ock Mor.

The first event occurred in 1352, in Guînes, France, south of Calais. An English archer named John Dancaster found himself captured by the French and unable to pay his ransom. The French released him on the condition that he remain and work for them. The chronicler Geoffrey le Baker of Oxford recounts what happened:

> There was an archer called John Dancaster who had previously been captured and imprisoned in the castle of Guînes. As he did not have the means to pay his ransom, he was set free by the French on the condition that he served as an archer for them. This fellow became acquainted with the lewd embraces of a washerwoman and learned from her of a wall that had been built across the bottom of the chief moat of the castle. It was two feet wide and extended from the rampart to the inner wall of the castle. It was so covered with water that it could not be seen, but it was not so submerged that a man crossing by it got wet further up than his knees. It had been made once upon a time for the use of fishermen and for that reason the wall was discontinued in the middle for the space of two feet.
>
> Armed now with this information from his strumpet,

J.W. Elliot

John Dancaster measured the height of the wall with a thread. Having discovered it, he one day slipped down from the wall, entrusting himself to God, and crossed the moat by the hidden wall. He hid until evening in the marshes, came to the vicinity of Calais by night and waited for broad daylight before he entered the town, as he would definitely not have been let in at any other time.

He told those who were greedy for booty and keen to take the castle by stealth, where an entrance was lying open for them. These thirty conspirators made ladders of the length measured by him, and, wearing black armor without any brightness, they came to the castle of Guînes by night, guided by John Dancaster. They climbed the wall with their ladders, knocked out the brains of a guard, who meeting them by chance was beginning to cry out and threw his body into the moat. In the hall, they found and slaughtered many unarmed men who were playing at che[ck]ers or dice and who were as panic-stricken as sheep in the presence of wolves. Then, easily breaking into chambers and turrets where ladies and some knights were sleeping, they became masters of all they wanted.

Finally, when all their prisoners, stripped of all their weapons, had been shut into one strong room, they set free those Englishmen who had been taken prisoner the previous year, fed and armed them, and put them in charge of their former masters. So in this way, they seized all the defen[s]es of the castle, while the Frenchmen in the town who were superintending the rebuilding of the ruins knew nothing of what was happening to the French in the castle. [*The Chronicle of Geoffrey le Baker of Swinbrook*, translated by David Preest (Woolbridge: The Boydell Press, 2012), 101.]

Other men joined them from Calais. When the French arrived to ask them who they were and why they had seized the castle, they replied they wouldn't tell them until they had enjoyed it for a while longer. The French sent to the English King to demand that he return the castle since it was taken during a truce. The King denied any knowledge of the plot and sent a letter with the French envoys ordering the archers to deliver the castle to its lawful owners. The English archers refused but said they would sell the castle to the King of England or anyone offering a higher price. The King of England then purchased the castle.

The French refused to accept the loss of Guînes, so they occupied a nearby monastery and fortified it with a fence and a moat. They then lay siege to Guînes and refused to let the occupants out or let supplies reach them from Calais. In response, the men of Calais, Oye, and Mark joined forces to attack the French position from behind, while the archers from Guînes attacked them from the front. Together, they overwhelmed the French and set fire to the monastery. Guînes remained in English hands until it fell to the French in 1558.

The second incident occurred in March of 1416, near the town of Valmont (or Ouainville). The French had long harbored a hatred of the English archers who wreaked such havoc on their horses, disrupting their cavalry charges and leading to the terrible slaughter of battles like Crécy and Agincourt. The French commander, the Count of Armagnac, surprised a raiding party of one thousand men led by the Earl of Dorset, with a force three times its size. The Earl had his archers dismount and form a line that succeeded in fending off successive French attacks with heavy losses to the French cavalry. When the French finally broke through and attacked the baggage train, Dorset retreated to a garden where he reorganized his men using the protection of a ditch and hedge.

Armagnac offered to accept the English surrender and promised the men-at-arms would be ransomed, but the archers would have their right hands amputated so they could never again draw a bow against the French. Dorset refused the offer and fought Armagnac to a standstill. Armagnac withdrew at nightfall to prepare for the final assault the next day, but Dorset took his men and slipped away under the cover of darkness. He retreated to the seaside in an attempt to reach the safety of Harfleur and its garrison.

They made it to the cliffs of St. Andress near Harfleur before a French detachment, led by Marshal de Loigny, intercepted them. The French charged down the cliffs in such a disorganized fashion that Dorset's men were able to mount a counterattack that routed the French force. Armagnac arrived with the main army, and the

English broke all military protocol by charging up the slope to rout the French army. The English garrison at Harfleur sent out a small force that completed the destruction of the French forces. By all accounts, this retreat in the face of an overwhelming enemy took considerable daring, skill, discipline, and dogged determination not to be defeated and mutilated.

I combined these two events to show that Redmond and his archers had achieved the same level of skill and cunning and were able to fight with the same discipline and loyalty that marked the English archers when they were at their best.

Archers, of course, were not always at their best, and there are plenty of examples in the history of the Hundred Years' War in which English archers not only failed, but they fell upon the unarmed population with a savagery that is hard to justify or explain. I didn't want Redmond or his men to descend to that level, so I intentionally placed restraints on the rapine and slaughter they might have inflicted on the inhabitants of Castle Windemere.

ABOUT J.W. ELLIOT

J.W. Elliot is a professional historian, martial artist, canoer, bow builder, knife maker, woodturner, and rock climber. He has a Ph.D. in Latin American and World History. He has lived in Idaho, Oklahoma, Brazil, Arizona, Portugal, and Massachusetts. He writes non-fiction works of history about the Inquisition, Columbus, and pirates. J.W. Elliot loves to travel and challenge himself in the outdoors.

Connect with J.W. Elliot online at:
www.JWElliot.com/contact-us

Books by J.W. Elliot
Available on Amazon and Audible

Archer of the Heathland
Prequel: *Intrigue*
Book I: *Deliverance*
Book II: *Betrayal*
Book III: *Vengeance*
Book IV: *Chronicles*
Book V: *Windemere*
Book VI: *Renegade*
Book VII: *Rook*

Worlds of Light
Book I: *The Cleansing*
Book II: *The Rending*
Book III: *The Unmaking*

The Ark Project
Prequel: *The Harvest*
Book I: *The Clone Paradox*
Book II: *The Covenant Protocol*

Heirs of Anarwyn
Book I: *Torn*
Book II: *Undead*
Book III: *Shattered*
Book IV: *Feral*
Book V: *Dyad*

The Miserable Life of Bernie LeBaron
Somewhere in the Mist
Walls of Glass

If you have enjoyed this book, please consider leaving an honest review on Amazon and sharing on your social media sites.

Please sign up for my newsletter where you can get a free short story and more free content at: www.JWElliot.com

Thanks for your support!

J.W. Elliot

Writing Awards

Winner of the New England Book Festival for Science Fiction 2021 for *The Clone Paradox (The Ark Project,* Book I).

Award Winning Finalist in the Fiction: Young Adult category of the 2021 **Best Book Awards** sponsored by American Book Fest for *Archer of the Heathland: Windemere.*

Award-Winning Finalist in the Young Adult category of the 2021 **American Fiction Awards** for *Walls of Glass.*

Award-Winning Finalist in the Science Fiction: General category of the 2021 **American Fiction Awards** for *The Clone Paradox (The Ark Project,* Book 1).

Chet Kevitt Award for contributions to Weymouth history for the publication of *The World of Credit in Colonial Massachusetts: James Richards and his Daybook, 1692-1711.* Awarded by the Weymouth Historical Commission, 2018.

Writers of the Future Contest
Honorable Mention for *Recalibration,* 2018.
Honorable Mention for *Ebony and Ice,* 2019.

Made in the USA
Coppell, TX
08 March 2023

13986155R00156